D.E. STEVENSON
THE BLUE SAPPHIRE

Born in Edinburgh in 1892, Dorothy Emily Stevenson came from a distinguished Scottish family, her father being David Alan Stevenson, the lighthouse engineer, first cousin to Robert Louis Stevenson.

In 1916 she married Major James Reid Peploe (nephew to the artist Samuel Peploe). After the First World War they lived near Glasgow and brought up two sons and a daughter. Dorothy wrote her first novel in the 1920's, and by the 1930's was a prolific bestseller, ultimately selling more than seven million books in her career. Among her many bestselling novels was the series featuring the popular "Mrs. Tim", the wife of a British Army officer. The author often returned to Scotland and Scottish themes in her romantic, witty and well-observed novels.

During the Second World War Dorothy Stevenson moved with her husband to Moffat in Scotland. It was here that most of her subsequent works were written. D.E. Stevenson died in Moffat in 1973.

NOVELS BY D.E. STEVENSON
Available from Dean Street Press

Mrs. Tim Carries on (1941)

Mrs. Tim Gets a Job (1947)

Mrs. Tim Flies Home (1952)

Smouldering Fire (1935)

Spring Magic (1942)

Vittoria Cottage (1949)

Music in the Hills (1950)

Winter and Rough Weather (1951)

The Fair Miss Fortune (written c. 1938, first published 2011)

Green Money (1939, aka *The Green Money*)

The English Air (1940)

Kate Hardy (1947)

Young Mrs. Savage (1948)

Five Windows (1953)

Charlotte Fairlie (1954, aka *The Enchanted Isle*, aka *Blow the Wind Southerly*)

The Tall Stranger (1957)

Anna and Her Daughters (1958)

The Musgraves (1960)

The Blue Sapphire (1963)

*(A complete D.E. Stevenson bibliography is included
at the end of this book.)*

D.E. STEVENSON

THE BLUE SAPPHIRE

DEAN STREET PRESS

A Furrowed Middlebrow Book
FM83

Published by Dean Street Press 2022

First published in 1963 by Collins

Cover by DSP

ISBN 978 1 915014 51 1

www.deanstreetpress.co.uk

PART ONE

CHAPTER 1

1

LONDON was enjoying the first day of spring; the clouds which had obscured the atmosphere for weeks had been swept away in the night and the old grey city was stretching herself and relaxing happily in mild air and golden sunshine. The sudden change was affecting everyone, people were walking along the streets more briskly, with cheerful faces and good-tempered mien.

No wonder the Ancients were sun-worshippers, thought Julia Harburn as she looked round at her fellow-passengers in the bus and listened to the scraps of conversation. Spring was not only a happy time in itself, it was full of the promise of approaching summer.

When the bus stopped at one of the entrances to Kensington Gardens a good many passengers got out. Amongst them were mothers with small children, and two little boys with a model yacht which they intended to sail on the Round Pond. Julia got out too, not because she wanted to amuse herself by walking in the gardens but because she had an appointment at three o'clock. It would have been pleasant to watch the children when they were let loose to run about and play, but there was no time to dawdle, for the bus had been held up in the traffic and she was a few minutes late.

Julia always met Morland on Thursday afternoons—it was the day when he escaped early from his office. If it were cold or rainy they met at a tea-shop and had tea together, but this morning Morland had rung up and said, 'It's lovely to-day, Julia. Let's meet at that seat in Kensington Gardens this afternoon. You know the one I mean.'

Of course Julia had known, for it was when they were sitting there that Morland had asked her to marry him.

Morland might have chosen a better place for his proposal; there were children playing with balls and shouting to each other; there were mothers with prams and girls strolling past with their arms round each other's waists; there were all the usual odds and ends of humanity which take their pleasure in London parks on fine afternoons, so there was no opportunity for any sort of demonstration. Morland had just taken her hand, given it a somewhat painful squeeze and said, 'You will, won't you? . . . Good!'

He might have said more, but at that moment an old gentleman sat down at the other end of the seat and looked at them sideways with an inquisitive stare in his pale-blue eyes, so they rose with one accord and walked on.

'There are too many people in the world,' declared Morland savagely.

Julia was very young and romantic, so she was considerably upset. A proposal of marriage should be made and accepted in a rose-garden by moonlight . . . at the very least it should be made in private and sealed with a kiss. Why, oh why, had Morland chosen to make it in a London park amongst a crowd of people?

However, in other ways the engagement was entirely satisfactory; their families had known each other for years. The Harburns lived in a pleasant old house in Manor Gardens, the Beverleys lived in a palatial modern flat in Springfield Mansions. They visited each other occasionally and sometimes played bridge together. Mrs. Beverley was fond of Julia and had decided long ago, when Julia was a child, that she would do very nicely for Morland, so when Julia's mother died Julia was invited to go for a little holiday with the Beverleys and it was then that she and Morland had become friends. Morland was a good deal older than Julia, but they were both 'only children,' which made a bond between them, and gradually their friendship had ripened into a closer relationship.

2

The engagement had taken place in the autumn; now it was spring, and Julia was on her way to the historic seat. She walked quickly, because she was late and she was aware that Morland did not like to be kept waiting . . . but Morland had not yet arrived at the rendezvous and the seat was unoccupied. Julia sat down.

Now that she had leisure to look about her Julia was enchanted, for the scene was gay with spring; the trees were budding, the grass was green, there were tulips standing up straight like regiments of well-drilled soldiers; there were children running and skipping like frisky lambs, and girls in cotton frocks all colours of the rainbow.

Julia herself was greeting the sunshine in a simple white frock and large straw hat with a sapphire-blue ribbon round the crown (it so happened that the ribbon matched her eyes; perhaps she was aware of this fortunate circumstance). She had dressed to please Morland, of course, but soon she became aware that quite a number of people were taking pleasure in her appearance. In fact it began to be rather uncomfortable sitting here all by herself . . . she wished Morland would come.

An old gentleman stopped and stared at her; he might have been the very same old gentleman who had intruded before at such an unfortunate moment, for he had the same wrinkled face, the same inquisitive pale-blue eyes. He stopped and stared and made a movement as if he intended to sit down beside Julia on the seat; but she returned his stare in such a forbidding manner that he changed his mind and walked on.

Three youths who were strolling along arm-in-arm looked at her hopefully, but Julia took no notice so they nudged each other and giggled and left her in peace.

Julia was just recovering from her alarm when a young man went past—a remarkably large young man with a tanned face and sun-bleached hair—he looked at her intently but did not stop. A few moments later he returned and looked at her again . . . and hesitated.

Julia was getting tired of all this; she wished Morland would come. She gazed at the young man's shoes; above the shoes she could see the turn-ups of light-grey flannel trousers. It would have been interesting to see the rest of the outfit but she resisted the temptation to raise her eyes. The shoes were very large; they remained stationary on the path for a few seconds and then moved on reluctantly. They moved a few paces and stopped. Their owner came back to the seat and sat down.

'You don't mind if I sit here, I hope,' said an unusually deep voice.

'I have no right to mind,' replied Julia coldly.

'That sounds as if you do.'

The voice seemed disappointed, so Julia said hastily, 'You see I'm waiting here for my fiancé.'

'Oh, I see.'

'There are lots of other seats,' said Julia pointedly.

'But this one is particularly nice.'

Julia remained silent. She had noticed before that he was large and fair; she noticed now that his face was frank and open; he really was rather nice but all the same she wished he would go away.

'It would be better for me to sit here till he comes,' said the young man in a casual tone.

Julia was quite startled. It seemed as if he had read her thoughts.

'You see,' he continued, 'if I don't sit here someone else is certain to come and sit down and I promise to buzz off the moment he comes—so it would be better, wouldn't it?'

This was perfectly true. As a matter of fact Julia had noticed that whereas before, people had stared at her in a rather too interested manner, they now seemed much less interested. The seat was fairly long, but the young man had spread himself sideways, and he was so large that there was no room for anyone else.

'You see what I mean?' he asked anxiously.

'Yes,' said Julia. She hesitated and then added, 'It's very kind of you.'

'Not at all. It's a pleasure . . . besides, it's absolutely necessary.'

'Necessary?'

'Yes. For instance those two fellows—ghastly types—would have sat down here if it hadn't been for me.'

Julia smiled; she had noticed the 'ghastly types.'

'You frightened them,' she said.

'Yes, I meant to frighten them. We didn't want them, did we?'

'No, of course not.'

'That's what I meant. It's absolutely necessary for you to have a watch-dog to show his teeth at people like that. It isn't pleasant for a girl like you to sit here alone.'

'I'm waiting for my fiancé.'

'Yes I know, but he shouldn't be late.'

Julia felt obliged to defend Morland. 'He can't help it,' she explained. 'Sometimes he gets held up. You see he's in his father's firm and he's hoping to be given a junior partnership so he has to do his best. He can't always get away at the right time.'

'Keeping you waiting!' exclaimed the young man indignantly.

'I've told you he can't help it! I don't really mind—not now.'

'Not now?' he asked.

'I mean people aren't so—so—'

'No, they aren't, are they?'

'Besides, it's nice sitting here in the sun.'

'It's lovely,' said the young man, smiling at her. 'I've been abroad for three years—just got home—and you can't think how lovely it is to see green grass and trees in bud and girls in pretty dresses and the sun shining so pleasantly; in Africa it glares at you—not pleasantly at all.'

'I'm glad you're enjoying it.'

'I'm enjoying it tremendously. The only trouble is I don't know anyone in London, so it's a bit lonely.'

'Yes, it must be.'

'I've been to one or two plays but it isn't so much fun going by yourself.'

Julia agreed again. She had never been to a play by herself, but she could see it would not be much fun. She was beginning to feel sorry for the young man—how sad to come all the way from Africa and have nobody to welcome you when you arrived!

'Haven't you got a home?' she asked.

'Oh yes, my people live in Devonshire and of course I'm going home as soon as I can. Brett is my name—Stephen Brett.' He paused and looked at Julia. Obviously he wanted to know her name and she saw no harm in telling him. Morland would be here at any moment and she would never see this poor lonely young man again, so what did it matter?

'Mine is Julia Harburn,' she said.

'Oh, thank you awfully. That *is* kind of you!' he exclaimed. 'It's nice to think that I know one person in London . . . makes it feel different, somehow. Thank you awfully much.'

His thanks for the small crumb she had given him were so exorbitant that she was slightly embarrassed and changed the subject by asking when he was going home.

'I'm not quite sure,' he replied. 'I've got some business to settle first. I want to get it over and done with so that I can go home with an easy mind.'

'Devonshire will be looking lovely now.'

'Yes,' he agreed. 'Our house is very old, it stands on a cliff overlooking the sea. There's an orchard at the back with old gnarled apple trees and cherries and plums. They'll all be in flower now.'

'You must be longing to get home.'

'Yes,' he said. 'At least I was. I mean, of course I want to get home, but—but I may be staying in Town longer than I expected, so perhaps I could see you again. I mean—'

Julia was not listening. She had seen Morland approaching. 'He's coming now,' she said urgently. 'You promised you would go, didn't you?'

Stephen Brett rose at once. 'Good-bye, Miss Harburn. Thank you for being—kind.'

She smiled up at him. 'Good-bye, Mr. Brett. Thank you for being a watch-dog.'

3

The two men passed each other on the path; one going, the other coming. They looked at each other appraisingly. It was rather interesting, because they were so unlike: the one large and fair, the other slender and dark; the one clad in light grey flannel, the other in conventional city clothes. Julia had a feeling that they did not approve of each other's appearance, but fortunately that did not matter in the least because it was most unlikely that that they would ever see each other again.

'Julia!' exclaimed Morland as he approached. 'I saw you talking to that fellow. Who was he?'

'Stephen Brett.'

'I didn't like the look of him at all. Where did you meet him?'

'I met him this afternoon for the first time.'

'Do you mean he just—picked you up?' asked Morland incredulously.

'Well, I suppose you could call it that. He sat down on the seat and we chatted a bit. He has just come back from Africa and knows nobody in London.'

'How extraordinary!'

'What's extraordinary?'

'You—talking to an absolute stranger like that!'

'He talked to me; I couldn't help it. As a matter of fact I was quite glad of his company, because he kept other people away.'

'What other people?'

'Everyone,' replied Julia vaguely. 'You see, I had to wait for nearly half an hour, so—'

'I couldn't help being late,' declared Morland. 'I was delayed. You know perfectly well that I'm not my own master. I can't pick up my hat and walk out of the office whenever I like. I thought you understood.'

'Oh, Morland, of course I understand! I'm not blaming you for being late. I'm only trying to explain why I was talking to him, that's all.'

'Surely you can sit on a seat for a few minutes without getting into conversation with a perfectly strange young man!'

Julia smiled. 'It isn't as easy as you seem to think.'

For a few moments Morland was silent—perhaps he had seen the point—then he exclaimed, 'But why did he rush off like that when he saw me coming?'

'Because I asked him to go.'

'You asked him to go when you saw me coming?' asked Morland incredulously.

'Yes,' nodded Julia.

'Why on earth did you do that?'

'Because I wanted to talk to you, of course. I wanted to talk to you about something important and I couldn't talk to you with that very large young man sitting and listening to every word, could I?'

There was a short silence.

'Something important?' asked Morland at last. 'What is it, Julia?'

There was quite a lot to tell him; Julia's father had decided to take a holiday from his business, so he and his young wife (Julia's stepmother) were going for a cruise in the Mediterranean.

'It has all been arranged suddenly,' explained Julia. 'They asked me to go with them, but I think it will be much nicer for them to go by themselves.'

'Well, perhaps,' agreed Morland. 'At any rate I'm very glad you aren't going, I should miss you frightfully; but what are you going to do? It will be dull for you alone in that big house.'

'Oh, I can't stay in Manor Gardens! The house is being painted and redecorated while they are away. I shall have to find a room somewhere and I want to get a job.'

'A job!' cried Morland. 'Julia, why on earth—'

'Because I'm tired of doing nothing,' she told him. 'Of course I had plenty to do when I was keeping house for Father but now it's quite different. Retta likes to run the house in her own way and it's right that she should.'

'You get on very well with Retta, don't you?'

'Oh yes.'

'Retta is devoted to you,' declared Morland. 'She said to me the other day that she would miss you dreadfully when we were married. She said all sorts of nice things about you.'

Julia was not surprised at this information. Of course Retta would say 'all sorts of nice things' about her to Morland. Retta wanted Julia and Morland to be married as soon as possible and made no secret of her desire. Only yesterday she had said with studied carelessness, 'I suppose you'll be fixing a day soon. You've been engaged for six months, haven't you?' and Julia had replied as usual, 'Morland thinks we should wait until he has been given his partnership in the firm.'

Julia was tired of saying the same thing; every time she said it she found it more difficult. She did not blame Retta for wanting to get rid of her—it was quite natural really—but it made her uncomfortable to feel she was *de trop*.

Morland had sat down on the seat by this time and was poking a hole in the gravel with the ferrule of his umbrella. 'I can't think why you want a job,' he said.

'I should be happier if I had something to do.'

'It would be much better to settle down at home and wait until we can be married. I expect I shall be given the partnership quite soon.'

'They would get on much better without me.'

'Why should you think that? Retta is very fond of you. She said so more than once. Besides, what sort of job do you think you could get?'

Julia found it difficult to answer the question, for she had had no training, nor any experience, and her education had been sketchy to say the least of it. Mr. Harburn was not interested in his daughter's education (it would have been different if Julia had been a son), and Mrs. Harburn had been delicate and had often gone abroad during the winter taking Julia with her for company in her travels. Julia had enjoyed it thoroughly, of course, but it had not been so pleasant to come home and return to school and to discover that her contemporaries had left her far behind. She was fond of reading and good at languages, but she was aware that these were unlikely to help her in her search for a good post.

'Oh well,' said Morland with a sigh, 'I suppose you could try to find something that would keep you busy in the mornings.'

'That isn't my idea at all,' declared Julia. 'I want a proper whole-time job because I shall want the money to pay for my board and lodging.'

'But you aren't proposing to leave home permanently are you? I thought it was only to be a temporary measure.'

'I've told you already, Morland. They'll get on much better without me. Retta likes to have things done in her own way and it's difficult for me not to interfere. I shall try to get a room in a boarding-house.'

'Oh, Julia! You wouldn't like it. You've always lived in a comfortable spacious house, so how could you be happy cooped up in one room? Unless you have good reasons for leaving home you had better give up the idea.'

Julia was silent. There was only one reason for Julia's decision to leave her father's comfortable house, and that was Retta. Retta there in her mother's place; sitting in her mother's seat; running the household in a careless haphazard manner, very different from the way in which it had been run when her mother was alive. Retta was by no means the cruel stepmother of fairy stories, but she and Julia had nothing in common. Retta did not like books, she never did any sort of needlework, she did not care for a good play. Poor Retta was often bored; in fact she was always bored unless she was entertaining her own particular friends— and her friends did not appeal to Julia. Sometimes Julia wondered why Retta had married her father. Probably it was because she was tired of fending for herself and wanted a comfortable home and a good position and plenty of money to spend on clothes. . . . Well, she had got all that, so what more did she want? It was doubtful if Retta herself could have answered the question.

'What on earth are you thinking about?' asked Morland.

'I don't believe you've heard a word I've been saying.'

Julia turned to him and tried to smile. 'Don't be angry with me,' she said pleadingly.

'Darling, I'm not angry—only worried. I'm worried because I can see there's something wrong.'

She hesitated. Dear Morland! But what could she tell him? There was nothing definite to tell him. Retta was not unkind; she just wanted Julia to get married; she wanted Julia out of her way; she was bored to death—and therefore difficult to live with; she had friends whom Julia did not like. What was there in all that? Nothing that would satisfy Morland . . . and of course Morland would find it difficult to believe that Retta was bored and difficult to live with, because she was always on her best behaviour when Morland was there.

'It's all right,' declared Julia, trying to speak lightly and cheerfully. 'There's nothing wrong except that I haven't got enough to do. Father and Retta will be much happier alone. It's natural.'

'Natural?'

'Yes, of course. When you and I are married you wouldn't like to have someone else living with us, would you?'

'There's something in that,' he admitted.

'I've been thinking about it,' she continued. 'It isn't a sudden idea. Now, when they're going away for a holiday, is a good opportunity to make the break. By the time they come back I shall have got a comfortable room and found something to do.'

Morland said nothing. She could see he thought it unlikely that she would be able to carry out her plans, and perhaps he was right. Julia was aware that it might be extremely difficult.

CHAPTER 2

1

MORLAND took Julia to dinner at his club, so it was after nine o'clock when she got home. She found Retta in the drawing-room yawning over a woman's magazine.

'This is a rotten book,' declared Retta, throwing it down. 'I can't think why I bought it; there isn't anything worth reading in it. I've been sitting here alone the whole evening.'

'Why don't you sit with Father in his study?'

'He doesn't want me,' said Retta frankly. 'He says I fidget. Well, you can't sit perfectly still without moving a muscle for hours on end. There isn't anything decent on TV either; just one of those tiresome plays. What have you been doing, Julia?'

'I went to dinner with Morland at his club.'

'He might have taken you somewhere amusing instead of that dreary old hole. I shall never forget how bored I was when he took us there to lunch; everyone in the place was over seventy—even the waiter had one foot in the grave. Oh, by the by, there was a phone message for you. It was a man with rather a nice voice.'

'Who was it?' asked Julia.

'He told me his name but I can't remember it. He said he had met you somewhere. I think it was at the Claytons' cocktail party on Friday night.'

'Did he say he'd met me at the Claytons'?' asked Julia patiently. She was quite used to having messages delivered to her in this casual manner and had schooled herself not to be annoyed.

'Yes, I think so—at any rate it doesn't matter, does it?'

'Did he leave a message for me?'

'No, not really. He seemed disappointed when I said you were out. He said you were the only person he knew in London.'

'Surely it couldn't have been Stephen Brett!'

'Why couldn't it? As a matter of fact that's exactly who it was. I remember now—Stephen Brett. His voice sounded rather nice, so I asked him to tea to-morrow.'

'You asked him to tea!'

'Yes, why not? He jumped at it and thanked me profusely; it was quite pathetic, really.'

'But, Retta, I scarcely know him!' exclaimed Julia in dismay.

'You'll know him better after to-morrow,' Retta pointed out. She hesitated, and then, misreading Julia's consternation, inquired, 'Does the man know you're engaged to be married?'

'Oh yes, I told him,' said Julia quickly. 'It's nothing like that. He's just a bit lonely, that's all. He has been out in Africa for years. His home is in Devonshire. He's going home when he gets some business matters settled.'

'You said you scarcely knew him, but you seem to know a lot about him! Well, I liked his voice and I thought he might be rather amusing so I asked him to tea. I'm sorry if I've done the wrong thing.'

'No, of course not. It was kind of you, Retta.'

'Don't mention it,' said Retta with another yawn. She added, 'I'm off to bed. It has been a long dull evening. Thank heaven we're going away for a holiday; I've had about all I can take.'

'Retta, I want to talk to you about my plans.'

'Well, don't be long; I'm terribly sleepy.'

'It won't take more than a few minutes. You know we decided that I had better try to find a room while you and Father are away? I've been thinking about it and I think it would be a good thing to make the arrangement permanent. You see, I should like to get a job if possible; I should be happier if I had something to do.'

There, it was out! Perhaps it was not a good time to spring the idea on Retta, when she was tired and sleepy, but it was difficult to get her alone; either she had friends to see her or else she was rushing out in a hurry to meet someone. To-night was an opportunity and Julia had seized it. Her little speech had been thought out carefully beforehand. She had delivered it and now waited anxiously for Retta's reaction.

'Yes, it isn't a bad idea,' said Retta in a thoughtful voice. 'But why on earth don't you get married if you really intend to get married?'

'Of course we intend to be married! I don't know what you mean.'

Retta laughed. 'You don't seem very keen to fix a day for the wedding; that's what I mean. If you really want to marry Morland you'll have to do something about it. I may not know much about books and music—you think I'm pretty dim—but I know a good deal about men, and you can take it from me that Morland needs a good shake-up.'

'A good shake-up!' echoed Julia in bewildered tones.

'Yes, he's thoroughly selfish and pleased with himself. If that's the sort of man you like, it's all right—none of my business.'

Julia was so stunned with amazement that she could scarcely speak. 'I thought—I thought you liked Morland!' she gasped.

'I don't dislike him,' replied Retta. 'He's always very pleasant to me. I'm just trying to tell you that if you want to marry him you had better take a firm line. It's a good thing to give men a fright now and then—keeps them up to the mark. You're much too soft with him, Julia.'

'But Retta, Morland thinks—'

'I know what you're going to say and I'm sick of hearing you say it: "Morland thinks we should wait until he gets his partnership." But why need you wait for that? What's the reason? I could understand it if the Beverleys were very badly off, but old Mr. Beverley is rolling in money, so he could easily raise Morland's screw.'

'We want to be able to buy a nice flat.'

'Why doesn't Mr. Beverley buy a flat for you and furnish it and give it to you as a wedding present? There's nothing to prevent him. The Beverleys like you and they want Morland to marry you, don't they? How long do they think a girl like you is going to hang about waiting for their precious son?'

'Oh, Retta, don't talk like that! I can't bear it!'

'All right, I won't say another word. I'm sorry if you're annoyed with me, but I've been thinking about it for some time and I decided to warn you, that's all.'

There was silence for a few moments.

Then Retta continued in quite a different tone. 'As a matter of fact, unless you're going to be married soon, it will be a very good plan for you to get a room somewhere and find a job, but you had better let me talk to Andrew about it or he may be upset.'

Julia agreed. She was only too pleased that Retta should speak to her father about her plans.

'You'll find a job all right if you aren't too choosy,' said Retta thoughtfully. 'You're a very good cook so you could go out and cook a slap-up dinner for people who wanted to throw a party. I used to know a girl who made a packet out of that. People get to know about you and recommend you to each other.'

'I suppose I could,' said Julia doubtfully.

'I'm sure you could . . . but the first thing is to find a room. You had better start looking for one to-morrow, but don't forget that man is coming to tea.'

'I shan't forget,' promised Julia, rising to go upstairs.

'Wait, Julia! You must have money. If you aren't going to live at home Andrew must give you a decent allowance; that goes without saying. I can give you fifty pounds to go on with.'

'It's very kind of you, but I've got enough of my own.'

'Don't be silly!' exclaimed Retta impatiently. 'You've got a hundred a year which belonged to your mother, but that won't go far. You can't expect to get a well-paid job straight off.'

'I'm sure I shall manage all right.'

'Not without money. I've tried living on a shoe-string so I know what I'm talking about.' Retta laughed and added frankly, 'I'd rather you took the fifty pounds; it will make me feel less like the stepmother in *Snow White and the Seven Dwarfs*.'

'Retta, are you sure you can spare it?'

'Yes, I can spare it all right. Andrew gives me as much as I want.'

There was no need to say more, for they understood each other perfectly . . . and the strange thing was, Julia had never liked Retta so much.

Queer, thought Julia, as she went upstairs to bed . . . very queer . . . she's willing to pay fifty pounds to get rid of me but I never liked her so much! I suppose it's queer of me to accept the money (I suppose I wouldn't take it if I had any proper pride), but I shall accept it because it will be useful and it will give me a nice safe feeling to have it in the bank.

2

Julia had burnt her boats; she must begin hunting for a room to-morrow. Fortunately there was no need to speak to her father about her plans; Retta was going to do that.

At the thought of her father Julia's heart failed her a little, and she wondered if it was right to desert him. He was a strange silent man, reserved and shut up inside himself. For as long as Julia could remember, he had been like that: silent, gloomy and reserved, not interested in anything that went on around him. When she was a child Julia had accepted this as natural (children take their parents and environment for granted), but later, when she met the fathers of her friends and saw how different they were, she realised that it was very unnatural indeed and she began to think of her father's reserve as 'a big brown blanket.' He was wrapped up so tightly in his big brown blanket that the real man was invisible; he seldom spoke, quite often he did not hear what was said to him. Julia sometimes looked at him as he sat at the head of the dining-room table, and wondered what he was thinking about.

She wondered whether he always wore the big brown blanket. Surely he did not wear it in his office—he was a lawyer, the senior partner in a large firm—surely he did not wear it when he went to lunch at his club.

Julia had hoped that things would improve when he married Retta, and for a few weeks it seemed that he was brighter and more alert; but quite soon he relapsed into his habitual condition of gloomy silence, spending his leisure hours shut up alone in his study, unwilling to be disturbed or distracted.

Would he be glad or sorry when he heard that his daughter intended to leave home? It was impossible to tell. One thing only was certain: Retta would be happier when she had gone, and perhaps if Retta were happier she would be more companionable . . . at least that was what Julia hoped with all her heart.

CHAPTER 3

1

LOOKING for rooms in London is a very tiring business. Julia spent the whole morning and most of the afternoon going from place to place and finding nothing to suit her; either the rooms were quite horrible, dark and incredibly dismal, or else they were far too expensive. She returned home about four o'clock dirty and discouraged. There was just time to wash and change before tea, and as she washed and changed and brushed her hair she began to think about Stephen Brett and the problems arising from Retta's impulsive invitation. She wondered how she should greet him; she wondered how he would behave.

Retta was at home for tea—perhaps because she was interested to see the man whose voice she had liked—and as Stephen Brett was ten minutes late, she and Julia were waiting for him in the drawing-room when he arrived.

He greeted Julia as if he knew her well; he sat down near the tea-table and looked perfectly at home in his surroundings. Julia noticed that he was wearing a well-tailored lounge suit—brown, with a faint blue stripe—and his brown shoes were the colour of chestnuts, polished and shining. There certainly was nothing to be ashamed of in his appearance.

'It was so kind of you to ask me, Mrs. Harburn,' said Stephen Brett as he accepted a cup of tea from Retta. 'I'm terribly sorry I'm late, but I had no idea it would take so long to get here. The crowds are awful—simply incredible. I expect Julia has told you I've been abroad for years.'

'She said you had been in Africa.'

'Yes, in the wilds,' he replied. 'I'm assistant manager of a mine; quite a good job and very interesting.'

'It must be terribly lonely!'

'Yes, but the odd thing is I find it even more lonely in London.'

Retta opened her eyes very wide and said, 'Oh yes, I know what you mean, Mr. Brett.'

Julia was silent. She had intended to call him Mr. Brett but he had referred to her as Julia. This meant she must call him Stephen otherwise Retta would think it queer. Julia was annoyed with the man, for he had put her in a false position. The whole thing was quite ridiculous, of course. There was no harm in it—none at all. She could not have refused to speak to the man when he had spoken to her pleasantly and politely. In fact the only mistake she had made was to tell him her name . . . and how could she possibly have foreseen the consequences? How could she have foreseen that he would take the trouble to find her? How had he found her?

'Yes, I'm going home next week,' Stephen was saying. 'My father and mother are anxious to see me, but I have business in Town and I thought it better to get it over and done with so that I can go home with an easy mind.'

'Much the best plan,' Retta told him. 'You'll enjoy your holiday ever so much more if you finish all your tiresome business first. What are you doing in Town—apart from business? Have you seen any plays?'

Stephen had seen two; he talked about them amusingly, but added that it was not much fun going to the theatre alone.

'You should take Julia,' suggested Retta.

'Oh yes, I should like to! What would you like to see, Julia?'

'I'm afraid I'm rather busy at the moment,' said Julia in a prim little voice.

Julia was really very angry indeed, shaking with rage. First he had put her in the wrong by pretending he knew her well, and now he was taking it for granted that she would go to the theatre with him! He had said, 'What would you like to see?' as if there were no doubt whatever about her acceptance . . . and he knew perfectly well that she was engaged to be married to Morland, which made it a lot worse. She only hoped to goodness the man would go away before Morland came, as he often did about half-past six on a Friday evening. Julia was quite speechless with apprehension when she thought of what might happen if Morland came and discovered Stephen Brett sitting in the drawing-room at Manor Gardens.

There had been a short silence after Julia's somewhat ungracious refusal of Stephen's invitation. Retta saved the situation by asking Mr. Brett to tell her 'all about Africa.'

'That's rather a tall order, Mrs. Harburn,' said Stephen, smiling cheerfully.

'Tell us about the place where you live. You said it was a coal mine.'

'No, a diamond mine.'

'Diamonds!' exclaimed Retta. 'How marvellous! I never knew you found diamonds down a mine. Do you find them yourself, Mr. Brett?'

'My work is mostly administrative.'

'What is the mine like? Does it glitter like Aladdin's Cave?'

'It's quite blinding,' declared Stephen with well-feigned gravity. 'Everyone who goes down the mine has to wear dark glasses.'

'I believe you're teasing me!' Retta exclaimed. 'Yes, I'm sure you are. Well, never mind, I can take a joke as well as most people . . . and just to show that I forgive you for being so naughty I shall call you Stephen.'

'That will be delightful.'

'And you must call me Retta, of course . . . unless you think I'm too old and ugly. Am I too old and ugly, Stephen?'

Stephen laughed. 'What am I to say to that except, "Please, Retta, may I have another cup of tea?"'

'Oh!' exclaimed Retta in a disappointed voice . . . and then she laughed and added: 'Oh, I see what you mean. That's rather clever of you, Stephen.'

'I'm a very clever man,' Stephen told her.

Julia was listening to all this in dismay. Of course it was Retta's usual manner, it was the nonsensical way she carried on with her own particular friends, but obviously Stephen Brett was not enjoying it. Why couldn't Retta see that Stephen Brett was different?

The conversation continued and Julia became more and more ashamed and uncomfortable; she tried to think of something to say, but her embarrassment made her dumb.

Presently Retta got up and said she must go, she had promised to meet some friends and take them to the new film at the Plaza.

'But you'll come and see us again soon, won't you?' she added.

Stephen replied that he would like nothing better. He rose politely and opened the door for Retta to go out.

Retta paused at the door and looked up at him, 'Don't go away and forget all about me, Stephen.'

'Oh no, I shan't forget you,' replied Stephen seriously.

'I'm not too busy to go out in the evening, Stephen, so if you're feeling lonely . . .'

'Thank you, Retta,' said Stephen.

2

When Retta had gone there was a short silence.

'I'm sorry,' said Julia at last. She could find nothing else to say.

'It's all right. Don't worry.'

There was another short silence.

'I'm afraid you're annoyed with me,' said Stephen. 'I mean you're annoyed with me for ringing up and wangling an invitation to tea.'

'You put me in a false position.'

'I'm terribly sorry about it, but what else could I do?'

'Why did you say you had met me at the Claytons' cocktail party?'

'I didn't—honestly. Mrs. Harburn said she supposed I had met you there and I didn't contradict her. It's very rude to contradict a lady,' he added with a smile.

Julia made no comment.

'There was no other way,' he pointed out. 'There was no other way of seeing you again—or at least none that I could think of. If I had known anyone in London I might have managed to get a proper introduction to you, but I don't know anyone at all. What could I do, Julia?'

He was so much in earnest that Julia's heart was melted. 'What did you do?' she asked.

'What did I do? Oh, I see what you mean! I just got hold of the telephone directory at my club.'

'You mean you rang up all the Harburns in London?'

Stephen smiled. 'It wasn't as bad as it sounds. There aren't very many and your father's name is Andrew.'

'What if his name had been Zebediah Smith?'

'It would have taken longer,' admitted Stephen.

Julia giggled; it was a charming little giggle, and it displayed her dimples, which were quite delightful.

'Hurrah, you aren't *really* cross with me!' exclaimed Stephen joyfully.

'Not as cross as I ought to be.'

'You ought not to be cross. I've explained, haven't I? You understand everything now . . . so perhaps you will come with me and see a play. Do say yes, Julia. Please say yes.'

'No,' said Julia firmly. 'I can't possibly; I'm engaged to be married. I told you that yesterday.'

'Surely he wouldn't mind, would he?'

'Of course he would mind.'

'Oh, Julia! Do you really mean that you can't come out with me? I just want to be friends with you, that's all.'

He looked so crestfallen that she almost relented. She certainly could not go out with him in the evening, because her evenings belonged to Morland, but perhaps she could meet Stephen somewhere and have lunch with him. . . . But no, that would be frightfully wrong, it would be deceitful, thought Julia, quite horrified for allowing such an idea to enter her mind.

'No, I'm afraid I can't,' said Julia firmly. 'Besides, you're going to Devonshire, aren't you?'

'I'm going on Tuesday. What about having lunch with me on Monday? You could manage that, couldn't you? I just want to be friends,' he repeated earnestly.

Julia shook her head. 'It wouldn't do; I'm engaged to Morland. He was very angry with me for talking to you.'

'Good heavens, he sounds like an Indian Rajah!'

'An Indian Rajah?'

'Yes, they keep their womenfolk in purdah and never allow them to talk to another man.'

Julia could not help laughing.

'Besides, it was his own fault,' continued Stephen. 'He shouldn't have been late. If I hadn't sat down on the seat and spoken to you someone else would have done so—probably one of those ghastly types with the patent-leather shoes. He should be very grateful to me.'

It was no good talking about it, so Julia changed the conversation; she began to tell him about her plans to leave home and find a job. They discussed the matter for some time. Stephen had all sorts of wild suggestions as to what she could do, but eventually decided that she should pose for advertisements of perfume or cosmetics; he had seen pictures in illustrated papers—dozens of them—and he was sure the advertisers would be only too pleased to engage Julia as a model. Julia laughed and said she thought of going out as a cook.

'But you don't mean it, do you?' asked Stephen. 'It's just a joke. You don't really want a job.'

'Of course I mean it.'

'I thought you were going to marry the Rajah.'

'Oh, Stephen! I'm afraid you'll have to go!' exclaimed Julia, glancing at the clock in sudden alarm. 'I'm terribly sorry, but you must. I had no idea it was so late.'

'It's only twenty-past six.'

'Yes, but Morland is coming. He often comes in on a Friday evening.'

'That's all right,' said Stephen cheerfully. 'As a matter of fact I'd rather like to meet the Rajah.'

Julia rose to her feet. 'Please go, Stephen.'

'But why? Why do you banish me whenever he appears?'

'I've told you. He was angry with me for talking to you; he doesn't like you.'

'Doesn't like me? But he only saw me for a split second!'

'Do please go quickly,' said Julia earnestly.

Stephen rose with reluctance. 'Perhaps you'd like me to go down the back stairs in case I meet the Rajah in the hall?' he suggested with elaborate sarcasm.

'Well perhaps . . . but no, it wouldn't do. Ellen might think it queer.'

Stephen looked at her and saw to his surprise that she was perfectly serious. 'Your life must be very difficult, Julia!' he exclaimed.

'Yes, it is. And you aren't making it any easier.'

There was no more to be said. He went as quickly as he could, running down the stairs and out of the front door into the street. He saw the Rajah approaching in the distance, so deliberately turned and walked in the opposite direction.

'I wonder,' said Stephen as he walked along. 'I wonder . . .'

A girl who happened to be passing at the time looked at him with interest and wondered what the tall, good-looking young man was wondering about.

CHAPTER 4

1

THE room was fairly large, but it was full of furniture, so there was not much space in it. The fitted carpet was decorated with an all-over pattern of pink roses and blue bows; there were lace curtains at the three windows, looped back with sashes of pink plush; the chairs and the sofa were upholstered in pink plush and had curly yellow wooden legs. Along the mantelshelf was a runner of pink plush with dangling yellow balls; there were photographs everywhere in plush and silver-filigree frames. In one corner of the room stood a round pedestal table with a pink plush cloth, and on the table was a dish of wax fruit with a glass cover. The walls were hung with pictures of dogs and children and a number of painted plates.

Julia had never seen a room like this before, but she was aware that there was nothing funny about it; the room was merely out of date; it had been left behind in the march of time. She wondered whether it had always been like this, unchanged since the young womanhood of Queen Victoria, or whether it had been artificially produced. . . . But how difficult it would be to produce it! Where in all the world could you buy things like these? Chairs with curly yellow legs and a sofa with hard plush cushions decorated with yellow woollen tassels!

A young girl in a clean white apron had opened the door to Julia and conducted her upstairs. 'You better wait 'ere,' she had said. 'Miss Martineau'll be down in a minit.' But a good many 'minits' had passed and the owner of the room had not yet appeared. Julia had had time to look round and wonder about it and take it all in; she had had time to peep out of one of the windows between the lace curtains to assure herself that she really was here and now, actually living in the middle of the twentieth century—for the room had such a strong atmosphere of the past that it was the sound of traffic which seemed unreal: the screech of brakes, the grinding of engines, and the sudden hoots of motor horns.

What would Miss Martineau be like, that was the question. It was even more important to have a pleasant landlady than a pleasant room. This was Julia's third day of hunting here, there and everywhere for a reasonably comfortable room and a reasonably pleasant landlady, and she was so discouraged by her fruitless search that she almost regretted her decision to leave home. But perhaps this would do. Perhaps Miss Martineau would be nice and the bedroom which she had advertised as being vacant would be nice too. Julia hoped so. She hoped so all the more because this house was in a street quite near Kensington High Street; it was a district which was conveniently central and it was not far from the gardens.

By this time Julia was tired of waiting for Miss Martineau to appear, so she sat down cautiously in one of the chairs. She had not done so before because they looked like museum pieces, not intended to be sat on, but to her surprise the chair was comfortable; the padded back, though hard, fitted her shoulders and the yellow wooden arms were in exactly the right place for her elbows to rest upon. She had sat in many a modern chair much less comfortable than this. (They liked comfort of course, thought Julia.)

Now that she was becoming used to the unfamiliar aspect of the room she realised that the whole room was comfortable . . . and cosy. Julia's eyes strayed up to the ceiling, in the centre of which there hung a brass chandelier decorated with clusters of crystal drops. It was a pretty thing; the drops flashed and glittered like diamonds. Yes, it was a very pretty thing and absolutely right for the room; and then she noticed that inside the chandelier there was an electric bulb. The discovery gave her quite a shock. Dreadful, thought Julia. Absolutely wrong . . . there ought to be candles!

Julia was still gazing in horror at the anachronism when the door opened and a woman came in. She was short and plump with a pink-and-white complexion and a head of unnaturally golden curls. Her light-blue eyes were bright and sparkling, best of all they were friendly.

'You wanted to see me,' she said. 'It's about the room, of course. Well, it's a nice room and it's on the top floor at the back, so it's quiet—if you don't mind the stairs. The ceiling slopes a bit but you can't have everything in this world, can you?'

Julia agreed that you could not.

'Miss May Martineau is what I call myself. It isn't my real name, of course, any more than yours is Julia Harburn.'

'But it is!' exclaimed Julia in astonishment.

'Well, you're lucky, I must say,' declared Miss Martineau. 'If your name was Eliza Potts you couldn't use it could you? Are you resting?'

'Did you say "resting"?' asked Julia in bewildered tones.

'Oh, I see,' said Miss Martineau, smiling. 'My mistake. I usually get stage people. We call it resting when we're out of a job.'

'I'm looking for a job of some sort.'

'It was silly of me,' declared Miss Martineau, gazing at her.

'If I'd looked at you properly I'd have seen that you've never been on the boards in your life.'

'Are you on the stage?'

'I used to be. Started as a fairy in a Christmas pantomime and went on from there. I once played Michael in *Peter Pan* . . . flying!' said Miss Martineau, standing on tiptoe and waving her arms. 'You wouldn't believe it, would you? There's too much solid flesh about me nowadays, it would take a crane to get me into the air!' She laughed merrily.

Julia laughed too. She could not help it.

'You've got a nice figure, dear,' said Miss Martineau. 'And you know how to wear your clothes. I always say it's half the battle if a girl knows how to wear her clothes.'

She smoothed her rounded hips and continued, 'Well, dear, when I started to put on weight I got the job of wardrobe-mistress with a touring company—looking after the costumes, you know. I'm clever with my needle, Mother taught me that. It was a hard job, packing and unpacking, darning tights and ironing dresses, but all the same I was happy. Sometimes I long for those days back again—it's a kind of homesickness, you know—but there isn't any future in it. You go on till you drop and you can't save a penny, so when you drop you might as well be dead. . . . But I don't know why I'm telling you all this, dear; you didn't come to listen to my life story. You better see the room, and if you like it we can talk about terms.'

They went upstairs together. Miss Martineau continued to talk, though breathlessly, for the stairs were very steep. Her monologue was broken with little puffs.

'It's a good—puff, puff—bed,' said Miss Martineau. 'I like to have—puff, puff—good beds. I always say you spend—puff, puff—a lot of time in bed, so you may as well—puff, puff—be comfortable.'

'What about meals?' asked Julia.

'You can have—puff, puff—breakfast if you like—and supper, but I don't—puff, puff—do lunches. I wouldn't do lunches—puff, puff—for the Queen!'

They had reached the top landing by this time. It was a wide landing with a fitted cupboard which stretched along the length of one wall. There were two doors. Overhead was a skylight through which streamed the rays of the noon-day sun.

Miss Martineau hesitated with her hand on the knob of the door. 'What about boy-friends, dear? I see you're wearing a ring.'

'Yes, I'm engaged.'

'Well, I have to be a bit particular—you couldn't have him to tea in your room or anything—but I'm sure he's a very nice respectable young man so if you wanted to have him along in the evening now and then I'd let you sit in the parlour.'

'That would be very nice,' said Julia, trying to stifle an involuntary giggle at the mere idea of entertaining Morland in her bedroom.

Miss Martineau threw open the door. 'There's the room,' she said. 'I dare say it isn't what you're accustomed to, but you might do worse.'

Julia went in. She saw at once that she might do a lot worse. The room was certainly not what she was accustomed to, but it was a good size and well-shaped, and although the ceiling sloped down at one end it did not offend her sense of proportion. The window was square and looked out onto huddled roofs; the furniture was reasonably good; best of all, everything was clean.

2

Miss Martineau's terms were higher than Julia had expected, or at least they were higher than she had intended to pay, but she had looked at so many horrible rooms and encountered so many disagreeable land-ladies that she decided to clinch the bargain. The place was clean, the bed was comfortable, and Miss Martineau was a pet. Julia had never met anyone like Miss Martineau before. Hitherto all the people with whom she had come in contact were silent people: her father was wrapped up in his brown blanket; Retta had little to say—or at least said very little to Julia; even Morland was not what one could call a conversationalist. The house at Manor Gardens was the sort of house where people spoke in low voices, footsteps were muffled by thick carpets, and the tick of clocks sounded loudly in the stillness.

Miss Martineau was a revelation—there was no other word for it. Julia had known her for about an hour, but already she felt she knew her intimately, already they were friends. So the terms were settled amicably and it was arranged that Julia should move into the room on Monday, which was the day Mr. and Mrs. Harburn were flying to Rome. Miss Martineau showed Julia where she could hang her frocks, in the capacious cupboard on the landing, and explained that although it really belonged to Peter there would be plenty of room for Julia's things and lots of spare hangers.

'I always say you can't have too many hangers,' declared Miss Martineau.

By this time Julia had learnt that Miss Martineau was really Mrs. Potts, that her husband had died some years ago and Peter was her only child.

'We'd have liked more,' she explained. 'But I was so ill when Peter was born and Norman was so frightened that he wouldn't risk another. He said if it didn't kill me it would kill him—so that was that. And to tell you the truth, Peter was just about all I could manage. You wouldn't believe the mischief that child got into! Sometimes I felt like screaming and climbing up the wall. There's just two rooms on this floor,' she added. 'Yours and Peter's. I never let Peter's room because I never know when it might be wanted—not much fun to come home and find a stranger in your room!'

'It would be horrid,' agreed Julia fervently.

As they came down the stairs together Julia explained her own affairs and discovered that Miss Martineau could listen, as well as she could talk.

'You're quite right, dulling,' she declared. 'I can see it's a bit of a wrench to leave your comfortable home, but it must be difficult for you to take a back seat after running the show, and they'll get on better alone. Two's company, you know.'

'That's what I thought.'

'And you don't have to worry about a job. I'll talk to some of my friends; we'll soon find something for you to do.'

Julia had taken an instinctive liking for her prospective landlady, and obviously the feeling was reciprocated, for as they were saying good-bye ('It's *au revoir* really,' said Miss Martineau) she squeezed Julia's hand and exclaimed, 'What a good thing I didn't let that room before! I nearly did, yesterday afternoon, but something prevented me clicking. I don't know what, really, because he seemed a nice young chap and he had very good references. I think it was partly because I didn't much like the idea of him and Peter up there on the top floor by themselves.' She laughed gaily. 'A regular old granny I am,' she added.

3

As this happened to be Thursday, Julia was due to meet Morland in Kensington Gardens at the usual hour, so instead of going home to lunch she went to a small restaurant in a back street which had been recommended to her by Miss Martineau.

'It's a funny little place,' Miss Martineau had said. 'And funny people go there. But the food is good, and it's cheap. The man is called Jacques— he's French, and he cooks the food himself.'

Julia discovered that this was true. Jacques not only cooked the food himself but superintended the service. He chatted to Julia in a friendly manner and was enchanted when he found she could speak to him in his own language. She decided that when she came to live at Miss Martineau's she would make a habit of lunching here.

By the time she had finished lunch it was half-past two, so Julia was early for her appointment; but Morland was already there, sitting on the seat. This was most unusual. Was it an accident that he happened to be early or was it because of what had happened last week? Perhaps Retta was right in saying that it was a good thing to give men a fright now and then to keep them up to the mark! Julia smiled to herself at the absurd idea and went forward smiling to greet Morland.

It was cooler to-day and inclined to be showery, so there were not so many people about, and it was easier to talk.

'I've something to tell you,' said Morland as they sat down together.

'Something nice?'

'Yes, in a way. As a matter of fact I'm half pleased and half sorry about it. I've got three weeks' holidays and Father wants me to go to Gleneagles with him to play golf.'

'But that's lovely for you! Why are you half sorry?'

'It means I shan't see you for ages,' he explained. 'And I'm not very happy about leaving you here alone while your parents are away. It will be dull for you, won't it? Mother is coming too and she suggested we should try to get a room for you, but there isn't one to be had. Unless there happens to be a cancellation—'

'Oh no!' exclaimed Julia. 'I mean it's very kind of you to think of it, but I couldn't possibly.'

'Well, we can't,' said Morland with a sigh. 'The hotel is full.'

Julia was glad the hotel was full; the idea of going to Gleneagles with the Beverleys did not appeal to her at all. Morland and his father would play golf all day and she would have been left to chat to Mrs. Beverley or to go out with her for drives in the car. Mrs. Beverley was a nice kind woman—nobody could be kinder—but she was a nonentity, with no mind of her own, so she was poor company. The idea crossed Julia's mind that it would be very much more amusing to spend all day in the company of Miss Martineau.

'Don't worry about me,' said Julia cheerfully. 'Just go and enjoy yourself and have a good time. I've managed to find a room which seems very nice indeed, so the next thing is I must find a job.'

'You've found a room!' exclaimed Morland in surprise.

'Yes, it's in a sort of boarding-house in a turning off Kensington High Street. The place is run by a woman called Miss Martineau, I liked her the moment I saw her. Oh, Morland, you must come and see her parlour! It's simply wonderful—a perfect period piece—all pink plush and yellow tassels and chairs with curly legs. She said I could have you now and then in the evening and she would let us sit in her parlour.'

'She said you could have me? What frightful cheek!'

'It wasn't really.' Julia giggled and added, 'She doesn't approve of boy-friends.'

'Julia! The woman sounds awful. What you want is a boarding-house run by a respectable woman who used to be a cook in good service. She would know what was what.'

'Try and find such a place,' said Julia bitterly. 'I've been hunting for days. Miss Martineau is good and kind, and very amusing into the bargain.'

'What are the other people like?'

'You mean the other boarders? They're stage people, so I shan't see much of them. They'll be asleep when I have my breakfast and they'll be out when I get back from work.'

'It sounds most unsuitable. I don't like the idea at all,' declared Morland, frowning. 'Don't you think it would be better for you to stay on at Manor Gardens until we're married?'

'We've been into all that before,' Julia pointed out. 'And anyhow I can't stay on there now—even if I wanted to—because I told Retta I intended to leave home and she was delighted.'

'She was delighted?'

'Yes. You see, Morland, you don't understand Retta in the very least.'

Morland was silent for a few moments. Then he said, 'What about your father?'

'I don't think he will mind,' replied Julia with a sigh. 'I never know what Father is thinking. Ellen is the only person who is sorry that I'm going away. There was a frightful scene when I told Ellen about it.'

This was not surprising, for Ellen had been with the Harburn family for most of her life. She had been with them before Julia was born; she had been Julia's nurse; she had helped to look after Mrs. Harburn during her last illness. Now Ellen had assumed the duties of cook-housekeeper at Manor Gardens and ruled the dailies who came in at various hours with a firm but kindly hand. In addition to her other multifarious duties Ellen kept an eye on her one-time nursling. There was nothing Ellen enjoyed more than chatting to Julia about 'the old days,' which in her opinion were very much better than the new regime.

'Ellen will miss you,' said Morland.

'I know, but I can't help that; besides, as I told her, it isn't as if I shall be going far away.'

'Oh—well,' said Morland rather unhappily. 'I don't like the sound of it much but I suppose you had better try it and see how you get on. You'll write and tell me what happens, won't you?'

'Yes, of course I'll write.'

By this time it was beginning to get rather cold, so Morland rose. 'We'll go home,' he said. 'It will be much more comfortable. The parents are out so we shall have the place to ourselves.'

Julia got up and followed him.

CHAPTER 5

1

MR. AND Mrs. Harburn flew to Rome to join their ship and Julia went to the airport to see them off. Her father had been told of her plans but had made no comment except to say that if she changed her mind and wanted to come home she could do so whenever she pleased and that he had given instructions to the bank to pay thirty pounds a month into her account. Julia knew he could easily afford it, so she accepted the allowance with suitable gratitude. (It would have been foolish not to accept it for she had made some inquiries about suitable posts and had discovered that women without any training were a glut on the market.)

I shan't starve anyhow, whatever happens, thought Julia as she stood and waved her handkerchief to the departing plane.

When the plane had vanished from sight Julia went home to pick up her luggage and say good-bye to Ellen.

Poor Ellen was very upset.

'I don't know what your pore dear mother would think,' declared Ellen. 'We can only 'ope she don't know nothing about it. That's all I can say.'

Unfortunately it was not all she could say; she said a great deal more, and Julia, who was really very fond of Ellen, was obliged to listen. She tried to comfort Ellen and repeated several times that she was not going far away, but Ellen would not be consoled.

Ellen said she didn't know how she was going to bear it; she wished she was dead, she wished she could leave Manor Gardens, she hadn't never liked 'that young woman' and didn't trust her a yard . . . and what 'Mr. 'Arburn' wanted to go and marry her for Ellen couldn't think.

'It's all 'is fault,' declared Ellen wildly. 'She wouldn't never 'ave dared turn you out if it 'adn't been for 'im. 'E's an unnatural father, that's what 'e is and always 'as been ever since you was born . . . never looked at you or bothered about you, never spoke to your pore dear mother for days, and all because you wasn't a boy. As if she could 'elp it! I can see 'er now lying in bed with tears pouring down 'er face because it wasn't a boy and the doctor said she couldn't never 'ave another. It wasn't for 'erself she minded; you was a sweet pretty baby and as good as gold and she loved you dearly.'

Julia had heard all this before; she was aware that she had been a severe disappointment to her father, but as it was not her fault she was not unduly perturbed.

'I suppose that's why Father has always been so unhappy,' she said thoughtfully. 'I mean because he had no son.'

'Don't you think it,' declared Ellen. 'Your father was queer before you was born. It's 'is nature to be shut up like that and never speak a civil word to nobody . . . besides, there was something else that preyed on 'is mind.'

'Something else?'

'I don't listen to gossip.'

'But, Ellen, what was it? I wish you'd tell me. I've often wondered why he wasn't cheerful and happy like other girls' fathers.'

'I've told you, Miss Julia. There was something that preyed on his mind,' repeated Ellen. 'P'raps I didn't ought to have told you—p'raps I've said more than I ought—but it's because I'm all upset this afternoon.'

'It worries me,' said Julia sadly. 'It has worried me for a long time. I hoped he would be happier when he married Retta.'

'If 'e couldn't be 'appy with your mother 'e couldn't be 'appy with nobody,' Ellen declared. 'She was a saint if ever there was one . . . but there ain't no call for you to blame yourself, Miss Julia. You did your duty to both of them as well as you could. You were a good daughter to your pore mother, going abroad with 'er and looking after 'er when she was ill. I'm sure I don't know what she'd 'ave done without you. And you were a good daughter to your father too—better than 'e deserved—doing the 'ousekeeping so well, and everything just as it was when your mother done it 'erself. You did your best, so don't you worry about it.'

Julia was silent for a few moments. She was sensible enough to realise that what Ellen had said was true; she had done her best for both her parents . . . neither of them needed her any more. It was sad to feel that she was not needed, and it was sad to be leaving the old house in Manor Gardens where she had lived all her life, but it was no use allowing herself to feel sentimental. Julia decided to leave her old life behind her and look forward to the future.

The taxi which had been ordered to take Julia and her luggage to Miss Martineau's house had now arrived, so Julia kissed Ellen fondly, and, repeating her assurances that she would come and see her soon, ran down the steps as quickly as she could and drove away.

2

As the taxi turned the corner and approached Miss Martineau's door Julia began to wonder how she would be able to get all her luggage upstairs. However, Miss Martineau had been watching for her arrival, and she ran out and persuaded the driver to carry it up, and told Julia exactly how much she was to pay him.

The sum seemed very little to Julia—considering those breakneck stairs—so she gave him a good deal more, and he went away quite cheerfully.

'You gave him more than I said,' declared Miss Martineau, wagging her finger at Julia. 'I saw him jump into his cab and he wouldn't have been so cock-a-hoop if you hadn't overpaid him. . . . But never mind, dulling, I like a girl to be generous. Mean people give me the shudders. 'When I was in rep we did a play about a miser, it was translated from French, and it was so awful I used to wake at night screaming blue murder thinking he was after me. Come upstairs,' she added. 'We're having tea in the parlour—just you and me—the others are out so I thought we'd be cosy and get to know each other properly.'

This kind welcome comforted Julia considerably; her spirits rose and she followed Miss Martineau into the parlour feeling much more cheerful. They sat down together and drank tea from delightful old cups of mid-Victorian bone china and ate an exceedingly good sponge-cake which Miss Martineau had made with her own hands from a very special mid-Victorian recipe.

'It all goes together,' Miss Martineau explained. 'If you have a room like this you must live up to it. Peter wanted to have a cocktail party but I said, "Well, you can have a cocktail party if you like but you can't have it in the parlour."'

'You were absolutely right,' declared Julia.

'Some people like this room and some don't.'

'I like it awfully.'

'I'm glad you like it,' said its owner smiling proudly. 'I didn't like it much at first, but it grows on you—at least it did on me. Peter says it's affected and artificial, but it isn't at all. It's absolutely real.'

'Real?' asked Julia.

'The furniture is real. It all belonged to Great-Aunt Anne and she left it to me in her will. It was in store for years and years, but when Norman and I bought this house we got it out and had it brought along. I thought it was hideous,' admitted Miss Martineau. 'I wanted to sell it and buy a nice new suite, but Norman liked it. Norman said it would be a joke to have a Victorian parlour, so he got pictures of what it ought to be like and arranged it all himself. We had everything except the wallpaper and the fireplace. Norman bought the fireplace at a sale and he found the wallpaper in a warehouse in Stepney; it was right at the back behind a lot of modern wallpapers. I let him do it just as he wanted, all except the lamps. I drew the line at oil-lamps—nasty smelly things! I had to draw the line,' said Miss Martineau earnestly. 'But I don't mind telling you that after he died I was sorry I hadn't let him. It was horrid of me, wasn't it?'

'It wasn't horrid a bit,' said Julia in comforting tones. 'Lamps are dangerous; they might have set the house on fire.'

'Yes, that's true,' agreed Miss Martineau more cheerfully.

She poured out another cup of tea. 'I've got a job for you if you want it,' she added.

'A job—for me!'

'If you want it,' repeated Miss Martineau in warning tones. 'You didn't say what sort of job you were looking for, did you?'

'Almost anything!'

'It's a friend of mine who has a hat shop in Kensington High Street. She's doing very well and she said to me yesterday she wanted another assistant and I said, "Well, I can't promise, but if you want a girl that's got style and knows how to wear her clothes I believe I might know one that would suit you. But you'd have to pay her," I said. "She's good class and you won't get a girl like that for twopence a week." That's what I told her. She's French, you see, and she likes a bargain; you have to be business-like dealing with people like that. First she said four pounds—and I laughed in her face—so then she said five and I said five-ten. So that's what it is . . . take it or leave it, dulling.'

'But she hasn't seen me!' cried Julia. 'And I've never done anything like that before!'

'Gracious me, anyone can sell hats!' cried Miss Martineau gaily. 'Anyone with a face like you and pretty curls!' and with that she leapt from her chair, seized an antimacassar, twisted it into a sort of turban and crossing the room to a gilt-framed mirror arranged it carefully upon her head. Then she turned, and suddenly she was a different person, languid and affected.

'The very latest from Paris,' she drawled, bending her head from one side to the other and patting her curls with the tips of her fingers. 'So chic, so becoming . . . the line so original, so intriguing! Let us see if it becomes Madame,' she added, removing it from her own head and settling it carefully upon Julia's. 'Beautiful!' she cried in sudden ecstasy. 'What could be better? It is Madame's colour; it enhances the loveliness of Madame's eyes; it shows off her delicious complexion! Let me pull it this way a trifle—no, that way! Exquisite!' cried Miss Martineau, clasping her hands and rolling her eyes. 'Such faultless taste! Such perfect line! Quite ravishing! It is Madame's *chapeau* . . . and only twenty guineas. Too expensive?' asked Miss Martineau in surprise. 'Oh no! Oh dear me, no! Twenty guineas isn't out of the way for such a beautiful *chapeau*. Oh, I *do* want Madame to have it! Well—for Madame—let us say eighteen-ten.'

By this time Julia was laughing so uncontrollably that 'the *chapeau*' fell off onto the floor.

Miss Martineau pounced upon it, shook it out, and replaced it on the back of the chair. 'That's the way to sell hats,' she said in her ordinary voice.

'Oh goodness! I don't know when I've laughed like this!' cried Julia holding her sides.

Miss Martineau chuckled. 'It wasn't very good,' she said. 'Not really *good*. I'm out of practice.'

Julia was still giggling feebly. 'Thank you for the lesson. I see the idea of course, but I'm not sure that I could do it.'

'Have a try,' suggested Miss Martineau.

CHAPTER 6

MADAME Claire wanted an assistant immediately, and as Julia was free and anxious to get settled as soon as possible it was arranged that she should go for a week's trial. She was somewhat alarmed at the idea of her new job, and said so to Miss Martineau as they breakfasted together in the dining-room.

'You'll do it easily,' declared her new friend encouragingly.

'If you can't do it I'll eat my hat—my *chapeau*, I mean. I've got a little present for you, just to bring you luck.'

The little present was a small pair of gilt scissors, shaped like a stork, with a long beak and a tiny red glass eye. It was a charming piece of nonsense; Julia was delighted with it and accepted it with becoming gratitude.

'Just to bring you luck,' nodded Miss Martineau. 'They belonged to Great-Aunt Anne—so they're really old—but they'll be useful. You must hang them round your waist with a piece of ribbon and they'll be handy when you want them.'

'It's very, very kind of you,' said Julia. 'I'm sure they'll bring me luck.'

Miss Martineau came out onto the steps to see her off. 'Don't you let her bully you,' she said, wagging an admonitory finger at her protégée. 'People don't value doormats; they just wipe their feet on them and pass on.'

Julia smiled at this as she went down the street; but although she had not far to go, the smile had faded and an expression of intense anxiety had taken its place by the time she arrived at the gaily-painted door of

Madame Claire's establishment. She was a little early, and at first she thought the shop was empty. Then she saw a spread-out newspaper and two long elegant legs clad in sheer nylon stockings coming out from beneath it. When the door-bell tinkled the lady who was reading the newspaper put it to one side and looked at Julia inquiringly. She had very black hair and dark brown eyes. Her face was pale, her eyebrows dark, her lips scarlet.

'I came to see Madame Claire,' said Julia timidly.

'That is me,' said the lady, rising and putting down the paper. 'It is early—but no matter. You would like to see some *chapeaux*?'

'I'm Julia Harburn. Miss Martineau said—'

'All, the good kind May!' exclaimed Madame Claire. 'You have come to help me! It is understood. Ivonne and Fifi, they have not yet arrived. They are late always. I myself will show you the little room where you will leave your coat and put on the overall.'

She hurried into the back premises and Julia followed.

Julia had not expected her new job to begin immediately without any sort of preparation. She had expected to be interviewed by her employer; she had expected some sort of explanation of what she was to do and how she was to do it. Instead of which, almost before she could get her breath, she found herself attired in a very pretty blue nylon overall showing hats to a stout lady with a square red face. (The other two girls had arrived by this time, but there was nothing French about them except their names.)

The stout lady, Julia's first customer, tried on a great many hats and eventually went away saying she would think about it.

This was not a good start, in fact it was so bad that, when Madame approached, Julia quite expected her to say that Julia must take off the overall, put on her coat and leave immediately never to return.

However, Madame did not say that. She said, 'It is not any use to trouble with that sort of person. You wasted your time being so kind and attentive . . . but how could you know? Soon you will know at a glance whether it is a *chapeau* the woman desires or whether she is too early for her appointment with the dentist . . . or to meet her friend at the little café round the corner.'

Julia laughed, partly in amusement and partly in relief. 'But what am I to say?'

'You will be tactful,' replied Madame. 'You will not say, "We have no *chapeaux* in this establishment to suit a square red face that will nevaire do. It is true, of course, the *chapeaux* in this establishment are designed for pretty faces, but the truth is not always wise. Look, Julie, here is a client who desires to buy a *chapeau*! You will sell her the little red straw on the stand in the corner, but you will show her some others first.'

Julia noticed that she had become 'Julie' and the pretty girl with dark hair who had just entered the 'establishment' was a 'client.' The girl was looking round rather vaguely, so Julia advanced upon her with a smile. 'Can I help you?' she asked ingratiatingly.

It was quite easy after that. Julia showed the client several hats, and then, taking the red one off the stand, said, 'I believe this is the very one! I'm sure it will suit you,' and so saying put it on herself.

'It's certainly very nice on you,' agreed the girl. 'I had better try it, hadn't I?'

'Yes, you should wear it like this,' replied Julia, arranging it carefully upon the head of the client.

Of course it suited her admirably . . . there was nothing much that Madame did not know about hats.

'Yes, it *is* nice,' said the client. 'I like it.'

Julia gave her the hand-mirror and she looked at the back.

'I like it,' repeated the client emphatically.

'It suits you awfully well,' declared Julia. Fortunately this was true, so she was able to say it with enthusiasm.

'I suppose it's frightfully expensive?'

'Oh, I don't think so. I'll just look at the label . . . no, it's only five guineas.'

'Oh dear, that's a lot to pay for a hat!'

Julia felt like saying she couldn't agree more; instead she said, 'But it's so becoming, isn't it?'

'Yes,' agreed the girl. 'Yes—well—I wonder.'

'Try it on again,' suggested Julia.

The client tried it on again. 'It really *is* rather nice, isn't it?'

'Yes, it is. I like the way it turns up at the side; quite an unusual line and very becoming.'

'Perhaps I had better have it.'

'I think you should—really,' declared Julia with absolute truth—for of course the girl should buy the hat, for Julia's sake if not for her own.

Madame had been watching, and, much to Julia's relief, she strolled over to put the finishing touch. 'The little *chapeau* is charming,' she said. 'It is a model from Paris—*très chic*. You have chosen well, Mademoiselle. Perhaps you would like to wear it?'

Yes, Mademoiselle would wear it and have her old hat sent home.

Madame watched while Julia took the address, made out the bill, received the money, gave the correct change, and showed her first client out of the door.

'That was nice, Julie,' she said. 'Very nice indeed.'

'She was easy,' replied Julia.

'She was easy because you are her own kind,' explained Madame. 'And because you treated her just right. It is very important to treat people just right. There are some who like to be flattered: "Oh, Madame! It is your *chapeau*! Who else could wear it with such elegance?" There are others who prefer to hear sense. There are those who cannot make up their minds and must have their minds made up for them, and again others who dislike to be pressed. There are all kinds of people,' declared Madame with a gesture of her expressive hands which seemed to embrace the whole of humanity. 'Remember that, Julie. It will not always be so easy as that young girl, nor so difficult as the fat lady, but I think you will do very nicely.'

'*Je vous remercie, Madame. Je ferai de mon mieux pour vous plaire.*'

These simple words acted like a charm. Immediately Madame broke into a torrent of French . . . if only she had known Julie spoke French! But she knew now, and they would converse together. Julie could not imagine how Madame had yearned for an assistant with whom she could converse in her own beautiful language. It had occurred to Madame to search for such a one in France, but there were difficulties. . . . Madame enumerated the difficulties volubly.

Julia commiserated and put in a few words whenever Madame paused for breath.

How was it that Julie spoke French so beautifully, Madame wanted to know.

Julia explained that her mother was a very good linguist. They had spoken French together and read it aloud to each other and had spent several winters in France because her mother was delicate and the climate of London did not suit her.

'She is better now, I hope?'

'She is dead, Madame.'

'*Ah, pauvre petite,*' said Madame, patting her on the shoulder. '*C'est vraiment triste de perdre sa mère.*'

The other girls were idle at the moment and were watching the little scene with disfavour. They were even less pleased when Madame told them to put away the hats which Julia's client had discarded, whilst she continued to converse in an excited manner with the new assistant.

'Tidying up after her!' whispered Ivonne to Fifi as she shut one of the drawers with a vigorous slam. 'That's what we've got to do . . . just because she can gabble in French.'

CHAPTER 7

1

MISS Martineau was sitting at the window in the dining-room when Julia returned from her first day at Madame Claire's. As a matter of fact Miss Martineau often sat there; it was a good point of vantage, for the dining-room was on the ground floor and its window looked out into the street. From here Miss Martineau could watch people passing and could see all that was going on. The dining-room was the same size as the parlour but it seemed much larger, for it contained less furniture and its furnishings were modern. It was used by Miss Martineau and her boarders as an all-purpose apartment, not only for eating but for sitting and talking and taking their ease. The telephone and the television cabinet were here, so also was Miss Martineau's somewhat untidy workbasket and various odds and ends belonging to her boarders. The parlour was used only for special occasions and sometimes in the evening when Miss Martineau wanted to be cosy.

This afternoon Miss Martineau was on the lookout for Julia and rushed out to meet her at the door.

'How did you get on?' she asked anxiously.

'Quite all right. I sold six hats,' replied Julia proudly. 'Madame was very kind and said I would do very nicely.'

People are always pleased when their arrangements prove successful and Miss Martineau was no exception to the rule. She beamed with delight. 'That's lovely!' she declared. 'I knew you could do it. I said so, didn't I? Come and talk to me, dulling, I want to hear all that happened—every single thing—but I must get on with my sewing. Look, I'm making this for Peter's birthday!'

'For Peter's birthday!' echoed Julia, surveying the peach-coloured nylon slip in amazement.

'What a job I had getting the nylon lace!' continued Miss Martineau. 'I tried half a dozen shops before I could get what I wanted. You see, I'm letting it into the bodice and I'm putting peach-coloured ribbon shoulder straps. It's sweet, isn't it? Do you think Peter will like it?'

'Peter!' gasped Julia.

Miss Martineau chuckled. 'Oh, I see,' she said. 'I thought I'd told you. I thought you understood. Come and sit down and I'll tell you all about it,' she added, taking up her sewing and preparing for a comfortable chat.

'It was like this,' continued Miss Martineau. 'When the baby was coming I said to Norman, "Now don't forget; if it's a boy it's to be Peter and if it's a girl it's to be Wendy."

'"All right," he said. "That suits me—but why make such a point about me remembering? You can remind me about it after it has arrived." "I might die," I said. Norman just told me not to be silly but I could see he was upset, so I didn't say another word.'

'Did you really think you were going to die?' asked Julia in horrified tones.

'Off and on I did,' nodded Miss Martineau. 'But I kept it to myself. I was sorry I'd said it, really, because Norman didn't forget. He was very fond of me, you see—sometimes when he thought I wasn't looking he would sit and gaze at me. Oh well, I didn't die,' she continued more cheerfully. 'Though between you and me I wasn't far off it. I had an awful time. When I came round and found I was alive and kicking I was quite surprised. Norman was there, holding my hand. He said, "The doc says it's Wendy. Are you pleased?" Pleased! I felt too ill to care. If he'd said it was a kitten I wouldn't have minded.'

'It was Wendy?' asked Julia in bewilderment. 'But I thought—'

'Yes, it was Wendy—at least it ought to have been—but one day, when the baby was six weeks old and we were going to have it christened, Norman said to me, "I know it's a girl but it isn't my idea of a Wendy. You can hear it bawling all over the house. It's more like a tiger-cub than a baby. I can't imagine that baby growing up domesticated, mending the boy's socks and doing the spring cleaning."

'I couldn't imagine it either, to tell you the truth. It was a fierce little creature with a lot of black hair and it got into the most awful rage if it had to wait for its bottle, clenched its fists and screamed itself crimson in the face. It wasn't cuddly and soft; it was independent. You felt from the very beginning that it could look out for itself. I said to Norman, "Well, I believe you're right, but I made up my mind it was to be Peter or Wendy so if it isn't Wendy it had better be Peter." Norman said that would be queer (he didn't like things to be queer) so I said, "It won't be queer if we spell it P—E—T—A." So that's what we did.'

'Oh, I see,' said Julia, who had been listening to the story with interest. 'It's a nice name, isn't it?'

'Yes, very nice—and most unusual.'

'She's a very unusual sort of girl,' said her mother. 'It certainly suits her a lot better than Wendy. She was a bit of a problem when she was a child. (I told you that, didn't I?) Independent, you know, and wild as heather, always wanting her own way . . . but I understand why she was like that, she was Peter to the life, so I just went on loving her and it turned out all right. She's still a bit wild and independent but she's got a kind heart; that's the main thing, isn't it? She'll be coming home one of these days, so you'll see her. It will be nice company for you to have a girl of your own age to chat to.'

Julia agreed politely, but she felt doubtful. What she had heard about Peta was somewhat alarming.

2

The other boarders in Miss Martineau's house were a cheerful lot, young and gay, but Julia saw very little of them for they were asleep in bed when Julia went off to work and when Julia returned they had gone to the theatre. Occasionally she heard them coming home late at night, talking and laughing, but more often she was asleep by that time and their voices did not disturb her. She wondered when Miss Martineau slept, for she was always there when the theatre-party came back and was up and about in good time to have breakfast with Julia; but on making tactful inquiries Julia discovered that she always had 'a little shut-eye' in the afternoon. All the same, Julia was slightly worried about it, and on Saturday night she told her hostess that she would not want breakfast on Sunday. She had decided to go to church early and have breakfast afterwards somewhere in town.

'Just as you like,' said Miss Martineau. 'I like going to church myself, but eight o'clock is a bit much when you've had a late night on Saturday. You can come home to lunch, if you don't mind cold ham and salad.'

'I thought you said you wouldn't do lunches for the Queen,' said Julia teasingly.

Miss Martineau chuckled. 'Well, I couldn't give the Queen cold ham and salad, could I, dulling?'

Meanwhile Julia was settling down in her new job and finding it very interesting indeed. She realised that Madame Claire's establishment must be a veritable gold-mine. Some of the hats came from wholesale manufacturers and some from well-known houses in Paris, but many of them were made by Madame with her own clever fingers. Quite often these consisted of a few artificial flowers and a piece of gauze or straw. The materials cost a few shillings and the 'creations' were sold for pounds. It seemed wrong, somehow, but Julia comforted herself by the reflection that the clients were paying for Madame's skilful work. Like a picture, thought Julia. How much did a picture cost in actual money? The canvas and paint were practically worthless. It was the skill of the painter which made the picture valuable.

CHAPTER 8

1

ON FRIDAY when Julia returned from work Miss Martineau rushed out of the dining-room to meet her.

'He's come!' she cried in excitement.

'Who's come?'

'Your young man, of course!' She approached nearer, and sinking her voice to a conspiratorial whisper she added, 'Such a nice young chap—just the very one—you couldn't do better.'

'But it can't be! He's at Gleneagles.'

'He's in the parlour, dulling. He's waiting for you. I gave him the *Telegraph* to keep him happy . . . but he's been waiting twenty minutes or more, so you better pop upstairs quickly.'

Julia could not understand it at all, something unforeseen must have happened; but Morland did not like to be kept waiting, so she popped upstairs as quickly as she could.

She opened the door. 'Morland—' she began breathlessly . . . and then stopped. Her visitor was Stephen Brett.

'Hallo, Julia!' said Stephen, throwing Miss Martineau's *Daily Telegraph* onto the floor and rising to meet her.

'Goodness, it's you!' she exclaimed. 'I thought you had gone home to Devonshire.'

'I went home and then I came back. That's the explanation.'

'But why?'

'Business and pleasure,' he told her. 'I did my business this morning so I thought I'd call in and see you this afternoon.'

'How did you find me?'

Stephen laughed. 'You're rather an elusive person, aren't you? This time it was quite easy, I just phoned up your house in Manor Gardens and asked for your address. I thought we might go out together and have dinner. What about it?'

'Oh no, I don't think so—'

'Why not? Do come, Julia. It would be fun.'

Julia hesitated. It would be fun . . . but what about Morland?

'Do come,' repeated Stephen. 'I've been busy all day so I've earned a little pleasure. Please come, Julia.'

Why not? thought Julia. Morland was at Gleneagles amusing himself by playing golf, so why shouldn't she amuse herself by going out with Stephen? She smiled suddenly and the enchanting dimples came and went.

'You will!' cried Stephen in delight. 'How lovely! Where shall we go? Would you like to go somewhere posh, like the Savoy, or—'

'Have you come into a fortune?' asked Julia, laughing.

'No, but I'm going to make one.'

'You're going to make a fortune?'

He nodded. 'Yes, but it's a secret. Perhaps I'll tell you some time.'

In spite of this mysterious boast Julia decided against 'somewhere posh' and, as Stephen happened to know of a quiet place where you could eat well and talk comfortably, they agreed to go there.

'Do you mind waiting? I'd like to change,' said Julia.

'I'll change too—but not a dinner-jacket of course—I'll nip back to the club and fetch you in about half an hour. Can do?'

'Can do,' nodded Julia.

He went off like a rocket, clattering down the stairs, and Julia sped up to her room.

2

Julia was in the middle of changing when there was a timid knock on the door and Miss Martineau's head appeared round the corner.

'Not a little tiff, dulling?' she asked anxiously.

'Goodness, no! I'm changing; we're going out to dinner.'

'Oh, lovely!' said Miss Martineau with a sigh of relief. 'I just wondered. He went off in such a hurry and banged the door. I hope you don't mind me asking.'

'I think it's sweet of you,' declared Julia as she sat down and began to draw on a pair of sheer nylon stockings. 'It was sweet of you to come up all those stairs . . . but that isn't Morland Beverley.'

'Not?'

'No, just a friend. He lives in Devonshire and he happened to be in Town for a few days on business, so he called to ask me to go out to dinner with him.'

'Very nice,' said Miss Martineau, nodding. 'Are you going to a smart place?'

'No, just a quiet place where we can talk.'

'Very nice,' repeated Miss Martineau emphatically. 'Can I help you, dulling? What are you going to wear?'

Julia was searching in her drawer for a suitable slip. She said, 'I think my little blue frock will do; it's hanging in Peta's cupboard.'

Miss Martineau fetched it. 'You *have* got nice things, haven't you?' she said admiringly. 'Let me pop it over your head. You don't wear eye-shadow do you? Well, perhaps you're right. Gentlemen don't like girls to look made-up.'

She continued to chat, but that did not interfere with her efficiency (she had not lost her skill in quick-change technique), so Julia was changed and ready in record time.

'You *do* look sweet,' declared Miss Martineau. 'I *do* hope you'll have a nice time, dulling. I always say it's quite a good thing for a girl to have two strings to her bow.'

Julia laughed and kissed her lightly on her soft pink cheek and ran downstairs before she could say another word.

3

The little restaurant was in a quiet street not far from Piccadilly and had two flourishing bay trees in wooden barrels outside the door. The dining-room was L-shaped with padded seats along the wails and there were small tables with shaded lamps.

Stephen and Julia were unfashionably early, so not many people were dining, and they were able to find a table in a quiet corner. Stephen insisted on ordering 'champers' to celebrate, and when Julia asked what they were celebrating he said 'Business and pleasure.'

They drank the toast solemnly.

After that Stephen became very gay (Julia thought he was excited about something and wondered what it was); his high spirits were infectious, so they teased each other and laughed and chatted in a very amusing manner.

Presently Stephen leant forward and said, 'I see you're still engaged to the Indian Rajah. I hope he won't come here to-night or I shall have to nip out by the service-door, shan't I?'

'He's at Gleneagles, playing golf.'

'Hurrah, we're safe!'

Julia's hand was lying on the table so he took it and looked at her ring. 'Diamonds, but not good water and badly cut. He should have given you a sapphire to match your eyes.'

She drew her hand away quickly.

'You're cross with me,' said Stephen sadly. 'But it's perfectly true. I know quite a lot about stones. Would you like to see a really fine stone, Julia?'

Without waiting for her reply he took a little chamois bag out of his pocket and shook it gently onto the white cloth. A sapphire about the size of a large pea rolled out and lay between them on the table.

'Oh, Stephen, how beautiful!' exclaimed Julia.

It certainly was beautiful. It was cornflower-blue and glowed as if it possessed an inward fire.

'Yes, it's a good one,' agreed Stephen. 'Not large, but absolutely flawless . . . which is very unusual. You don't often find a sapphire without tiny feathers or clouds.'

'Feathers or clouds?'

'Little rents or fissures or cloudy spots, sometimes so slight as to be almost invisible, but all the same they take away from the lovely velvety appearance. This one is quite perfect.' He rolled it over with his finger. 'I've just had it cut,' he added.

'It almost looks as if it might burn a hole in the cloth!'

'Do you like it, Julia?'

'Of course I like it! I think it's perfectly lovely.'

'That's the stone I would give you if you were engaged to me.'

'But I'm not!' exclaimed Julia in alarm.

'No. It's a pity, isn't it?'

'Don't be silly!' she cried. 'And do put it away quickly. I'm sure it must be very valuable.'

He took it up, but instead of putting it away he dropped it into her hand. 'Why not have it—and me?'

'That isn't a very funny joke, Stephen.'

'It isn't a joke at all,' he told her gravely. 'The moment I saw you sitting on that seat in the park I knew you were the girl I wanted to marry.'

'Stephen, please! If I'd known you were going to be silly I wouldn't have come out with you. You know I'm engaged to be married.'

'It isn't irrevocable—being engaged.'

'It is, to me,' declared Julia breathlessly. 'I'm that sort of person. Besides, Morland and I love each other—we've known each other for years. I've seen you three times. I think you must be mad!'

'Mad about you,' he said in a low voice. He added, 'Of course I'm mad to speak to you like this. Forgive me, Julia.'

'Forgive you?'

'Yes, please! We'll say no more about it. We'll go back to where we were. We'll just be friends. Is that right?'

'Yes—if you promise to be sensible.'

'I promise. Cross my heart,' said Stephen earnestly.

For a few moments there was silence. The sapphire still lay upon the table; Julia had dropped it as if it were burning her hand.

'You had better put it away, hadn't you?' said Julia at last.

'Yes, of course,' he agreed. He took up the little chamois bag and showed it to Julia. 'It's neat, isn't it?' he said. 'Mother made it for me.'

Certainly it was very neat indeed; made of soft chamois leather, stitched in the tiniest of stitches with a soft little cord to draw it together at the neck.

'Beautifully made,' agreed Julia.

'Mother is very clever at that sort of thing,' said her son proudly. 'She made a tapestry picture—designed it herself—and it really is a work of art. It won a prize in a big exhibition of needlework. Do you know what she was going to do with it? She was going to put it on a stool for people to sit on! Did you ever hear such nonsense? But I soon put a stop to that. I made her give it to me and I'm having it framed so that we can hang it on the wall. I'd like to show it to you some time.'

Julia said she would like to see it, which was perfectly true; she was very much interested in needlework and it was evident from the appearance of the delightful little bag that Mrs. Brett must be an adept.

This little interlude had changed the subject and eased the embarrassment which Stephen's sudden madness had produced. He put away the sapphire in the little bag and asked Julia if she would like a peach.

'Oh yes—if they aren't too expensive,' she replied.

Stephen ordered them and a dish of fresh ripe peaches was placed upon the table, together with fruit-plates and finger-bowls.

They ate the peaches, which were ripe and luscious, and talked about various matters. Stephen said he wanted to buy a car but must wait until he had made his fortune. Julia laughed and asked how he proposed to do that.

'Are you interested in money?' asked Stephen seriously.

'What do you mean?'

'Would you like to make a lot of money?'

'Who wouldn't!' said Julia. 'But it would depend how, of course,' she added quickly.

'Quite honestly,' said Stephen, smiling. 'It's just a business matter. I'll tell you about it if you like, but it's a dead secret. It really is a dead secret, Julia. You must promise not to breathe a word about it to a single creature.'

Julia hesitated. It sounded very mysterious. But why not? Money was useful. It would be extremely pleasant to have a lot of money. 'All right,' she said. 'I promise faithfully; but if I don't like the idea—'

'Oh, you needn't do it if you'd rather not!'

At this moment the waiter came with the coffee. He removed the fruit-plates and finger-bowls and went away.

When he had gone Stephen leant forward and said, 'Listen carefully, Julia. That sapphire came from a place in Africa. I've been there and I've seen the place where it was found. For some reason the workings have been abandoned, nobody has been there for years, but there's still a company in existence which owns the property. You can buy shares in it for half nothing.'

'You mean there are lots of sapphires there and nobody knows?'

He smiled. 'You're pretty quick at the uptake, aren't you? Yes, that's the position more or less. I've scraped together every penny I can lay hands on and I'm buying shares on Monday morning; Father is doing the same. When people begin to hear about it the shares are bound to go up—see?'

Julia saw. She said slowly, 'I haven't much money to come and go on. I suppose it's quite safe?'

'Well, I'm putting my shirt on it,' he told her. 'Of course you needn't do it if you don't want to. I just thought I'd tip you the wink.'

'I wonder . . .' said Julia thoughtfully. She still saw, in her mind's eye, the sapphire lying on the table glowing with its soft blue light . . . and there were lots of others where that came from, hidden in the bowels of the earth. 'It would be silly not to, wouldn't it?' she added as if she were thinking aloud.

'It's for you to decide,' said Stephen. 'Supposing you think it over, Julia. We could meet to-morrow. There really isn't time to tell you all about it to-night. It would be much better for you to know the whole story before you decide.'

Julia agreed. To-morrow was Saturday, a half-holiday at Madame Claire's; they arranged to meet and have lunch together at Stephen's club so that he could tell her the whole story. Certainly there was no time now; for the restaurant was filled to overflowing and the waiter was hovering with the bill.

Stephen beckoned to him and paid it with a lordly air. Julia was horrified to see a sheaf of notes disappearing on the plate.

'Stephen, what a lot!' she whispered.

'Don't worry. It's been worth every penny; we'll do it again when I've made my pile.' He helped her to put on her coat and they went out into the street.

4

The air was so fresh and lovely after the stuffy atmosphere of the crowded restaurant that Stephen suggested they should walk for a little and Julia agreed. Stephen drew her hand through his arm and they strolled along together.

'This is fun,' said Stephen. 'There's something exciting about London at night especially to a fellow who has just come back from an isolated spot in darkest Africa . . . and especially if he has a girl to share the fun.'

'It's fun for the girl too,' said Julia lightly. 'Especially if she isn't used to walking in London at night. Tell me about darkest Africa, Stephen.'

'Not now,' he said. 'Darkest Africa belongs to the story I'm going to tell you to-morrow; I want to forget about it to-night and enjoy myself. Shall we walk round Piccadilly Circus?'

They walked round Piccadilly Circus, looking at the lights, jostled by the crowds. It would not have been very pleasant if Julia had not had an arm to hold onto, but the arm was safe and strong, so she found it very pleasant indeed. Although she had lived in London all her life she had never before strolled round the busy streets at night; perhaps she would never do it again, for she could not imagine Morland strolling amongst the crowd. Morland would be amazed that anyone should do such a thing for pleasure.

There were all sorts of funny little incidents to see and to point out to each other, and there were pathetic little incidents too. There was an old man trying to cross the crowded street; Stephen took him by the arm and piloted him to safety. There was a woman with a whining child; she was dragging him along and shaking him impatiently.

'Horrible little brat!' said Stephen.

'He's tired,' said Julia. 'He ought to have been in bed long ago. It's the woman who is horrible.'

'Are you tired, Julia?' he asked. 'If you aren't tired we might walk a bit farther, but say if you're tired and we'll take a taxi.'

Julia was not tired (fortunately she was wearing comfortable shoes), so they walked to Trafalgar Square and looked at the lions.

'Not like real lions,' said Stephen critically. 'I suppose they're heraldic beasts. Landseer designed them, didn't he? I wonder if he'd ever seen a real live lion in his life.'

'In the Zoo, perhaps,' said Julia, giggling. She added, 'But I like them.'

'Oh, so do I. They're very dignified and impressive. Do you think they'd like me to give their love to the next real live lion I happen to meet?'

'Not their love!' exclaimed Julia. 'They might like you to convey their greetings.'

They were both laughing as they walked on.

'This is grand,' declared Stephen. 'When I go back to my little bungalow in the wilds I shall think of this and remember every moment. It *is* good of you, Julia.'

'But I'm enjoying myself!'

'I know. That makes it all the better; if you weren't enjoying yourself it wouldn't be any fun at all. Shall we walk down to the river?'

Julia was beginning to feel tired, so it seemed a long way to the river, but presently they came to the bridge and stood there looking at the Palace of Westminster and the Abbey. Big Ben began to strike so they were silent, listening to the solemn sound. It struck eleven.

'The eleventh hour,' said Stephen.

Julia asked him what he meant, but he could not explain.

CHAPTER 9

1

SATURDAY morning was very busy at Madame Claire's establishment, so Julia was late in getting away and late for her appointment with Stephen. She had said half past one, but it was ten minutes to two when she arrived at the club, breathless with haste. However, she need not have worried, for Stephen was quite unperturbed and assured her cheerfully that it did not matter in the least. He had booked a table in the small dining-room where members were allowed to entertain their female friends, so they went in and sat down and ordered their meal.

'Not a very enlivening sort of place, I'm afraid,' said Stephen, looking round. 'But it's quiet, so we can talk as much as we like.'

'I was dreaming of sapphires all night,' declared Julia. 'I've been thinking about sapphires, whenever I had a moment to think, all the morning. Go on, Stephen, I want to hear about the place where the sapphire was found and how you found it.'

'Yes,' agreed Stephen. 'But let me eat my steak first. It looks rather good and I'm hungry.'

Julia could hardly object to this request (she had kept him waiting for twenty minutes), so she ate her own steak, which was excellent, and possessed her soul in patience. Stephen had chosen biscuits and cheese to follow but when he had stayed the pangs of hunger he began his story.

'Now then,' he said. 'You remember I told you I was the assistant manager of a diamond mine? What happened was I got ten days' leave, so a friend of mine, James Rafferty, suggested we should go on safari— that's a camping expedition—and take some boys and ponies to carry the tents and stores. Jim had heard about the workings at Coribunda from one of his boys (one of his servants, you know), so we decided to go and have a look at the place. It's a wild spot, miles from anywhere, and there's very little water to be had, so we made our camp near a stream, about fifteen miles short of Coribunda. We spent the night there and the next morning very early Jim and I rode over to the place alone. There were several reasons for going alone; one was that it was better to leave the boys where we knew there was water, and another was that there was something mysterious about the Coribunda workings and we didn't want the boys poking about and getting in our way.'

'Something mysterious?'

'Yes,' said Stephen, nodding. 'The place had been abandoned, you see. We wondered why. Of course it was just curiosity on our part, but we thought it would be interesting to have a look.'

'Oh, Stephen, how thrilling! Did you find the sapphire yourself?'

'No, my dear little innocent! You don't just dig a hole in the ground and find a gem of purest water; that only happens in fairy tales. You've got to know where to look.'

'How do you know where to look?'

'Because you know what sort of rocks to look for—at least, if you're a mining engineer you do,' said Stephen, laughing at her.

'I know,' declared Julia. 'You found a vein of—of whatever it's called.'

'Oh, you *do* know something about it.'

'We did geology at school and I liked it,' said Julia defiantly.

'Bless me! What next? I'm learning a lot about you.'

'Go on with the story, Stephen. I didn't mean to interrupt. . . . I'm dying to know how you found the sapphire.'

'We didn't find it,' he said. 'We poked about for a bit looking at the workings and the more we looked the more we wondered why they had been abandoned. I know a certain amount about corundum; Jim knows a lot more, and—'

'Corundum?'

'Sapphires and rubies,' explained Stephen. 'They aren't found in mines, like diamonds, they're found quite near the surface in different kinds of rocks—crystalline rocks, mostly. Well, as I was saying, we're both interested in the subject and we agreed that Coribunda was a place where we'd expect to find exceedingly good stones.'

'But you didn't find any?'

'No, we found an old man with a broken leg.'

'A black man?'

'Yes, with grey woolly hair. As a matter of fact we very nearly didn't find him. We had had a look round and eaten our sandwiches and discussed our ideas about the place and we were just coming away. Jim was already mounted on his pony, and I was just mounting, when I thought I heard a groan. Jim said I had imagined it—the place was absolutely deserted—but I thought I had better make sure. So I went back and hunted about, and found him lying in the shadow of a rock.

'It was touch and go,' said Stephen thoughtfully. 'It really was touch and go. What a lot of things hung upon that moment! I can see myself now with one foot in the stirrup and Jim saying, "Come on, Steve. Don't be an ass," and me saying, "But I'd better have a look—just in case." Supposing I hadn't gone back? What a frightful thought!'

'You mean you saved his life?'

'No,' said Stephen. 'No, we couldn't do much, really. He was half-dead with thirst. We gave him water and made a sort of shelter for him and Jim set his leg. Jim is the sort of chap that can turn his hand to anything. Then Jim rode off to our camp to get help and I stayed behind.

'It was dark by this time, but presently the moon rose from behind the hill and everything was silver and black—awfully eerie—the ruined huts and the tunnels in the hill and the great heaps of rubble! The poor old creature was pretty far through, but he talked a bit off and on. I sat beside him and listened. It was ghastly,' declared Stephen. 'Simply ghastly. There was nothing I could do for him except give him a drink now and then out of my water-bottle. He told me he had worked at Coribunda when the place was first started—long long ago, he said, before the evil spirits came.'

'The evil spirits?'

'Yes, he said the workings at Coribunda were haunted by devils. I know it sounds silly,' admitted Stephen, 'but everything was so quiet and eerie that I almost believed it was true. He said there were sapphires there—beautiful stones—but the devils guarded them and made all sorts of queer things happen so that they shouldn't be found.'

'Stephen, how amazing!'

'All sorts of amazing things happen in Africa. It's an amazing country. Well, the night wore on and the old chap went on talking. He said he had come back to Coribunda to look for sapphires himself because he was so old that he wasn't frightened of evil spirits any more. He said he remembered a blue vein where he had been working before the evil spirits frightened everybody away. It was all rather muddled,' explained Stephen, frowning thoughtfully. 'Part of the time his mind wandered, and he was sort of delirious, but I gathered that he and his fellow workers had been so terrified by the "devils" that they had deserted in a body one night and made their way home to their own little villages. It must have been a nasty shock for the manager when he woke up in the morning and found them gone.'

'Tell me about the blue vein,' said Julia, who was more interested in the sapphire than in the feelings of the manager.

'Yes,' agreed Stephen. 'The old chap had always remembered the blue vein and that's why he came back. He found his way to the place and started work on his own, but of course it was a foolish thing to do and extremely dangerous—'

'Why was it dangerous?' Julia wanted to know.

'Because the workings had been deserted for years and the ground had sunk a bit and the rocks had become loosened. So it wasn't surprising that quite suddenly there was an avalanche of rocks and stones which knocked him over and broke his leg. It was quite a natural thing to happen (in fact it was just what I should have expected to happen), but of course he put it down to the "devils." He kept on saying that the devils had got him because he had taken their stone. Somehow or other he managed to crawl out, but when he found he couldn't walk he knew he was done for. He dragged himself into the shade of a rock and lay down and waited for death.'

'Awful!' said Julia in a whisper.

'Yes, awful,' agreed Stephen. 'But there's a queer philosophy about those people, a sort of fatalism. They don't rebel against the inevitable. He knew the "devils" had got him and he accepted his fate quite calmly.'

'What a good thing you found him!'

'It was a good thing for me that I found him—the best thing I ever did in my life—but it wasn't much use to him. It was too late. I don't know how long he had lain there without food or water—several days at least. When we found him he was too far gone; there was nothing I could do, nothing except sit beside him and give him a drink now and then and wait for Jim.'

2

There was silence for a few moments.

At last Julia said, 'You still haven't told me how you found the sapphire, Stephen.'

'The old chap had found it. He had it hidden in his hair.'

'Hidden in his hair?' asked Julia incredulously.

'Yes, it's a favourite place for hiding things. They keep all sorts of treasures hidden in their woolly matted hair—livestock too, of course," said Stephen with a little grimace of disgust.

'However, we won't think about that. My old man was no exception to the rule. It was just after sunrise; I had been trying to settle him more comfortably and given him a drink, when he began scratching about in his hair. First he produced a small silver pencil-case—goodness knows where he had got it—and then a little compass, quite a cheap one made of brass, and then he produced the sapphire. He put them all into my hand and said they were for me.'

'Oh, Stephen, how pathetic! It was because you had been kind to him.'

'Yes, and because he knew he was dying. The sapphire looked like a pebble. I mean it was only because I knew about precious stones that I realised what it was (you can't tell the value of a stone until it has been cut). But what really interested me was the fact that he had found it in the Coribunda workings.

He swore by all his gods that he had found it in the blue vein and he declared that if the 'devils' had not made the stones fall down and hurt his leg he could have got more—two or three or five, he said, holding up his fingers.

'After that he was unconscious for a long time—at least it seemed a long time to me; and Jim came back with some boys and a litter and plenty of food and water, but by that time he was far too ill to be moved. All we could do was to wait with him till he died. He regained consciousness just before the end and said that he had given his treasures to me—all of them—because I had given him water out of my own water-bottle. That seemed to have made a great impression upon him; he kept saying it over and over again. He said water was the greatest treasure in the world. Well, of course it is, if you're dying of thirst.'

'Yes, of course,' said Julia. She added thoughtfully, 'We take water for granted, don't we? I mean we don't really value it enough.'

'No, we don't value it nearly enough,' agreed Stephen emphatically.

At this moment the waiter appeared and cleared away the remains of the meal in a significant manner.

'I suppose you want us to go?' asked Stephen.

'The Ladies' Lounge would be more comfortable, sir.'

'Is it full of lounging ladies? Because if so we shall remain here.'

'No, sir, it's empty,' replied the waiter without a smile.

'Oh well, in that case we'll go and lounge there ourselves—shall we, Julia?'

Julia nodded and gathered up her bag and gloves and followed Stephen into the Ladies' Lounge. They sat down together on a very large sofa and Stephen continued his tale.

'After the old chap died we had another look round the workings. Jim found traces of the blue vein but we didn't touch it; we had to be careful because the stones kept rolling down in avalanches wherever we went. Jim thought the sapphire looked pretty good, so we decided that the best thing was for me to get leave and come home and have it cut and I could see the directors of Coribunda and tell them about the place and advise them to have the workings properly surveyed . . . and that's what I did.'

'That was your business in London?'

'Yes, that was my business.'

'They must have been frightfully pleased.'

'Not at all; they were very stuffy. To tell you the truth they were quite nasty. They wanted to know what right I had to snoop round the Coribunda workings. One of them asked what I was getting out of it. Their attitude annoyed me. My first idea had been to show them the stone but they were so unpleasant that I didn't. They would just have said I had stolen it; they might have made me give it to them.'

'They couldn't!' cried Julia indignantly. 'The old man had given it to you. It was yours!'

'I wasn't quite sure of the legal aspect,' said Stephen slowly.

'I suppose, strictly speaking, the old chap had no right to it; but the whole place was deserted, so anyone who felt inclined could have taken it. The old chap had lost his life in getting the stone and had given it to me with his last breath, so I felt I had a moral right to it, if you see what I mean. Certainly I had more right to it than those stuffed owls in the London office.'

'Of course you had!'

'Well anyhow, I kept it in my pocket and didn't say a word about it. I just told them that Jim and I—both of us mining engineers—were of the opinion that there were sapphires at Coribunda and advised them to get the place surveyed. Then I came away and left them arguing about it.'

'Are they going to do it?'

'They've done it. They got the surveyor's report yesterday.'

'Was it a good report?' asked Julia eagerly.

'Excellent—as far as it went. There are sapphires at Coribunda. The surveyor sent a couple of stones which he and his assistants discovered in the famous blue vein. Of course they haven't been cut yet, but they look pretty good. That made the directors sit up and take notice!'

'I don't wonder!' exclaimed Julia. 'It's frightfully thrilling, isn't it?' She hesitated and then said slowly, 'I wonder why the workings were abandoned.'

'Yes, why? That's the question,' said Stephen. He added, 'But Julia, all this is frightfully secret . . . top secret. You understand, don't you? Not a word to anyone on your life.'

'Not a word.'

There was silence.

'Stephen, I've decided,' said Julia at last. 'I want to buy those shares. What am I to do? I'm frightfully ignorant about business.'

'Are you sure?'

'Absolutely certain,' she declared. Now that she had decided she was beginning to feel excited about it; what fun it would be to buy shares in those sapphires! She had the money Retta had given her and her father's cheque; she also had a little in her current account at the bank. She would put it all into the sapphires, every penny. What fun it would be!

'You had better do it through your bank,' said Stephen in thoughtful tones. 'Go and see the manager on Monday morning and ask him to get a stockbroker to buy shares in the Coribunda Sapphire Company. He'll probably take a fit.'

'A fit?'

'It's a moribund concern.'

'Oh yes, I see,' said Julia, smiling. 'Nobody knows about it, of course. I'll take a bottle of smelling salts with me for Mr. Silver.'

Stephen smiled too. 'What a good name for the manager of a bank! But you'll be careful what you say to him, won't you, Julia? Don't mention my name.'

'I'll be very careful indeed. Thank you awfully much, Stephen. It was kind of you to tell me, and—'

'You can thank me when you've made your pile—and you *will* make a pile, if you do exactly as I say. Buy them on Monday morning and hang onto them until I tell you to sell. Then sell them straight away.'

'Sell them?' asked Julia in surprise.

'Yes, but not until I tell you, see?'

'It seems funny—' began Julia.

'It isn't funny. It's business,' declared Stephen. 'Be sure to go and see Mr. Silver early on Monday morning and say you want them at once. He'll make an awful fuss about it. He'll say you're mad . . . or at least he'll say in a very serious voice, "I think it would be a very undesirable investment, Miss Harburn."'

'Well, I suppose I can do what I like with my own money,' said Julia, laughing.

CHAPTER 10

1

'BUT, Mr. Silver, I can do what I like with my own money, can't I?' said Julia.

It was Monday morning; she was sitting in Mr. Silver's comfortable office at the bank and was finding him every bit as difficult as Stephen had predicted. He had not actually taken a fit when he heard her request but he had said in a serious voice, 'I shouldn't advise it, Miss Harburn. In my opinion it would be a very undesirable investment. I feel sure your father wouldn't approve.'

Of course it would have been easier if she could have told him why she wished to put her money into the Coribunda Sapphire Company—but of course she couldn't! She could only keep on saying that she wanted to do it. At last she had become slightly annoyed with Mr. Silver and had asked him whether or not she could do as she liked with her own money.

'Yes, of course,' agreed Mr. Silver. 'I'm just trying to warn you that the shares are practically worthless, so unless you have inside information . . .' He paused and looked at her.

Her face was absolutely blank.

'Perhaps your father advised you to buy them.'

Julia smiled. The idea of her father advising her to buy shares in a moribund sapphire company was really very amusing indeed.

Mr. Silver saw the smile and misread it. 'That would be different,' he said.

'I'm afraid I can't tell you,' said Julia. 'I just want to buy shares in it, and I want to buy them at once—this morning. If you can't do it for me perhaps you could tell me where to go.'

'I can do it through our brokers,' he replied, heaving a sigh of defeat.

'At once?'

'Yes, I can ring them up immediately. How many shares do you want?'

'As many as I can buy for a hundred pounds.'

'A hundred pounds! Don't you think that's rather a large sum to risk in such a—'

'If I had more I would risk more.'

He gazed at her in a baffled way; at one moment she seemed foolish to the point of idiocy and the next moment she seemed very much all there, but it was obvious that she was supremely confident—or perhaps stubborn was the word—he had done his best but he had not been able to shake her determination.

'I'm sure you must be very busy,' said Julia, and she tapped her foot on the floor as much as to say that if he were not busy she was.

Mr. Silver sighed. 'But Miss Harburn, that will mean that your account will be slightly overdrawn.'

'Oh dear!' she exclaimed. 'Does it matter frightfully?'

It did not matter, of course; Mr. Harburn's account was in a very healthy condition and this was his only child, and what was more, he had signed a bank order to pay thirty pounds on the first of every month into his daughter's account. Only one thing was worrying Mr. Silver: would Mr. Harburn be annoyed when he learnt that his daughter had been allowed to throw away a hundred pounds?

But wait a moment, thought Mr. Silver. Perhaps Mr. Harburn had inside information about Coribunda. How else could the girl have heard about it except from her father? He remembered the enigmatic smile . . . yes, that must be the explanation. And if so, thought Mr. Silver, if Mr. Harburn (who was an extremely cautious man) were advising his daughter to buy Coribundas, it might be worth while for Mr. Silver to do the same. Yes, definitely! Foolish not to! thought Mr. Silver.

'Does it matter frightfully?' repeated Julia. 'You see, if I could make it up to a hundred pounds it would be a round sum; besides, I shall get more when I sell them.'

This naive statement tipped the balance; Mr. Silver was converted.

'It doesn't matter in the least,' he assured her. 'It's only seven or eight pounds, so—'

'You'll get it all back, of course,' said Julia earnestly.

Mr. Silver smiled; she really was an absolute innocent. 'I haven't a doubt of it, Miss Harburn,' he declared.

'And you'll do it now?'

'Yes, immediately.'

2

Julia had obtained permission to absent herself from Madame Claire's establishment on the plea of important business; and the business having been carried out successfully, she hurried back and proceeded to sell hats.

At first it had been a little difficult, but now it had become easy and interesting. Truth to tell, Julia enjoyed her job. The 'lesson' which Miss Martineau had given her helped quite a lot, for although it had been highly exaggerated and exceedingly funny there was a certain amount of sense at the bottom of the nonsense. Julia often thought of it with an inward quiver of laughter when she put on a *chapeau* and turned her head to display its beauties to one of Madame's clients.

The following morning Julia rang up Mr. Silver to see what had happened.

'I have written to you,' he said. 'In matters such as this it is wiser to write than to telephone.'

When Julia returned from work the letter had arrived.

'A letter for you,' said Miss Martineau, handing it to her. 'It's from the bank, dulling. I wonder what it can be about.'

Julia had discovered that Miss Martineau was interested in everything that went on in her house and especially interested in letters that came to her boarders; if any of her boarders received a postcard or left a letter lying about Miss Martineau had no qualms about reading it . . . no qualms at all. Julia had received a highly-coloured postcard of the Colosseum at Rome from Retta, and Miss Martineau had handed it to Julia saying, 'They've had a good trip and the hotel is very comfortable, isn't that nice?'

At first Julia had been slightly taken aback; but, on reflection, she realised that it was just because Miss Martineau was interested in her affairs. It was nice of her to be interested, and as Julia had no secrets it did not matter. Now, however, Julia had a secret which she was sworn to keep, so she took Mr. Silver's letter and ran upstairs to her room where she could read it in private. She saw with astonishment that her hundred pounds had been sufficient to buy eight hundred shares in the Coribunda Sapphire Company. It seemed incredible.

Mr. Silver's letter was rather curt. He merely said that the one pound shares were standing at two and sixpence.

The fact was, Mr. Silver was annoyed with Miss Harburn and extremely worried about his own five hundred pounds which, in a moment of madness, he had invested in Coribundas and which he could ill-afford to lose.

Julia was not in the least worried, she was excited. It was thrilling, a sort of gamble—like putting money on a horse, but much safer, of course.

'You're in good form this morning, dulling,' said Miss Martineau as they breakfasted together. 'Anything nice happened?'

'Yes, but I can't tell you, Miss Martineau. It's a secret.'

'You can call me May,' said Miss Martineau. 'Much cosier, and I'll call you Julia, dulling. It's a pretty name and it suits you. How are you getting on with Jeanne?'

'Jeanne?'

'Jeanne Kessell—that's her real name. When I want to make her mad I call her Mrs. Kettle. She doesn't overwork you, I hope.'

Julia had got it now. 'Oh no, we get on swimmingly. I'm really quite good at selling hats, thanks to your lesson, and we speak French together, so—'

'French!' cried Miss Martineau. 'You can talk French? Real French, I mean?'

'Yes, Mother taught me. She was at school in Paris; she spoke French beautifully, and we used to go abroad quite often in the winter.'

'Dulling!' exclaimed Miss Martineau in dismay. 'Why didn't you tell me before that you could talk real French? I'd have stood out for six pounds; she'd have given it like a shot! Oh dear, what can we do about it?'

'We can't do anything,' said Julia giggling. 'Never mind, Miss M-May, I'm going to make lots of money soon,'

'How?' asked May with eager interest.

'Well, that's the secret,' explained Julia. 'I'd tell you if I could.'

3

As usual Julia arrived early at Madame Claire's. She made a point of going early, for, being the newest assistant, it was her job to take the hats out of the cupboards and arrange the stands. Madame herself was always early, but it was easy for her: she had an extremely comfortable little flat above the shop, so all she had to do was to walk downstairs and there she was. It was very different for Ivonne and Fifi, who were obliged to come by bus; at this hour of the morning the buses were always over-crowded.

When Julia arrived Madame Claire was there as usual, sitting and reading the morning paper, obviously deeply interested in the news, so Julia proceeded to arrange the hats without speaking to her.

Presently she looked up and said, 'Do you ever make investment of your money, Julie? I find it very interesting. It is good to see one's shares go up, but very bad when they go down. I am a business woman, you see.'

'Where do you see the shares go up and down, Madame?'

'In the financial news, of course. To-day some of my shares go up, which is very nice. It is a good day for me,' she added gaily.

'I wonder if I might look at the financial news for a moment?'

'You have made a small investment?'

'Yes.'

'I am glad,' declared Madame, handing her the paper. 'It is good to be a business woman. In France we are very practical; we learn when we are young so when we are older we know how to take care of our money. It is not so in England.'

'I am trying to learn, but I'm afraid I don't know very much about business,' said Julia.

'*Incroyable!*' cried Madame. 'Come, Julie, I will give you a little lesson.'

Julia leant upon the back of Madame's chair and received her lesson with suitable gratitude. It was not as difficult to understand as she had expected, the list of companies and the prices at which the shares had changed hands. She was obliged to reveal the name of her small investment—there was no getting out of it.

'Coribunda!' exclaimed Madame scornfully. 'Foolish child! Those shares are rubbish! There it is—three and twopence!'

'It isn't very much,' agreed Julia trying to keep the excitement out of her voice. Of course she was excited. She had paid two and sixpence for her shares, so already, in one day, she had made eightpence—and she had eight hundred shares! How much was that? But she could not do it in her head, and anyhow there was no time—the other two girls came in, and Madame, throwing down her paper, began to rage and storm at them.

'Again late!' she cried. 'Is it for this that I pay good money? Day after day you are late for your work. Nine o'clock is the hour—not ten minutes past nine—and always the same excuse. I am tired of hearing the bus was crowded. Look at Julie! She is nevaire late. . . .'

'She doesn't have to catch a bus,' muttered Fifi.

'Is it my wish that you should live in some out-of-the-way suburb?' inquired Madame. 'It matters nothing to me where you live. It matters a great deal that you should be here at the right hour. When I engaged you it was agreed that you should be here at nine o'clock. The same arrangement was made with Julie and Julie is always punctual. Julie is a business woman like me. We know the right thing, we business women; we are punctual; we make a small investment; we do not spend all our money on trashy clothes.' She looked them up and down and snorted contemptuously. 'Trashy clothes,' she repeated. 'It angers me to see good money thrown away on trashy clothes. That little frock which you buy in a chain-store—you are pleased with it, Fifi? You get it cheap because it is shoddy material and in a week it will become shabby and out of shape. And Ivonne's shoes with the stiletto heels and the pointed toes which she gets in another department—they will fall to pieces when it rains! Is that good business? Do you think Julie would wear a shoddy frock or shoes which are made of brown paper? No, she is much too sensible. Quick, put on the overalls and hide the miserable little frocks!'

They slunk away, sullen and dejected. If it had not been for the fact that they were getting 'good money' in Madame's establishment they would not have stood it for a moment.

This was not the first time the new assistant had been held up as a pattern. It was embarrassing and made her position difficult; Julia wished Madame were not so foolish. Already the two girls had teamed up against her and were causing trouble in various ways. They were jealous because she was Madame's 'pet'; they were jealous because Madame spoke French to her in a rapid torrent which they could not understand. They were annoyed because Julia made a point of coming early to arrange the hats for Madame and because she often stayed late to tidy up and leave everything in good order. Before Julia's advent Madame had been obliged to do this herself, so naturally she was delighted when she found that her new assistant was willing to come early and stay late and take the tiresome duties off her shoulders.

'Sucking up,' said Fifi scornfully.

'It won't last,' declared Ivonne. 'You mark my words, she'll do something silly and get the sack.'

They were speaking to each other, but Julia knew she was intended to hear. She would have liked to explain that she was just trying to learn her job and earn her living; she would have liked to ask them to be friends with her . . . but of course it would be useless.

4

It was ten days since Julia had left home and she had not yet found time to visit Ellen. She was busy all day and was too tired after her work to make the necessary effort . . . and it would be an effort to return to her old home. Julia did not want to go; she had left her old life behind her and it would awaken unhappy memories to return. However, she had promised Ellen and the matter was on her conscience, so one fine evening after supper she set forth to perform her duty.

The house in Manor Gardens was in process of being painted: some of the window-frames had been finished and were glistening with new green paint, others had been scraped and looked extremely shabby. The interior of the house was even worse, for the old paper had been torn off the walls and was lying in heaps on the floors.

To Julia's surprise Ellen seemed quite cheerful, and although she complained bitterly about the mess, and the bother of having to make tea for the painters, Julia knew her well enough to see that in reality she was enjoying their company and would be sorry when they had finished their job and gone away.

The kitchen seemed to be the only room which was clean and comfortable, so they sat there together and talked. Julia had been thinking about Ellen's reference to some trouble which had preyed upon her father's mind and had decided to find out more about it. This would not be easy, of course, for Ellen liked to be mysterious and was given to exaggeration, so you could not believe all she said; but there might be something at the bottom of it. If only she could get to the root of the trouble Julia felt that she might be able to make contact with her father and help him. There was something preying on his mind—that was what Ellen had said. The phrase had haunted Julia. What could it be?

For some time Julia was obliged to listen to long stories about the delinquent painters (what they had done and what they had left undone and what Ellen had said to them when they came into her nice clean kitchen with their dirty boots), but at last she managed to guide the conversation into the right channel. Even then she had to be very careful, for if Ellen thought she was being pumped she was liable to dry up at a moment's notice.

'You've been here a long time, haven't you, Ellen?' said Julia.

'That's right. I came before you were born and I've been 'ere ever since.'

'I've been wondering about Father's old home in Scotland.'

'What were you wondering?'

'Oh, nothing much . . . only it seems queer that he never talks about it. You often tell me about your home, Ellen, and about your relations. You often go and see your sisters, don't you? Hasn't Father got any relations in Scotland?'

'None that I ever 'eard tell of.'

'It seems funny.'

'I don't know nothing, Miss Julia,' declared Ellen. 'All I know about is that picture I found in the attic.'

Julia had never heard of the picture before. 'Oh, yes,' she said. 'It was a very valuable picture, wasn't it?'

'Well, I don't know about valuable,' replied Ellen doubtfully. 'If it was valuable why was it stuffed away in the attic with a whole lot of old junk? I found it when I was spring-cleaning—years ago, it was.'

'It was a portrait, wasn't it?' asked Julia.

'A portrait? Whatever made you think that? It was a picture of a great big lovely 'ouse. It seemed funny being left up there in the attic so I brought it down and showed it to your mother . . . but I wished I'd left it alone.'

Julia was silent. It was no use asking questions.

'She was upset when she saw it,' continued Ellen thoughtfully.

'She said it was a picture of 'Arburn 'Ouse, where your father used to live when 'e was a boy. I thought it was such a nice picture that 'e might of liked to 'ang it up in 'is study, but she said I was to take it away and put it back where I found it and never talk about it again—quite vexed with me she was—so that's what I did.'

'A picture of Harburn House!' exclaimed Julia. 'Oh, Ellen, how interesting!'

'A lovely picture,' said Ellen, nodding. 'A great big beautiful 'ouse it was, with trees and gardings round it.'

'I should like to see the picture.'

'Well, you can't,' replied Ellen, smiling grimly. 'It's been tore up in little bits.'

'Torn up!'

Ellen nodded. 'I told you I put it back in the attic. Well, the next day I went up to the attic again, just to 'ave another look at it, and the nice frame was empty. There was one or two little bits of the picture on the floor and the rest of it was in the waste-paper basket.'

'In Father's study?'

'Yes, 'e'd gone and tore it up 'imself with 'is own 'ands.'

'But why?' cried Julia in astonishment.

'Ask me another. I'd been told I wasn't to talk about it ever again so I didn't. It wasn't no business of mine.'

Julia sighed. There were all sorts of questions she would have liked to ask but she was aware that the subject was closed.

'You 'aven't told me nothing about the 'at-shop,' said Ellen. 'It seems funny you working in a 'at-shop. Does Mr. Beverley know about it?'

Obviously there was nothing more to be got out of Ellen to-night, so Julia made the best of it and entertained her with stories about some of the amusing things that had happened in Madame Claire's establishment until it was time to go, and as it was dark by this time, Ellen walked to the corner with her and saw her safely into the bus.

It was only afterwards, when she had time to think about it properly, that Julia realised what an extraordinary tale she had heard from Ellen about the picture of Harburn House. She had hoped to clear up the mystery but the mystery had deepened. Of course she had known before that her father had been born and brought up in Scotland, but he had never spoken to her of his boyhood nor mentioned his home. Somehow Julia had received the impression that he was ashamed of his home . . . but now she realised that this was wrong. He could not be ashamed of 'a great big beautiful house with trees and gardens round it.' Why had he torn up the picture of Harburn House? Did he hate the place so much . . . or did he love it so much that he could not bear to be reminded of it?

Julia had always been frightened of her father—too frightened to speak to him about anything except everyday affairs—but now that she had escaped from the uncomfortable atmosphere of Manor Gardens she felt quite different. She decided that she had been foolish and she made up her mind that when he came home she would go and see him and ask him about Harburn House. It was natural, wasn't it, that she should want to know about his life when he was a boy? Yes, she would go and speak to him bravely; she would try to make contact with the man inside the big brown blanket. She would try to get to the bottom of the mystery.

CHAPTER 11

1

ONE morning the break at eleven for coffee was interrupted by the arrival of the Honourable Mrs. de Courcy, who was said to be 'the fourth best-dressed woman in London.' Madame Claire always attended to this client herself, but that did not mean her assistants could relax: far from it—they were kept on their toes running hither and thither to fetch what was wanted. To-day it was 'Julie' who was chosen to be chief assistant and to act as model. Madame produced her most cherished creations, which were displayed only to her most favoured clients, and arranged them upon 'Julie's' head. 'Julie' was ordered to turn round slowly whilst the Honourable Mrs. de Courcy surveyed them critically through her lorgnette.

'No,' said the Honourable Mrs. de Courcy. 'No, that won't do. . . . No, I don't like that either. . . . No, that isn't what I want at all. Haven't you got anything else to show me?'

'Julie, faites vite!' whispered Madame. *'Cherchez le petit chapeau en paille noire—il est dans l'atelier. Il n'est pas encore fini, mais n'importe.'*

Julia dashed upstairs to the workroom, found the little black straw, seized a spray of gardenias which happened to be lying on the table, and was back in record time.

'Good,' said Madame, taking it from her. 'And the flowers—yes.' She placed the little hat upon Julia's head and pinned on the spray of gardenias.

'Well, perhaps,' said the honourable client doubtfully. 'The line is quite good but it's a little severe.'

'An eye-veil?' suggested Madame Claire.

'No, no. They're quite out.'

'Just a wisp of veiling would soften the line,' said Madame Claire. She seized another hat and pressed it into Julia's hand. 'You have your scissors?' she asked.

Of course Julia had her scissors. She snipped the veil from the hat and smoothed it out. Madame took it and pinned it onto the little black straw, gathering it into a soft fold at the back.

'Not bad,' said the Honourable Mrs. de Courcy. She added, 'I'll try it on.'

It was Madame Claire's habit to place her creations upon the heads of her clients with her own hands, but to-day she merely watched anxiously while the Honourable Mrs. de Courcy took the little black straw and put it on. Julia watched too, not anxiously but with eager interest.

The whole affair was interesting to Julia. Usually Madame talked incessantly to her clients, praising their style and taste (in fact she behaved more or less like the vendor of *chapeaux* in Miss Martineau's sketch), but that sort of nonsense would not have gone down with the Honourable Mrs. de Courcy; it would have annoyed her and put her off completely, and Madame Claire knew this perfectly well. To-day Madame was serious and business-like, she accepted this client as her equal and deferred to her judgment.

The little black straw suited the client admirably; it was most becoming . . . but Madame Claire remained silent.

The client turned this way and that. She adjusted the spray of gardenias and considered the matter.

'*Où est la glâce à main, Julie?*' whispered Madame Claire.

Julie had the mirror ready. As the lady took it from her, their eyes met for a moment and Julia was aware that she had been seen quite clearly and—if seen again—would be remembered.

'The back is really quite good,' said the Honourable Mrs. de Courcy.

'It is not finished,' said Madame Claire. 'I intended a little twist of velvet—'

'No, too heavy.'

'Yes, perhaps. May I arrange the veil?'

'Don't spoil it. I like the informal effect.'

'It is very good.'

'I suppose you're going to charge me the earth.'

'No, no, not to you, Madame!' exclaimed Madame Claire in horrified tones. 'To you, ten guineas.'

'You're a robber,' said the client casually. 'You ought to let me have it for nothing.'

Madame Claire rolled her eyes heavenwards. 'Oh, Madame! How delightful to make you a little present! But, alas, one must eat. There is the bread and butter. . . .'

'And sometimes a little jam,' suggested the Honourable Mrs. de Courcy, smiling wickedly. 'Sometimes just a little, little smear of jam.'

Madame Claire dismissed 'Julie' from the conference with a side-long glance and the tweak of an eyebrow, so Julia left them to it; but as she went into the cloakroom to brush and comb her hair (which was absolutely necessary after she had been used by Madame as a model) she overheard the following little exchange:

'I haven't seen her before. She's French, I suppose.'

'Julie is Parisienne, like me, Madame. She has been with me two short weeks; but already, as you see, she is worth her salt.'

Julia smiled to herself; so she was Parisienne, was she?—and worth her salt? In that case perhaps a little more salt might be extracted from Madame's well-stocked cellar. She had discovered that the other girls were receiving a good deal more salt than herself.

The joke was that Jeanne Kessell was definitely not a Parisienne but hailed from the neighbourhood of Strasbourg. You could tell by her accent, or at least Julia could tell . . . not that she would have told, not even to May. If Jeanne Kessell liked to pretend she hailed from Paris she could go on pretending as long as she liked. Her guilty secret was perfectly safe with 'Julie.'

2

Miss Martineau (or May, as Julia must remember) was in the dining-room as usual when Julia returned from work. There was a lot to tell her to-day: first about the Honourable Mrs. de Courcy; Julia remembered every word that had been said and gave a little sketch of the affair, play-ing the parts of Madame Claire and the Honourable Mrs. de Courcy in turn. May laughed till the tears streamed down her face making furrows in the powder.

'Oh dear,' she said as she repaired the damage. 'You only want a little training and you could make a hit on the boards. . . . But better not,' she added hastily. 'It's too chancy and there isn't any future in it.'

After that, Julia told May about the remark she had overheard, and May agreed that something must be done about that. Perhaps it might be a good plan to pop along after supper and have a chat with Jeanne.

Lastly Julia disclosed to May the difficulties of her position. It was becoming more and more unpleasant; the jealousy of the two girls, caused by Madame's favouritism, had been augmented by her deroga-tory remarks about their new frocks.

'Jeanne is a fool,' declared May. 'I mean, of course I know she's clever—much cleverer than I am—but she's a fool all the same. I'm not a bit clever but I can see that much.'

'You're wise,' said Julia. 'That's the difference.'

'Wise? Well, nobody's ever told me that before, dulling,' said May in astonishment.

CHAPTER 12

1

THE next few days were very exciting. Coribundas went up and then went down a little; then they went up again. Julia had a letter from Mr. Silver saying Coribundas were standing at five and sixpence so Miss Harburn had more than doubled her capital and it would be advisable to take her profit. Julia phoned to him at once from a call-box at the corner and said he was not to sell them.

'Are you sure, Miss Harburn?' he asked.

Miss Harburn was absolutely certain. 'I'll tell you when to sell them,' she said firmly.

Mr. Silver had been on the point of instructing his brokers to sell his own holding, but now he hesitated. There was someone behind Miss Harburn, that was evident, and who could it be but her father? He decided to hang on a bit.

Madame Claire was interested too. She had been following the fluctuations of 'Julie's small investment' and was generous enough to admit that Coribundas might not be such rubbish.

'It is good that they go up,' she said. 'But sometimes it is what you call a ramp. Yes, a ramp. Then in a little while they go down with a bang and you are in the soup, so it is better to sell before that happens, Julie.'

'What is a ramp, Madame?' asked Julia doubtfully. She was beginning to suspect that Madame Claire did not know quite as much about business matters as she pretended.

'If somebody says there are sapphires and it is not true, then it is a ramp.'

'But they would know!'

'Not always. There was one time when I invested some money in a diamond mine and it was a ramp. They had put salt in it.'

'Salt?'

'Yes, alas, I lost my money.'

'But if there really are sapphires?'

'It may be salt, Julie.'

Julia did not understand, but she knew quite definitely that there were sapphires at Coribunda—not salt. Had she not actually seen a most beautiful sapphire with her own eyes?

She held her peace.

2

Coribundas went back to four and ninepence and then soared to ten and a penny. Several times that day Mr. Silver put out his hand to the telephone which stood upon his desk . . . and drew it back. But when the shares reached twelve and sixpence he could delay no longer; the anxiety was getting him down and interfering with his sleep, so he sold his holding.

Mr. Silver had made a very good profit on his Coribunda shares and was pleased about it—very pleased indeed; he was not quite so pleased when Coribundas rocketed to eighteen and threepence.

Julia had been following the reports with delight. Unlike Mr. Silver she had no qualms at all. She watched her horse galloping along, taking the hurdles in his stride; she dreamt about sapphires at night and thought about them frequently during the day. It was tremendous fun.

Julia was surprised and distressed when she received a telegram from Devonshire which bore one word and one word only. The word was SELL.

Sell? thought Julia. Sell her beautiful sapphire horse which was galloping along so bravely! Why should she? It seemed silly. Coribunda was full of perfectly lovely sapphires, so surely it would be a good thing to have shares in it and keep them. She went to bed determined not to sell her sapphire horse, but when she got up in the morning she had changed her mind (I suppose I had better do what Stephen says, she thought). Very reluctantly she rang up Mr. Silver and gave the order to sell.

'Sell them at once,' said Julia. 'Sell them this morning. It's very important. I've just heard from—from the person who told me to buy them.'

'Very well, Miss Harburn.'

What a fool I've been! thought Mr. Silver as he put down the receiver.

Coribundas had dropped back a little, so Julia's shares in the Coribunda Sapphire Company were sold for seventeen and sixpence. She did not know how much she had made, but obviously it was a lot. That night when she was alone in her bedroom she took pencil and paper and tried to figure it out, but as she had never been good at arithmetic and had not done this sort of sum for years she found it difficult.

At first she could not believe the answer but when she had repeated her calculations several times she came to the conclusion that it must be right; the hundred pounds which she had invested had become seven hundred pounds.

It really was staggering. What an easy way to make money! And what fun it had been! But of course it was not every day that a thing like this happened . . . and of course someone must lose. For instance what about the people who sold their shares for half a crown? Worse still, what about the people who had bought shares at seventeen and sixpence? Julia wondered who they were, she felt extremely worried about the poor things. She hoped they were all very wealthy, in which case it would not matter so much.

Although Julia had sold her sapphire horse she still continued to take an interest in its fortunes and still continued to come down a few minutes early for breakfast in order to have a quick glance at May's *Daily Telegraph*. The day after she had sold her shares Coribundas dropped to fifteen and tenpence; the next day, with a bump, to eight and five.

Julia's horse seemed to have gone lame; she felt very sorry about it.

CHAPTER 13

1

CONTRARY to her usual custom Madame Claire was not in her establishment when Julia went in. She came running down the stairs with the morning paper in her hand.

'Julie!' she cried. 'What did I tell you! The Coribunda is rubbish! It was a ramp. Many people will have got their fingers pinched. You must sell your small investment at once—'

'I sold my shares when they were seventeen and sixpence,' said Julia smugly.

'Vraiment?'

'Oui, Madam, vraiment,' replied Julia as she began to open the cupboards and take the hats from the shelves.

Madame was almost incredulous. 'Ma foi!' she exclaimed. 'Vous êtes une bonne femme d'affaires, sans aucun doute!'

'A friend told me to sell, so I sold. I don't understand it in the very least,' said Julia frankly.

'What do you not understand, Julie?'

'I don't understand why the shares are going down.'

'It was a ramp,' declared Madame.

The conversation was cut short by the arrival of a client—not an important client, of course (important clients did not arrive at nine o'clock in the morning), but merely a young woman who wished to buy a hat. Naturally Madame did not concern herself with such small fry so it was left to Julia to deal with her.

Several times that day Julia thought of Stephen. She wondered if she should write and thank him . . . but perhaps she had better not. She was still debating the matter as she walked home and he was so much in her thoughts that she was not surprised when May rushed out and met her in the hall to tell her that he had called.

'He's here!' cried May excitedly. 'He's taking you out to dinner. He's all togged up like the Duke of Edinburgh with a flower in his button-hole. Oh dear, he *does* look beautiful! I put him in the parlour. You had better pop up, dulling. I'll come and help you change; we don't want to keep him waiting too long, do we?'

Julia popped up and there was Stephen! Her first thought was that May had not exaggerated in the slightest; her second was to hold out her hands and say thank you.

'I've been longing to thank you,' she declared. 'I wanted to write, and then I thought perhaps I shouldn't.'

'Why not?' asked Stephen, taking her hands and smiling down into her upturned face.

'Because it's such a dead secret, of course.'

'It isn't a secret any more.'

'Oh, I see.'

'You sold all right?'

'Yes, I've got seven hundred pounds! Isn't it marvellous? And it has been such fun—so exciting!'

'Has it?'

'Yes, watching them go up and down and then up and up and up.'

'You've been following them, have you?'

'Every day,' nodded Julia. 'I've learnt quite a lot. What an easy way of making money, isn't it?'

'But, look here! You mustn't try speculating on your own. It's fright-fully risky. The thing to do is to put your pile into something safe.'

'Oh, I know,' she agreed. 'I've learnt enough about business to know that I don't know much.'

'Some people never learn as much as that.'

'Stephen, tell me, what did it mean? Was it a ramp?'

'A ramp? No, of course not.'

'Someone said they put salt in it.'

'Salt!' cried Stephen. 'You mean the workings were salted? Goodness no, what a frightful idea! Who said so?'

'It was Madame Claire—but I don't think she knew what it meant. Neither do I. What does it mean, Stephen? Why did the shares go up and down like that?'

'Oh, for goodness' sake, Julia! What a girl you are! Sometimes you seem extraordinarily clever and other times you seem practically half-witted.'

'Thanks awfully,' said Julia, laughing. 'As a matter of fact I'm neither the one nor the other. I'm just a reasonably intelligent person. I've learnt a little about business but not enough. Stephen, did you make a lot of money?'

'Enough to stand you a slap-up dinner,' declared Stephen, laughing. 'It was a promise, wasn't it? Cut along, you reasonably intelligent person, and make yourself beautiful.'

She went to the door and paused. 'I shall wear my new frock,' she said. 'I got it yesterday. Madame came and helped me to choose it so I got it at trade price. It really is *rather* nice, so I shan't disgrace you.'

'Disgrace me?'

'May said you were togged up like the Duke of Edinburgh!' Julia heard him chuckling as she ran upstairs to change.

2

While Stephen was waiting he had time to think. He was not usually introspective—nor retrospective—his habit of mind was to live in the present rather than to dwell upon the past. But it so happened that when Stephen was dressing in the room at his club, getting ready to take Julia out to dinner, he looked at his engagement book to make certain of the exact hour at which he was trysted to meet the directors of the Coribunda Sapphire Company the following morning (an engagement which he was so loath to fulfil that an attack of chicken-pox or some such highly infectious complaint would have been a welcome alternative). Stephen had noticed the date and suddenly had thought, 'By Jove, if this isn't the very day a year ago when I found that poor old blighter!'

So while he was dressing, Stephen's thoughts had gone back to that ghastly vigil with the dying man. He remembered the bright moon shining down on the tumbled heaps of rock and the half-delirious jumble of words which fell disjointedly from the poor cracked lips . . . mostly about

devils. Naturally Stephen did not believe that the workings at Coribunda
were infested with devils, but all the same . . . Gosh, how frightened I
was! he thought.

He had found himself starting and looking round suddenly; thinking he had heard a queer noise; almost expecting to see a ghostly shape
rising from a hole in the ground . . . or a hideous face peering at him
from the ruins of a hut.

What a long night it had seemed! The longest night he had ever
spent in all his life! Having missed the war, by being too young, he had
never seen a man die—and he did not want to. Obviously this man was
going to die and Stephen felt inadequate to cope with the situation. If
he could have done something to help, if he could have given the poor
creature some sort of dope to ease his pain, it would not have been so
frightful. But he had nothing except water, and not too much of that, so
he was obliged to deal it out sparingly. His own throat was parched by
this time, but that did not matter.

He had expected Jim to return in a few hours, but time passed and
Jim did not come. He began to wonder what could have happened—some
accident, perhaps. Jim's pony might have stumbled and thrown him.
Even at this very moment Jim might be lying somewhere unconscious,
having been unable to reach the camp. What then? thought Stephen.
What indeed? The idea was too ghastly to bear thinking about . . . too
ghastly to bear thinking about. . . .

All the same, Stephen could not help thinking about it, and presently he rose and began searching about for water; if only he could find
a spring—the merest trickle—it would solve most of his difficulties and
anxieties. Surely there must be water somewhere; surely they must have
had water here when the Coribunda workings were in full swing? But all
he had found was a large iron tank which had been tipped over. (Perhaps
by a devil?) There was a residue of water in it, green slimy water from
which rose a nauseating stink; Stephen turned away in disgust.

When he went back to his post he found that his patient had rolled
over in delirium. Stephen straightened him out and took his hand. The
hand was as hot as fire and clung to his fingers desperately.

'I thought you were gone,' said the hoarse, choking voice.

'I just went to have a look round, that's all. I shan't leave you,' Stephen
told him as he bent over him and moistened his lips. There was not
much left in the bottle now and the glaring sun was rising like a fire in
the eastern sky.

It was then that the old chap had groped about in his woolly hair and produced his treasures . . . and of course the stone that had been the beginning of the whole thing.

That night! thought Stephen, as he tied his white tie with meticulous care. That night—just a year ago—and now this!

This, said Stephen to himself: dining Julia, the lovely darling, with lots of money in my pocket, enough and to spare, so that I needn't think about money at all. Then perhaps we could go and dance somewhere. I wonder if she would. That long-nosed city type wouldn't like it much—but who cares? I wonder if she's really fond of the Rajah. It doesn't seem possible! But she's frightfully loyal. She's the sort that would stick to her word through thick and thin; she's the sort that would do what she thought was right if it killed her. I wouldn't have her different, of course; I wouldn't alter a hair of her lovely head, but . . . oh well, it's a problem. He sighed. I shall tell Mother about it, he thought. She might be able to advise me. Even if she can't advise me it would be a comfort to talk about it. I could tell her the whole thing. I could even tell her about seeing the darling sitting on that seat in the park and falling in love with her straight off, head over heels. Mother would understand. Yes, that's what I'll do when I get home.

Stephen was ready by this time—bathed and shaved, his hair brushed, his tie properly adjusted—ready, all except the tail-coat which was hanging on the back of the chair. It had come that morning from the tailor in Savile Row. He put it on and regarded himself critically in the mirror. Not bad, he thought, smiling at his reflection. It pays to go to the best place if you can afford it.

Seizing his light coat he ran downstairs and hailed a passing taxi; he was on his way to Julia.

All this passed through Stephen's mind while he was waiting for Julia in Miss Martineau's Victorian parlour. He had expected to have to wait quite a long time for Julia (he did not mind in the very least how long he had to wait), but in less than half an hour the door opened and there she was.

Stephen had told her to make herself beautiful, and she had taken him at his word.

She was beautiful—absolutely beautiful—thought Stephen, gazing at the vision in stunned amazement.

'Will I do?' asked Julia, feigning anxiety. It was rather naughty of her, of course, because although Stephen had said nothing it was perfectly obvious what he was thinking; besides, May had told her—and she had seen herself in the long mirror in Peta's room.

Stephen did not reply to the question. He was speechless.

'Well, come on,' said Julia, smiling kindly. 'We'd better go, hadn't we?'

CHAPTER 14

1

JULIA had dined with Stephen before and had enjoyed it immensely, but it was even better to-night. For to-night was a very special night; it was a celebration. Both were excited, both were wearing new clothes and were pleased with their own and each other's appearance.

In spite of having dwelt for years in the wilderness Stephen knew exactly how to behave; he treated his lady like a queen and the waiters with just the right amount of gracious condescension to obtain the best service. Even the lordly wine-waiter was impressed by Stephen's magnificence. Who are they? he wondered as he hastened to fetch the gold-necked bottle and to bestow it with tender care in the ice-pail.

Quite a number of other people were wondering the same thing: who were they? Various suggestions as to their identity were whispered and discussed at the adjoining tables.

Stephen and Julia were quite unconscious of the interest they were arousing; they were too much interested in each other's conversation; they were enjoying themselves immensely. Julia was retailing the story about the Honourable Mrs. de Courcy, and who could blame her if she retold it with advantages?

Presently Stephen leant across the table and said, 'Isn't this a joke?'

'It's terrific fun, but why a joke?' asked Julia.

'Because if they could have seen me this time last year they would have thrown me out of the place. I was in rags and as dirty as a tinker. It was exactly a year ago to-day that we found that old man at Coribunda.'

Julia gazed at him, wide-eyed. 'We ought to be very grateful to that old man, because if it hadn't been for him—'

'Oh, I know,' agreed Stephen. 'I've thought of that often. I was thinking about it to-night when I was dressing. If I hadn't found that poor old chap none of this would have happened. It was because he gave me the sapphire and I came home to have it cut that I found you sitting in Kensington Gardens. If it hadn't been for him—'

'We shouldn't be here to-night,' nodded Julia. 'It's queer, isn't it?' she added thoughtfully.

'Very queer. That old man—and now this.'

They were silent for a few moments, looking round at the beautifully decorated room full of beautifully decorated people.

'I wish you would explain why the shares went up and down,' said Julia at last. 'I'm not really half-witted, it's just that I don't understand. You said it wasn't a ramp.'

Stephen took up a fork and began to draw a little pattern on the gleaming white tablecloth. 'It wasn't a ramp,' he said slowly. 'There are sapphires at Coribunda—good ones. The surveyor's report was excellent.'

'Stephen, you'll cut the cloth!' exclaimed Julia in alarm.

'Oh, sorry!' said Stephen. 'It's a bad habit of mine—doodling, you know.'

'Well, if the surveyor's report was excellent that's all right, isn't it?' asked Julia.

'Yes, that's why the shares went up. When people got to know about the report they started buying the shares. One fellow said to another, "I'll tell you something, old boy. You know the Coribunda Company? Well, they've discovered that the place is stiff with sapphires. Take my tip and buy." Then the other fellow told his pals about it. That's how things get round. People saw the shares rising, and bought and went on buying.'

'I see that, I can understand that. But why did they go down?'

'They went up too high,' he told her. 'There are a lot of mugs in this world and the mugs thought (if they ever stopped to think) that all you have to do when you find precious stones is to go and pick them up. They never realised that new equipment would have to be bought and transported to one of the wildest places in Africa; they never realised that you must have people to work there and suitable accommodation in which to house them.'

'And the old man said there were devils!'

Stephen laughed. 'I know it seems ridiculous, but actually it's a tremendously important point. In fact you've laid that little finger of yours on the biggest snag of the lot. Jim thinks so and Jim knows Africa better than most. Jim thinks that although there are sapphires in the Coribunda workings it will be dashed difficult to get them out. He says . . . but you'd better keep this dark,' said Stephen, lowering his voice. 'He says he wouldn't take on the job of manager at Coribunda for any money they liked to offer.'

'Oh dear, what a pity! Those beautiful sapphires!'

'Yes, what a pity,' agreed Stephen, smiling. 'All those beautiful sapphires waiting for somebody to get them out and have them cut and polished and made into engagement rings for girls with sapphire-blue eyes! Oh dear, *what* a pity!'

'How are your parents, Stephen?' asked Julia.

Stephen's eyes twinkled. They were grey with little brown flecks in them. He said, 'The parents are as fit as fiddles, thank you, and of course they're very happy about the money. It will make a lot of difference to them. The old house was getting terribly shabby so they're planning to have it put in proper order; in fact the whole place should be renovated and restored. It has been going downhill for years. There's only one fly in the ointment; you won't believe me when I tell you what Mother is worrying about!'

'The people who lost their money,' said Julia confidently. 'The people who bought shares at seventeen and sixpence.'

'Well, I'm dashed! And you don't even *know* Mother! Surely you can't mean *you're* worrying about the mugs?'

'Well—yes,' admitted Julia. 'I can't help wondering who they are and being sorry for them. I keep on hoping they're very rich, in which case it wouldn't matter so much.'

'They're all as rich as Croesus,' declared Stephen. 'They've all got more money than they know what to do with—every one of them.'

Julia did not laugh. She frowned and sighed. 'I hope so,' she said. 'If they were poor it would be frightful. Oh, Stephen, I couldn't bear it if they were poor.'

'Goodness! That's just the way Mother goes on! Do you know this, Julia, you and Mother would simply love each other. I know you would! What about coming down to Gemscoombe for a visit?'

She shook her head.

'Julia, couldn't you? It would be so lovely. You'd adore Gemscoombe; it's an old house and very attractive, set high up on a cliff overlooking the sea. We could bathe and have picnics and go for spins together—it's lovely country—and I promise to be terribly good and sensible all the time. We'd just be good friends,' declared Stephen earnestly. 'We'd just be pals, that's all. That chap is chasing a little white ball at Gleneagles so he couldn't object to your having a holiday at Gemscoombe, could he?'

'It's very kind of you, Stephen, and of course I should love it, but you see I've got a job, and I must—'

'But just for a week,' he urged. 'Just for a little short week. Surely you could get a week's holiday.'

'I've got a job,' repeated Julia in regretful tones; truth to tell she was very much tempted by the joys which Stephen had offered. 'I've got a job, Stephen, and I've only had it for a fortnight; I don't see how I could ask for a holiday so soon.'

'It isn't a very important job, is it?'

'Perhaps not,' she agreed. 'I dare say it seems a silly sort of job to you—selling hats—but it suits me and really and truly there's quite a lot in it. There's psychology in it.'

He thought for a moment or two and then nodded. 'I can see there might be.'

'That's what makes it interesting.'

'What are you paid for selling hats?'

'Eight pounds a week,' said Julia proudly . . . and so she was, for May had managed to persuade Jeanne Kessel to part with this princely sum. (May had popped round to see her friend and had returned from the interview in triumph. 'Jeanne is raising your screw to eight pounds, dulling. Isn't that nice?' she had said.)

'Well, I suppose eight pounds isn't too bad,' admitted Stephen.

'It's splendid,' declared Julia. 'And I've got all that lovely money in the bank! I'm rich, Stephen.'

'Beyond the dreams of avarice,' agreed Stephen, chuckling.

2

The moment had now come for Stephen to suggest that they might go on somewhere else and dance. He suggested it with more confidence than he felt, for he was doubtful whether she would agree.

Julia hesitated—but not for long. Why shouldn't she dance? It was more than likely that Morland was dancing at Gleneagles.

'But where?' asked Julia. 'I mean I don't know much about these places and I don't suppose you do either.'

'I'll ask that commissionaire at the door. He's sure to know the best place.'

Naturally he knew the best place, commissionaires know everything, and one glance at this couple was sufficient to assure him that only the very best place would be good enough for them; he named the very best place in a confidential undertone.

'You're sure it's the best?' asked Stephen anxiously. 'It's quite all right, I mean? Not rowdy or anything?'

Rowdy! The commissionaire's eyebrows nearly disappeared into his hair. As if he would have recommended a rowdy place! 'I think it will suit your requirements, sir; it is occasionally patronised by royalty,' replied the commissionaire accepting Stephen's gratuity with gracious condescension.

There was nothing more to be said . . . which was fortunate, because Stephen was trying to stifle an attack of the giggles; Julia was in the same condition, so they fled out through the revolving doors into the street.

'Oh, Julia!' gasped Stephen. 'Wasn't he priceless?'

'Priceless,' agreed Julia in a choking voice.

The best place to dance in London was very pleasant indeed; there were shaded lights and an exceedingly good band, the floor was like satin. It was so delightful that Julia was surprised to find it was not overcrowded; there were just enough people and no more. Stephen was not surprised; it was he who had paid for the privilege of entry; he had arranged the matter with a very grand gentleman while his partner was titivating in the ladies' room.

'I'm afraid I'm frightfully out of practice,' said Stephen as they took the floor.

'Weren't there dances in Africa?'

'Not this sort.'

'Witch-dances, perhaps?'

'Yes, but I didn't take part.'

They both laughed. They were so excited that even this nonsense seemed witty. . . . Stephen suddenly remembered the last time he had danced. Jim had taken him to the place (a basement room in Jo'burg) and they had danced with sixpenny partners to the strains of a radio-gram. It was stifling, hot and airless, and soon the proceedings became so rowdy that even Jim, who was tough as blazes, had agreed that it might be better to quit before they became involved in a stand-up fight. That was the last time Stephen had danced; if you could call it dancing. Stephen smiled to himself as he guided his partner round the room.

'You don't seem out of practice,' his partner said.

'Anyone with two feet can dance with a feather,' he replied.

After that they scarcely talked at all but just danced and sat at a little table and drank iced lemon-squash and then danced again.

'I suppose we ought to go home,' said Julia at last.

'We should, really,' agreed Stephen reluctantly. 'I've been asked to meet the Coribunda directors to-morrow morning and I shall have to have all my wits about me . . . and I'm going home to-morrow afternoon.

I meant to spend several days in Town, but Father wants me to see the builder about the roof. I shall have to go.'

'Yes, of course you must go.'

'It means I shan't see you again for at least a week, probably more,' continued Stephen in lugubrious tones. 'Of course I can dash up to Town and see you when it has all been settled.'

'Yes,' said Julia doubtfully.

'Home to-morrow! Isn't life sickening?' exclaimed Stephen.

'We've had a lovely, lovely evening.'

'We'll have another lovely, lovely evening soon, won't we?'

Julia was silent. Of course when Morland came home she would not be free to go out with Stephen; she would be spending her evenings with Morland. She wondered whether she should mention this to Stephen but she decided it would be better to write. She could explain it more easily in a letter, and to-night had been so perfect that it seemed a shame to spoil it.

Yes, thought Julia, she would write to Stephen at Gemscoombe and explain that she would not be able to go out with him again.

CHAPTER 15

1

JULIA had received a good many letters from Morland telling her about his doings at Gleneagles; chiefly about his golf. His game was improving with daily practice and tuition from the pro. He had met some kindred spirits in the hotel. Their name was Foster, two brothers and a sister, all very good players. Morland had been playing four-ball matches with them nearly every day. The Fosters had a beautiful house at Sandwich which of course accounted for their proficiency in the game. Morland's letters were well written and well expressed, but somehow they were rather unsatisfactory, for although they contained a great deal of information it was not the kind of information that Julia wanted. Julia was not a golfer and she did not know the Fosters; she would rather have heard about Morland's thoughts than about his deeds of prowess on the golf course; she would rather have heard little details about his daily life than about the magnificence of the Fosters' residence at Sandwich.

(Of course Morland Beverley was by no means unique; quite a number of people who write letters to their friends are concerned to describe their own interests without pausing to think whether or not their news is likely to be of interest to the recipients.)

Julia's letters to Morland were quite different; they flowed from her pen rapidly and occasionally a trifle incoherently. She told Morland that she missed him very much and often thought of him, especially on Thursday afternoons; she told him about her job and how interesting it was; she told him about May Martineau and the boarders . . . but she did not mention Stephen. She had tried several times to tell Morland about Stephen, but it was too difficult in a letter, so she decided to wait until Morland returned. She realised that if she did not mention Stephen she could not mention Coribunda . . . but perhaps that was just as well, for she had a feeling that Morland would not approve of her little flutter on the Stock Exchange. All that must wait until Morland came home, when she could explain it properly and make sure that he understood. She salved her conscience by saying in her letter that she had lots and lots of things to tell him when he came home—and of course he would be home quite soon now, for his three weeks' holiday was almost at an end.

Several days later Julia received another letter from Morland in which he said that his father's health had benefited greatly from the change of air and the bracing climate so they had arranged to extend their holiday at Gleneagles for another week. In some ways this was delightful, but unfortunately it meant that another week must pass before he and Julia could meet. However, it could not be helped and the week would soon pass, especially if they had good weather.

Julia received this letter at breakfast and told May the news.

'Oh dear!' said May. 'That's a pity, isn't it? And your other nice young man has gone home to Devonshire!'

'Yes, it is rather a pity,' agreed Julia thoughtfully as she gathered up her letter and hastened away to her work.

2

This was Saturday, a half holiday at Madame Claire's. Julia wanted to be there early, because she had mislaid her scissors (the dear little gilt bird which May had given her) and intended to have a good hunt for them before the others arrived.

The scissors were a most important part of Julia's equipment and she always kept them hanging round her waist on a ribbon. Not only were they useful to Julia herself, they had become extremely useful to

Madame Claire, who frequently mislaid her own scissors and might require them at any moment.

Madame would cry, 'Scissors, scissors!' in urgent tones, or sometimes, *'Julie, vite! Le petit oiseau d'or!'*

When Julia went in, Madame was sitting reading the morning paper as usual, so Julia did not bother her but got on with her daily task of taking the hats from the shelves in the big glass-fronted cupboards and arranging them on the stands. Having done so she began her search.

'What do you seek, Julie?' inquired Madame.

'My scissors, Madame. I don't know where I can have put them.'

'Le petit oiseau d'or?'

Julia nodded sadly. 'Of course I can easily get another pair of scissors, but May gave me the little gilt bird; it's very old and rather valuable. Perhaps it was silly of me to use a valuable pair of scissors, but May said the little gilt bird would bring me luck.'

'Voici le petit oiseau d'or!' exclaimed Madame, producing Julia's treasure from her handbag.

'Oh, Madame, how lovely! Where did you find it?'

'Where do you think? No, Julie, you will never guess. I found it in the pocket of the pink overall.'

'But the pink overall belongs to Fifi—' began Julia in bewilderment.

'You do not understand?' asked Madame with a wicked little smile. 'Me, I understand very easily.'

Julia stood and looked at her blankly. 'Oh, Madame, you don't mean she—'

'Stole it,' nodded Madame.

'But it's impossible! I can't believe it!'

'Oh, she is not really a thief, that one. The money is safe with her. It was just to cause annoyance to one who is attentive to my wishes, to one who is always ready with the little gold bird when I call for scissors in a hurry.'

'Oh dear,' said Julia sadly. 'Of course I knew they hated me.'

'They are jealous, Julie.'

'I know, but what am I to do?'

'You will do nothing,' said Madame, picking up her paper. 'They will get over it in time.'

'You think so?'

'I'm sure of it. Meanwhile you will go on as usual, my child. You will hang the little gold bird round your waist with the little black ribbon and you will say nothing about it—nothing at all. That will puzzle Fifi

and perhaps it will frighten her. It will do no harm to give Fifi a fright,'
added Madame, chuckling.

Julia did as she was told, but she was very unhappy about it. She
would have liked to believe that it was an accident; and perhaps it was.
For instance Fifi might have found the scissors lying about and put them
in her pocket intending to give them to their rightful owner at the first
opportunity—and forgotten. Yes, it might easily have happened like that.
It must have happened like that, thought Julia.

Fifi was unusually late that morning (it was nearly half-past nine
when she arrived), so she hurried in, disappeared into the cloakroom
and emerged a few moments later fresh and smiling. She had expected
a stern reproof from Madame for being so late, but she escaped her
deserts, for already there were several clients in the establishment and
everyone was busy.

Presently Madame called out, 'Julie, your scissors! Where is the
little gold bird?'

Of course Madame had done it on purpose; Julia knew that (it was
the sort of joke Madame enjoyed). Julia did not like it at all but there
was nothing to be done except to produce the scissors.

'So nice,' declared Madame as, quite unnecessarily, she snipped a
tiny piece of ribbon from one of her creations. 'Such a dear little gold
bird! So useful! Always ready when I need him! You must take great care
of him, Julie. It would be a thousand pities to lose him.'

Julia glanced at Fifi . . . and wished she had not done so. The girl's
natural colour had faded leaving two patches of pink rouge. With her
round face and staring eyes she reminded Julia of an old-fashioned
Dutch doll. Worst of all she put her hand into her overall pocket and
brought it out empty.

Julia was afraid Fifi was about to faint, but she pulled herself together.
Just for a few moments there was silence and then everything went on
as before. Business as usual; the selling of little hats and big hats, hats
of all colours and shapes, placed upon the clients' heads and arranged
in the most becoming manner; disapproved and discarded, quite often
approved and bought.

3

Madame Claire's establishment was so busy to-day that there was no
proper eleven o'clock break. Julia and Ivonne happened to be disengaged
at the same moment, so they rushed into the little cloakroom and made

themselves some coffee from the tin of Nescafé which stood on the shelf. There was no time to chat even if they had wanted to; they drank their coffee hastily and went back to work. Perhaps Ivonne knew, or perhaps not. Julia could not tell.

Soon after that a middle-aged lady in a well-cut tweed suit came in. Obviously she was 'a country lady' (as Madame put it), and as a rule it was Julia's task to deal with 'country ladies' but Julia was engaged with another client—a tiresome and extremely disagreeable client—so Madame went forward herself.

'Can I help you, Madame?' asked Madame sweetly.

'I want a hat,' said the 'country lady' bluntly.

Julia was interested in the lady, there was something vaguely familiar about her, but her own disagreeable client was demanding all her attention. It was not until the disagreeable client had tried on at least six hats, decided that none of them would do and swept out of the establishment saying that she could not think why her sister-in-law had recommended it to her, that Julia was free to watch what was going on at the other end of the room.

How clever Madame was! She was 'just right' with the country lady, showing her a selection of neat little felts exactly suited to her style, not pressing her nor hurrying her but giving her plenty of time to make the correct decision. Presently the lady decided upon a dark red felt, quite plain except for a very small silver buckle. Madame assured her it was very becoming . . . which indeed it was. The lady said she would wear it, and gave the address of her hotel, where the old hat was to be sent.

Whilst the bill was being made out she glanced at Julia and smiled a little shyly; then she paid the bill, and Madame showed her out.

Odd, thought Julia. I believe I've seen her before—somewhere—and it almost looked as if she had the same feeling about me.

'She is a country lady,' said Madame as Julia went to help her to put away the little felt hats. *'Elle est gentille, n'est ce pas? Elle n'a pas de chic, mais elle a l'air d'une grande dame.'*

Julia agreed that the newly departed client was all that Madame had said: nice, not chic, but with the air of a great lady. Then, remembering the shy little smile, she thought, no, not 'great,' exactly, that's wrong.

CHAPTER 16

1

ON SATURDAYS it was Julia's duty to put all the hats away in the cupboards for the week-end and to cover the furniture with dust-sheets. The other girls were supposed to help her but they never did . . . and Julia did not object. As a matter of fact she preferred to do it herself rather than to have reluctant assistants. The task took some time, so it was getting on for two o'clock before she was ready to go. She locked the door carefully and walked away.

'Miss Harburn!' said a voice behind her.

Julia turned and saw the lady in the red felt hat.

'It is Miss Harburn, isn't it?' asked the lady.

'Yes, Julia Harburn.'

'I was sure it was. I hope you don't mind my speaking to you like this?'

'No, of course not! I had a sort of feeling that I knew you.'

'No, we've never met. My son told me about you so I thought I'd like to speak to you, that's all. . . . Oh, how silly of me! I should have told you I'm Mrs. Brett.'

'Stephen's mother!'

'Yes,' said Stephen's mother, smiling.

By this time they were walking along the street together.

'So that's why I had a sort of feeling I'd seen you before!'

'You mean he's like me? I always think he's more like his father.'

'He's like you—quite definitely,' said Julia. She hesitated and then added, 'I'm so glad you spoke to me, Mrs. Brett. I suppose Stephen told you I was working at Madame Claire's?'

'Yes, he told me. I came up to Town for a few days to do some shopping and I wanted a hat—and I thought I should like to see you, so I thought . . .'

'You thought you would kill two birds with one stone,' suggested Julia.

Mrs. Brett laughed. 'Yes, something like that, but I wouldn't have put it so rudely.' She added, 'Where are we going, Miss Harburn?'

This was quite a natural question, because Julia was striding along in a purposeful manner as if she were making for a definite goal. As a matter of fact she was making for Jacques's, the little restaurant where she usually had lunch. By this time she and Jacques were fast friends; he reserved a special table for her and gave her special terms. She explained this to Mrs. Brett, adding that she had been detained shutting up the shop for Madame Claire so she was extremely hungry.

'I'm simply ravenous,' declared Mrs. Brett. 'May I come there with you?'

'Yes, of course! That would be lovely. The only thing is I don't know whether . . .'

'Wouldn't there be room for me?'

'It isn't that,' Julia explained. 'It's just . . . well it's just that I don't know whether you would like it. I mean it isn't a very good place to go.'

'But you often go there?'

'Yes, but I don't mind the queer people. I go because it's very convenient. The place is clean and the food is good, so—'

'Let's go there,' said Mrs. Brett. 'I don't mind queer people. What I want is good food—lots of good food—and I want it soon.'

(It was no wonder that Mrs. Brett felt like that, for she had been hanging about outside Madame Claire's establishment for nearly an hour waiting for Miss Harburn to come out. She had walked up and down; she had peered into the neighbouring shop windows until she was tired of seeing the tastefully displayed merchandise. Several times she had decided she must have missed Miss Harburn, but on peeping in through the window she had seen her quarry was still there, putting away hats in cupboards and drawers and covering the stands with dust-sheets. Most people would have given up the exhausting business long before, but there are no limits to the endurance of a mother when the happiness and well-being of an adored son are at stake.)

'Well, if you're sure you don't mind having lunch in rather a queer little place—this is it,' said Julia, pushing open the door and holding it for her companion.

It was a very small place but most of the regular customers had fed already so it was not overcrowded. Jacques received them himself with a beaming smile; conducted them to a table in the corner; took their order and hurried away. Soon the two hungry ladies were eating the *Plat du Jour*, which consisted of braised pigeons with mushrooms and sauté potatoes.

'Exceedingly good,' declared Mrs. Brett. 'I'm so glad we came here. What do you say to a bottle of white wine, Miss Harburn?'

Julia laughed and said, 'Yes.'

'The sapphire is beautiful, isn't it?' said Mrs. Brett.

'It's perfectly lovely,' Julia replied. 'Stephen put it down on the table and it lay there glowing like a red-hot coal . . . a blue red-hot coal if you know what I mean.'

'I know exactly what you mean. A blue red-hot coal describes it exactly . . . and such a gorgeous colour! It makes me think of the sea at Gemscoombe on a summer's afternoon.'

'The sea?' asked Julia doubtfully.

Mrs. Brett nodded. 'I've seen it just that colour—deep cornflower blue. You must come and stay with us when you get your holiday and then you'll believe me.'

'I'm afraid I shan't be getting a holiday for ages. You see, I've just started work . . . and of course I'm engaged to be married. You know that, I expect.'

'Yes, Stephen told me. Are you going to be married soon?'

'Not for some time,' replied Julia. 'We're waiting until my fiancé is given a junior partnership in his father's firm. We don't know when that will be.'

2

Mrs. Brett and Julia chatted agreeably of one thing and another as they enjoyed their belated meal. Not unnaturally they chatted about Stephen.

'I should have liked to have several children,' said Mrs. Brett. 'I had three brothers and we had the greatest fun together, so I felt very sorry for Stephen being an only child. Fortunately he had Wodge.'

'A dog?' asked Julia with interest.

'No, a boy.' She laughed and added, 'An imaginary boy. They used to play together for hours and hours quite happily. I was so grateful to Wodge. I believe he was almost as real to me as he was to Stephen . . . and he was absolutely real to Stephen.'

'Tell me more about Wodge. Why was he called Wodge?'

'I don't know,' said Mrs. Brett, frowning thoughtfully. 'He was always called Wodge. As a matter of fact—strictly in confidence—I believe Stephen still has Wodge. I believe Wodge was in Africa with Stephen and kept an eye on him and looked after him when he had that horrible adventure at Coribunda.'

'A sort of guardian angel,' suggested Julia.

'Well—sort of,' agreed Mrs. Brett. She laughed merrily and added, 'But who ever heard of a guardian angel called Wodge?'

Julia laughed too, and admitted that it certainly was an odd name for a guardian angel.

'Don't tell Stephen I told you about him, will you?' said Mrs. Brett. 'I expect he would be very cross with me. He would think it silly. Perhaps it is rather silly.'

'It isn't silly at all,' declared Julia emphatically. 'I was an only child and I used to have an imaginary sister, but she wasn't nearly as nice as Wodge.'

It was now Julia's turn to talk, so she told Mrs. Brett about May Martineau and her Victorian parlour and the chandelier with the crystal drops.

'How interesting! I wish I could see that room!' exclaimed Mrs. Brett.

They had been talking without a pause and getting on splendidly, but when the coffee was brought Mrs. Brett suddenly became silent; and not only silent but deaf. It was evident that she did not hear a word Julia was saying. She had picked up a fork and was drawing little patterns on the cloth . . . just like Stephen, thought Julia, smiling to herself. Of course she could not prevent Mrs. Brett from doodling, and fortunately it did not matter here. Jacques's table-cloths were very different from the beautiful white gleaming table-cloth in the restaurant where she and Stephen had celebrated their winnings in the Coribunda Stakes.

'Julia,' said Mrs. Brett at last. 'I hope you don't mind my calling you Julia? You see, Stephen has talked to me about you such a lot.'

'Of course you must call me Julia.'

'You see,' said Mrs. Brett, raising her eyes and looking at Julia for a moment. 'You see, Julia, the fact is I came to London on purpose to talk to you; the other things were just excuses. I wanted to talk to you, but I wasn't sure whether I would be able to say what I wanted to say until I had seen you. When I saw you I thought I could.'

Julia was silent. She wondered what was coming.

'It's just this,' said Mrs. Brett, drawing industriously.

'Stephen said you weren't very happy at home. He said rather a strange thing about your stepmother. He said she was "a fast worker," and when I asked him what it meant he wouldn't tell me.'

'I'm afraid it means she's rather—rather—I mean she makes friends—too quickly—'

'Yes, I see,' said Mrs. Brett, nodding. 'I was afraid it meant something like that. I've been thinking about it a great deal and worrying about you.'

'About me?' asked Julia in surprise.

'Was it very interfering of me? You see I had heard so much about you that I felt I knew you quite well . . . and you have no mother. I just thought, *perhaps* that girl needs a friend, so I thought the best thing to do was to come and see you and make sure. Because if you needed a friend, an older woman whom you could rely on if you weren't very happy or anything, I might be some use.'

'Oh, Mrs. Brett—'

'You see what I mean, don't you?' said Mrs. Brett earnestly. 'You see what I meant when I said that I wasn't sure whether I would be able to say what I wanted to say until I had seen you? If I had found that you were an independent sort of girl, quite happy and contented, I wouldn't have said a word; but it seemed to me that you looked—you looked rather forlorn. . . . No, no!' exclaimed Mrs. Brett impatiently. 'Forlorn isn't quite the right word. Oh dear, I wish I were better at explaining things! When I saw you in that hat-shop I thought you looked as if you didn't quite belong to your surroundings; I thought you looked as if something had happened that had distressed you.'

'Something had happened; something rather horrid.'

'Yes—well, you can tell me or not as you like. I just want you to feel that if you ever need a friend—someone of your own kind—there's Alison Brett. If you want to leave that place, and have nowhere to go, you can ring up and say you're coming. That's all.'

There were tears in Julia's eyes. She said with difficulty, 'I do need a friend . . . like you.'

'That's lovely,' said Mrs. Brett, nodding.

'But you understand, don't you?' said Julia hastily. 'I've told you I'm engaged to be married.'

'Yes, of course,' agreed Mrs. Brett. 'This is between you and me. It's a woman's arrangement. It has nothing to do with Stephen—except of course that I should never have known anything about you if it hadn't been for him. If you come and stay at Gemscoombe, as I hope you will, it will be as my guest—to see me and talk to me. As a matter of fact Stephen may not be there at all unless you come fairly soon, I'm afraid he will be going back to that horrible place in Africa next month.'

'Going back to Africa!'

'I'm afraid so,' said Mrs. Brett with a sigh. 'He has got that job, you see. It's a good job; he likes it and he likes the people. Mr. Sloane the manager is very nice to Stephen so it would be a pity to give it up. I suggested he should get a job in this country, but he says it wouldn't be nearly so interesting, because all the mines here are fully developed. Stephen likes breaking new ground.'

'It would be nice if he could get a job in this country,' said Julia in rather a sad little voice. 'I mean nice for you,' she added quickly.

'Lovely for us,' agreed Mrs. Brett.

Julia happened to be looking at Mrs. Brett when she said this, so she happened to notice that Mrs. Brett was smiling to herself in a somewhat enigmatic manner. Her eyes were exactly like Stephen's, thought Julia. Grey with little brown flecks in them and liable to twinkle when their owner was amused.

'But of course our arrangement has nothing whatever to do with Stephen,' said Mrs. Brett. 'As I said before, it's a woman's arrangement. It has nothing to do with anyone except Julia Harburn and Alison Brett.'

'Thank you very very much,' said Julia holding out her hand.

Mrs. Brett gave it a little squeeze. 'What nice hands! Nice long slender fingers! Do you play the violin, Julia?'

Julia shook her head. 'Mother tried to teach me to play the piano but she gave it up in despair. I haven't any accomplishments.'

'But you can speak French beautifully. You were speaking French to Jacques.'

'Oh, languages are easy!'

'Not to everyone. I suppose that's how you got that job in the hat-shop?'

'Well, not exactly, but it's the reason why Madame Claire likes me and it's the reason why the other girls hate me.'

'Hate you!' exclaimed Mrs. Brett in a startled tone.

'Mrs. Brett, I'd like to tell you about what happened this morning.'

'I was hoping you would. Can we go on talking here . . . or where?'

'Jacques won't mind,' replied Julia.

3

The restaurant was empty except for themselves, so Julia rested her elbows on the table and without more ado proceeded to tell her new friend about the little pair of gilt scissors. She had them with her in her bag, so she produced them and laid them on the table.

'Perfectly charming,' declared Mrs. Brett taking them up and examining them with the air of an expert. 'Eighteenth century, I should think—probably French. Quite valuable.'

The story took some time to tell, because such a lot of things had to be explained if Mrs. Brett was to understand it properly (and it was quite useless to tell it at all unless it was thoroughly understood); but Mrs. Brett was an admirable audience, listening carefully and occasionally asking a question.

By the time Julia had finished, Mrs. Brett had a complete grasp of Julia's problem, and, curiously enough, Julia herself understood it much more clearly.

When she had finished there was silence while Mrs. Brett thought about it.

At last she said, 'Will you be able to bear it, Julia?'

'Not if it goes on,' replied Julia without hesitation. 'Madame said they would get over it in time. Do you think she's right?'

'You may be able to win them round—I'm sure you could if Madame were sensible—but meanwhile it will be very unpleasant for you. Oh dear, I don't like it at all!'

'I suppose I could find some other job,' said Julia thoughtfully. 'The trouble is I'm rather an idiot, completely untrained, and I can do this job rather well. Quite honestly I'm good at selling hats, and it interests me. It seems so foolish to give it up. What else could I do?'

'Yes, I see. Well, perhaps you should go on trying for a bit, but you needn't worry about getting another job. If you find you can't bear it you must let me know and come to Gemscoombe. I mean come and stay until you're married. It would be delightful to have you for as long as you like.'

Julia was about to reply to this extremely kind and obviously sincere invitation when Jacques approached the table, and apologising profusely, began to explain his difficulties in rapid French. He was devastated to be obliged to disturb the two ladies in the middle of their obviously so important conversation, but what was he to do? The waiter had gone home and he himself must commence his preparations for dinner. It was therefore necessary that the restaurant should be closed, the blinds drawn down and the door shut. He did not want to hurry the ladies (it would be unpardonable), but perhaps in about ten minutes, if that were possible. . . .

Julia replied that she understood perfectly and ten minutes would be ample time for the conclusion of their conversation.

'We've got ten minutes,' she said to her companion, smiling apologetically.

'Yes, I gathered that much. I can understand French fairly well if they don't talk too quickly. Unfortunately they usually talk much too quickly.'

'Would you like to come home with me?' asked Julia, who was unwilling to part from her new-found friend. 'I mean to Miss Martineau's. It isn't very far, and you said you would like to see her Victorian parlour.'

'Not to-day, I think. For one thing I must go back to the hotel and rest (Town is so noisy and bustling, frightfully tiring for a country cousin), and for another thing I don't want anyone to know we've met. I'm sure Miss Martineau is very nice. She sounds an absolute pet. But she talks a lot, doesn't she? If Stephen happened to call and see you, as he did before, she might happen to mention that she had met his mother.'

Julia was obliged to admit that this was so.

'It's like this you see,' explained Mrs. Brett. 'Harry and Stephen are both under the impression that I came to Town to buy a hat. Men are so dim, aren't they? Very clever in some ways, of course, but fortunately very very dim in others. You would never believe that I would come all the way from Devonshire to London to buy a hat, would you?'

Julia giggled.

'No, of course you wouldn't,' nodded Mrs. Brett. 'You have only to look at me and you can see I'm not that sort of person.

Harry has lived with me for thirty-two years but he believed it, and so did Stephen. They teased me about it—but very kindly. Harry gave me fifty pounds and they both came to the station and saw me off. They're perfect dears, both of them. I wouldn't be deceitful, of course,' declared Mrs. Brett. 'I've bought a hat and I'm very pleased with it, so that's all right. I wouldn't be deceitful for worlds, but when you live in a house with men you've got to have your own little secrets. You simply can't tell them everything. You see that, don't you, Julia?'

'The truth and nothing but the truth, but not the whole truth,' suggested Julia.

'How well you understand!' exclaimed Mrs. Brett with a sigh of relief.

The ten minutes respite was now over, so they gathered up their gloves and bags and emerged into the sunlit street.

'Don't forget what I told you,' said Mrs. Brett.

'I'm not likely to forget,' declared Julia.

They kissed each other affectionately and parted.

CHAPTER 17

1

JULIA thought a great deal about her conversation with Mrs. Brett; it had given her a feeling of safety. She had been wondering what she could do if Ivonne and Fifi continued to be so unpleasant, for she knew that if she were obliged to leave Madame Claire's it would be very difficult indeed to get another post, and although she had money in the bank it would not last for ever. Would she have to go home with her tail between her legs? Horrible thought! There was Morland of course, but Morland would advise her to go home. He had done so before and would do so again. Some day she and Morland would be married, but not until he had got his partnership, and when would that be? Julia was quite determined not to press Morland to 'fix a day,' as Retta had advised. She would marry Morland, but not until he wanted to marry her.

All this had worried Julia, but now there was no longer any need to worry, for if things became too difficult she could ring up Mrs. Brett and go to Gemscoombe. She could stay there as long as she liked. Yes, Mrs. Brett's invitation had given Julia a nice safe feeling. She had liked Mrs. Brett immensely and Mrs. Brett had liked her; that was evident. Mrs. Brett had said that she and Julia were the same kind of people . . . she could not have said anything nicer.

On Sunday afternoon May suggested that she and Julia should have an outing together.

'We might go to Kew,' said May thoughtfully. 'The flowers will be nice just now and you can get a good tea at the restaurant.'

Julia was delighted at the idea of an outing with May (custom had not staled her infinite variety). 'Yes, let's,' she said. 'It will be fun. I haven't been to Kew since I was a child.'

Usually May rested in the afternoon, but she had decided that poor darling Julia must be feeling dull without either of her young men, so she had suggested the expedition to amuse her. However, she soon discovered that Julia was not dull; quite the contrary.

'You're in very good form this afternoon,' said May as they alighted from the bus at the entrance to the gardens.

'Yes, I'm happy,' Julia agreed. 'You see, I was a bit worried about something, but now I needn't worry any more.'

'I suppose it's because your young man will be coming home from Scotland soon.'

'No, not exactly—there was something else—but of course it will be lovely to see Morland again. I feel as if he had been away for months.'

Of course May was dying to know what the 'something else' could be, but she did not like to ask.

'Months and months,' continued Julia thoughtfully. 'I feel as if Morland had been thousands of miles away . . . at the North Pole or somewhere like that. It's because so much has happened, I suppose.'

'Yes, that's the reason. Time is funny; isn't it? Sometimes it tears along like mad and sometimes it crawls like a snail.'

'And not always because you're happy or unhappy.'

'That's right,' agreed May. 'But it always crawls if you're waiting for someone and watching the clock. Have you noticed that, dulling?'

Julia had noticed this strange phenomenon.

Julia and May were good companions; they strolled round the gardens admiring the flowers. Neither of them knew very much about flowers, for both had been born and bred in London, but that did not prevent them from enjoying their beauty and fragrance. Julia commented upon this fortunate circumstance and May agreed.

'Look at those!' May exclaimed. 'I don't know what they are but they're lovely, aren't they?' She pointed to a bed of small bushy plants bearing enormous blossoms; some were deep pink, others were white as snow.

They stood for a few moments looking at the unknown flowers in delight and watching an elderly gentleman who was examining the labels and making notes in a little book.

'He knows all about them,' whispered Julia reverently.

'Yes, but he likes the labels best,' replied May with one of her fat chuckles.

There were dozens of children running about the gardens; some were wearing little frocks or suits but most of them were in scanty bathing costumes and were enjoying the warmth of the sunshine on their naked limbs. Julia envied them and said so.

'Yes, it would be nice,' nodded May. 'But people would be a bit surprised if they saw me turning somersaults in my birthday suit. Oh dear, I'm tired and hot,' she added.

Fortunately they were not far from a restaurant, so they went and sat down under a large coloured umbrella. May ordered tea and cream buns and Julia ordered a glass of iced lemon squash.

The expedition was so successful and they had enjoyed themselves so much that they agreed to come again soon. It was only afterwards that Julia remembered she would not be able to take part in another expedition to Kew because Morland would be home next Sunday and would take her out in his car.

2

Several days passed without anything very important happening, but Thursday was eventful, to say the least of it. To begin with, Julia's alarm clock failed her so she was very late in waking. She had no time for her usual bath but washed and dressed hastily and ran downstairs flustered and upset.

May was standing in the hall. 'Oh, there you are!' she exclaimed. 'I was just coming to see what had happened.'

'The clock didn't go off, that's what happened. I'm terribly late.'

'Never mind, dulling. Breakfast is all ready, so—'

'I haven't time for breakfast.'

'But you must!' cried May in consternation. 'You can't go to work without having something to eat!'

'I'll just have a cup of coffee,' declared Julia. 'I haven't time for anything else, and anyhow I'm not a bit hungry.'

May followed Julia into the dining-room. She had a letter in her hand.

'Is the letter for me?' asked Julia as she poured out her coffee.

'Yes, but it isn't from your young man,' replied May turning it over and examining it carefully. 'It isn't from your father either, because it hasn't got a foreign stamp. I can't make out the postmark, it's quite a long word beginning L-E-D, and it's been forwarded from Manor Gardens. Who is it from, I wonder.'

'I haven't the slightest idea,' said Julia crossly.

'Funny spidery writing,' added May as she handed the letter to it's owner.

Julia took it and put it in her bag.

'Aren't you going to open it?' asked May in a disappointed tone.

'I haven't time.'

'But it may be important!'

Julia took no notice; she was annoyed with May. Although she had decided that it was nice of May to be interested in her affairs, it was aggravating to see one's correspondence handled and examined and commented upon before one had had the chance to look at it oneself. . . . Julia already was out of temper, and this seemed the last straw. She drank a cup of coffee hastily, collected her belongings and fled.

It was almost nine o'clock when she arrived at Madame Claire's establishment. Madame had begun to arrange the hats with her own hands and was extremely cross at having to perform the unaccustomed task.

'What do you think I pay you for?' exclaimed Madame. 'Do I pay you eight pounds a week so that I may have the pleasure of doing your work myself?'

Julia did not reply. It was unfair of Madame to be cross; Julia was not late. Madame was cross because Julia was not early. . . . But everything was unfair this morning, thought Julia as she put on her overall. Everything was horrible. . . . It was absolutely disgusting to think that she would have to spend all day selling hats. She was sick and tired of the job.

There had been no time to read the letter, of course, but she had seen at a glance that the writing on the envelope was completely unknown. It was not from Morland nor from Stephen; not from her father nor Retta nor from any of her friends. All through that morning while Julia was selling hats she kept thinking off and on about the letter.

Presently Julia began to feel a little queer; she had risen in a hurry and had had no breakfast; she had been flustered and upset. That had passed now, leaving her in a strange dreamy condition which was not unpleasant. Fortunately by this time she was so used to selling hats that she could have sold them in her sleep.

Who can it be from? thought Julia as she put on a little bonnet of twisted straw trimmed with ox-eye daisies and turned to display its beauties to one of Madame's clients.

'It's very pretty. Do you think it would suit me?' asked the client eagerly.

'You could try it,' suggested Julia, smiling dreamily and thinking how lovely it would be if the letter were from a fairy godmother.

'Yes, I'll try it,' said the client.

Oh, I hope it's from a fairy godmother, thought Julia as she arranged the little bonnet on the client's stringy hair and presented her with the hand-mirror.

'It doesn't look quite the same,' said the client in a disappointed voice.

This was true, of course. 'No, it isn't quite your style,' agreed Julia. 'Let's try this blue one; I think it would suit you better.'

She arranged the blue hat on the client's head. (A fairy god-mother, she thought. Perhaps she wants me to go with her for a cruise in the Mediterranean . . . or possibly to the South Seas. How lovely it would be to get away from everyone and everything!)

'Yes, it's rather nice,' said the client. 'The only thing is I didn't really want a blue one. I might try that white one over there, or the one with the pansies.'

Although aware that neither would be the slightest use Julia fetched them at once. The client tried them on, hesitated for a few moments and then discarded them. She tried on several other hats—all quite hopeless—and eventually decided to have the blue one.

3

Julia spent the morning dreaming the wildest dreams about the mysterious letter. It seemed a very long morning, but at last it was one o'clock, the establishment was closed for an hour, and she was free. She hurried round to the little restaurant as usual.

Jacques was busy to-day, there was no time for him to linger and chat with his favourite customer, so she made her way to the table which was always reserved for her and, because by this time she was exceedingly hungry, she ordered beef-steak-pie and vegetables.

There was now time to read the letter, so Julia took it out of her bag. For some reason or other she was reluctant to open it . . . perhaps because the opening of it had been so long delayed and she had entertained so many absurd and extravagant ideas about it. She held it in her hand, looking at it and wondering. May had said the writing was 'spidery,' but to Julia it looked shaky and uncertain. Perhaps the person who had written it was ill.

I'm just being silly! thought Julia, and with that she seized a teaspoon, inserted the handle in the flap of the envelope and opened the letter.

> The Square House,
> Leddiesford,
> Scotland

My dear Julia,

Perhaps you will wonder who is writing to you. I am your father's elder brother. You may not have heard about me before because I had a serious quarrel with your parents. We were young and hot-blooded in those days. Now that I am old and ill I regret my part in the quarrel deeply and sincerely. It distresses me to feel that I am at loggerheads with anybody—especially with my nearest relations—so I should like to put an end to the stupid feud. I have written to your father several times but I have had no reply so now I am writing to ask you if you will be kind enough to come and see me. I was obliged to sell Harburn House which belonged to our family for generations so I am living in a small house in the town with a housekeeper to look after me.

I hope you will come—even if it were only for a short visit. I would like to see your mother's daughter before I die.

> Yours sincerely,
> RANDAL HARBURN

Julia had thought of half a dozen different explanations but never of anything like this. She had never heard of her father's brother—never knew that he existed.

Randal, thought Julia. Somehow the name seemed familiar; she began to have a feeling that she had heard it before; she began to have a vague recollection of hearing her parents mention the name, but it was so long ago that she could not remember what they had said. The impression left on her mind was somehow rather unpleasant.

Yes, definitely unpleasant, but that was natural if there had been a 'serious quarrel.'

Julia had nothing to do with the quarrel, had never heard of it, did not know what it was about . . . and most certainly she did not want to go to this unknown place and stay with this unknown uncle.

I can't go, of course, thought Julia with a sigh of relief. It's quite impossible. I shall have to write and explain that I've got a job and I can't get away.

Then she read the letter again and thought, *but I must go*!

Yes, she would have to go . . . there was no getting out of it. When a man is old and ill and writes to say he wants to see you before he dies you have no choice in the matter. If Julia refused to go and the man died she would have it on her conscience for the rest of her life!

Julia sat and stared at the letter in dismay.

It was not until the waiter brought her bill that she suddenly came to her senses and realised it was nearly two o'clock.

4

What an awful day! thought Julia, as she hastened back to Madame Claire's. Late all the time, rushing hither and thither and never catching up with the clock!

Madame was in her establishment when Julia arrived hot and breathless.

'I'm sorry,' began Julia. 'I'm terribly sorry. Everything seems to have gone wrong to-day!'

'Some days are like that,' said Madame quite kindly. 'To-day is not a good day for me either. I was a little cross this morning because you were late, but you must not be upset about it. Some of my shares have gone down a little; that was the reason.'

'Madame!' exclaimed Julia. 'I've had a letter. I'm terribly worried about it.'

'It is bad news?'

'No—at least I mean yes,' said Julia breathlessly. 'It's from my uncle who lives in Scotland. He's very ill. He says he wants to see me before he dies.'

'*Mais ce sont de mauvaises nouvelles!*' exclaimed Madame in dismay. 'My poor Julie, no wonder you are distressed!'

'I don't know what to do. I'm afraid I shall have to go and see him.'

'*Cela va sans dire! Naturellement vous devez aller le voir* . . . it would be very wrong to refuse such a request.'

'That's what I thought. I don't want to go, but—'

'But you must, my child. You must certainly go, but I hope you will return to me when he is better.'

'Yes, of course,' agreed Julia with a sigh of relief.

'That is settled, then.'

'*Oh, Madame, comme vous êtes bonne!*'

'It is good to be kind to those who are in trouble. Naturally it will be very inconvenient for me to do without you, I shall miss you greatly, but I hope it need not be for long.'

'Not more than a week,' declared Julia. 'It's just to see him, that's all.'

'*Pauvre vieillard,*' said Madame sadly. 'Has he no family? Has he no wife, no children?'

'No, he lives alone with a housekeeper to look after him.'

Madame shook her head. 'How lonely he must be! How natural that he should want to see his little niece! Yes, Julie, you must go and comfort him; it would be very wicked of me to prevent you from doing your duty. When will you go, my child?'

Julia thought for a moment. To-day was Thursday, Morland was coming home on Sunday, and she must see Morland before she went. 'Perhaps I had better go on Tuesday,' said Julia reluctantly. 'He's ill, you see.'

'Yes, let it be Tuesday,' Madame agreed. 'You will come here to-morrow and on Saturday morning. On Monday you can pack and make all your arrangements.'

'Oh, how kind you are!' repeated Julia. 'It is such a relief to my mind. I was afraid you would say . . .'

'You were afraid I would say you must not go?' asked Madame, smiling. 'Am I such a gorgon?'

Julia was still thanking Madame and assuring her that never for a moment had she thought her a gorgon, when the entry of a client cut short the conversation.

As usual, May was awaiting Julia's return. She was waiting more eagerly than usual because she wanted to hear about the mysterious letter; it had intrigued her so much that she had been thinking about it all day . . . and, as Julia was feeling remorseful over her bad temper, she produced the letter and gave it to May to read.

'Poor old man!' exclaimed May. 'You'll have to go, won't you, dulling?'

'Yes, I'll have to go, but I needn't stay long, of course.'

'A feud,' said May, reading the letter again more carefully. 'It's very romantic, isn't it? I once read a book about Scotland; there was a lot in it about feuds . . . Scotch clans having feuds with each other and shooting each other and burning down each other's houses.'

Julia smiled. 'I don't think it's that kind of feud.'

'Well, I hope not,' declared May looking somewhat apprehensive. 'You don't want to get mixed up in that kind of thing, do you? What about your young man, dulling? He won't like you going off to Scotland, will he?'

'Morland will understand. I'm glad he's coming on Sunday because he'll be able to find out about trains and make the arrangements for me. He's very good at all that sort of thing.'

'Good,' nodded May. 'I like a man to be efficient and practical. Norman was like that, very good at arranging things.'

Julia nodded.

'You'd better look out the things you want to take with you,' continued May. 'I can wash your jumpers to-morrow and press your frocks.'

'Oh, May, how kind of you!'

'It's nothing—I'd like to do it,' declared May. 'I like doing things for people.'

It was true that May liked doing things for people—Julia knew it. She said very seriously, 'You've done a lot for me. I don't mean just washing nylons, I mean you've helped me to see life in a different way. You've given me confidence in myself.'

'I believe you *are* different,' said May looking at her in surprise. 'But it isn't me—not really. It's being on your own. There's nothing like being on your own and earning money, for giving a girl confidence in herself.'

'It's you,' declared Julia, giving May a hug and laughing.

'It's because I can say anything I like to you without thinking. That's the reason I'm different.'

CHAPTER 18

MORLAND had written to say that they were returning home on Sunday and he would call and see Julia on Sunday evening; he was longing to tell her all his news. On hearing this, May said they must sit in the parlour; she would light the fire so that they would be nice and cosy, and perhaps Mr. Beverley would like a glass of beer.

Julia accepted the offer of the parlour gratefully but refused the other amenities; Morland did not like beer, and objected to fires during the summer. At the Beverleys' flat, fires were never to be seen from May until September. The flat was centrally-heated, of course.

'Well, just as you like, dulling,' said May in doubtful tones. 'I always say there's nothing so nice as a fire in the evening if you want to have a cosy chat.'

Julia was inclined to agree—like May she was a fire-worshipper—but she knew that Morland did not share this weakness.

From eight o'clock onwards Julia sat in the dining-room with her eyes glued to the window, but it was nearly nine when Morland's car drew up at the door. She rushed out and met him on the steps.

'Oh, Morland, how lovely!' she cried.

'Julia, darling!' exclaimed Morland. 'It seems ages since I saw you!'

'Yes, ages! How well you look! You're frightfully brown!'

'Of course I'm brown; I've been out all day and every day. It has been a splendid holiday, I wish you could have been with us. I'm afraid you must have felt very lonely and dull.'

'Not really,' replied Julia. 'I've had a lot to do. For one thing I've been very busy learning my new job. I've made a lot of money—I must tell you about that—but first of all I want to tell you about a letter I got on Thursday; it has been worrying me a lot.'

By this time they had climbed the stairs and Julia opened the door of the parlour.

'What an extraordinary room!' Morland exclaimed. 'I never saw anything like it in all my life!'

Julia giggled. 'That's because you weren't alive in eighteen-sixty—or thereabouts,' she told him. 'If you had been alive in those days you would have lived in a room exactly like this.'

'I doubt it,' said Morland, looking round disdainfully. 'It's too full of furniture . . . and what ugly furniture! So garish! No, I don't like it at all.'

Julia could not really blame him for his first reaction to the Victorian parlour (hers had been much the same), so she just smiled and said,

'It grows on you, Morland. There's something rather comfortable and cosy about it.'

'Well, never mind that,' he replied. 'Let's sit down together on the sofa and talk. I've got such a lot to tell you.'

'So have I!' Julia exclaimed. 'There are all sorts of things I couldn't tell you in my letters. It's so difficult to explain things properly in a letter. First of all I want to tell you—'

'Yes, I know,' he agreed. 'I couldn't possibly tell you all we did in my letters. I had a wonderful time. We had several wet days, but rain doesn't matter if you're really keen, so we played every single day. The Fosters were keen too—you remember I told you about them, Julia?'

'Yes,' said Julia.

'Mona and I played in the mixed foursomes together; we were the runners-up. She drives a nice straight ball and her short game is simply marvellous. If we had had any luck at all we should have won quite easily.'

'How nice!' said Julia. 'It must have been fun.'

'Tremendous fun . . . and of course it was very good for my game, playing with the Fosters. Nothing improves one's game so much as playing with people better than oneself. The Fosters said I only needed regular practice to be a really fine player.'

'How nice!' said Julia. 'I'm so glad you enjoyed it.'

'I must tell you about one game we had,' continued Morland eagerly. 'It was a four-ball match; I played with Bob Foster against Jack and Mona. For the first few holes Bob was completely off his game, which was most unusual. He sliced into a bunker at the third and he lost his ball at the fourth. Poor old Bob couldn't do anything right! They were four up at the tenth, but after that his game improved and we stuck to it. . . .'

Unfortunately Julia was not a golfer, so she ceased to listen and never heard what happened. She was waiting for Morland to stop talking, so that she could tell him her news.

'Well, it's over,' said Morland at last. 'It was the best holiday I ever had, but all the same it's delightful to come home. We must arrange to do some things together. You must take up golf, Julia; it would be nice if you could play with me occasionally. We must arrange for you to have lessons. You'd like that, wouldn't you?'

'I don't think I should be much good—' began Julia doubtfully.

'You would soon learn,' Morland told her. 'The Fosters have asked us to go to Sandwich next week-end. I told them about you and they're very anxious to meet you. That will be fun, won't it? Perhaps it would be a good plan for you to get a set of clubs and Mona could give you some lessons to start you off. Her style is perfect.'

'I'm afraid I can't go next week-end, Morland. You see—'

'You can't go!' he exclaimed. 'But I said we would go!'

'I'm terribly sorry, but you see—'

'Why can't you go?'

'Well, that's what I wanted to tell you. I'm going to Scotland on Tuesday. I had a letter from—'

'You're what? You don't mean to say you're going away for a holiday the moment I've come home?'

'Not a holiday—I don't want to go—but I'm afraid I must—only for a week, of course,' said Julia incoherently.

Morland's arm had been round her shoulders but now he removed it. 'I don't know what you mean,' he said. 'I've been looking forward to seeing you. I thought you were looking forward to seeing me.'

'Yes, of course I was!' she cried. 'I've told you I don't want to go to Scotland, I'd much rather not, but—'

'I don't understand.'

'It's this letter,' she told him, trying to speak calmly. 'I just got it on Thursday so I couldn't tell you about it before. You'll see why I've got to go if you read it. The letter explains everything. Read it, Morland.'

He took the letter and read it carefully; then he looked up and frowned. 'Who is this man? I never heard of him before.'

'Neither had I. At least I just have a vague recollection of hearing Mother and Father mention his name . . . but the letter explains that, doesn't it? He says they had a serious quarrel.'

'What did they quarrel about? It must have been something pretty bad; your father didn't answer his letters.'

'I know,' agreed Julia. 'But he's sorry. He says he regrets it deeply. He can't say more than that. If people are sorry you have to forgive them no matter what they've done.'

'Your father hasn't forgiven him.'

'I'm afraid it looks like that.'

'Of course it looks like that,' said Morland impatiently.

'Your father will be very angry if you go to Scotland and stay with the man.'

Julia was silent. She had thought of this herself (her father's reaction was one of the first things she had thought of), but she had decided that this was her own affair and she must do what she believed to be right.

'Never mind,' said Morland, patting her hand comfortingly.

'You hadn't considered the matter carefully; so like a woman to rush into things without careful consideration! This man sits down and writes you a pathetic letter and you decide you must dash off and see him at once. You're just being sentimental, that's all.'

'No, Morland—honestly! I've thought about it a lot. I don't want to go but I feel I ought to.'

'You don't want to go and there is no reason for you to go. In fact there is every reason why you should not. You can put it out of your head and think no more about it.'

'I can't do that.'

'Well, write to him, then. You can write and say you're very sorry to hear he is ill but you can't get away at present. That's perfectly true, isn't it? You can hardly ask for a holiday when you've only just started work. It wouldn't be the right thing. I wasn't in favour of your taking a job—you know that, Julia—but if you take a job you ought to stick into it and do it properly.'

'Oh, I know,' agreed Julia. 'Of course I wouldn't ask for a holiday in ordinary circumstances. It's because he's ill. Madame was very kind when I told her about it; she's quite willing to give me a week's holiday.'

'But I am not willing to give you a week's holiday,' said Morland, smiling at her. 'I want you to come to the Fosters' with me on Saturday.'

'Morland, this is serious,' declared Julia very seriously. She took up the letter and read aloud, '"I would like to see your mother's daughter before I die." I can't refuse, can I?'

'Sentimental nonsense! And why does he say "your mother's daughter"? He's your father's brother isn't he?'

'I don't know why he says that,' admitted Julia. 'All I know is that I can't possibly refuse to go and see him.'

'Julia, I don't want you to go.'

'But it's settled. I've written and told him—'

'You must send a wire and say you can't.'

'But, why? What's the reason?'

'Because I don't want you to go. That's enough reason, isn't it?'

She looked at him in despair. 'Don't you understand?' she said pleadingly. 'Oh, Morland, I was sure you would understand.'

'It is you who doesn't understand,' declared Morland. 'Listen to me, Julia. I don't want you to go because I've just come home and I've been looking forward to seeing you and because I want to take you to Sandwich next week-end and introduce you to my friends, but chiefly because it would be the height of folly to offend your father. He might stop your allowance and where would you be then? You hadn't thought of that, had you?'

'Yes, I thought of that, but I could manage all right without it. I'm making enough money to live on.'

'Julia, you must be mad! Think of the future.'

'The future?'

'Yes, you are your father's only child, so it's only reasonable to suppose that he has made suitable provision for your future. It would be madness to offend him.'

'I don't want to offend him, but I can't refuse to go.'

'Not even if I ask you?'

'Morland!' she cried. 'I'm sorry—frightfully sorry—but I must go and see him. I must, really.'

'Why?' demanded Morland. 'Why must you go?'

'I've told you! He's ill—'

'Why must you go?' repeated Morland.

'Because—because I'm a Christian!' exclaimed Julia in desperation.

'Do you mean that I'm not a Christian?'

'No, of course I didn't mean that! I only meant . . .' But what had she meant?

'I should be interested to know that you meant,' said Morland coldly.

'I can't—explain,' declared Julia breathlessly. 'It's because he's ill. He might die. If I didn't go—and he died—I should never be happy again.'

'What an absurd thing to say! You would forget all about him in a month.'

'I should never, never forget him! Oh, Morland, don't you understand?'

'No, I don't,' replied Morland angrily. 'I can't see any sense in quarrelling with your father for the sake of an old man you've never even heard of.'

'I don't want to quarrel with Father, but—but—'

'And what about me? Do you want to quarrel with me?'

She looked at him in dismay. 'Morland!'

'That's what you're doing, isn't it? You're quarrelling with me.'

'Oh, no!' she cried.

'Yes, you are. You won't take my advice; you say I'm not a Christian; that's quarrelling, isn't it?'

'I didn't mean—'

'And all because of this mad idea that you've got into your head. It's a mad idea,' he repeated furiously. 'You must give it up and be sensible. I don't want to hear any more about it.'

'It isn't mad,' she said in a low voice. 'It's a feeling; deep down inside me. I *can't* give way to you in this.'

'You mean you won't,' said Morland, rising from the sofa. 'You won't take my advice. Well, Julia, all I can say is, if you won't take my advice in a small matter like this I don't see much prospect of our happiness in the future.'

It was not a small matter to Julia. It was a deep-down feeling—a matter of principle—but she had explained this already. She too, rose from the sofa, so that they stood face to face. She took off the ring and held it out to him in the palm of her hand.

'Do you mean this?' he asked incredulously.

'I thought that was what you meant.'

'I just meant—'

Julia was angry now. She interrupted him. 'You just meant that I must do exactly what you say whether I think it right or not. You're right, Morland. There isn't any prospect of our happiness in the future. Take it, please.'

He took it. There was nothing else for him to do . . . except climb down and grovel. He certainly did not intend to do that! Besides, she was so stubborn. He had never before found her stubborn. What would she be like when they were married? In his own home his father was the arbiter; his father said what was to be done and it was done as a matter of course. His mother would no more have thought of voicing her own ideas than of flying to the moon. That was the right thing, thought Morland. It was in the Bible: 'Wives submit yourselves unto your husbands.' He might not be a Christian, thought Morland bitterly, but he knew that much. It was a pity Julia did not read her Bible more carefully.

'I think you had better go now,' said Julia.

He turned and went to the door—and paused—and looked back. She was still standing there, gazing down at the carpet. There was something pathetic in her attitude; she was like a drooping flower. He very nearly ran back and took her in his arms . . . but it was no good giving in like that. If he gave in now he would always have to give in.

'Julia,' he began. 'If you change your mind—'

'I can't,' she said in a low voice. 'I've told you. I can't do something I know to be wrong, not even to please you.'

'Julia, listen—'

'Good-bye, Morland.'

He went out and shut the door.

CHAPTER 19

1

WHEN Morland had gone Julia remained standing quite still in the middle of the room. She stood there until she heard his car drive away and then sat down and hid her face in her hands; she was not crying, she just felt dazed. Presently she heard the door open and looked up quickly . . . perhaps he had come back! But it was May, her round pink face wearing a look of consternation.

'Julia, what happened?' she exclaimed.

Julia could not speak. She held out her left hand.

'Yes, I saw,' said May. (Of course she had seen. It was the first thing she had looked at when she came into the room and found 'the poor dulling' in a limp heap in the corner of the sofa.) 'Yes, I saw,' she babbled. 'But it's all right, dulling. There isn't any need to take on about it. You mustn't be upset. I always say there's as good fish in the sea. . . . And anyhow you can have him back to-morrow if you hold up your little finger. He was as pale as death and he couldn't find the keyhole of his car. People often have little tiffs and it all comes right in the end. Just lie down on the sofa for a minute and I'll get something that'll do you good.'

May hastened away and presently returned with a large red-rubber hot-water bottle and a medicine glass full of white cloudy liquid.

Julia drank the liquid, which was exceedingly nasty, and hugged the hot-water bottle.

'There now,' said May, sitting down beside her on a little stool and holding her hand. 'You'll feel better soon. There's nothing like sal volatile to buck you up when you're a bit upset; I always keep a bottle handy. Peta says it's old-fashioned, but what does that matter? Why, only the other day there was a dog-fight just outside the dining-room window—it was Miss Winkler's little terrier and another dog—and poor Miss Winkler was so upset I made her come into the dining-room and sit down. "Just you wait a minute, dear," I said. "I'll get you something that'll do you good." And it did,' added May triumphantly. 'She felt better in half no time.'

Julia smiled a wan smile at the idea of her disagreement with Morland being compared with a dog-fight.

'There, you're better already!' declared May. 'Sal volatile is wonderful. If we just had a fire we'd be nice and cosy—but you wouldn't let me, would you?'

'You're just as cosy as a fire.'

'That's nice, dulling,' said May, smiling, and patting her hand. 'I suppose he was cross when you said you were going to Scotland. I was afraid he might be a little cross.'

'But I couldn't put it off, could I? You can see from the letter that he's very ill. . . . Supposing he died!'

May nodded. 'You'd never forgive yourself, would you?'

'Never! But Morland didn't understand. He didn't even try to understand what I felt about it.'

'Oh dear, what a pity! But men are like that—at least some men are—they only understand what they want to understand. That's the trouble.'

'I thought I could rely on Morland.'

'Yes, I know you did,' said May, soothingly. 'Never mind, dulling. You can have him back whenever you like.'

'But it wouldn't be any good! He expected me to do exactly what he wanted whether I thought it right or not . . . and of course it would be worse if we were married because I should have to promise to obey him. . . . I couldn't do it, May!'

May nodded in a thoughtful manner.

'I shall never marry anyone,' declared Julia hysterically. 'I shall never give up my freedom to do what I think right.'

May did not know what to say to this declaration of independence, so very wisely she said nothing, but continued to pat Julia's hand.

2

In spite of May's endeavours to console her, Julia went up to bed feeling tired and miserable. It was not so much the breaking off of her engagement that upset her, it was the discovery that Morland was quite different from what she had thought. She had known him for years, she had been engaged to him for months, but now she felt that she had never really known him at all. She had been so sure that he would understand; she had imagined him saying, 'Oh poor darling, what a nuisance having to go! Never mind, it's only for a week.' But instead of being loving and sympathetic he had been selfish and dictatorial. He had said, 'I don't want you to go; that's enough reason, isn't it?'

By this time Julia was in bed; she lay there feeling rather forlorn . . . and there was a queer kind of blankness in her heart when she thought of the future. For months and months her future had been full of Morland, so naturally the space he had occupied was empty. It was a dreary prospect to face the future alone but she must summon up her courage and face it. Morland had said that there was no prospect of happiness for them if they were married—or at least that was what he had meant—and Julia had seen at once that this was true.

What Morland wanted was a wife exactly like his mother; a wife who would say 'Yes, dear.' Julia had often smiled to herself when she heard Mrs. Beverley say 'Yes, dear' and had despised her just a little for having no mind of her own . . . but perhaps poor Mrs. Beverley had become a 'Yes, dear' sort of wife because it was the only way to live comfortably with a 'Do this' sort of husband!

I might have got like that! thought Julia.

Yes, it was true, Julia might have got like that (in fact, now that she came to think of it she realised that she had been saying 'Yes, dear' to Morland for months), because Julia loved peace and would go to almost any lengths to preserve it—almost any lengths—but there came a time when it would be wrong to say, 'Yes, dear' . . . and that time had come.

Julia tried to think why she had been so certain that she must not give way. She had said, when pressed for her reason, 'Because I'm a Christian.' She had been pushed beyond the limit of her endurance and the words had burst out without thinking . . . but of course it was true. That really was the answer; for if you were a Christian you had to forgive people who showed contrition, no matter what they had done. She had no idea what 'Uncle Randal' had done, but he was sorry and wanted to end the feud. If you did not forgive other people you could not expect forgiveness from God . . . awful thought! Awful in the real meaning of the word.

Of course the feud had nothing to do with Julia; she was concerned merely with the fact that 'Uncle Randal' was ill and had asked her to go and see him. Could any woman calling herself a Christian refuse such a request?

'I was sick and ye visited me' . . . there you had a perfectly clear definition of Christian behaviour.

Julia heaved a sigh of relief. Yes, she had been right not to give in to Morland; and, if her father were angry with her, she could not help that either. She had known she was right but there had been a nagging little doubt at the back of her mind. The doubt was banished now—quite gone—so she turned over in bed, snuggled down and went to sleep.

On Monday Julia was busy all day, making her arrangements, packing and writing letters. She wrote to Stephen, telling him that she was going to Scotland to pay a short visit to her uncle, who was very ill and wanted to see her; she did not mention Morland. She wrote to Ellen; there was no time to go and see her. Finally she wrote to her father. He and Retta had left Rome and were now cruising in the Mediterranean; they were due at Athens in a few days. This letter was by far the most difficult to compose. Julia spent a long time wondering what she should say, but eventually she got down to it. She explained that she had received a letter from Uncle Randal; he was very ill and wanted to see her, so she felt it her duty to go. She did not expect to be away for more than a week. (Should she say more? But what more could she say? Better leave it at that, she thought.) There was still some space left upon the air-mail letter so she filled it by expressing her hopes that they were both enjoying the cruise.

When Julia read the letter over she was dissatisfied with it, for she felt it to be insincere; but she did not see how insincerity could be avoided. Besides, she could not rewrite it, because she had not got another air-mail letter and it must be posted to-night. In fact it must be posted at once or it would not reach Athens in time. She ran out to the pillar-box and posted it.

PART TWO

CHAPTER 20

1

THE journey north seemed very long, especially the last part, when Julia was obliged to change from the comfortable express into a small old-fashioned train which dawdled along and stopped at every station. She might have enjoyed it and been interested in the unfamiliar aspect of the country if her heart had not been so heavy. The distant future still seemed bleak; the near future was alarming—and became more alarming every minute—for Julia had no idea what sort of place lay at the end of her journey, nor what 'Uncle Randal' would be like. Perhaps he would be a disagreeable old man! Perhaps he would be lying in bed, at his last gasp! Perhaps he would be queer and terrifying! . . . but no, that was silly, thought Julia, trying to summon up her courage.

Julia found his letter in her bag and read it again for perhaps the twentieth time. She almost knew it by heart, but all the same she read it again carefully and it comforted her—for it was kind. In fact it was very kind indeed and, although written in a shaky hand, it was perfectly sensible.

The journey had gone on for so long that Julia was surprised when the train stopped again at another little station and she heard a man shouting, 'Leddiesford! Leddiesford!' She had to collect her things and scrambled out in a hurry.

The train trailed away and vanished. Julia stood on the platform feeling tired and dirty and very lonely and miserable. What next? she wondered . . . but the question had scarcely crossed her mind when her arm was seized in a firm grasp and a voice said, 'You'll be Miss Julia?'

Julia turned and saw an elderly woman with pink cheeks and brown eyes and curly grey hair; she was dressed in a black cloth coat with a brown fur collar and a black straw hat (which would have given Madame Claire a migraine).

'You'll be tired to death!' declared the woman compassionately. 'Poor lassie, coming all that long way on your own. Oh, I'm that glad to see you! He'd have come to meet you himself but he's not so well. He'll have told you in his letter.'

'Oh, I never expected him to meet me!'

'He'd have come if he could. I'm Mrs. Walker that looks after him— or tries to—but when folks are ill they need their own flesh and blood. Never heed the luggage, Miss Julia. Andrew'll bring it. I've got a taxi waiting in the yard.'

'How is Uncle Randal?' asked Julia when she could get a word in.

'Off and on,' was the reply. 'He had an awful bad turn last week— that was when he wrote you—but he's keeping better the last few days. When he got your letter to say you were coming he was that excited you would scarcely believe it—neither to haud nor to bind!' She laughed, 'But you'll not know what that means, Miss Julia. Och, and I'd made up my mind to speak proper English to you! I can do it fine when I remember.

'Andra!' she cried loudly. 'Will ye tell me what ye're daein' wi' yon luggage! We're not wantin' tae staun' here waitin' on ye the hale nicht!' She turned back to Julia and added, 'That'll sort him. You get into the taxi, Miss Julia. It's too cold standing about.'

Julia felt quite dazed by the flow of talk, but she no longer felt like a very small mouse that had ventured too far from its hole and did not know how to get back.

Meanwhile Andrew had appeared with the zip-bag and the suitcase, and having stowed them into the taxi appeared to be arguing with Mrs. Walker about the inadequacy of his tip; but as Julia could not understand a word they were saying she could not be certain of this.

2

'Well, that's that,' declared Mrs. Walker as she climbed into the taxi. 'Saxpence was quite enough for all he did, the idle loon! The train was a wee bit late but it's not far. I'm just hoping he'll not have climbed up the stair again while I was away. You could have knocked me down with a feather when I found him in your room this morning; he's not been up the stair for months. "Maggie," he says. "You're to put two bottles in the bed and she'll need another blanket. It's colder here than London, You've put clean paper in the drawers, I hope." Him, to say that!' exclaimed Mrs. Walker with a fat chuckle. 'Him that has taken no interest in anything except his books the whole live-long winter!'

'How kind,' murmured Julia. 'But, oh dear, I hope it wasn't too much for him!'

'It did him good, Miss Julia, and that's the truth; but when he rose from his chair after his dinner and said he was away to the garden to pick a few roses for a vase there was nothing for it but to put my foot down.'

Julia was about to reply when the taxi drew up at a dilapidated gate. Mrs. Walker dismounted, pushed the gate open and hurried up the stone-paved path, taking off her gloves and muttering something about supper. The taxi-driver collected the luggage and hastened after her. They both disappeared into the house.

Somewhat surprised at being deserted in this summary fashion, Julia followed more slowly, looking about her with interest. Although it was getting late by this time there was still light enough to see that The Square House was indeed a square house, standing by itself in a small garden with other houses not so uncompromisingly square on either side. There was a neglected look about the place; the paint was shabby, the garden untended . . . but there was a delightful pink rose-bush on a trellis in the corner and a cluster of lily-of-the-valley beside the path, struggling amongst a tangle of weeds.

The door of the house was open, so Julia went in. She stood in the hall and looked about, uncertain where to go. It was a square hall with doors on either side and a staircase with a wooden banister leading up to the first floor. The hall was furnished with a grandfather clock in a beautifully polished mahogany case, and a large mahogany chest. The carpet on the floor was faded and threadbare.

As Julia stood there, taking it all in, the clock struck eight in charming silvery tones and, almost as if it were a signal, one of the doors opened and a voice exclaimed, 'Julia!'

It was Uncle Randal, of course—who else could it be? So Julia turned and held out her hand.

'My dear child!' said Uncle Randal, taking it in a warm clasp. 'I never knew you had arrived! What on earth possessed Maggie to leave you standing in the hall?'

'She murmured something about supper.'

'Oh, that's it! The creature gets flustered,' explained Uncle Randal, drawing her into the room and shutting the door.

'But I haven't paid the taxi!'

'We needn't bother,' said Uncle Randal comfortably. 'He knows he'll get his money. Come and sit down by the fire. I dare say you're not used to fires at this time of year, but old bones feel the cold more than young ones, and a good log fire is a pretty thing to watch, so I just coddle myself a bit.' While he was talking he arranged a chair near the fire for Julia and sat down in what was obviously his own, an old-fashioned wing-chair upholstered in faded brown tapestry with a high back and padded arms.

'Now then, let's look at each other,' he said.

Julia smiled. She had dreaded this meeting, but there was nothing alarming about Uncle Randal, and, except for the fact that he was pale and unnaturally thin, he did not look ill. His hair was grey and silvery; his features were cleanly cut; the grey eyes were twinkling beneath the rather bushy grey eyebrows; the mouth was wide, and just at the moment it was curving up at the corners.

'Well, Julia?' asked Uncle Randal.

'You aren't a bit like Father!' exclaimed Julia impulsively.

'But you're like your mother,' said Uncle Randal, nodding. Then he leaned forward, stirred the fire gently with the poker and began to question her about her journey. Had it been comfortable? Had it seemed very long? Journeys always seemed longer when one did not know where one was going—at least that was his experience—and especially when there was an ogre to be met with when one arrived.

Julia said where was the ogre? She had not seen him yet . . . which made Uncle Randal laugh.

After this it was easy to talk. They discussed journeys. Uncle Randal asked whether she thought it was better to travel cheerfully than to arrive.

'No, I don't,' said Julia with decision. 'I've often wondered what on earth he meant when he said that.'

'I know exactly what he meant,' replied Uncle Randal.

'I've knocked about all over the world, just as he did, and I can assure you that travelling cheerfully is delightful.'

'Arriving is delightful,' retorted Julia, looking round with a contented air. 'Especially when you receive a nice warm welcome.'

'Oh, Julia!' he cried. 'What am I to say to that? You've swept the ground from beneath my feet, you wicked wee lassie!'

Julia giggled and as usual her dimples came and went. It was rather fun to be called 'a wicked wee lassie.'

3

They had not been talking for long when the door opened and Mrs. Walker announced that supper was on the table.

'It will have to wait,' said Uncle Randal. 'Miss Julia will want to see her room and tidy up after her journey. You left her standing in the hall, Maggie.'

'Maircy, so I did!' exclaimed Mrs. Walker in dismay. 'I felt the smell of burning as I came in at the door and it clean went out of my head that Miss Julia wouldna ken the way!'

'It doesn't matter a bit,' declared Julia.

Mrs. Walker continued to apologise and explain; and Julia, following her up the stairs, repeated that it did not matter, it was quite all right and of course she understood.

'You'll be quick, won't you, Miss Julia? I mean you'll not change— except maybe your shoes. It's a brace of nice trout that Neil caught this morning and they'll not improve with getting cold. I just mashed the potatoes—he likes them mashed—there was only one had stuck a wee bit to the bottom of the pot . . . and Dr. Cairn brought a lettuce from his garden . . . and Mrs. Inglis came along with a batch of scones. I'll not say they're as light as mine, but the creature meant well; she kenned fine I'd be busy with you arriving and all.'

'People seem very kind,' said Julia.

'And so they should be! He's done enough for them in all conscience!'

Already Julia had discovered that 'he' was Uncle Randal; already she had caught the infection and found herself using the pronoun in and out of season. She had been taught in her childhood that the habit was disrespectful ('She's the cat's aunt,' Ellen had said); but Mrs. Walker's use of the pronoun was the reverse of disrespectful, indeed you could almost imagine that she used it with a capital letter. He was her sun and moon and stars; he was her last thought when she laid her head upon the pillow and went to sleep, her first thought when she awoke in the morning. Only God was higher in Mrs. Walker's estimation, and to be quite honest, Mrs. Walker thought more often of Mr. Randal Harburn than of God. Of course Julia did not realise all this that first evening, but she realised it quite soon. Some people might have deplored this preoccupation with the needs of an earthly master, but Julia had a feeling that God would understand.

When Julia went down Uncle Randal was sitting at the dining-room table, doing the crossword puzzle in *The Scotsman*. He put it away and looked up cheerfully.

'I hope Maggie didn't hurry you,' he said.

CHAPTER 21

1

JULIA had gone to bed weary from her long day's journey, but she slept soundly and wakened rested and refreshed. For a minute or two she lay and looked round the room; she had been too tired to look at it properly last night. It was a square room. (Everything in The Square House was square, thought Julia, smiling at the ridiculous thought . . . except Mrs. Walker, of course; she was round and comfortable.) The furniture was old-fashioned, large and solid and shining with polish. The bedstead was brass with polished brass knobs. The wallpaper, the curtains, the carpet on the floor, were all so faded that their original pattern had almost disappeared, but everything was scrupulously clean—clean with a cleanliness that was impossible to achieve in Town no matter how hard one tried.

The sun was pouring in through the large open window, filling the room with golden light. Julia sprang out of bed and ran to the window and found that it looked out to the front. The stone-paved path led down to the ramshackle gate and on each side was the square patch of garden. She had seen this last night; she had seen the weedy garden and the pink rosebush. A beech hedge which badly needed trimming divided the garden from the wide road, which was empty and very quiet. She sniffed the air; it was cool and clear like a drink of spring water.

Julia was still kneeling at the window with her arms on the sill when the door of her room was opened very softly and Mrs. Walker's head appeared round the edge.

'Maircy!' she exclaimed. 'I thought you'd be sleeping! You'll get your death at the open window, Miss Julia. Away back to bed and I'll bring your breakfast.'

'But I can easily get up! I was just going to—'

'You'll take it in bed while you're here,' said Mrs. Walker firmly. 'It'll do you good after racketing about in London, and I'm not wanting you downstairs—that's the truth.'

Obviously it was the truth. If there was any woman on earth more truthful, more straightforward and honest, more the-same-all-through than Maggie Walker, Julia had still to meet that remarkable woman. So Julia found her dressing-jacket and went back to bed.

Quite soon Mrs. Walker returned with a very large tray which she placed on the chest of drawers while she arranged Julia's pillows. A wooden bed-table was settled firmly across her knees and the tray laid carefully upon the top of it.

'There! that's fine,' said Mrs. Walker complacently. 'I've given you a wee bell to ring if you're wanting more.'

'More!' exclaimed Julia, looking at the tray in astonishment. It contained a glass of orange juice; a bowl of porridge; a covered dish with three large rashers of bacon; scones and butter; marmalade and honey; a teapot with a woolly crochet jacket; milk and sugar and a jug of cream. There was also a small brass bell which Mrs. Walker pointed to with pride, repeating her injunction that Miss Julia was to ring loudly— give it a good shake—if she wanted more.

'Maybe you'll feel like an egg,' added Mrs. Walker.

'I shall feel as full as an egg if I eat all this!'

Mrs. Walker chuckled. 'You're an awful lassie!' she declared. 'I'll tell him what you said. He's fine this morning.'

'None the worse of all he did yesterday?'

'Not him. I was a bit scared, to tell you the truth—what with all his stravaigling and the stir and excitement—but he's just grand. He's taking porridge to his breakfast and toast and marmalade and he's wanting up.'

'Wanting up?' asked Julia with a puzzled frown.

'He's wanting to get up out of his bed and put his clothes on,' explained Mrs. Walker loudly and clearly—as if her listener were hard of hearing and not quite right in the head. Fortunately she went away quite quickly after that, so there was no need for Julia to control her giggles.

2

'Stravaigling,' thought Julia as she walked into the little town of Leddiesford with Mrs. Walker's shopping-basket on her arm. It was a good word, and so descriptive that it required no explanation even to someone who had never met with it before; but on thinking it over seriously she decided that it did not describe this morning's expedition. No, 'stravaigling' had a leisurely wandering sort of feeling about it and Julia was hurrying hither and thither, consulting the list of 'messages' and looking at the names displayed above the doors of the shops.

The list was written in a clear round hand and the instructions were lucid. In fact it was an admirable guide. It was headed, 'Green-grocer—Macfarlane. Six bananas—yellow with brown spots—bring. One cabbage—send to-morrow.' What could have been clearer? It was absolutely fool-proof. Fool-proof, thought Julia, smiling as she remembered the little scene which had been, enacted in the kitchen that morning.

Julia had risen (after demolishing her gargantuan breakfast), dressed and made her bed and carried the tray downstairs.

'Where shall I put it, Mrs. Walker?' she had asked.

'Och, Miss Julia! You should never have carried yon heavy tray down the stair! I was coming to fetch it when I'd got the sink cleaned.'

'Can I help you?' Julia had asked.

'I'm not needing help,' was the frank reply. 'I can manage fine on my own—I'm not in my dotage yet—and to tell the truth, Miss Julia, I'm not wanting you under my feet the whole morning; so just you put on your hat and away out for a walk. I'll not let him up till dinner-time—one o'clock, that is—but I'll need to hurry for there's the messages to do,' she added, glancing at the clock and frowning.

'Shopping?' asked Julia. 'Well, I could do that for you, couldn't I?'

Mrs. Walker was doubtful about it. How would Miss Julia find her way to the town? How would she know which shops to go to? How would she carry the heavy basket home? Finally, however, Mrs. Walker's objections were overborne; she put on her spectacles and, seating herself at the kitchen table, she had made out the fool-proof list.

3

Julia had had no difficulty in finding her way to the town. When she had walked to the end of the road she had seen Leddiesford before her eyes lying in a hollow in the fold of the hills with the river wandering through it like a silver ribbon. She had seen the grey stone houses, surrounded with trees, and a couple of church spires, and she had seen the railway-station at which she had arrived last night. All she had to do was to follow her nose down the hill and through the outskirts of the town until she came to the wide, paved street with shops at either side which obviously was the High Street.

It was a novel experience for Julia to shop in a small town and she was enjoying herself immensely. Already she had collected 'Bananas—yellow with brown spots' from Mr. Macfarlane and instructed him to send a cabbage to-morrow; she had found the bookstall and had collected *The People's Friend* and *Blackwood's*. (The incongruity of these two papers amused Julia considerably.) She was now dashing across the wide street and into 'Grocer—Menzies' where there was a long list of comestibles to be sent and half a pound of rice marked 'bring.' Julia was about to give Uncle Randal's name and address to the smiling youth behind the counter when she saw that already he had written 'Harburn, Square House,' in his order book and was awaiting instructions. Now, how on earth did he know that? wondered Julia as she dictated her requirements.

She soon discovered that everyone 'knew that,' and everyone was desirous to be helpful. When her turn came to be served at 'Butcher—Wilson' and she hesitated over the unknown word 'gigot,' an unknown woman, looking over her shoulder, said kindly, 'It's a jiggot, Miss Harburn. French, you know. We've stolen a wheen o' words from the Frenchies.' And a little old man with a hooky nose remarked that no doubt Miss Harburn would be accustomed to calling it a leg of mutton.

'Oh, thank you,' said Julia. 'Yes, but I'll remember it next time.'

Of course Julia would remember it—the little incident was much too mysterious for her to forget a word of what had been said—besides, she was always ready to learn a new language. She was one of those fortunate people who find languages easy and fascinating. In addition to French, which she could speak like a Frenchwoman (as Madame Claire had discovered) she had a good working knowledge of German, and could converse fluently and idiomatically, if not very grammatically, in Spanish.

As she walked along, looking for 'Brown—Milk,' Julia decided that this dialect was not just English pronounced in a peculiar way. For one thing the construction of the sentences was different, and for another there was a large vocabulary of fascinating words which gave it a salty tang . . . and the odd thing was, you could hear at least three grades of speech shading into each other. Take Mrs. Walker for instance: when Mrs. Walker 'remembered,' she could speak normal English with scarcely any accent at all; and when she liked she could speak in a language absolutely incomprehensible to English ears (she had done so to the porter at the station); her own ordinary, comfortable way of speaking was somewhere in between. Even Uncle Randal had different ways of speaking, the way he spoke to 'Maggie' and the way he spoke to Julia. So far Julia had not heard him speak in the absolutely incomprehensible way, but quite probably he could. These were Julia's first impressions of the country and the people and the language. She found it all very strange.

It should not have been strange, thought Julia, for it was her father's home. He was Uncle Randal's brother, though it was difficult to remember this because they were so different.

This was her father's home! He had been born and bred at Harburn House, a few miles from the town. How very queer to think of him here, in Leddiesford, walking about in this wide pleasant street! The street and the houses were unfamiliar to Julia's eyes—foreign-looking, somehow—but they must have been very familiar to him! Why had he never spoken about Leddiesford? Why did he never mention his boyhood?

Poor Father! What was he doing now? Had he emerged from his brown blanket to enjoy the sunshine and the Mediterranean breezes? Was Retta being kind and companionable? By this time he would have received her airmail letter, so probably—almost certainly—he was angry and upset. Oh dear, what a pity it all was!

Having walked the length of the High Street twice without having found 'Brown—Milk' Julia was obliged to ask the way from a passer-by. (It was quite absurd not to have thought of this before, but her mind had been occupied with other things.) She was directed to a side street and here she found the little dairy quite easily. A girl of about her own age, who was going in before her, held the door open and said with a shy smile, 'Are you wanting in?'

Julia nodded and smiled and thanked her.

'Wanting in,' thought Julia. It came into the same category as 'wanting up' of course. No doubt you could say 'wanting out' and 'wanting down.' What a useful word!

A few moments later the round fat lady behind the counter was smiling and saying, 'Are you wanting cream, Miss Harburn?' and Julia, with a glance at the fool-proof list, saw that she was.

'Tell me,' said Julia to the round fat lady. 'How did you know I was Miss Harburn?'

'Who else could you be?' asked the round fat lady in surprise.

This was unanswerable, of course; Julia could not imagine herself being anyone else, so she turned her steps homewards with the mystery unsolved.

4

Mrs. Walker had warned Julia that the basket would be heavy, and although it did not seem so at first, it became heavier as she walked along. She changed it from one hand to the other but still it was heavy. She was toiling up the hill when a small brown van passed her; it had 'MUSSEL—FISHMONGER' in large letters on the side. She was just thinking what a good name it was for a fishmonger when the van drew up at the curb and a head topped with a mop of flaming red hair appeared at the window.

'Will I give you a lift?' inquired its owner.

'That's very kind of you,' said Julia, who now discovered herself to be gazing into a pair of very bright blue eyes.

'Not at all,' declared her benefactor. He leapt from the van, took her basket and opened the other door.

'It is very kind indeed,' said Julia as she got in and sat down. She noticed that the van smelt strongly of fish, but that was natural, and she really was extremely grateful for the kindness which had prompted the boy to stop. She was surprised, also, for she saw that he was a youth of about eighteen—not much more, anyhow—and in her experience youths were not usually so thoughtful and considerate.

'You'll have been doing the messages?' suggested the youth as he let in the clutch and drove on.

Julia admitted that this was so.

'It's not a bad wee town,' said the youth. 'There's some that say it's dull in Leddiesford, but there's a lot goes on. To-night there's a whist drive at the Town Hall. Are you fond of whist?'

'I've never played whist.'

'Is that so? I suppose folks in London are too busy to play whist—going to theatres and that. There's a dramatic society in Leddiesford and it's not bad at all. Mind you it'll not be up to London or Edinburgh, but it's not too bad. It's Bridie's plays we do mostly. Maybe you'll have seen some of Bridie's plays? They're real good.'

'Oh yes, I have,' declared Julia. 'I've seen several; I think they're very interesting. They give you something to think about. I saw *Daphne Laureola*.'

'We've not tried that—it's a bit too difficult—but we've done *The Anatomist . . .*'

They continued to discuss the plays of James Bridie.

It passed through Julia's mind that if she had been told several days ago that she would be sitting in a fish-van beside a red-haired boy talking about the plays of James Bridie she would not have believed her informant, but to-day it did not seem strange at all. Indeed she was so interested in the conversation that she had not mentioned where she was going. She was about to remedy this omission when the van drew up at the gate to The Square House.

'Here you are, Miss Harburn,' said her companion cheerfully. 'I'll just carry the basket through to Mrs. Walker; it's too heavy for a lady like yourself.'

'Oh, thank you!' exclaimed Julia. 'I didn't notice where we had got to. Please don't bother about the basket; I can easily carry it into the house.'

'Please yourself,' said the red-haired boy cheerfully.

They shook hands.

'Thank you very, very much,' repeated Julia. She hesitated for a moment and then asked, 'Why is it that everyone in Leddiesford knows me?'

She waited eagerly for the reply, for he was such an intelligent boy that now at last she would receive an intelligent answer to the problem which had been puzzling her so much.

He smiled at her, 'Oh, that's easy answered, Miss Harburn. It's because nobody in Leddiesford is acquainted with you,' and so saying he drove off quickly and left her standing at the gate, more bewildered than before.

This is Looking-Glass Country, thought Julia. Everybody knows me because nobody is acquainted with me! It just doesn't make sense.

It was only afterwards—some time afterwards when Julia had begun to understand the way of things in Leddiesford—that she realised the red-haired boy's answer to her question was perfectly sensible and correct. In Leddiesford everybody knew everybody, therefore if they saw somebody with whom they were not acquainted it was only reasonable to suppose she was 'Mr. Harburn's niece from London that's staying at The Square House.'

CHAPTER 22

UNCLE Randal had got up for dinner at one o'clock; but he always rested in the afternoon, so Julia went out and weeded one of the beds in the neglected garden. It was a task which she had never attempted before but which she found unexpectedly enjoyable. The sun was shining, the birds were singing, and a perky robin, who thought the earth was being turned for his benefit, came quite near and gorged himself with worms. When she had finished, the bed looked a great deal neater, but it was rather bare and she wondered whether she should buy some packets of flower-seeds. Being a Londoner born and bred she was abysmally ignorant on the subject, but she had seen dozens of packets with gaily coloured pictures of all sorts and kinds of flowers (she had noticed them that morning when she was searching for Brown—Milk). All you had to do was to put the seeds in the ground and wait for them to come up. What could be easier? And how nice they would look, thought Julia, envisaging the bare beds in Uncle Randal's garden chock-full of brilliant flowers. It would be a lovely surprise for Uncle Randal.

At four o'clock Julia began to think of tea, so she decided to go and see what Mrs. Walker was doing about it. She was surprised to discover Mrs. Walker and a young man sitting at the kitchen table enjoying a substantial meal.

'Oh, it's Mr. Logan,' said Mrs. Walker, and added in a flustered manner, 'He comes in for a wee crack now and then.'

Somehow Julia had a feeling that Mrs. Walker was slightly ashamed of being discovered drinking tea with Mr. Logan . . . and certainly he looked rather disreputable, for he had taken off his jacket and his braces were to be seen displayed over a shabby grey pullover. Julia noticed that he was wearing no shoes and there was a large hole in the heel of his sock. However, in spite of his unconventional attire, his lean brown face and merry brown eyes showed no trace of embarrassment. He rose politely and bowed at Mrs. Walker's somewhat informal introduction.

'He's brought us a burrd,' added Mrs. Walker, gesturing towards a mass of brown feathers lying on the draining-board of the sink.

'Oh, how very kind,' said Julia.

'Poached, of course,' explained Mr. Logan.

'It'll not taste any the worse of that,' said Mrs. Walker, laughing.

Mr. Logan laughed too, so Julia smiled. It seemed rather queer, but so many things were queer that she did not know where she was at all. She felt like Alice at the Mad Hatter's tea-party—yes, that was exactly how she felt—and the feeling was considerably augmented when Mr. Logan moved his cup and saucer and plate to make room for her at the table and pulled up another chair.

'Come on, Maggie,' he said as he made these arrangements.

'What are you thinking about? You're not very hospitable, are you? Have you not got another cup in yon big brown teapot that you're so proud of?'

'Och, I never thocht!' exclaimed Mrs. Walker.

She stood there all of a dither while Mr. Logan padded over to the cupboard and returned with a cup and saucer and a plate, saying as he laid them on the table, 'Maggie Walker, use the brains that were given you to think with. You know well enough that he doesn't take tea in the afternoon.'

'I was going to give Miss Julia her tea in the room.'

'Oh, I dare say Miss Julia'll not be too proud to drink a cup of tea with a poacher.'

'No, of course not,' said Julia hastily.

'Och, Neil!' cried Mrs. Walker. 'You're an awful laddie for a joke!' She added, 'Maircy! Look at yon hole in your heel! Is there nobody at Dunraggit can use a darning needle?'

By this time Julia was seated at the kitchen table. Mrs. Walker was offering her hot buttered scones, and Mr. Logan was pouring tea into her cup from the comfortable-looking brown teapot.

'This is a good pourer,' remarked Mr. Logan examining the spout with interest.

'Well, I would hope so,' its owner replied. 'What use would a teapot be if you couldna' pour tea from its spout?'

'There's some that dribble,' he told her as he helped himself to a scone and plastered it with an extra coating of butter. 'Believe you me, when I was in Edinburgh I went to a shop to get a teapot and half the pots in the shop dribbled.'

'How did you know that, may I ask?'

'I tried them. I made the girl fill them with water—'

'Maircy, you had a cheek! It's a wonder she did it!'

'She was a wee bit thrawn about it,' admitted Mr. Logan, smiling reminiscently. 'But I got my way.'

'When do you not get your way!'

'The experiment was well worth the trouble,' declared Mr. Logan. 'As I told you before, half the pots in the place dribbled out of the corners of their silly mouths.'

'Oh, I know!' exclaimed Julia, who felt it was high time for her to take part in the conversation. 'I bought a teapot in London and it dribbled all over the place . . . and what's more, the tea-leaves came through the spout into the cups.'

120 | D.E. STEVENSON

'Look at that, now!' cried Mrs. Walker in horror.

'*Regardez-moi ça,*' said Mr. Logan *sotto voce.*

Julia glanced at him in astonishment and saw that he was looking at her with twinkling eyes.

'French!' said Mrs. Walker scornfully. 'I've told you often enough that it's not the right thing to talk foreign languages to folk that canna' understand them. Miss Julia will think—'

'But Miss Julia understands perfectly. Miss Julia looks slightly bewildered, not because she doesn't understand French, but because it seems rather strange to hear it from the lips of a disreputable-looking poacher.' He continued, turning to Julia: 'If you stay here long—as I sincerely hope you will—you'll discover a close link between the French language and the speech of the people of Leddiesford.'

'Dinna' heed him, Miss Julia!' cried Mrs. Walker in dismay. 'He's just joking with you. He can talk like a book when it pleases him but he's not meaning any harm.'

'He only does it to annoy because he knows it teases,' agreed Mr. Logan, smiling.

'But it doesn't tease me a bit,' declared Julia earnestly. 'It's frightfully interesting. There was a woman in the town this morning who said the same thing in different words.'

'What words?' asked Mr. Logan, leaning forward and planting his elbows firmly on the table.

'She said, "We've stolen a wheen o' words from the Frenchies."'

'Quite good,' nodded Mr. Logan appreciatively. 'Allow me to compliment you on your accent.'

'"I wondered how—and why—'

'It's partly the Auld Alliance and partly trade in wines and silks and such like. Not always legitimate trade, if you take my meaning.'

'Smugglers?'

'Yes, smugglers and Jacobites . . . we'll discuss the whole matter another time. It's a fascinating subject.' He rose as he spoke.

'Your coat'll not be dry yet,' said Mrs. Walker firmly. 'Nor your shoes neither.'

'I'll just need to wear them wet,' he told her. 'I must get home, Maggie. I've a lot of work to get through to-night.'

'You'll not go home in yon socks. They're just a disgrace. I'll get you a pair out of his drawer and you'll leave those ones to be washed and mended.'

'What a woman!' said Mr. Logan, shaking his head sadly.

Julia had finished her tea and thought it a good moment to take her departure; so while Mrs. Walker was away, looking out a pair of Mr. Harburn's socks to lend her visitor, she rose and said good-bye.

'*Au revoir,*' said the visitor, taking her hand. 'You'll stay as long as you can, won't you? It's good for him to have one of his own kin near him just now.'

'Only a week,' replied Julia. 'You see, I've got a job in London.'

'You've got an important job here,' said Mr. Logan earnestly.

Julia had been bewildered before, but now she was even more bewildered. First she had thought Mrs. Walker's guest a disreputable character (Mrs. Walker had seemed ashamed of being discovered entertaining him to tea); then she had thought he must be a relation of Mrs. Walker's, for he had seemed so at home in her kitchen. Then he had suddenly become an entirely different sort of person; he had spoken French with an impeccable accent and read Julia's thoughts in a way that was quite alarming. Finally he had 'talked like a book,' as Mrs. Walker put it, and shown a knowledge and understanding of the history of his country which she had found immensely interesting.

Who was he, what was he, Julia wondered. However, it was no good trying to understand, because every endeavour she made to get things clear took her deeper into the bog of bewilderment; and as Mrs. Walker had now returned with a pair of grey woollen socks, she said good-bye again and went away quickly . . . but not quickly enough to escape the astonishing sight of Mrs. Walker on her knees before her visitor helping him to change his socks.

CHAPTER 23

UNCLE Randal had his supper in bed; he was a wee bit tired, explained Mrs. Walker.

'He's wanting up,' she added, 'but he's on a diet and it's not very tasty. Maybe he'll eat a bit more if he has it in his bed. I'll get him up when he's finished and he can come through to the room and talk to you. That's what he's wanting to do.'

So Julia had her supper alone in the dining-room and then went into Uncle Randal's study (which Mrs. Walker always referred to as 'the room') and waited for him to come.

Julia had seen this apartment last night, of course—was it really only last night that she had arrived?—but she had been too interested in

Uncle Randal himself to take in his surroundings, so now she sat down in a big chair by the fire and looked about her.

It was a man's den, she decided; the sort of place where a man could take his ease. Brown was the predominant colour: a brown fitted carpet; large brown leather chairs and a brown leather sofa with velvet cushions. There was a solid table in the middle of the room. Uncle Randal's own chair, which she had noticed last night, was equipped with an adjustable lamp and book-rest. The whole of one wall was fitted with shelves which were full of books. The furniture was worn and shabby, like everything else in The Square House, but not too shabby to be comfortable.

Julia had been sitting here for some time when the door opened and Uncle Randal came in. He looked less tired and was smiling cheerfully.

'Hallo, Julia,' he said. 'I'm a very poor host, I'm afraid. I wanted to get up and have supper with you but Maggie wouldn't let me. However, here I am, ready for a chat.' He sat down in his chair and added, 'We've a lot to talk about, haven't we?'

'Yes,' agreed Julia. There were so many things she wanted to ask Uncle Randal that she did not know where to begin.

'I'm very glad you've come,' he continued. 'To tell the truth I was doubtful about writing to ask you; I was afraid Andrew would object, but it seems I did him an injustice.'

'An injustice?'

'I mean he's sent a dove with an olive branch. That's right, isn't it?'

Julia looked at him in dismay. 'You mean Father sent me? Oh no, I'm terribly sorry, but—but he didn't. He doesn't even know I've come.'

'Doesn't know you've come?'

'He and Retta are away from home, cruising in the Mediterranean, so I couldn't ask him. Oh dear, I can see you're terribly disappointed! I'm so sorry.'

'A wee bit disappointed,' he admitted. 'I'm anxious to be friends with Andrew. When you get near your end you see things differently; you look at things in a clearer light. Feuds are foolish and bad, they should be forgiven and forgotten. It's worst of all when it's a feud between two brothers that have grown up together and loved each other dearly.' He sighed and added, 'I've done my best. I've written three times. I doubt if I can do any more.'

'You had no answer?'

He shook his head. 'But, Julia! What will Andrew say when he hears you've come?'

She looked down at her hands and replied in a low voice, 'I don't know. I wrote and told him but there hasn't been time for a reply.'

'Do you think he'll approve?'

It was no good telling a lie, so she was silent.

'I see,' said Uncle Randal thoughtfully. 'I'm seeing a good deal, Julia. I was an old fool to write to you and make bad blood between you and your father. I should have left it alone. I wanted to make things better but it seems I've made them worse. Why did you come, my dear?'

'You said you were ill and wanted to see me.'

'So you packed your bag and came?'

'Yes, of course!'

'Yes, of course,' he echoed, smiling at her very kindly. 'You said to yourself, "Here's a poor old man who is nearing his end and wants to see me; I'd never forgive myself if he went and died, so there's nothing for it but to go and—"'

'Uncle Randal!' she exclaimed.

'Maybe you said to yourself, "It's a Christian duty to visit the sick"?'

'It is!' cried Julia impulsively.

'So we're told on the very best authority.'

'But I'm glad I came, not only because . . .'

'I'm glad too, not only because . . .' he told her with a little chuckle. 'Of course I shouldn't be glad. It's sheer wickedness on my part; but there's a kind of poetic justice about the whole affair that appeals to the lower part of my nature.'

'Poetic justice?' asked Julia.

'Just that. Oh me, oh my!' said Uncle Randal, shaking his head and smiling. 'There's an awful lot of wickedness in a man's lower nature.'

'Do you mean it's wicked of you to be glad I've come?'

'I do indeed. The right thing to do would be to pack you up and send you home to-morrow.'

'Why?' asked Julia in dismay.

'To make it up with your father, of course. He might not be angry with you if I packed you off home in disgrace; he could take it out on me.'

'I shan't go—at least not if you want me.'

'Want you!' he exclaimed. 'You're a delight to me. It's a joy to look at you and listen to your pretty voice. I've not got many joys at the moment.'

'Well, that's settled then,' said Julia. She said it lightly, but in fact she was more than a little embarrassed by the charming compliment—But no, it was not really a compliment at all!

He was simply speaking the truth straight from his heart. How strange that he could do it like that, without the slightest sign of self-consciousness. One had always heard that the Scot was a reserved sort of person—dour was the word—but dour was certainly not the word for Uncle Randal.

They were silent for a while. Then he said, 'Did Andrew ever speak of me?'

'Never,' replied Julia. 'I didn't know—I didn't know anything about you.'

'Not even that I existed?'

'No, not really. It was only after I got your letter and thought about it that I vaguely remembered hearing Father and Mother saying something about "Randal." It was the name I remembered, that was all.'

He sighed. 'Perhaps it's as well. They wouldn't have said much good of me.'

Julia hoped he would tell her more, but he was gazing at the fire in silence. What could they have quarrelled about, she wondered. What could it be? Now that she was getting to know him she could not believe that Uncle Randal had done anything very bad. Nothing that would justify an age-long feud; nothing that could not be forgiven. She looked at the thin worn face and the kindly eyes with the little wrinkles round them which had come from smiles. Suddenly she burst out impulsively, 'Uncle Randal, I don't believe you ever did anything bad!'

'Landsakes, Julia!' he exclaimed, looking up and laughing.

'Never did anything bad! What a thing to say to a man! Is there a man on this earth who could lay his hand on his heart and make such a claim? If there is I'd like to see him. I'd like to see him, but I'm not sure I'd like him much; he'd be a queer uncanny being.'

'You mean he wouldn't be human?'

'Of course he wouldn't be human. "To err is human, to forgive divine." Do you know Alexander Pope, Julia? No, you're a bit young for Pope. It was Shelley I liked when I was your age, and Keats and Byron. Then I came onto Browning—there's good meat in Browning if you take the trouble to understand—but now it's Pope. Would you get him for me, Julia?'

Julia rose and went to the book-shelves. She was aware that Uncle Randal had changed the subject because he did not want to talk about the quarrel. I wonder if I shall ever know what happened, she thought, as she looked along the shelf for the book he had asked for.

'No, he's above that at the other end,' said Uncle Randal, pointing. 'He's a bit shabby, poor fellow, but that's because he's read.'

'So he doesn't mind being shabby,' said Julia standing on tiptoe to reach the shelf and bringing the well-worn copy of *Pope's Poetical Works* to its owner.

'No, he doesn't mind a bit,' agreed Uncle Randal, turning over the leaves with his long thin fingers. 'To tell you the truth it always grieves me when I see a book that's never read. There's something a bit pathetic about its crisp leaves and immaculate binding. Poor thing! What's a book for if it's not to be read and enjoyed? Well, I won't bore you reading screeds of Pope—it would be an ill return for your kindness in coming all this way to see me—but there's just a wee bit in "An Essay on Man" that comforts me a good deal in these days when the newspapers make such uncomfortable reading:

> *All Nature is but art unknown to thee;*
> *All chance, direction which thou canst not see;*
> *All discord, harmony not understood;*
> *All partial evil, universal good;*
> *And spite of pride in erring reason's spite,*
> *One truth is clear, Whatever is, is right.'*

Julia was leaning on the back of his chair following the lines, so although some of it was difficult to understand, she grasped its meaning.

'"Whatever is, is right,"' she said doubtfully. 'But I wish they hadn't invented nuclear fission.'

'They wouldn't have been given the brains to invent it if it hadn't been intended.'

'Well . . . perhaps.'

'There's no perhaps about it. If we have any faith at all we've got to believe that. What do you make of "All chance, direction which thou canst not see"?'

Julia hesitated. She thought of Stephen finding that poor old man with the woolly hair. It was touch and go, Stephen had said.

The finding of him had led to the meeting of Julia and Stephen; the sapphire horse; the renovations at Gemscoombe House. Surely that was 'direction which thou canst not see'?

'Yes,' said Julia. 'I know of one thing at least that looked like chance and turned out well for a lot of people.'

'Do you, now? That's interesting.'

'I'm not so sure about "All discord, harmony not understood,"' declared Julia. 'No, I'm sure that isn't true,' she added, her thoughts switching to Fifi, who did her best to create discord and succeeded only too well.

'Och, away, lassie!' exclaimed Uncle Randal, laughing. 'You're trying to shake my faith in my favourite philosopher.'

Julia smiled in sympathy. 'I'd like to read some more. Would you mind if I took the book up to bed with me?'

'Of course not. Take anything you like,' he replied, waving his hand and making her free of his shelves.

Soon after this Mrs. Walker came in. She pointed to the clock and said it was half past nine.

'Oh, Maggie! But I'm enjoying myself!' exclaimed Uncle Randal reproachfully.

'That's easy seen, but you've been up long enough. You know as well as me what happens when you're over-tired. Miss Julia will be off to her bed too, no doubt,' added Mrs. Walker, as she shepherded him away.

He paused at the door to look back at Julia with a twinkle in his eye. 'Don't you forget to take Pope to bed with you, Julia. He'll enjoy it, I'm sure of that,' said Uncle Randal.

Of course he meant I'll enjoy it, thought Julia, as she tucked Pope under her arm and went upstairs to bed.

CHAPTER 24

1

THE next day was dull and rainy. Julia was disappointed, for she had intended to walk to the woods; Mrs. Walker had assured her it was a nice morning's walk and would keep her out of the way till dinner-time, but Mrs. Walker was bound to admit that it would not be a nice walk to-day.

'You'll just need to keep your bed till I get the room dusted,' said Mrs. Walker with a sigh.

'I'll dust the room,' Julia told her.

A long argument ensued, but in the end, somewhat to her own surprise, Julia was victorious and, armed with a couple of large yellow dusters and a sweeper, started upon her task. She was standing upon a ladder dusting the books on Uncle Randal's top shelf when the door opened and Mr. Logan came in.

'Good morning,' he said. 'You seem busy.'

'Good morning. Yes, I'm very busy. Do you want to see Mrs. Walker? She's in the kitchen.'

'I want to see you,' he replied. 'What you're doing is a waste of time, you know. You're merely disturbing the dust, moving it from one flat surface to another. There's no sense in it.'

'No sense in it?'

'Very little sense. Anyway I want to talk to you about something important, so please come down and listen.'

There was so much urgency in Mr. Logan's voice that Julia felt bound to comply. She was still puzzled about him. She was even more puzzled than before, for to-day he was different again . . . and, now that she had descended from the ladder and was able to look at him properly, she was quite taken aback; the man she had taken for a disreputable character was attired in a well-cut tweed sports jacket, a blue linen shirt and a silk tie and a pair of grey flannel trousers, spotlessly clean and neatly pressed.

'I see you're surprised at the transformation,' he said. 'The poacher is on his way to Edinburgh, so he had to get cleaned up.'

'He isn't a poacher at all,' said Julia, smiling.

'It depends what you mean by a poacher. I had no right to kill that bird so if you don't mind we'll just keep quiet about it.'

Julia nodded, 'I suppose you shot it on someone else's ground.'

'Good heavens, no! What a frightful thought. It was on my own moor—Dunraggit. It's just a little matter of dates, that's all.'

'Dates?'

'Yes, but it was an old cock, so my sin is not terribly black, and if Maggie stews it carefully it will make a nice change for her lord and master. He's very partial to grouse. That's the whole explanation, see?'

Julia did not see.

'The twelfth of August,' said Mr. Logan impatiently. 'The glorious twelfth is the day upon which grouse shooting begins.'

'Oh yes,' said Julia with dawning comprehension. 'Yes, of course. How silly of me!'

'Well, never mind. I want to talk to you about something much more important.'

'Yes?' asked Julia inquiringly.

She sat down as she spoke and immediately Mr. Logan followed suit, subsiding gracefully into a large chair and crossing his legs.

'It's about Uncle Ran,' said Mr. Logan. 'He's not my uncle of course but I've always called him that. He's a wonderful person. You don't know him properly yet, but you'll soon realise what a wonderful person he is. I'm terribly worried about him, Julia.'

Her name fell from his lips so naturally that it was a moment or two before she realised what he had said. Yesterday he had called her 'Miss Julia'—just as Mrs. Walker did—and that had seemed right. This morning it seemed quite natural that he should call her 'Julia.' It was not because he was wearing different clothes, not even because he was speaking differently; his whole personality seemed to have changed. He was one sort of person sitting at the kitchen table and having tea with Maggie Walker, and quite a different sort of person lounging gracefully in Uncle Randal's comfortable leather chair.

'I'm terribly worried about him,' repeated the puzzling young man. 'You can see how ill he is, can't you?'

'He's very thin,' agreed Julia. 'But he's so cheerful and bright. I know he was very ill last week when he wrote to me, but I thought he was getting better. Why are you so worried about him, Mr. Logan?'

'Neil is the name.'

Julia smiled. 'All right,' she said.

'I'm worried about him because he's not getting better,' declared Neil Logan. 'He's seriously ill and the old doc hasn't the slightest idea what's the matter with him.'

'You don't mean—'

'Oh, he thinks he knows what's the matter, and he thinks there's no hope, so he thinks the best thing to do is to dope Uncle Ran when necessary and let him die in peace.'

Julia gazed at her informant with wide horrified eyes.

'Yes, it's grim,' he agreed. 'Perhaps I had better explain that I'm a student at Edinburgh University—medicine and surgery—taking my finals next month; so I know what I'm talking about.'

'You ought to speak to the doctor!'

'Speak to him! I've spoken till I'm tired. He won't tell me a thing, but I know from his prescriptions what he thinks. You see, Julia, the chemist is a pal of mine. As a matter of fact I made friends with him so that I could check what Uncle Randal was being given . . . but keep that under your hat.'

'Yes, of course, but—'

'Listen, Julia. In simple words the old doc thinks it's an inoperable tumour on the liver. My diagnosis is entirely different—'

'But that's dreadful!' cried Julia. 'He must see a specialist. He should be X-rayed and—and properly examined!'

'Of course he should be,' agreed Neil eagerly. 'That's what I've said all along. He should see MacTavish. Honestly, Julia, MacTavish is marvellous. He's simply marvellous in every way, not only as a surgeon but as a man. There's nobody like him—nobody. I've seen him operate—absolutely brilliant! You wouldn't believe me if I told you some of the things he's done. For instance . . . but it would be no good,' declared Neil, pulling himself up short. 'You wouldn't understand a word I was saying . . . besides, there's no time. I've got to go to Edinburgh to see an old professor and I mustn't be late for my appointment. I came here to see you first because I had to see you—I just had to see you! You understand, don't you, Julia? You've got to persuade Uncle Ran to see MacTavish.'

'Oh, but I don't think—'

'You must!' cried Neil, sitting forward in his chair and squeezing his hands together. 'You simply must! You're the only hope! When I heard you were coming I thought, if this girl has any guts she may be able to work it. That's what I thought.'

'But I told you! I've got a job in London so I can't possibly stay here for more than a week. There wouldn't be time—'

'Is the job more important than saving a man's life?'

She gazed at him in dismay.

'That's what it comes to. The old doc is sitting back and letting him die.'

'You mean an operation could save him?'

'Yes, if it's gall-bladder . . . and I'm practically certain that's what it is.'

'But Neil, why can't you persuade him? You know him much better than I do.'

'That's just it!' cried Neil in agonised tones. 'I've done my damnedest to persuade him, but he won't listen to me; he thinks I'm still a kid. You know how it is when people have known you all your life, don't you? They know you've got brains—they can't help knowing because they know you've passed every exam you've ever sat with flying colours. They know you're mad keen on your profession and you've worked like a dog and you're all set for first class honours in your finals, but all the same they won't believe you know anything at all.'

Julia gazed at him in astonishment.

'It's all true,' he told her. 'I'm not conceited or anything like that—I didn't make my brains—I'm just being realistic. I'm not telling you in a boasting way, though it may sound like boasting to you. I'm just telling you because you simply must believe that I know what I'm talking about. I don't care what I do or say if I can get Uncle Ran to consult MacTavish. Do you believe me, Julia?'

It was impossible not to believe him. There was truth and sincerity, there was desperate urgency in every line of his tense body.

'Yes,' said Julia. 'I believe every word you've said.'

'Thank God for that!'

'But what can I do? Why should he listen to me?'

'You can try to make him—and anyway I've got somebody on my side. It's been awful trying to fight the battle alone. I've talked to Uncle Ran; I've tackled the old doc. They won't take me seriously. I've thought of all sorts of plans. One night when I was lying awake in bed I even thought of kidnapping him, doping him and taking him to Edinburgh in my car—absolutely ridiculous, of course, but you think of the most ridiculous things when you're desperate. I had the plan all worked out— how to get Maggie out of the way and everything—but of course in the morning I saw what a fool I'd been.'

Poor Neil, she thought. Aloud she said, 'You're terribly fond of him, aren't you?'

'I love him better than anybody else in the world.'

There was silence for a few moments and then Neil rose and stretched his cramped limbs. 'I must go,' he said. 'You'll try to persuade him, won't you?'

'Yes, I'll try.'

He held out his hand and they shook hands gravely.

It was not until he had gone and she heard the sound of a noisy little car speeding down the road that she realised what she had let herself in for: she had promised to try to persuade Uncle Randal to see this mysterious MacTavish, who was 'brilliant,' and if Uncle Randal consented the surgeon might advise an operation (in Neil's opinion this was a foregone conclusion, and somehow she had a great deal of faith in Neil's opinion). What then? thought Julia. If Uncle Randal was to have a serious operation at her instigation could she say good-bye and leave him to it?

But I must go home, thought Julia (oddly enough May Martineau's house had become home). I'll lose my job if I don't go home. I can't stay here indefinitely . . . that's what it means, really. It means staying here until he's better, and we don't know when that will be. It may be weeks and weeks!

The study was only half dusted, so Julia rose and went on with her task—but alas not very thoroughly, for she was turning it all over in her mind; thinking that perhaps Uncle Randal might refuse definitely to see MacTavish, or perhaps MacTavish might not advise an operation, or perhaps Neil was entirely wrong and Uncle Randal might regain his health and strength without having another opinion at all.

2

Uncle Randal got up for lunch—or dinner, as Mrs. Walker called it—but Julia had not made up her mind how to tackle the subject of MacTavish. She had decided she must think about it seriously and choose a suitable opportunity when they would be free from interruption. Meanwhile Julia wanted to know the origin of the name 'Leddiesford,' which seemed to her delightful.

'Lady's ford,' he told her. 'It's supposed to be the place where Mary, Queen of Scots, crossed the river. Some people say it was on her way to Dunbar to visit Bothwell, others say differently, but there are parts of the town which are very much older and the ford was there long before the unfortunate lady was born or thought of. Unless the name was changed, which seems unlikely, we've got to thank some other lady for naming the little place.'

'Who could it be?' asked Julia with interest.

Uncle Randal smiled. 'To tell you the truth I like to think it was the saintly Queen Margaret, though that's going a bit far back in time. She died in ten ninety-three. Of course the ford would be there, and where there was a ford you would find an inn of sorts, and maybe a small village . . . but whether the wise and wonderful Margaret happened to ride in this direction and cross the river and give the place its name, nobody can tell.'

'You like to think it, Uncle Randal.'

'Yes, I do. Skene says, "Perhaps there is no more beautiful character recorded in history than that of Margaret." If you're interested you can read about her in Skene's *Celtic Scotland*.'

'I'm interested in that sort of history—I mean history about places I know—but I never could remember dates,' said Julia frankly.

'Battle of Hastings, ten sixty-six, and all that!' said Uncle Randal, laughing. 'There's not much glamour about it, is there? History books for schools are too condensed. If they gave you a rousing account of the battle you'd remember it . . . but there's no time, Julia, no time for anything except names and dates and battles and pacts.'

'I remember a pact called the Diet of Worms,' said Julia thoughtfully.

'It would be a deal more interesting than my diet, anyway,' said Uncle Randal ruefully as he went away to have his afternoon rest.

3

Julia spent the afternoon weeding the garden (for the rain had cleared and the sun was shining) and she had tea with Mrs. Walker in the kitchen.

'You can say Maggie, Miss Julia,' said Maggie Walker in an off-hand manner. 'I'm used to Maggie and it sounds more friendly-like.'

'Oh, yes, I'd like to,' said Julia, who, to tell the truth, had had some trouble in preventing herself from 'saying Maggie' before.

By the time they had finished tea and Julia had been allowed to dry the dishes her quick ear had caught the rhythm of Maggie's speech . . . for now that they were friends, doing a little job of work together, Maggie had forgotten to 'remember to talk proper English' and was chatting away comfortably in her own comfortable way.

'Sammy Tamson was in this afternoon when you were weeding the gairden,' said Maggie. 'No, Miss Julia, dinna bother to put the cups away. I'll do it later masel' and then they'll be on the right hooks. In he came with a fine blue suit and a stiff white collar. Och, he's a grand man noo by his own way o' thinking—with a caird in his pouch—and it signed with his name, Samuel Thomson. "My land!" I says, "so they've made you an elder!" and he says, all niminy-piminy, "I'm hoping you'll be coming to church on Sunday, Mrs. Walker. We've not seen you for a while." "And you'll not see me for a while," says I. That was the truth, Miss Julia. I'm all for going to the kirk on the Sabbath; I like fine to hear a good sermon and to lift ma voice in a psalm; but if it means I've tae leave him his lee lane my hairt's not in it nor my mind neether and Mr. Johnstone's fine arguments would just go over ma heid. I'd be sitting wondering whether he'd be well enough; I'd be thinking he'd be up from his bed and getting into some kind o' pickle with me not there to see to him. "No, no, Sammy Tamson," I says. " I'm better at hame where I'm needed. I can sit and read a psalm or a parable with my ears open for his step in the passage or the tinkle of his bell." "But this'll not do, Mrs. Walker," he says—and begins his piece about the need for going to church if we're proper Christians and so on and so forth. I was that riled wi' the man I could have skelped him. "Och, away!" I says. "I'm not needing you to lairn me my Christian duties, elder or no. They must be haird put to it if they chose you for the job, I mind when you were a bairn wi' a snotty nose and wet breeks mair often than not."'

Julia did not understand all of it, but she had given up asking for explanations because it broke the spell. It reminded Maggie that her listener hailed from south of the Border and her conversation immediately became more conventional and not nearly so amusing. So Julia just listened, putting in a word or two when Maggie paused for breath and giggling softly to herself at intervals. But on this occasion Julia had understood quite enough to realise that Maggie enjoyed going to church if she could go with an easy mind.

'You could go to church on Sunday, couldn't you?' suggested Julia. 'I mean I shall be here. He'd be all right with me, wouldn't he?'

'Well, it's an idea,' admitted Maggie, as she swilled out the sink and hung up the washing-cloth to dry. 'But there's the dinner to see to, Miss Julia.'

'I could do it if you told me what to do.'

'He'd maybe not like it,' said Maggie doubtfully. 'It would vex him to think of you toiling and moiling in the kitchen. No, Miss Julia, I'm better at hame.'

'Isn't there an evening service? That would be quite easy, wouldn't it?'

Maggie hesitated. 'Well, I might,' she said. 'There'd just be the supper and I could leave it ready set. There'd be nothing except to heat his Bengers. Could you do that, d'you think?'

Julia professed herself capable of heating his Bengers and promised faithfully not to let it come to the boil, so the matter was settled. And immediately Maggie turned off her iron (which she had just that moment turned on) and began to search all round the kitchen; pulling out the drawers in the dresser; taking down the ornaments on the chimney-piece and peeping inside; looking behind the photograph of her mother which stood on the shelf, and beneath the wireless set in the corner. The search, which had started in a leisurely manner, became more and more frantic, and when she had looked in every conceivable place she began looking in the same places all over again.

'Noo, where did I lay it?' murmured Maggie to herself.

'It wis on the table when he left—I mind that. I mind lookin' at it and thinkin' I'd no be needin' it. Did I put it at the back o' the fire? Na, na, I wouldn't ha' din that!'

'Are you looking for something important?' asked Julia, quite unnecessarily one might think.

'It's a mystery to me,' declared Maggie, rummaging wildly in the drawer of the dresser, where already she had rummaged twice. 'I niver thocht I'd be needin' it—so I niver bothered. Where, in the name o' goodness, can I ha' laid it!'

Julia had no suggestions to offer. It seemed to her that Maggie had looked in every possible place and as she had no idea what Maggie was looking for—and did not like to ask—she could be of no help whatever.

This being so she rose and went to the door.

Maggie was still searching feverishly. She was muttering, 'I canna gang wantin' ma caird! Na, na, I canna gang wantin' ma caird!'

CHAPTER 25

WHEN Julia went into the study Uncle Randal was already there, sitting in his usual place with a book upon the adjustable book-rest. He seemed so engrossed that she did not interrupt him but crept in quietly and sat down in the chair opposite without a word. She was thinking about what Maggie had said and wondering what it meant, when Uncle Randal looked up and took off his spectacles.

'Well, Julia, what are you thinking about so seriously?'

'Maggie has lost something,' replied Julia. 'I don't know what it is, but it's something very important.'

'Did she not tell you what it was?'

'Yes, but I couldn't understand. Usually I can understand Maggie pretty well, but this afternoon she was worried about the thing she had lost, hunting madly and muttering to herself.'

'It's the key of the store cupboard,' suggested Uncle Randal.

'Well—perhaps—but I don't think so.'

'It's her post office savings book?'

'No, I'm sure it isn't that.'

'What did she say?'

'She said,' replied Julia, trying to reproduce the accent and intonation of Maggie's incomprehensible mutter, 'she said, "I canna gang wantin' ma caird." She said it twice and I haven't the slightest—'

The remainder of the sentence was drowned by Uncle Randal's laughter. He laughed and laughed; his face became pink all over and tears streamed from his eyes. Julia was quite alarmed; so alarmed that the laughter (which is usually so infectious) did not infect her in the least.

'Oh, Julia!' sobbed Uncle Randal. 'Oh, lassie, you'll be the death of me! It's the funniest—thing—to hear—poor Maggie—coming from your mouth! Don't say it—again! For pity's sake don't—say it again—it's more than—I could hear!'

She remained silent and waited while he recovered himself. Presently the spasms subsided, and except for an occasional chuckle he was quiet.

He mopped his eyes. 'Well, well,' he said. 'It's years since I laughed like that, but it's done me good. The translation is, "I cannot go without my card."' He chuckled again but managed to control himself.

'But I still don't understand,' declared Julia in bewilderment.

'Let's see if I can read the riddle. I'll make a shot at it, anyway. I wouldn't wonder if you and Maggie had arranged between you that she would attend kirk on Sunday morning and you would be left at home to mind the baby.'

'How did you guess?'

'I was always a great hand at riddles.'

'But it's Sunday evening,' said Julia. 'You see, she thinks I might be capable of heating your Bengers without letting it come to the boil.'

'Obviously she has a very high opinion of your capabilities.'

Julia giggled. Now that he was better she had begun to see the funny side of it.

'So now you know all about it,' declared Uncle Randal.

'Not quite,' she replied. 'I mean why must she have a card to go to church? Surely anyone can go whenever they like.'

'Of course they can. She could get a card at the door if she asked for it, but you may have noticed that our friend likes to do the right thing, and the right thing is to hand your card to the elder as you enter the building.'

'Every Sunday?' asked Julia incredulously.

'No, no. Three times a year on Communion Sunday. It's just a custom.'

'I see,' said Julia; it seemed to her rather a queer custom . . . but of course it was Looking-Glass Country.

'Was Neil here this morning?' asked Uncle Randal after a short silence. 'I found a book I'd lent him on the table. Did he bring it himself?'

'Yes', he came in on his way to Edinburgh.'

'What do you think of Neil? Nice lad, isn't he?'

'Very nice,' agreed Julia. Even as she said it Julia realised the inadequacy of the description. In fact it was ludicrously inapt. There was a fierce power in Neil (like a tiger, thought Julia); he possessed outstanding ability; he was full of humour and intuition . . . and, there was no doubt about it, he had exercised a sort of hypnotic influence upon Julia so that she had been forced to believe every word he said and had agreed to do exactly as he wanted. Yes, thought Julia, Neil Logan was one of the most extraordinary personalities she had ever met with in her life . . . and she had said he was 'very nice.'

'Well, what's the verdict?' asked Uncle Randal.

Julia woke up. 'He—puzzled me,' she said.

'That's not to be wondered at. He's a strange mixture, is Neil, but all the ingredients are pretty good. Maggie loves him of course; she used to be his nurse.'

'Oh, that accounts for a lot!'

'Yes, you should hear him chatting to her in her own idiom!'

'I did,' said Julia, nodding. 'When he was talking to Maggie he seemed the same sort of person—if you know what I mean.'

'Exactly. Neil's idea is that you should adapt yourself to your company. If you're chatting to a tinker on the road, be a tinker on the road. If you're chatting to an old man like Uncle Ran, be an old man like Uncle Ran. Oh, he can do it, too,' declared Uncle Randal, chuckling. 'He's good company, is Neil. He says you can get on better with people if you speak to them in their own tongue; that's Neil's idea.'

'Yes, I see,' said Julia in doubtful tones. She was thinking of Ellen. Would Ellen be pleased if Julia started speaking to her in her own tongue?

'But you don't agree?' suggested Uncle Randal.

'It's different here,' said Julia thoughtfully. 'Everything is different. I feel like Alice Through the Looking-Glass.'

'Everything the wrong way round.'

'The other way round,' said Julia, smiling.

Uncle Randal nodded. 'I'm glad of that. Perhaps you'll get used to us in time.'

This was the moment when Julia should have said, 'I must go home on Tuesday,' but she hesitated, and the moment passed.

Uncle Randal was wearing a puzzled frown. 'Let me see,' he said. 'How does it go?

"You are old, Uncle Randal," the maiden said,
"And your hair has become very white.
And yet you incessantly stand on your head;
Do you think at your age it is right?"
"In my youth," Uncle Randal replied to the girl,
"I feared it might injure the brain,
But now I am hoping to make my hair curl
So I do it again and again."'

Julia was laughing and Uncle Randal laughed too; so he could not continue the poem. They were both laughing merrily when Maggie came in with a large tray.

'There, you're better!' she exclaimed. 'I just knew the moment I saw her step off the train that she'd do you more good than all the bottles and pills that Dr. Cairn prescribes.'

'Yes, I'm better,' admitted Uncle Randal. 'Prescriptions are never much use for a pain in the wame, are they, Maggie?'

'You should know,' said Maggie significantly. She added, 'I've brought in your suppers. It'll be more comfortable for you to take your suppers here by the fire. I'll push in the table a wee bit.' She nodded significantly at Julia. 'I found it,' she said.

'Oh good! Where did you find it?'

'Beneath the tea-cloth,' chuckled Maggie. 'Did you ever hear the like! There was me searching high and low and wondering where I'd laid it . . . and it was there all the time, lying on the table where Sammy Tamson put it down. I'd just let it lie and spread the cloth over it, ye see. You could have knocked me down with a feather when I took the cloth to fold it away in the drawer—and there was ma caird!'

'She's a good kind soul,' said Uncle Randal, when Maggie had set the table and gone away. 'I'm fortunate in my friends, Julia.'

'They're fortunate in having you,' she told him. 'It always works both ways.'

'I'm no use to anybody; just a nuisance.'

'That isn't true and you know it!' cried Julia indignantly. 'Maggie adores you, she enjoys taking care of you, and Neil loves you better than anybody else in the world.'

'Neil—said that?'

'Those very words.'

'Poor laddie,' said Uncle Randal sadly. 'Yes, he's a lonely creature. His parents died years ago and Dunraggit is a big draughty place. He'd be better to let it; he'll need to let it when he gets his degree and finds a post as assistant to a doctor. Let's hope he finds one quickly, for he's not got two pennies to rub together.'

'He'll get a good post quite easily; he's frightfully clever. Anyone can see that.'

'Well, maybe. He was always getting prizes at school.'

'Uncle Randal,' said Julia earnestly. 'Neil thinks you should consult Mr. MacTavish.'

'Oh, he's been on at me about that—and now he's on at you! What a laddie! Can he not let the old horse die in peace in his own stable?'

'No, he can't, and neither can I!' cried Julia.

'What! Both of you?'

'Yes, both of us.'

'Surely it's early days to be allies.'

'I know, but—but he opened his heart to me. He's desperate.'

'Desperate?'

'Absolutely desperate,' declared Julia. 'He lies awake at night thinking out plans to get you to go to Edinburgh and see that man. Uncle Randal, listen! He even thought of kidnapping you and taking you to Edinburgh in his car. Of course, in the morning, he saw it was silly; but it shows how desperate he is.'

'Good heavens!'

'It shows how desperate he is,' repeated Julia earnestly.

Uncle Randal sighed. 'It shows Neil is nothing but a boy. Cairn is an old friend and an experienced doctor and he's dead against the idea. He thinks it would be a waste of time.'

'He said that to you!'

'No, no, of course not. He wrapped it all up very carefully, but that's what he meant.'

'I think it's disgraceful! If he doesn't know what's the matter with you he should advise you to have another opinion.'

'But it's not that at all, my dear. Cairn knows what's wrong and wants to spare me the fatigue. He's a nice kind creature. He comes along in the evenings now and then and sits and chats. Sometimes we play chess together.' Uncle Randal smiled and added, 'He's not what you'd call a first-class chess player, for he never sees beyond the end of his nose, but he does his best.'

'Perhaps he isn't a first-class doctor, Uncle Randal.'

He looked at her doubtfully. 'You mean the two things go together? That's a bit far-fetched.'

'No, I didn't mean that exactly. I meant it would be a man's nature to be far-seeing or not far-seeing,' she replied.

Uncle Randal leaned forward and stirred the fire. 'Well, that's as may be,' he said. 'At any rate he's a nice kind creature and he's all for leaving me in peace.'

Uncle Randal may have thought the argument finished, but Julia had another shot in her locker.

'Perhaps Dr. Cairn doesn't love you better than anybody else in the world,' she suggested in a thoughtful voice.

'Good gracious! Of course not! Why should he? The man has his own family—'

'And Neil has nobody but you.'

Uncle Randal was silent. Julia also was silent; what more could she say? She applied herself to the dissection of the finnan-haddock which Maggie had seen fit to provide for her supper. It was very tasty but it seemed to have an awful lot of bones, and as Julia had not dealt with a finnan-haddock before she was having some difficulty with it. She noticed that her host was toying with a piece of steamed fish, pushing it about his plate as if he loathed the sight of it.

'If I were not here you would throw that into the fire, wouldn't you?' she exclaimed.

He started and looked up like a guilty child. 'Well, I can't deny it,' he replied ruefully. 'I'm sick and tired of steamed fish. It's all I can do to swallow it—and that's the truth, as Maggie would say. If you'd just shut your eyes for a minute I'd be grateful. Maggie would be grieved if she saw it lying on my plate.'

Julia was of the opinion that if Uncle Randal were sick and tired of steamed fish it was unlikely to do him any good, so she shut her eyes as requested, but she could not shut her ears . . . she heard the fire make a sizzling noise.

'That's fine,' declared Uncle Randal. 'Maggie will be pleased.'

'But I'm not pleased,' Julia told him. 'If you can't bear the sight of steamed fish it isn't the right kind of food for you.'

There was silence for a few moments and then they began to talk of other matters. Julia told him that she had been given permission to 'say Maggie,' and asked if she might 'say Uncle Ran, like Neil.'

'Yes, why not?' replied Uncle Randal. 'It's a nice wee name and very suitable.'

'Suitable?'

Uncle Randal chuckled. 'Because Uncle ran,' he explained. 'Long, long ago Uncle could run with the best of them. You wouldn't think it now to see him creeping about like an elderly snail . . . but it's true. Uncle ran with the Edinburgh Harriers, and many a good time he had and many good friends he made! He'll not forget those days; he often thinks of them. Some of the friends are gone now, but there are still some left; there's Andy Hepburn and Henry Baird . . . but what's the use of telling you a string of names? There's not much interest in that.'

'Tell me about the good times,' suggested Julia.

Uncle Randal did not need much pressing; he began to tell her about some of the cross-country runs and the amusing things that had happened, and his recollections were so interesting that they lasted until Maggie came to fetch him to bed.

CHAPTER 26

The following morning when Maggie appeared as usual with Julia's breakfast there was a large bulky letter upon the tray.

'Oh, a letter!' exclaimed Julia.

'Postie has just been,' said Maggie. She arranged the tray as usual and went away.

Meanwhile Julia had discovered that the letter was from Stephen; it had been sent to May Martineau's and redirected to The Square House. She opened it as she sipped her orange juice, and saw it was a very long letter and contained several sheets of typescript on very thin paper. She read the letter first:

Gemscoombe

My dear Julia,

It was good of you to write and let me know you were going to Scotland, but it was a very short letter and you did not give me your address. I was waiting to hear from you again but I expect you have been too busy to write letters, so I am sending this to Miss Martineau's, marked 'please forward.' I feel inclined to say—like the Irishman—'Let me know if you don't get this' but, being an ordinary common or garden Englishman, I shall just say, 'Let me know if you do'! I hope your uncle is better—or at least improving. From what you said in your letter I am afraid he must be seriously ill.

You remember I told you I had to go to that meeting of the directors of Coribunda? It was just as bad as I expected if not worse. However, I have done what I believed to be my duty and warned them of the difficulties that lie ahead. I enclose a copy of the statement which I gave the directors to digest at their leisure. I did not intend to write it but Father advised me to do so and helped me to compose it. I don't know whether it will interest you—if not, just tear it up—no need to return it. Mother made me send it to you, she said you would like to read it. She also said I was to give you her love. I dare say this seems funny to you but of course I have told her a lot about you—I told her about how we met and she took it in her stride! I hope you don't mind my having told her.

Oh, Julia, I wish you were here instead of hundreds of miles away in Scotland! It is such lovely weather, mild and balmy with a little breeze off the sea, and the sunshine is kind. Perhaps you will think 'kind' is a strange word to use of sunshine but I can't think of a better one. In Africa the sunshine is cruel and glaring and dries you up and hurts your eyes. Yesterday morning I woke early and went down to bathe before breakfast. There is a path down the cliff and a little sandy bay and a rock from which you can dive into deep clear water. I was out of practice so I went in with a splash and came up gasping. It was a good deal colder than I expected—I suppose it feels colder because I was out in Africa for so long—all the same I enjoyed it and felt warm and tingly afterwards and braced up for the day's work.

If you think I am having an idle holiday you couldn't be more wrong! The builder has come at last and is re-slating the roof. In my opinion he is a plausible rascal so it is a good thing I am here to keep an eye on him and see what he is doing. This old house began life as a small inn, frequented by smugglers, and has been enlarged and added to so often that the roof is very strange indeed. There are ups and downs and flat places and little gables in unexpected corners and several unnecessary chimneys. I mean there are no fireplaces in the house connected with them. Parts of the roof are perfectly sound and other parts exceedingly old and rotten. When I was a boy I loved crawling about on the roof, it was a wonderful place to play, but now I am not enjoying it at all. However, it must be done, and of course it is quite impossible for Father, so I am afraid it looks as if I shall be stuck down here for ten days at least. After that I shall try to run up to Town for a long week-end and shall look forward to seeing you. Perhaps we could have another celebration. If we can't think of anything else to celebrate we could celebrate your return from Scotland! Our last celebration was great. I often chuckle to myself when I think of that terribly grand commissionaire who looked as if he had been melted and poured into his uniform and how we nearly disgraced ourselves by laughing at the wrong moment—and I often think about the evening when we walked round Piccadilly Circus and visited the lions in Trafalgar Square and then on to Westminster Bridge and heard Big Ben strike eleven. It was kind of you to enjoy it with me, Julia, but I am sure you understood. I had been living for so long in a solitary spot, miles from civilisation, that it was a wonderful experience to walk in London, jostled by the crowd, with a girl on my arm. When I told Mother about it she said it was very inconsiderate of me to make you walk so far in your evening shoes, but you were not wearing evening shoes—they were sensible shoes. I looked at your shoes before I suggested we should walk. I am telling you this because Mother was so horrified and I should not like you to think I had been inconsiderate.

My parents are very keen for me to stay at home for the whole summer and I have agreed. I have written to the manager of the Dickenson Mine to ask for an extension of my leave. I expect he will grant it, because he is a decent chap, but if not it will be quite easy for me to get another post. Mining engineers don't grow on blackberry bushes! At any rate I must stay here for the summer. You see there is so much to be done. Not only the house but the whole estate has been neglected for years because there was no money for repairs. Now, thanks to the sapphire, we can put everything in proper order. How amazing it is! If I had not gone back and found the old chap none of this would have happened. I had my foot in the stirrup! If I had mounted and ridden away I should never have found you sitting on that seat in Kensington Gardens. I feel quite frightened when I think about it.

Please write and tell me how you are and what you are doing. I have never been to Scotland so I can't imagine you at all. Just a short letter will do if you are too busy to write a long one.

Yours ever,

STEPHEN

2

Julia read the letter with pleasure; it was a nice friendly letter and very interesting indeed. Of course Stephen believed her to be engaged to Morland and she did not intend to undeceive him—not yet. There were various reasons for this decision: to begin with, it was less than a week since her engagement had been broken off. It felt a great deal longer, but that was because so much had happened and because Julia was so far away from her previous life, not only far away in a geographical sense but also in her own private feelings. She had expected that she would continue to think of Morland and to miss him, but for the last few days she had not thought of him at all. Her new friends and her new experiences had filled her life completely. Now that she thought of Morland and of all the months when they had seen each other nearly every day she felt ashamed of being so—yes, so fickle, thought Julia. It really was horrid of her! However, perhaps it was just as well, because she and Morland were quite unsuited to each other—it was a good thing that they had made the discovery in time—Morland would find a girl who would say 'Yes, dear' on every possible occasion and they would be perfectly happy together. Meanwhile Julia must think of Uncle Randal and of how she could persuade him to have another opinion. She had begun her campaign last night; she did not think her arguments had made much impression upon him but she must go on trying . . . and she would go on trying, for she was now convinced that Dr. Cairn was no use at all. He might be 'a nice kind creature,' but what use was a doctor who could not see further than the end of his own nose?

Having made up her mind that she must continue her campaign Julia realised that it was necessary for her to remain indefinitely at Leddiesford. Whether or not she were successful it would be impossible for her to walk out and leave Uncle Randal to his fate. Neil had been right in saying that she had an important job here; certainly it was a great deal more important than selling hats. This meant she must write to May at once and also to Madame Claire and explain the whole situation. She must do that to-day. And she would write to Stephen—quite a short letter would do—telling him about Uncle Randal's illness, which was even more serious than she had expected, and saying that he might have to undergo an operation. She would not mention Morland at all; that was the best way.

Stephen's letter was lying on the tray, so she took it up and read it again more carefully. Yes, it was a kind friendly letter and quite sensible—until the very end. The end was not quite so sensible. Of course lots of people signed themselves 'yours ever'; it was the sort of thing to write when you could not make up your mind how to end. You thought of various endings and dismissed them as being too affectionate or, alternatively, too stiff. Then you just dashed off 'yours ever' without meaning it in the very least (Julia had done this herself to several of her friends without having the slightest intention of remaining theirs for ever); but if you dashed it off like that, was it likely you would inscribe the words in large roman capitals?

No, it was not. So it really was rather naughty of Stephen (when he believed her to be engaged to be married to another man). It was rather naughty, but rather nice too, thought Julia smiling to herself. At any rate it showed that although she was 'hundreds of miles away in Scotland' he had not forgotten her.

Turning back to Stephen's description of Gemscoombe, Julia reread the bit about the roof. 'Parts of the roof are perfectly sound and other parts exceedingly old and rotten.' It sounded frightfully dangerous, thought Julia frowning. How awful if poor Stephen fell through one of those horrible rotten parts and broke his leg or something! She decided to tell him in her letter that he must be very careful.

All this time Julia had been stowing away her breakfast and had now reached the stage of scones and honey. It crossed her mind that if she stayed here long she would put on a lot of weight; however, it could not be helped. The air of Leddiesford made her hungry and Maggie Walker's scones were delicious.

Julia took up the thin sheets of typescript, and unfolding them carefully began to read Stephen's statement to the Directors of the Coribunda Sapphire Company, which ran as follows:

Gemscoombe,

Devonshire

The Coribunda Sapphire Co.

Dear Sirs,

I understand that you wish me to give you my advice about reopening the workings of the Coribunda mine. It is difficult for me to do this as there are so many factors to be taken into consideration, so perhaps the best plan is for me to tell you of my own experiences in the district and leave you to consider the matter at leisure. I am, as you are aware, assistant manager of the Dickenson Diamond Mine situated not far from Kimberley. About this time last year I was given ten days' leave of absence and, as it was too short a holiday to come home, I decided to go on safari with a friend, James Rafferty, a mining engineer like myself. We took some ponies and half a dozen boys and set out to visit the Coribunda Sapphire workings which we knew to have been abandoned some years previously. We are both interested in corundum (i.e. rubies and sapphires), and as we were aware that good specimens of sapphire had been found at Coribunda we wondered why the workings had been discontinued. We did not hurry and it took us several days to reach the district. We made our camp about fifteen miles short of our objective, where there was a good water supply, and the following morning James Rafferty and I rode over to Coribunda leaving the boys in camp. When we arrived at the workings we found the huts and equipment were all falling to pieces; the whole place looked derelict, but it interested us greatly because it seemed to us a most promising situation for sapphires. The workings had taken place in the side of a small kopje of igneous rock, we found gneiss and granite and qualities of quartz sand. There was an auriferous drift such as is found in the gold fields of Victoria. No doubt you are aware that drifts of this nature yield very fine sapphires in Australia, so it is reasonable to suppose that this type of geological formation should yield good sapphires in Africa.

Perhaps I should point out that corundum is not found in deep mines—like gold and diamonds—but in crystalline rocks which lie nearer the surface, frequently in beds of rivers and basaltic detritus.

At Coribunda numerous shallow tunnels had been bored in the hill, but it was difficult to explore them because the roof had not been shored up properly and had fallen in. For this reason we could not determine their extent. At one place there was a blue vein in the roof which looked very promising indeed, but it would have been extremely dangerous to touch it without proper equipment as the roof might have fallen in and buried us alive. We spent some time looking about but could do nothing useful.

I am aware that this information may be redundant as you have had the workings surveyed by an expert and have had his report. My object is merely to inform you of the experiences of my friend James Rafferty and myself.

All this is very hopeful but I feel I should not be doing my duty if I did not show you the reverse side of the picture. I have said that the huts and equipment were falling to pieces, so you will realise that new huts would have to be erected and new equipment purchased and everything would have to be brought to the site. Coribunda is one of the wildest and most desolate spots in Africa and would, in my opinion, be a miserable place to live. One cannot help wondering whether it would be possible to get a good manager to live there and settle down. It would be necessary to have an assistant manager and at least two overseers to prevent pilfering. Suitable accommodation would have to be built for them and a small hospital to deal with injuries, etc. This would cost a great deal of money.

There is another snag, even more formidable. When we were coming away from the Coribunda workings we discovered an old native dying of thirst and starvation. He told us he had been employed in the workings and was sure there were sapphires to be found, but he also told us that he and his fellow workers had deserted the place because it was haunted by evil spirits. To anyone not acquainted with the place and having no experience of the weird and wonderful 'magic' practised by African witch-doctors the idea may seem ludicrous, but to those who have witnessed some of their 'magic' it does not seem ludicrous at all. For instance I have seen a man pine away to a shadow and lie down and die for no reason except that a witch-doctor, more than fifty miles away, had willed his death. I have seen other things happen, equally mysterious and inexplicable. But whether or not we believe in African magic is not the point. The point is that the natives believe in it. The native workers at Coribunda believed the place to be haunted by evil spirits so they deserted in a body. Rumours get about like wildfire, and once a place has a bad name—in this case the reputation of being haunted—it is difficult to recruit suitable workers and perhaps even more difficult to keep them. You could get riff-raff of course, but when you are searching for precious stones you want a respectable team of workers.

I should like to make it clear that it does not matter to me personally whether or not you decide to resume workings at Coribunda. I have no interest in it financially—or otherwise. You asked for my advice. I believe there are good sapphires at Coribunda but I feel certain that it will be difficult and costly to get them out.

Yours faithfully,

STEPHEN BRETT

The statement was extremely interesting, and in Julia's opinion it was admirably clear and well thought out. She had known quite a lot before, but this description seemed to bring it all into focus. She could almost see the tumbledown buildings and the tunnels in the hill. What would the directors do, she wondered. Would they go on with the project or not? She hoped they would. It was sad to think of hundreds of sapphires waiting to be found and cut and polished into beautiful, shining, sparkling gems.

3

JULIA was still thinking about the sapphires when Maggie came in for the breakfast-tray, but before removing it she stood at the end of the bed and delivered a message:

'He'd like to see you about ten if convenient,' said Maggie solemnly. 'But I'm to say not to bother if you'd rather not see him in his bed and not to bother if you're busy and not to bother if you're wanting to go out and—'

'Oh, Maggie, of course I'll go in and see him!'

'I knew you would,' declared Maggie, beaming with delight. 'I said you would. I said, "Miss Julia's not the girl that would stick at going into a gentleman's bedroom." That's what I said.'

'No, of course not! I mean—' said Julia, trying to stifle an involuntary giggle—'I mean of course I'll go in and see him. Tell him I'd like to.'

Maggie nodded.

'About ten, you said,' continued Julia, glancing at the clock. 'Goodness, I'm awfully late this morning! It's because I've had such an interesting letter. I'd better get up at once.'

'There's no hurry, Miss Julia. A quarter past will do as well.'

The letter was strewn all over the bed. She collected the sheets and folded them and put them back in the envelope. How different people were! thought Julia. May Martineau would have shown eager interest in the letter and would not have been satisfied until she knew all about it, but Maggie had shown no interest at all. Maggie had kept her eyes turned in the other direction so that they might not fall, even for a moment, upon the scattered sheets. In Maggie's opinion it would not be 'the right thing' to show any interest . . . and of course Maggie was absolutely correct.

Having put her letter in the drawer of her dressing-table Julia hesitated and wondered if she should lock it—but there was no need to lock it—none whatever. Maggie would no sooner have thought of prying into somebody else's private correspondence than she would have thought of stealing a five-pound note . . . and the idea of Maggie stealing a five-pound note was simply ludicrous! The idea of May stealing a five-pound note was equally ludicrous, but she saw nothing wrong in reading other people's letters.

Very interesting and very, very queer, thought Julia.

She was dressed and ready by this time, and as it was just after ten o'clock she ran downstairs and tapped on Uncle Randal's door.

Uncle Randal was lying in bed propped up with pillows. His face looked wan and haggard this morning and he admitted that he had slept badly.

'I was thinking,' he explained. 'It began with Cairn and his chess; as I told you, he never sees beyond the end of his nose. Well, it seemed a bit far-fetched when you said a man who's not far-seeing at chess is not likely to be far-seeing as a doctor, but I'm bound to admit there's a certain amount of sense in it. Then there's the steamed fish,' continued Uncle Randal, with a shudder. 'Well, the less said about that the better, but there's sense in what you said about that too . . . . And then there's Neil. To tell you the truth I never thought of Neil needing me—he always seemed an independent sort of lad—but it seems he does. You said he was desperate, and that idea of kidnapping me looks as if it were affecting his brain. What did he think I'd be doing while he dragged me out of my bed and carried me away to his car? What did he think Maggie would be doing? Tell me that. It was a daft idea, Julia.'

Julia remained silent. She had decided not to mention the details of Neil's plan.

'It was a daft idea, Julia,' repeated Uncle Randal with an anxious frown.

'Yes, but when you're feeling desperate all sorts of—of daft ideas come into your head, don't they? Especially in the middle of the night when you can't sleep.'

'He's lying awake at night?'

'Yes, for hours and hours, worrying about you.'

'That's bad,' said Uncle Randal. 'That's very bad. Neil will need a clear head if he's to do well in those exams.'

'Frightfully important exams,' Julia reminded him.

'Yes, that's true,' he agreed.

'His whole career depends upon them.'

'Yes. Listen, Julia, do you think it would relieve his mind if I consented to see that man?'

'I'm sure it would.'

Uncle Randal heaved a sigh. 'Well then, there's nothing else for it. I'll need to see that man. You'd better arrange it with Neil . . . but mind this, Julia, I'll not go unless Cairn agrees to it. He's a good friend and I wouldn't hurt him for the world.'

'Neil will arrange it all,' declared Julia with conviction. She could not imagine Neil being stumped by little things like these.

'Yes,' said Uncle Randal. 'But there's no hurry about it, Julia.'

'No, of course not,' she agreed. She had been about to rush off and phone to Neil at once, but she realised that they must be careful, so she stayed where she was and chatted about other matters . . . and meanwhile she looked round the room.

It was a room on the ground floor looking out onto the back garden. The window was masked by a couple of laurel bushes which made it dark and airless. It was also exceedingly dismal, thought Julia in some distress. It was the room of a man who did not value comfort or at least had no idea how to achieve it. Maggie had told her that she had been obliged to move him down from the upstairs bedroom to save him the stairs and this was the only room available, but surely something could have been done to make it more comfortable! It was frightful to think of him lying here for days on end in such miserable surroundings: the drab drugget on the floor; the drab paper on the walls; the narrow iron bed—quite frightful! He was badly off, but it would not take much money to make the room brighter. I could do it myself, thought Julia remembering her nest-egg in the bank. Yes, I could do it myself quite easily . . . and if he has to go to a hospital in Edinburgh I can have it all done while he is away. Maggie can help me.

By this time Uncle Randal was looking more cheerful, so Julia left him and went to phone to Neil and explain what she had been able to accomplish.

CHAPTER 27

THIS was Julia's third day at The Square House, but already she had been absorbed into its atmosphere and a routine had been established. She did the 'messages' in the morning, had dinner with Uncle Randal, and weeded the garden in the afternoon. To-day, however, instead of weeding the garden she settled down at the solid table in the study and wrote letters to May Martineau, to Madame Claire and to Stephen. She had expected to polish them off quite quickly, but she found she had a good deal to say, so it was four o'clock by the time she had finished her letters and ran out to post them in the pillar-box at the corner of the road.

Usually Julia had tea with Maggie, but on this particular afternoon Mrs. Inglis had come in for a crack with her old crony, so Julia was banished to the study.

'It's a pity, Miss Julia,' said Maggie. 'But you'll need to take your tea in the room. You'll understand it wouldna be the right thing for you to take your tea in the kitchen with Mrs. Inglis there.'

Julia understood perfectly and was not sorry to be banished, for she was half-way through *Villette*, which she had found on Uncle Randal's shelves. Lucy Snowe was annoying, of course (Julia would have liked to take her and shake her and tell her not to be a silly little ass), but all the same she was so enthralled by the creature's misadventures that it was difficult to put the book down. She propped it against the teapot and sipped her tea. It was most enjoyable.

By this time Lucy was in desperate straits; she had fallen in love and the wretched man, having led her on in a shameless manner, had now forsaken her. He had failed to keep his appointment with her and had gone away without saying good-bye.

Various other frightful things had happened to poor Lucy and she had gone to bed 'haunted by quick scorpions,' when the door opened and Neil came in.

Lucy's troubles were immediately forgotten.

'Oh, Neil, have you seen the doctor?' Julia exclaimed. 'You had better fetch another cup and—'

'Too much bother,' said Neil, sinking gratefully into a big chair. 'I'll just have it in the slop-bowl. Lucky you haven't used it!'

She was about to expostulate but already Neil had leaned forward and was pouring out his tea, adding milk and five lumps of sugar.

'It's bigger than those silly cups,' he explained, taking the bowl in his two hands and drinking the syrupy liquid with enjoyment. 'I had no time for lunch,' he added, seizing a buttered scone and devouring it ravenously.

In view of his starving condition Julia forgave him and smiled at him in a friendly manner.

There was a short silence while the pangs of hunger were alleviated.

'I couldn't get hold of the old doc,' said Neil at last. 'Mrs. Cairn said he'd gone to Dunbar on business. I wonder what he's doing at Dunbar.'

'Business, perhaps,' suggested Julia.

'Think you're funny, don't you? Well, you are funny,' declared Neil with a wide grin. 'You amuse me a lot.'

'I find you rather boring,' declared Julia, giggling and displaying her dimples in her usual attractive way.

Neil laughed delightedly and poured out another bowl of tea.

'Six lumps of sugar!' exclaimed Julia, raising her eyebrows.

'I've used up a great deal of energy this afternoon. That's why I require so much sugar. What have you been doing?'

'Writing letters,' she replied. 'I've realised that you were right. I can't go home on Tuesday; in fact I shall have to stay here with Uncle Ran until he's better.'

'That's grand!' he exclaimed. 'That's splendid! Julia, I didn't want to say much on the telephone this morning because in a place like Leddies-ford you never know whether somebody may be listening, but it was marvellous that you were able to persuade Uncle Ran. How did you manage it?'

'Remember, Neil, it's only on condition that Dr. Cairn agrees.'

'I know—and anyway we couldn't get MacTavish without his sanc-tion—but I'll make him agree,' declared Neil emphatically. 'You've done your bit, Julia, and I'll do mine. I intend to be on his doorstep at eight-thirty to-morrow morning. He's not likely to be out before that.'

Julia thought it most unlikely.

'How did you manage it?' asked Neil.

He had asked this question before and Julia had evaded it. She did not intend to answer it now, so she offered him another scone.

'It's a secret, is it?' asked Neil as he accepted the offering. 'Well, never mind, I shall worm it out of you in time. I like to know things—all sorts of things—for one thing I'd like to know why you've gone all grand.'

'Gone all grand?'

'Having tea all by yourself in state. I thought you always had it in the kitchen.'

This was easily explained so Julia explained it.

'No, of course it wouldn't be the right thing,' said Neil seriously. 'And anyway the two old girls wouldn't want you.' He took the last scone, crammed it into his mouth and added none too clearly, 'They're probably talking obstetrics.'

'Did you say obstetrics?'

'M'h'm. People having babies. They wouldn't want a young and innocent maiden listening in.'

Julia giggled.

'It's a silly giggle but there's something rather attractive about it,' said Neil, looking at her critically.

'Thank you.'

'Don't mention it. I'm glad we're cousins.'

'Cousins? But we aren't cousins!'

'We share Uncle Ran. You can't share an uncle unless you're cousins. If you think about it you'll realise that it's impossible for two people to have the same uncle unless they're cousins.'

'But he isn't really your uncle.'

'He was my uncle long before you knew anything about him,' retorted Neil with some heat.

'All the same—'

'Listen, Julia. I've been thinking about it and I'm sure we're cousins. The Logans and the Harburns have been living in this district within a few miles of each other for generations so it goes without saying that they must have intermarried. At some time or other, perhaps four or five generations ago, a Neil Logan must have married a Miss Harburn—or a Randal Harburn a Miss Logan. See what I mean?'

At first Julia had thought he was joking but she now perceived that he was perfectly serious. She had heard of 'Scotch cousins' but she had not realised that the relationship was quite so far-reaching.

'I've got a tree as long as your arm,' continued Neil. 'It's rolled up in a tin case and I've never bothered to look at it, but I'll have a go at it when I can spare a moment; meanwhile let's be cousins, Julia. I've got no cousins—at least none that I know of—and I've always thought it would be a nice pleasant relationship. What about it?'

'All right,' said Julia, laughing. 'I haven't got any either. What are cousins supposed to do?'

'Oh, just stand by in an emergency, that's all.' Neil rose and added that he had wasted the whole day trying to get hold of the old doc so he must do some work. 'I shall probably work till midnight,' he added. 'It's nice and quiet in the evening. I'll just look in and see Uncle Ran for a minute and then I'll be off.'

When Neil had gone Julia returned to *Villette* . . . but somehow the spell had been broken and she did not really mind what happened to Lucy Snowe.

CHAPTER 28

As USUAL Uncle Randal came into the study for supper, and he and Julia had it together by the fire. It had been a warm day, but now it had become cooler and was raining, so the gentle log fire was very pleasant. Julia was glad to find that he did not seem to be worrying about the prospect of seeing Mr. MacTavish; he was talking about his travels, which had been extensive, and talking in a most interesting way. Julia had never before come into close contact with a man so widely read and widely travelled and she found his conversation absorbing.

'Have you ever been in South Africa?' she asked.

'Yes, but it's a long time ago,' he replied, smiling. 'It's an amazing country. There's a queer sort of fascination about the veldt and the kopjes and the blazing sunshine. I went on safari with two other fellows that I happened to pick up in Johannesburg. They were interested in precious stones and they infected me with their enthusiasm—'

'Precious stones!' exclaimed Julia. 'Oh, I'm tremendously interested in them too, especially sapphires.'

'Sapphires,' he said. 'Yes . . . sapphires. I'll tell you about sapphires . . . some time. I'm not . . . feeling very well . . . just now. . . .'

She looked up in dismay. His face had gone a queer colour—grey like ashes—and there were beads of perspiration on his forehead. His hands were clutching the arms of his chair.

'Uncle Ran!' cried Julia.

'Call Maggie!' he exclaimed breathlessly 'It's all right, dear child. Don't be—frightened—but—just call Maggie—quickly.'

Julia ran to call her. She was not in the kitchen but was coming downstairs carrying a pile of linen in her arms. When she saw Julia's face she dropped the linen in a heap and rushed into the study. Julia followed and saw her bending over him, murmuring to him, holding his hand, trying to raise him from the chair.

'It's one of his turns, Miss Julia!' she exclaimed. 'We must get him to his bed. Take hold of his other arm.'

He was groaning with pain, bent almost double, but he was so light—so terrifyingly light—that between them there was no difficulty in getting him out of his chair. They half-carried him across the hall and into his room and laid him on the bed. He rolled over and buried his face in the pillow.

'Phone the doctor,' cried Maggie. 'Quick, Miss Julia! It's three-two-nine. Tell him to come at once.'

Julia ran to the phone. Her hand was shaking as she took up the receiver . . . and she remembered suddenly that the doctor had gone to Dunbar! Fortunately he had just returned, and said he would come. For a moment Julia hesitated and then ran back to see if there was anything more she could do to help. The door was locked. She could hear half-strangled groans and Maggie's voice, soothing and encouraging.

Julia tapped gently and in a moment or two Maggie opened the door.

'Is he coming?' she asked.

'Yes, at once. Can I help?'

'He's not wanting you to come in. You can fill a hot-water bottle—two of them—and put on the kettle. The doctor will need a glass of boiling water for his needle.'

'Yes, of course!' Julia went into the kitchen, filled the kettle and put it on the stove, and found the hot-water bottles. Quite soon she heard the doctor come in at the front door and go straight into the bedroom. By this time the kettle was boiling so she filled the glass and the hot-water bottles and carried them to the door. When she tapped, Maggie came and took them from her.

'Can't I do anything?' asked Julia miserably.

'There's nothing anybody can do,' replied Maggie, closing the door.

Julia stood in the hall twisting her hands together; tears were running down her checks. He was dying—she was sure of that.

Uncle Randal was dying . . . and she loved him dearly. She only realised now—when he was dying—how much she loved him. She could hear the sound of moaning; it went on and on growing more feeble until at last the dreadful sound ceased and there was silence. . . .

A few moments later the door opened and the doctor came out. 'Dr. Cairn, what's happened?' she exclaimed.

'He'll be all right now,' replied Dr. Cairn. 'I've given him a shot of morphia. There's no need to worry. You're Miss Harburn, I suppose.'

'Yes.'

'Good evening,' he said, smiling at her and taking up his hat which was lying on the hall table.

'I should like to speak to you for a minute.'

'Some other time,' he replied, nodding. 'We'll have a chat some other time, Miss Harburn. I've been out all day and I'm anxious to get home.'

'Please, Dr. Cairn, just for a few minutes,' said Julia. She opened the door of the study and waited.

Dr. Cairn hesitated and then went in reluctantly. He said, 'I'm sorry you got a fright, Miss Harburn. These attacks are very alarming.'

'Very alarming indeed. They can't be allowed to go on.'

'There's nothing to be done. I can assure you that I've—'

'Oh, I know,' said Julia earnestly. 'You've been very kind and attentive—my uncle says so—and I'm sure you've done all you possibly can. That's why I want him to have further advice.'

'It has been considered,' he told her. 'Naturally it has been considered most carefully, but Mr. Harburn is not very keen to have further advice. It would mean that he would have to go into hospital and undergo a great deal of discomfort and fatigue . . . all for no object. Believe me, I am every bit as distressed as yourself about my old friend's condition.'

'I can't believe that.'

'Miss Harburn! What do you mean?'

Julia raised her eyes and looked him straight in the face. 'He's my uncle and I love him,' she said.

'Yes, of course,' said Dr. Cairn rather uncomfortably. 'Yes, well, perhaps I had better explain.' He proceeded to explain and Julia listened. He explained that he had been attending Mr. Harburn for over a year, seeing him regularly. At first the attacks of pain had been slight and infrequent, but from the beginning of the illness there had been little doubt of its nature, and soon it became evident to Dr. Cairn that his old friend was suffering from an incurable disease. It was then that he had suggested a visit to Edinburgh to obtain further advice, but finding his old friend disinclined to make the effort Dr. Cairn had not pressed it, for he was convinced it would merely confirm his own opinion—and what use was that? What was the use of persuading Mr. Harburn to go into hospital and undergo all the worry and discomfort of X-ray examinations and tests? Dr. Cairn explained that he had had forty years of medical practice and that in most cases he was only too ready to call in a specialist, but in this case it would do more harm than good.

'Much more harm than good,' declared Dr. Cairn emphatically.

'The fuss and worry and fatigue would be the worst thing possible. Surely you can understand that, Miss Harburn?'

Dr. Cairn was so sure and so absolutely sincere that Julia was almost convinced—almost but not quite. She remembered Neil.

'Yes, I understand,' said Julia. 'But all the same I should like another opinion.'

Dr. Cairn turned away. He walked to the end of the room.

'I can't refuse, of course,' he said. 'I can only tell you that you're making a great mistake. Mr. Harburn is in a very precarious condition; he could never stand a serious operation—if that's what you're thinking of.'

'I just want another opinion, that's all. I want him to see Mr. MacTavish.'

'MacTavish?'

'Yes.'

Dr. Cairn walked to the door. 'Very well, have it your own way!' he said angrily.

Julia could not let him go like this. She ran after him and put her hand on his arm. 'Please don't be angry with me! ' she exclaimed. 'It's just—it's just—I do love him so much. That's why I feel—I feel we must do everything possible. You understand, don't you? Please say you understand.' She looked up at him, her eyes brimming with tears.

'You're making a mistake,' he said gruffly.

'Dr. Cairn, you have a daughter, haven't you?'

'A daughter? What has that got to do with it? I don't know what you mean.'

'I just mean that if you were terribly ill she would want to do everything in her power . . .'

He hesitated. 'I suppose she would,' he said in a surprised sort of voice.

'You know she would.'

'Yes, it's true. Isabel is like that—she's all for doing things—but you don't know Isabel, do you?'

'I'm sure she loves you . . . and I love Uncle Randal.'

'Well, well,' he said. 'I see we'll have to arrange it.'

'And you aren't angry with me?'

'No, not angry.' He gave her shoulder a little pat and went away.

Chapter 29

When Dr. Cairn had gone Julia sank into a chair; she felt exhausted—absolutely down and out—and now that she had won the battle, she began to have doubts. She began to have frightful, horrible, terrifying doubts. She was panic-stricken. She had pitted her youth and ignorance against the knowledge and experience of forty years! How could she have been so mad? But thank goodness, it was not too late; she could phone to Dr. Cairn and tell him she had changed her mind.

Julia rose and went to the phone; but with her hand outstretched to take up the receiver, she suddenly thought of Neil. Neil, thought Julia, hesitating.

There was no reason why she should not speak to him now, this very minute, for it was only half past ten and Neil had said he would be working until midnight. She took up the receiver and gave Neil's number and waited. She could hear the bell ringing and ringing . . . she had almost given up hope of an answer when she heard his voice.

'Who is it?' asked Neil crossly.

'Neil, I've done it,' gasped Julia. 'I've spoken to Dr. Cairn. Neil, I'm terrified! Perhaps we shouldn't do it. Perhaps he'll die! It will be my fault if he dies. Neil, I can't bear it! What am I to do!'

'I'll come at once,' said Neil's voice in her ear. 'Sit down quietly and wait till I come. I'll be there in ten minutes.'

'Neil!' she cried. 'What am I to do? Do you think I should . . . Neil, are you there?'

There was no reply—not a sound—so she jabbed the receiver up and down in a frenzy of impatience. Presently the operator's voice said, 'Number, please.'

'I was talking to seven-one-seven. You've cut us off.'

'They've cut off,' said the operator wearily. 'Will I ring them again?'

'Yes—no,' said Julia. 'No, it's all right. Don't bother.'

Of course it was all right—how foolish she had been!—Neil had said he was coming so he was coming; he was on his way. He had said she was to sit down quietly and wait, so she sat down quietly . . . and waited.

Julia had left the door of the study open, so that she could hear Neil arriving; she could hear the clock in the hall ticking away slowly . . . tick-tock, tick-tock, tick-tock. Ten minutes, she thought. Ten minutes was not long but it seemed a long time when you were waiting.

Suddenly Julia was shaking all over; it was a most extraordinary sensation—as if some outside force had taken hold of her and was shaking her—it lasted for a few moments and then passed.

Don't be silly, she told herself. There's nothing the matter with you. Try to be calm. Neil is coming. He can't be here in ten minutes, of course, but it doesn't matter . . . just wait quietly.

She waited quietly for a little while and then without the slightest warning another spasm gripped her and shook her unmercifully. It was more violent than before and lasted longer. When it had passed she lay back in the chair and closed her eyes. The clock continued to tick patiently. She fixed her mind on the clock. How many years had it been ticking on, night and day, never hurrying, never stopping? It was a nice quiet peaceful sound, tick-tock, tick-tock, tick-tock. The clock was old; it was a grandfather's clock. Quite likely it had belonged to her own grandfather. It had stood in the hall at Harburn House when her father and Uncle Randal were little boys. They must have looked at it often and listened to it ticking . . . what a strange idea! Julia lay and listened to it.

There was another sound now, the sound of a car in the distance. Could it be Neil? The car approached rapidly—yes, it was Neil's car—there was no mistaking that strange rattling noise! The car stopped at the gate; a door banged; there were flying footsteps on the path . . . Neil was in the room, bending over her, when another shudder began.

This spasm was the worst of all; it shook her from head to foot. Her teeth were chattering, she was helpless in its grip.

'I don't know—what's the matter—with me,' she gasped.

'You've had a fright, that's all,' said Neil comfortingly. 'It's nothing to worry about.'

The spasm left her as limp as a rag. She lay there helpless. Neil was rolling up her sleeve.

'What are—you doing?' she whispered.

'I'm going to give you an injection—just a tiny prick—you'll scarcely feel it.'

Her arm was dabbed with something cold and then there was the prick of the needle.

'You'll be all right in a few minutes,' Neil told her.

'Neil,' she whispered. 'He was terribly, terribly ill—frightful pain—'

'I know. Terrifying,' said Neil. He sat on the arm of the chair and held her head against his side.

'I spoke—to the doctor.'

'Don't talk, Julia. Just rest quietly.'

'But I want to tell you—'

'Don't talk,' repeated Neil. 'I understand what happened. The old doc came and doped him, so then you tackled the old doc and made him agree to having MacTavish.'

'Perhaps we shouldn't—'

'Of course we should! We must. It's the right thing to do. You're a marvel, Julia. You're an absolute trump—that's what you are.'

There was silence. Neil was still holding her and rocking her gently to and fro.

A peaceful feeling was beginning to creep over Julia. Her limbs felt queer and her eyelids became heavy. She said vaguely, 'You've doped me.'

'Just a little,' he told her. 'Just a very little. You won't go out completely. Don't worry.'

She was not worrying in the least, she was comfortable and relaxed, quite happy and peaceful. She was almost asleep.

'You had better go to bed,' said Neil suddenly, and with that he picked her up as if she were a child of six years old and carried her out of the room.

That wakened her. 'Neil, you can't! I'm heavy!'

'Heavier than I expected,' he admitted. 'Put your arm round my neck . . . that's better . . . up we go!'

Up they went, slowly and steadily. The door of her room was ajar; Neil kicked it open, walked in and laid her on the bed.

'There,' he said. 'Nothing very difficult about that.'

'Frightfully strong,' murmured Julia, looking at him admiringly.

'Fairly strong,' he agreed, stretching his arms. 'You see I know exactly how to use my muscles and I keep them in good trim; that's the secret. Lie still,' he added. 'Don't move. I'll send up Maggie to help you, and I'll stay with Uncle Ran till she comes down. Selfish old besom, she might have spared a thought for you! Just one thought!' added Neil savagely.

'She was frightfully upset.'

'Oh, I know. There's only one person in Maggie's world; everybody else can go hang for all she cares. Don't let her dose you with any of her nauseous mixtures—hartshorn or sal volatile—or anything—she can give you a glass of hot milk if you want it, but nothing else.'

'Yes,' said Julia. Her eyes seemed to be shutting and it was difficult to speak. 'Thank you awfully—awfully much,' she said slowly and indistinctly.

'Cousins,' said Neil.

'Cousins,' agreed Julia with a deep sigh.

2

Julia knew no more until she awoke to find her room full of bright sunshine and Maggie standing beside her bed. Maggie's face, usually so round and rosy, was pale and pinched and there were blue shadows beneath her eyes.

'Uncle Randal!' exclaimed Julia, staring up in alarm.

'He's not so bad,' said Maggie. 'He's wonderful, considering . . . but oh, Miss Julia, what an awful turn he had!'

'It was frightful! Maggie, is he better this morning?'

'He's weak, of course, like he always is after one of his turns, but he's lying in his bed quite peaceful, talking a bit and asking after you. Oh, Miss Julia!' exclaimed Maggie, her voice trembling a little. 'He was terrible bad last night! I was scared to death. I just felt I couldna leave him for a minute and I was dragging my mattress into his room, so that I could lie beside him on the floor, when Neil came down the stair with a face like thunder. He said you were ill and it was all my blame and I should have spared a thought for you. Oh, he was in a fearful rage!'

'Was I ill?' asked Julia, trying to remember what had happened.

'I'd have said you were dead drunk,' replied Maggie frankly.

'That was the way you looked to me—but it seems Neil gave you some drug to make you sleepy. "It was just a prick, Maggie," he said. "You can get her into her bed and she'll be fine in the morning." Just a prick!' said Maggie scornfully. 'It must have been a mighty big prick, that's all I can say . . . and what right had Neil to be pricking you when he's not a doctor?'

'Oh yes, I remember. I felt awfully queer and ill so he gave me an injection and carried me upstairs. I don't remember anything after that.'

'Carried you upstairs? The thing's impossible. You were dead drunk with yon queer drug he gave you. Dead drunk, that's what you were. It took me all my time to get your clothes off you, and your nightdress on, and roll you over between the sheets . . . and you as limp as a rag doll, smiling away to yourself as though you were having a nice dream.'

'I can't remember a thing about it.'

'Och, what a night I've had!' exclaimed poor Maggie.

'There was him lying below and you lying above, and me up and down the stair wondering which of you was the worst and what I ought to do, wondering what kind of queer drug Neil had given you and what like you would be in the morning.'

'I feel perfectly well,' said Julia, stretching her arms and yawning. 'Just a bit sleepy, that's all. I'll get up in a few minutes and come down and sit with him while you have a rest. What time is it?'

'It's eleven o'clock.'

'Eleven o'clock!'

'Very near. I've been wondering if you would ever wake again. The doctor was here at nine and I was minded to ask him to have a look at you but I was scared it might get Neil into trouble.'

'Oh, poor Maggie!'

'He'd no right to do it,' declared Maggie. 'I'm real mad with Neil— frightening folk out of their wits!'

'But I really was ill, Maggie. I don't know what was the matter with me but it was horrible. I never felt so queer before in all my life . . . and Neil cured me.'

'H'm'h!' said Maggie, snorting scornfully.

'I'm as fit as a fiddle so you needn't worry about me any more. I'll come down and help you.'

'There's no need, Miss Julia. Neil sent Mrs. Lean over from Dunraggit; she's a capable wee body and kind-hairted forbye. She'll see to the dinner and look after him and let me get to my bed. I'll not be sorry to get to my bed,' added Maggie with a groan.

CHAPTER 30

IT WAS Monday afternoon. By this time The Square House was itself again, and, except for the fact that Uncle Randal was still in bed, it had settled into its usual routine. Maggie had done her washing in the morning and the clothes had dried so quickly in the summer breeze that they were ready for ironing. Maggie had spread her ironing blanket on the kitchen table and was thumping away with her heavy iron; Julia was sitting in the basket-chair mending a large pile of grey woollen socks.

The scene was one of peaceful domestic activity.

'It's a pity you couldn't go to church yesterday,' Julia remarked.

'I wasna wanting to. I just felt I couldna take my eyes off him for a minute . . . and anyway I'd have been thinking about him all the time.'

Maggie's iron went thump, thump, thump.

'Miss Julia,' she said. 'Are you sure you'd not like me to give yon petticoat a wee press? It'll not take me any time at all when I've done his pyjamas.'

'Maggie, I've told you nylons shouldn't be pressed.'

'They needn't be pressed,' declared Maggie, making the all-important distinction, 'but it brings them up so nice.'

'It spoils them,' said Julia with a sigh. The matter of Julia's nylon underwear had already been discussed, *ad nauseam*.

Thump, thump, thump.

'I suppose these socks belong to Neil,' said Julia, looking with dismay at an enormous hole which it was inconceivable to suppose had been made by Uncle Randal.

'Aye, they're Neil's. I said I'd do them for Mrs. Lean as a sort of wee return for Saturday.'

'Oh, I see. Yes, that was quite right. What a nice woman she is!'

'She's not bad at all,' agreed Maggie, thumping away briskly. 'I was real glad to see her wee smiling face. I was just about the end of my tether.'

'I know. Poor Maggie!'

'Miss Julia, I'm real worried. Do you think Dr. Cairn is giving him the right medicine? That was an awful bad turn he took on Friday. He's not getting any better,' declared Maggie with her usual habit of understatement. 'He's not getting any better,' she repeated in a trembling voice.

'I know,' agreed Julia. 'But we're going to take him to see a very good doctor in Edinburgh.'

'Oh, Miss Julia, that will be grand! Neil has been on about it for months but they wouldna heed him. Did you speak to Dr. Cairn?'

'Yes, I told him I insisted on having further advice,' declared Julia, raising her chin. 'I had to be very firm about it.'

'Maircy, I never thought you had it in you!' exclaimed Maggie admiringly.

Julia knew that Maggie was by no means the only person who thought her soft and pliable . . . and they were right, up to a point; but occasionally they got a surprise. Occasionally it was absolutely necessary to make a stand even if it half-killed you!

'Will it be MacTavish?' asked Maggie eagerly.

'Yes. Dr. Cairn has written to him and Neil has gone up to Edinburgh to see him this afternoon.'

'Oh, Miss Julia! That's wonderful! It's just wonderful . . . and it's you that's done it. Yes, it's you that's done the whole thing.'

'But, Maggie, we mustn't be too—I mean we mustn't put too much faith in Mr. MacTavish. He isn't a magician, you know.'

'He is—almost,' declared Maggie. 'They think the world of him at the Royal. Mrs. Inglis was telling me. Her sister-in-law's nephew that's a doctor in the out-patients is never done talking about MacTavish. They're all just crazy about the man. Mrs. Inglis was saying that MacTavish is wanting an assistant to help him with his operations and they're all wondering who it will be. Bill Grainger would like it himself, and maybe he'll get it, for he's a clever one is Bill and he's had a lot of experience . . . and what's more he's helped MacTavish with some of his operations.'

'Who is Bill Grainger?'

'I've told you, Miss Julia. He's Mrs. Inglis's sister-in-law's nephew.' Thump, thump, thump. 'I hope he'll get it,' continued Maggie. 'It would be a fine feather in his cap; but there's several others better qualified than him, so there's no telling.'

'Why do they all want the job?'

'It's because he's a grand surgeon, that's why, Miss Julia. There's nobody like him. There was a wee boy came over from America—his father was a millionaire—and MacTavish cut his hairt open and sewed it up again. Bill Grainger was there and saw it with his own eyes. What do you think of that, Miss Julia? Did you ever hear the like? And the wee boy got better and was up from his bed, running about as cheery as you please. Mrs. Inglis was saying that MacTavish got two thousand dollars for the job . . . but, mind you, it may be wrong. I'm not believing everything I hear.'

'It sounds a lot of money.'

Thump, thump. 'Dollars,' said Maggie. 'It's not pounds. I'm not very sure how much it would be in pounds.'

Julia was not very sure either, so she did not venture an opinion, and for a few minutes there was silence.

'Maggie,' said Julia very seriously. 'I'm sure Mr. MacTavish is very clever, but all the same he can't work miracles. We must remember that. I think we must be prepared . . .'

Maggie put her iron on the trivet and stood up very straight.

'I know what you're meaning, Miss Julia,' she said in a queer strained voice. 'There's no need for you to be warning me. D'you think I'm so blind that I canna see what's before my eyes? He's that thin and frail you'd think a wee breath of wind would blow him away—there's nobody kens that better nor me—but there's something being done about it at last. *There's something being done.* All these months he's been taking turns . . . and every one worse than before. All these weary months he's been getting frailer and frailer. A year ago he could still walk to the town and enjoy a crack with folks . . . and then he could do nae mair than walk to the road-end to post his letters . . . and then it came that he would just take a wee dander round the gairden . . . and then,' said Maggie in a shaky voice, 'and then he was not on for that, even. I would put out a chair beneath the tree and he would sit and watch the burrds and maybe scatter a han'ful of crumbs for them to peck. He's just been dying,' said Maggie, dashing the tears from her eyes and groping for the handle of her iron. 'He's just been dying . . . and nothing being done.'

Julia could not speak. Even if she could have spoken she would not have known what to say; somehow she knew quite definitely that Maggie would dislike any demonstration of sympathy.

'This iron is too hot for his semmit,' said Maggie. 'I'll need to leave it and finish his shirts.'

'What a long time it takes to iron a shirt!'

'It does, if you do it right. I like to do them nice for him—as nice as I can.'

(Yes, of course she did, thought Julia.)

Thump, thump, thump. 'Not that he cares,' added Maggie.

'He'd put them on, rough-dried, and never notice. He's not the one to notice things like that.'

'If he has to go to a nursing home for—for treatment or anything, we might have his bedroom done up.'

'Well, there now! I never thought on that.'

'It's so dreary, isn't it? And it would be a nice surprise for him when he comes home.'

'So it would. Maybe we could get the walls papered, Miss Julia. Would it cost a lot of money?'

'I don't think so.'

'You could get Alec Fleming to do it. He's a real good painter and he wouldna charge as much as the Edinburgh shops.'

Julia nodded. 'Yes, a local man would be best. We must get a new carpet, Maggie.'

'And curtains,' said Maggie eagerly. 'If we got some nice bright chintz I could borrow Mrs. Inglis's sewing-machine and run them up in no time.'

They continued to discuss plans for the project—it was to be a secret of course—and Julia was glad she had suggested it, not only for Uncle Randal's sake but also Maggie Walker's. The task of doing up Uncle Randal's bedroom would give her something to think about, something to keep her busy while her master was away.

Julia had finished darning the socks by this time, so she rose to go.

'Miss Julia,' said Maggie, continuing to iron his shirt industriously. 'Miss Julia, I'm not very good at "thank-you," but that's not to say I dinna feel it in my hairt. You've done mair nor anybody for him.'

'Sometimes I wonder if I've done the right thing,' said Julia with a little tremble in her voice. 'I mean supposing . . .'

'We'll not suppose anything,' said Maggie firmly. 'We'll just hope and pray and keep our fingers crossed. That's what we'll do, Miss Julia.'

'Yes,' said Julia. For some reason or other this curious mixture of Christian faith and pagan superstition comforted her considerably.

CHAPTER 31

1

IT WAS a lovely morning, warm and bright; the sunshine was streaming in through the open windows of the study. Julia was sitting at the table darning some pillow-cases; Neil was sitting in a big leather chair trying to read the morning paper and obviously failing in the attempt. They were anxiously awaiting the arrival of Mr. MacTavish.

'Isn't he wonderful!' exclaimed Neil. 'Isn't he simply splendid! Fancy his coming all this way to see Uncle Ran! I never asked him to come, of course; I never thought of it. I just gave him Dr. Cairn's letter and told him what I could and explained that Uncle Ran was still in bed after that frightful attack on Friday night and it might be a week before he was able to come to Edinburgh . . . and do you know what he said? He said, "Well, in that case, the mountain will have to go to Mahomet." Wasn't it splendid of him, Julia? I told you he was wonderful, didn't I?'

'At least twenty times,' said Julia, nodding.

'I expect he'll be here soon,' said Neil, throwing the paper onto the floor in an untidy heap. 'He's always punctual unless something unforeseen happens. If something unforeseen happens he can't help it. People come hundreds of miles to see him. That's why it's so wonderful of him to come all this way to see Uncle Ran.'

'It's only fifteen miles and he has got a Bentley, so it isn't—'

'How do you know he has got a Bentley?'

'Because it has just stopped at the gate.'

Neil rushed out of the room to greet his hero but Julia remained where she was, sewing industriously, as if her very life depended upon the work. She heard the sound of voices in the hall, she heard Uncle

Randal's door opening and shutting; she was still sewing industriously when Neil returned.

'He wants to see Uncle Ran alone,' explained Neil. 'I thought he might want me to be there, but he doesn't. We'll just have to wait.'

'Yes,' agreed Julia, taking up her little gilt scissors to snip off a thread. 'We'll just have to wait.'

For a few moments Neil stood and looked out of the window and then he began to prowl up and down the room like a caged tiger.

'He has come!' exclaimed Neil. 'When I opened the door and saw him coming up the path I could scarcely believe my eyes!'

'He said he was coming, didn't he?'

'Oh, I know, but all the same . . . I mean he's so famous and so frightfully busy. I don't know how he gets through all his work.'

'He won't be so busy when he gets an assistant.'

'How do you know he's looking for an assistant?' asked Neil in astonishment.

'Maggie told me.'

'Maggie told you! How on earth did Maggie know?'

'Mrs. Inglis's sister-in-law's nephew said so.'

'Who the heck is he?'

'His name is Bill Grainger,' replied Julia. She was talking for talking's sake, hoping to interest Neil so that he would stop prowling up and down the room. Her nerves were at stretching point, ready to snap at any moment . . . and then I shall be really cross with him, she thought. She did not want to be cross with Neil, for she knew what he was suffering. She herself was suffering agonies of impatience and apprehension and of course it was worse for Neil. She herself loved Uncle Ran dearly—it was incredible that she had known him for little more than a week—but Neil had known him and loved him for years and years and years; he was part of Neil's life.

'Did you say Mrs. Inglis is related to Bill Grainger?' asked Neil, pausing in his walk and gazing at Julia incredulously.

'If you call it "related,"' she replied. 'I mean if a sister-in-law's nephew is a relation—'

'What an extraordinary thing!'

'Why so extraordinary?'

'Because she's a horrible old woman—I can't stand the sight of her—and Bill is a frightfully decent chap.'

'It isn't unknown for a frightfully decent chap to have unpleasant relations. Besides, she isn't a relation, she's only his aunt's sister-in-law.'

Neil took no notice of this remark, he had resumed his walk. He said, 'I've always liked Bill—everybody likes him. He's clever and very capable and he's had a great deal of experience. Perhaps MacTavish will offer Bill the job—nobody could possibly be better qualified—but as a matter of fact I don't believe Bill would take it; he has a very good job already.'

'He would take it.'

'How do you know?'

'Mrs. Inglis told Maggie.'

'Mrs. Inglis told Maggie!' echoed Neil with a mirthless laugh. 'Well, all I can say is MacTavish will be a fool if he doesn't take Bill Grainger.'

'You had better tell him so,' suggested Julia sweetly.

'Really, Julia, you are the limit! I don't know what's the matter with you to-day!'

'You're the matter with me,' she retorted. 'It's driving me mad to see you prowling up and down like that.'

'Oh, I see,' said Neil. 'Yes, I suppose it is rather annoying.' He sat down beside Julia at the table and took up one of the pillow-cases.

'It's beautiful linen, isn't it?' said Julia. 'Terribly old, of course. You can't get linen like this nowadays.'

'How neatly you've mended it! The stitches are so tiny that the darn is scarcely visible.'

'That's the whole idea.'

'Oh, I know, but isn't it rather a waste of time? You could be making something useful, couldn't you?'

'Or I could be prowling up and down the room and wearing out the carpet.'

'Touché!' exclaimed Neil with his sudden grin.

They were silent for a few moments, listening.

'I thought I heard something,' said Neil.

'It's Maggie, in the kitchen,' said Julia. 'The door of the cupboard makes a squeak like that.'

'Anyway it's too soon; he won't have finished yet. It'll take him a long time to examine Uncle Ran and have a chat and everything. He's frightfully careful and thorough, so we'd better make up our minds to wait patiently.'

'Yes, let's do that.'

Julia was about to resume her task when Neil seized one of her hands and looked at it critically.

'You've got nice hands,' he said.

Julia was so thankful that he had found something to amuse him that she made no objection but allowed him to do as he liked with her hand.

'Well made,' said Neil, stretching it out and folding it up and flexing the fingers. 'A woman's hand is beautiful when it's well-made like yours; so delicate and yet so strong, so exquisitely designed for its purpose. I remember one of the first things I was given to dissect was a woman's hand.'

'Neil!' cried Julia, pulling it away from him in horror.

'What's the matter? You've got to have bodies to dissect when you're doing anatomy. Surely you know that much! All right, we won't talk about it if it revolts you . . . but I can't see why it should. You've been wearing a ring on your engagement finger, Julia.'

'How do you know?'

'I could feel the ridge. I suppose you've broken it off.'

'Really, Neil, I don't think that's your business!'

'Everything is my business,' he told her. 'I'm terribly interested in people. "The proper study of mankind is man." I study their bodies and I study their minds; all terribly interesting. I'm not sure that their minds aren't more interesting than their bodies . . . to watch what they do and find out why they do it. Why did you chuck him, Julia?'

'I didn't!' exclaimed Julia, taken by surprise.

'He broke it off?' asked Neil, raising his eyebrows. 'How very strange! I can scarcely believe it. Why did he do that, I wonder. Perhaps he didn't like the idea of your coming to Leddiesford; was that the reason?'

'Neil, I've told you it isn't your business.'

'But it is,' declared Neil seriously. 'It is my business. It would half kill Uncle Ran if he knew. It upset him frightfully to think he had been the cause of a breach between you and your father; this would be worse.'

Julia's eyes flashed. She exclaimed, 'He won't know—ever—unless you tell him, of course!'

'All right, don't bite me.'

Neil was silent for a few moments. Then he said, 'Why did you come?'

'Why did I come?'

'Yes, why did you? It seems—it seems out of character, somehow. You're a gentle sort of person. I can't imagine you quarrelling with everybody belonging to you and dashing off at a moment's notice.'

'Can't you?'

'Did you think it was your duty or something?'

'He wrote and said he was ill and wanted to see me.'

'Yes, I know, but why did you come?'

Neil's eyes were fixed on her inquiringly; he really wanted to know
. . . so perhaps she ought to tell him. She did not want to tell him because
it was such a very private thing but it would be cowardly to evade the
question.

'Why did you come?' repeated Neil.

'I came—' said Julia slowly—'I came because if I had refused to come
I couldn't have gone on calling myself a Christian.'

Neil was silent with astonishment for at least fifteen seconds; it was
quite a long time for Neil to be silent.

'Gosh!' he exclaimed at last. 'Then you really believe in—in all that!'

'Don't you?'

'Oh yes, of course. I mean—vaguely. I mean if you'd asked me if I
were a Christian I would have said I was. I'm not an atheist or anything.
I rather like going to church if there's anything special on; for instance
St. Giles on Armistice Sunday when it's packed with people and they
put on a really good show. The music is good, too. I like good music; I
like a good rousing psalm . . . but all that doesn't seem to have much to
do with real life.'

'I think it has everything to do with real life.'

'Yes, I can see that,' he said, looking at her as if he had never seen
her before.

There was silence. They both listened intently but there was not a
sound to be heard.

'What a long time he's taking!' exclaimed Neil, getting up and beginning to prowl up and down again.

'You said he would take a long time,' Julia pointed out.

'I know . . . but it's ages. Look here, Julia, we had better decide what
we're going to do.'

'It depends on what he says, doesn't it?'

'Yes, but if he wants to operate; that's the point. Uncle Ran hasn't
much money—neither have I, worse luck—so I suppose he had better
go to a hospital. You get very good treatment, of course, but it would be
a bit noisy and he's used to peace and quiet. It would be frightfully bad
for him if he couldn't sleep . . . but a nursing home would cost the earth.
Then there's MacTavish. Of course MacTavish gets a huge fee for private
patients. It's a problem, isn't it?'

'I've got money.'

'Really!' cried Neil, pausing in his walk. 'You mean you've got money
of your own?'

'Yes.'

'Julia, how marvellous! You're an angel in disguise! You've been sent straight from heaven! Gosh, what a load off my mind! I've been thinking about it and worrying about it and wondering if there was anything I could sell. I had to sell the Raeburn to pay for repairs to the roof—Dunraggit runs away with a lot of money in upkeep—and you see it just might make all the difference if we could possibly get a quiet room for him in—'

'Hush!' exclaimed Julia, holding up her hand. 'Yes, there he is. I can hear him coming out of—'

Neil turned and rushed into the hall.

2

Several minutes passed before Neil returned to the study with his hero. Julia had been waiting in a fever of anxiety; she was so distraught that she could not sit still. She had risen and was standing looking out of the window when the door opened and they came in.

Neil's hero was quite different from Julia's expectations (why had she expected him to be tall and dark and good-looking?); he was thickset with very broad shoulders. In fact her first impression was that Mr. MacTavish was a dwarf. He was not really a dwarf, for he was as tall as Neil, but the tremendously broad shoulders and unusually long arms looked as though they ought to belong to a giant. His face was square with a straight-lipped mouth and a firm chin, his brown hair sprang from his broad forehead as if every separate hair were alive. His whole personality was so full of vital force that even if you were blind (thought Julia) you would know he had come into the room.

'Mr. MacTavish, Miss Harburn,' said Neil proudly.

They shook hands.

'Mr. MacTavish thinks—' began Neil.

'Now then, Logan, I'm quite capable of telling Miss Harburn what I think. Sit down quietly and try to hold your tongue. I know it's difficult for you.'

'Sorry, sir,' said Neil humbly—yes, humbly.

They all sat down.

'Well, Miss Harburn, I dare say you think I've been a long time with your uncle, but these things can't be hurried, you see. It's my way to go into things thoroughly—or not at all. I've examined Mr. Harburn and had a long talk with him—a very interesting talk. Of course you'll understand that it's impossible for me to give a definite opinion until I've had him under observation and made the usual tests, but it looks as if the gall-bladder is the source of the trouble. I say it looks like that.'

'That's what I've said all along!' cried Neil excitedly.

'When I want your opinion I'll ask for it,' said Mr. MacTavish firmly, but quite kindly.

'Sorry, sir.'

'I say it looks like that,' repeated the great man (and he must be a very great man, thought Julia). 'In fact I'll go so far as to say I shall be surprised if we find the condition diagnosed by Dr. Cairn. . . . That's between ourselves. You'll not mention that, Logan.'

'No, sir.'

'Not a word about the gall-bladder.'

'No, sir.'

'You can tell Dr. Cairn I was sorry to miss him, but I've seen his patient and I would like to have him in a nursing home for a few days and put him under observation. There's no need to say more.'

'No, sir.'

'Tell him I'll be writing to him myself.'

'Yes, sir.'

'Now, Miss Harburn,' said the great man. 'I'm sorry about it, but I'm afraid we've got to face the fact that your uncle's condition is very serious indeed.'

'Oh, I know!' exclaimed Julia. 'Maggie said . . .'

'What did Maggie say?'

Julia looked at him in surprise, but his face was perfectly serious.

'What did Maggie say?' he repeated. 'I've known at least half a dozen Maggies and I've always found their opinions well worth listening to.'

Julia tried to tell him what Maggie had said about Uncle Ran; how he had become 'frailer and frailer,' less able to do things, less interested in what went on. She found it difficult, for her voice began to tremble, but Mr. MacTavish was listening so intently that she was obliged to go on to the very end.' Maggie said, "He's just been dying,"' whispered Julia.

Mr. MacTavish nodded. 'Maggie was right . . . but we'll not let him die if we can help it. The first thing is to make certain what the trouble is and then we must go ahead. Now Miss Harburn, I want to explain to you in simple words that the removal of the gall-bladder is a serious operation, but as a rule not dangerous. It's done every day with excellent results. In this case, however, the condition has been neglected and has gone on too long. Much too long,' declared the surgeon with sudden heat.

'Much—too—long!' He banged on the table with his fist. 'It's deplorable! It's little short of culpable homicide in my opinion.'

'I did my best—' began Neil and stopped.

'Well now,' said Mr. MacTavish more quietly. 'Well, that's between ourselves, you understand. I wouldn't have said it if I hadn't got worked up about it . . . but it's no good getting worked up about it. We've got to keep calm and do the best we can in the circumstances. The fact is that in consequence of the delay Mr. Harburn is in very poor condition to stand an operation of any sort whatever. I'm not in favour of operating—'

'But you must!' cried Neil. 'It's the only hope—'

Mr. MacTavish quelled him with a look. 'I'm not in favour of operating upon a patient in very poor condition if there's any alternative. What I would like to do is to put Mr. Harburn on a diet for some weeks and build him up, but in view of the severe attacks which are occurring more and more frequently the risk of delay would be very great.' He looked at Julia and waited.

'You must do what you think best, Mr. MacTavish.'

He nodded. 'That's all I want; a clear field of action to do as I think best. I'll see if there's a room in the Westchester Home; I'll speak to Matron. There's a quiet room at the back that I like for my serious cases, and a special nurse. If I can fix up everything satisfactorily we'll have him in at once.'

He turned to Neil. 'I'll let you know as soon as possible. You're on the telephone, I suppose?'

'Yes, sir.'

'You'll bring Mr. Harburn to Edinburgh yourself.'

'Yes, sir.'

'But you'll not bring him in that rattletrap of yours.'

'No, sir.'

'Nor in an ambulance either. Mr. Harburn would dislike an ambulance and there's no need to upset him.'

'No, sir.'

'Can you beg, borrow or steal a reasonably comfortable motor car for the occasion?'

'Yes, sir.'

'What's the matter with you, Logan?' demanded Mr. MacTavish. 'Have you lost your wits? I'm tired of this "yes, sir" and "no, sir"! You can usually find something reasonable to say.'

'But you told me—' began Neil in astonishment.

'So I did! So I did! I told you to hold your tongue—I'd clean forgotten! I'm losing my memory, Logan. That's the only explanation. I'm going downhill fast. What I need is a young assistant to keep me up to the mark and I've got my eye on the very one. He's not taken his finals yet so I'll need to wait for him, but that can't be helped. I expect you know the man; Neil Logan, he's called.'

Neil stood and gaped. His mouth opened and shut but not a sound came out of it. His face went crimson to the roots of his hair. Julia saw that his eyes were swimming with tears.

Perhaps Mr. MacTavish saw it too, for he waved his hand and said, 'Away with you, lad! Go and have a look at the patient; he may need something done for him.'

Neil turned and blundered out of the room.

'Oh, Mr. MacTavish, you've made Neil terribly happy!' exclaimed Julia. She was surprised to discover that her eyes, too, were swimming with tears.

'I'm lucky to get him,' replied Mr. MacTavish seriously.

'I've had my eye on the lad for some time; he's the right stuff. There's a brilliant future before Neil Logan. It would be easy enough to get an experienced man, but I prefer to catch him young and train him in the way he should go.

'Well, now, Miss Harburn, I take it you're Mr. Harburn's nearest relative?'

'There's my father,' said Julia doubtfully. 'But he's abroad at the moment and anyhow I don't think—'

'You'll have to do,' Mr. MacTavish told her. 'There's no time to waste chasing your father all over the Continent. If you approve of the arrangements I suggested we'll just go ahead.'

'Yes, of course I approve. The only thing is . . .' She hesitated.

'Money, I suppose? Well, I dare say we could get a private ward at the Royal, but—'

'How much would it cost?' asked Julia, in a voice that was scarcely more than a whisper. 'You see I've got—I've got nearly seven hundred pounds in the bank. Perhaps I could borrow—I mean the bank let me borrow a little before, but—but it's different now. I mean I don't quite know—'

He took her hand and smiled, 'There's no need to worry. It'll not cost the half of seven hundred pounds.'

'But Mrs. Walker said . . . and Neil said . . .'

'It doesn't matter what anybody says—except what I say. Keep that in mind.'

She raised her eyes to his. 'Oh, of course I know *that*!' cried Julia.

Mr. MacTavish gave her hand a little squeeze. 'Lassie, I love you,' he declared, and away he went. She heard him go out of the front door and down the path with long strides. She heard the purr of the engine as he drove away . . . it was a very different sound from poor Neil's rattletrap.

But he couldn't have said that, thought Julia. He couldn't possibly; it must have been something else.

3

Julia was still standing in the middle of the room, wondering what it was that Mr. MacTavish had said—if he had not said what she thought he had said—when Neil came back.

'Where is he?' asked Neil. 'Good lord, he hasn't gone, has he?'

'He seemed to be in rather a hurry.'

'But—but I never told him! I never thanked him! I never even said I'd do it! Oh, what a fool I am! What a fool!' cried Neil and he wrung his hands—a gesture which Julia had never before seen actually performed in real life.

'Oh, Julia!' cried Neil. 'The prize of a lifetime offered to me on a plate . . . and I stood there gawping like a ninny!'

'Calm yourself, Neil.'

'Calm myself? How can I? Don't you realise what it would mean to be assistant to a man like that—to watch him at work—to be allowed to help him? I'd give anything—anything on earth—for the job.'

'Well, you've got it, haven't you?'

'What do you mean? I made a complete fool of myself. Even if he wanted me before, he doesn't want me now! I stood there opening and shutting my mouth like—like a cod-fish!'

'You were surprised, that's all.'

'Surprised?' cried Neil, throwing himself into a chair.

'Surprised? I was astonished, amazed, flabbergasted, utterly taken aback, dumbfounded. I could scarcely believe my ears. I couldn't have spoken a word to save my life.'

'Anyone could see that.'

'Do you think he realised it, Julia?'

'He understood perfectly.'

'How do you know?'

'Because I told him.'

'You told him? What did you say?'

'I said, "You've made Neil terribly happy."'

'Oh, Julia!' cried Neil, 'how marvellous of you! You couldn't have said anything better. If you'd thought for a hundred years you couldn't have found anything more perfect. I said you were an angel straight from heaven—and you are! Oh, Julia, I could kiss you!'

She laughed.

'What did he say?' demanded Neil. 'What did he say?'

'He said, "I'm lucky to get him."'

'He said that! Really and truthfully? Oh, heavens! Lucky to get me! Lucky—to—get—me! He could get anybody he liked—anybody! Oh, Julia!' cried Neil, in sudden alarm. 'Supposing I'm not a success? Supposing I can't do what he expects? Supposing I put my foot in it and do something silly?'

'Supposing you try not to talk so much?' suggested Julia, who was getting a little tired of Neil's hysterics. She did not wait for Neil's reaction but went out and shut the door.

4

Having dealt with Neil it was now necessary for Julia to pay a visit to Uncle Randal. She found him lying on his back gazing at the ceiling, but when Julia went over to the bed he looked up at her and smiled.

'I'm a bit tired,' he told her. 'That man put me through the hoop. He explored me, Julia. There's no other word for it. He explored every inch of my body. He can see with his hands.'

'I think I know what you mean,' said Julia thoughtfully.

'I said to him, "You can see right through me, can't you?" and he said, "There's not much of you to see through. What have they been giving you to eat?"'

'So you told him?'

Uncle Ran chuckled. 'There's to be no more steamed fish. He gave me a list of what I'm to eat and what I'm not to eat—it's there on the table—and I'm to get up and move about. I'm to get up to supper to-night and if it's fine and sunny to-morrow I'm to go out and sit in the garden for half an hour . . . and he wants those laurel bushes cut down—the ones at the window. He said if he'd the time to spare he'd cut them down himself and make a bonfire. Oh, he's a great man is Mr. MacTavish.'

Julia agreed wholeheartedly. He was great but he was not too great to concern himself with details . . . or perhaps it was part of his greatness that no detail escaped his eagle eye. The laurel bushes were already doomed, of course (Julia had sentenced them to extinction). Mr. MacTavish had merely hastened their end.

'Maybe you could get a man to cut down the laurel bushes,' said Uncle Randal anxiously. 'Mr. MacTavish was very keen on it.'

'Maybe,' said Julia teasingly. 'Maybe I could get a man to cut them down or maybe I could hire an elephant to tear them up by the roots or maybe I could borrow a saw and have a go at them myself.'

'Oh, Julia, you're an awful lassie for a joke!' exclaimed Uncle Randal, laughing heartily. 'I believe the elephant would be the best. I've seen them in Burma tearing up trees by the roots so if you could just hire one for half an hour he'd make short work of the laurels.'

'I'll ring up the Zoo,' said Julia, joining in the laughter; she took the diet-sheet and hurried away to consult Maggie about food, to tell her all the arrangements that had been made and to ask her to borrow a small saw from Mrs. Inglis's husband, who, being 'in the forestry,' was sure to have one handy. Julia was aware that it would be exceedingly difficult to get a man to cut down the laurel bushes and equally difficult to hire an elephant to tear them up, and she was determined that the laurel bushes should be removed that very night.

Chapter 32

1

Mr. MacTavish was not the man to let the grass grow under his feet. Everybody knew this, so nobody was surprised when all the arrangements he had suggested were completed in two days and Neil was informed of the fact. Neil was able to borrow a reasonably comfortable motor car from his friend the chemist in Leddiesford, and called at The Square House the following morning.

It had been decided that Maggie was to go with Uncle Randal to get him comfortably settled, so Julia saw the little party off at the gate and remained at home.

As Julia went in at the door she realised that there was a queer feeling in The Square House; it was empty. Of course she had known the house was empty, but she had never expected to feel this quite palpable and extremely eerie feeling. Several times, when Maggie had been out, Julia had been left alone in the house with Uncle Ran—Uncle Ran in bed and fast asleep—and the house had not felt empty. Julia decided that even if she had not known that Uncle Ran was not there in bed she would know for certain he was not there.

The clock was ticking much more loudly than usual; tick-tock, tick-tock, tick-tock. She stood and looked at it. She must remember to wind it on Sunday; Uncle Ran had shown her how to do it. It would be dreadful if she forgot—absolutely frightful. When Julia was a small child Ellen used to sing her an old old song, 'The clock stopped, never to go again, when . . .'

Julia decided not to think about that. No, it was a silly old song—nothing in it at all. She would just make a point of remembering to wind the clock on Sunday.

Fortunately there was plenty for Julia to do. She had decided to get the local painters to decorate Uncle Randal's bedroom; she had consulted Mr. Fleming and had found him extremely co-operative. He was coming himself and bringing a man with him, so they would soon get the old paper stripped off and the new paper hung. Julia had chosen a pale-grey paper with a faint white pattern which, with white paint and bright chintz curtains, would transform the dismal apartment into a very pleasant bedroom. They were coming in the afternoon, so Julia set to work to move the furniture into the middle of the room and cover it with dust-sheets.

The task was almost completed when the postman called.

'Mr. Harburn will be away to Edinburgh,' he said as he handed Julia the letters. 'Is it to-morrow that he's to have his operation?'

By this time Julia was quite used to everybody in Leddiesford knowing everything—and knowing it all slightly wrong—so she explained that Mr. Harburn had gone to Edinburgh 'for observation' and she was not yet certain whether an operation would be necessary.

'MacTavish will do it,' declared the postman with conviction. 'He's a great man for the knife. D'you know this, Miss Harburn, he cut out my cousin's wife's stomach and she was fine after it—just fine.'

He swung his bag onto his shoulder and went off cheerfully.

2

Three letters had come by the post; one for Uncle Randal and two for Julia herself. Hers were from May Martineau and Stephen. There was still no letter from her father; she had written to him twice and told him about Uncle Randal's illness but had had no reply. He was angry with her, that was evident. Well, she had known he would be angry, and anyhow she was very glad she had come.

Having made up her mind to this Julia went into the study and sat down to read her letters. She put Stephen's aside and opened May Martineau's first. May had covered six sheets of paper with her large sprawling writing, and as she had written without regard for punctuation—except for an occasional dash or a full stop—her letter was a little difficult to read. There was no date and no heading; the letter began at the very top of the first page.

Dear darling Julia,

Thank you so much for your letter. I was very interested to hear all your news. I have not got much time and I have a lot to tell you so I am writing this very quickly. I hope you will be able to read it all right. I am so sorry to hear about your uncle. Well of course you can't leave him and come home when he is so dreadfully ill—it would not be like you to do a thing like that so you will just have to stay till he is better but I hope that will be soon. About your room darling. I wish I could say I will just keep it empty but I can't unless you pay a little—what about half? I don't suppose you are paying your uncle so perhaps you could manage that. If not just say and I will let it temporarily and you can have it when you come home. You said you were writing to Jeanne but I thought there was no harm in me popping in to have a chat so that is what I did last night after supper and there she was in her workroom making a nonsense of a hat with a little bit of veiling and black velvet ribbon. It will cost her about 15s. and she will sell it to someone for goodness knows what. She really is clever isn't she darling—and she must be making a pot of money. Well she had just got your letter and was quite upset—said she missed you talking French and everything and she had been looking forward to Tuesday but you must do your duty as a Christian. She is an R.C. of course and they think a lot about being kind to people who are ill. Perhaps it would be a good thing if some of us thought more about it and went to see people and took them flowers and grapes. She said she would get someone temporarily and wait for you to come back when he is better. Well she couldn't say more could she? I could see she was *keen* for you to come back. Well I don't wonder Jeanne is fond of you. I am sorry you are away just now because Peta is here. She arrived quite suddenly on Monday night without letting me know. I said surely you could have sent a P.C. but she said not to fuss. She brought a young man—or at least he brought her in his car all the way from Newcastle so

178 | D.E. STEVENSON

I had to give him supper and a bed. Peta wanted him to have your room but I wouldn't let him because all your nice things are there and I had never seen him before. Peta said he was all right but she is apt to be a bit impulsive about people—either likes people straight off or can't bear the sight of them—Norman was like that too and got taken in more than once. Besides between you and me and the bedpost he seemed rather gone on Peta—I could tell by the sloppy way he looked at her when he thought I was not looking—so I would not have been happy with him upstairs on the top landing if you see what I mean. Of course Peta thinks she can look after herself like they all do nowadays but human nature is still human nature in spite of girls going about in trousers. She said I was a square so I said well darling I may be a square or a round or an oblong but if the little back room on the ground floor isn't good enough he better go and get a room at the Ritz. We had a little tiff but it soon blew over—all the sooner because she wanted to borrow a fiver. I miss you very much darling and the house seems very quiet—I don't mean you were noisy but it was nice having you to chat to at breakfast and supper. I have not had the parlour fire since you left except on Sunday when Miss Winkler came to tea. I told you about Miss Winkler and the dog-fight didn't I? Well there have been two dog-fights since you went away—such a barking and howling and snarling just outside the window as you never heard in your life. It is because the gentleman next door has a lady dog so they all come and sit outside the area gate when she is interesting. I always say you should send them to the vet especially in town. Perhaps I will just mention it to him in case he has not noticed. I sent on a letter to you two or three days ago. It was from Devonshire so I expect it was that nice young chap who took you out to dinner. I never can remember names but the one I said was like the Duke unless you know someone else in Devonshire of course. It was a very fat letter so I hope it was nice darling. I must stop now because Peta wants me to go out and help her choose a little frock. She is resting you see—if you can call it resting when she is on the go from morning to night but Peta never was one for a quiet life.

With much love dear darling Julia and please write soon if it is only a P.C. to say you are all right—and about the room.

Ever yours lovingly,

MAY

PS. Jeanne said you were a business woman and you made a lot of money with some shares. Perhaps that was the *secret*—but if that was the secret why did you tell Jeanne? Never mind darling I know lots of things about you that *she* doesn't know.

PPS. Peta says I better not speak to the gentleman next door about the dogs in case he is *coarse* so perhaps I better not. I don't suppose it will last much longer. What do you think about it? Be sure to write soon.

Although it could not be classed as first-rate in penmanship or erudition, May's letter possessed the most important characteristic of all letters, for it brought the writer clearly to the reader's mind. Julia decided she must write to May and tell her everything—everything that had happened. She must explain to May about 'the secret' and why she had mentioned it to 'Jeanne.' Poor May, the postscript showed she was a little hurt about it. That would never do! Julia reread the postscript more carefully and realised that May was very hurt indeed, so she must write at once . . . and she must tell May to pack up all the things she had left behind and let the room. Julia did not feel very happy about this; it had been a nice safe sort of feeling to know that she had a room in May's house to which she could return whenever she wanted, but it was not fair to May to keep it indefinitely . . . yes, the room must be let. Then Julia reread May's post-postscript—and giggled. So like May! So like dear May! In fact the whole letter was so like dear May that Julia could imagine herself sitting in May's parlour and listening to her chattering. She tried to imagine May here, sitting in Uncle Randal's study and chattering, but this flight of imagination was beyond her. May in Looking-Glass Country was unimaginable. May sitting in the kitchen talking to Maggie? No, no, no, they would hate each other! They would despise each other! It was a frightful thought.

Fortunately there was no chance of May coming to Looking-Glass Country, so there was no need to worry.

3

Julia was now ready to open Stephen's letter and enjoy it at her leisure:

> Gemscoombe,
> Devonshire

My dear Julia,

It was so nice getting your letter. I didn't open it at breakfast (I have breakfast with Father—Mother has hers in bed) but put it in my pocket and came out to a little shelf of rock in the cliff where I used to sit when I was a kid and read *Treasure Island* and *Westward Ho!* I'm sitting there now, answering your letter, with the waves lapping on the shore below and the seagulls soaring overhead and screaming and diving into the sea—so you must excuse rather an unconventional kind of letter, Julia. I was a bit disappointed when I saw how short it was—your letter, I mean—but when I read it I understood. I do feel so dreadfully sorry you are having such an anxious time; it is terrible when people we love are very ill. I remember when Mother was very ill and had to have a serious operation I nearly went mad with worry. I didn't realise that you were so fond of your uncle. As a matter of fact you never mentioned him to me; I'm sure you didn't, because I should have remembered; but I can see that he means a lot to you and I do hope and pray that the operation will be successful and he will make a good recovery. It is wonderful what a good surgeon can do nowadays and there are all sorts of new inventions like penicillin and oxygen and blood transfusions. I know about them because Mother had them when she was so desperately ill and they saved her life . . . and now, here she is, thank God, as fit as a fiddle!

So we must hope that all will go well with your Uncle Randal. I want you to know that I understand and am thinking about you, Julia—and hoping and praying and feeling sorry.

You ask in your letter whether Gemscoombe is so called because precious stones were found in the district, but I'm afraid the name has a less respectable derivation! Still it is interesting so I hasten to tell you that it is an abbreviation of Gentlemen's coombe. The 'Gentlemen' were smugglers of course. You remember Kipling's poem.

> *Five and twenty ponies*
> *Trotting through the dark—*
> *Brandy for the Parson,*
> *Baccy for the Clerk;*
> *Laces for a lady, letters for a spy,*
> *Watch the wall, my darling, while the Gentlemen go by!*

There are huge cellars underneath the house where the 'Gentlemen' stored their brandy until it could be taken away and distributed, and there is an underground passage leading from the cellars down to the cove—all very nice and convenient. Unfortunately the roof of the passage became unsafe and my grandfather had the door in the cellar blocked up with masonry. So now you know all about it. Last week I went up to London for a couple of nights to see our lawyer about some business and while I was there I called in at the British Museum and asked about sapphires. They had piles of books about precious stones so I found out quite a lot that I didn't know before. There was one very old book which gave the history of sapphires and all sorts of interesting stories about them. From the descriptions of the stone it seems obvious that our modern 'blue sapphire' is in reality the gem which the Ancients called the hyacinthus; there are fascinating legends about it—more than about any other precious stone. For instance the Ancients believed that the hyacinthus possessed magical properties and bestowed health, beauty, riches, honour, good fortune and healing powers upon its wearer. And an old writer called Solinus said, 'This is a gem that feels the influence of the air and sympathises with the heavens and does not shine equally if the sky be cloudy or bright.' I like that awfully—don't you? The early Christians valued it too and made it the symbol of St. Andrew and Heavenly Faith. I spent the whole morning taking copious notes and came home with my head full of blue, blue sapphires! Well, of course we don't believe in all those queer old superstitions—they are just fairy tales, aren't they?—so perhaps you will think I'm a bit crazy to send you the sapphire (which I'm doing by registered post). You can send it straight back if you don't want it or you can keep it as long as you like. I don't suppose you will want to keep it after you are married. I offered it to you before but that really *was* crazy—almost unpardonable, but fortunately not quite. You forgave me, didn't you? This time I'm offering it to you as a loan with no strings attached—absolutely no strings. Of course you don't believe it has magic properties but perhaps it will remind you that a friend is thinking about you. I hope so anyhow.

The tide is coming up so if I don't move quickly I shall have to swim ... besides I want this letter to catch the twelve o'clock post. The sapphire will follow when I can get it sealed up and registered.

YOURS EVER,

STEPHEN

Julia was smiling as she finished reading Stephen's letter, but her eyes were soft and shiny. It was such a nice kind comforting letter; he really was a dear and it was lovely of him to think of sending her the sapphire—yes it was lovely. She remembered how beautiful it was. Of course she would not 'send it straight back,' she would keep it for a while. (She was not going to be married, but Stephen did not know that.) She would keep it safely until—well, until Uncle Ran was better. Of course all those old superstitions were fairy tales, as Stephen had said, but all the same. . . . And anyhow, thought Julia, it would be comforting to have something so beautiful to remind her that a friend was thinking about her—and praying—and feeling sorry.

Julia read the letter again. In fact she read it several times and every time she read it she liked it better. It was an unconventional kind of letter—as Stephen had said—but that made it all the nicer. It was full of Stephen's personality; she could almost hear Stephen's unusually deep voice talking to her; she could imagine him sitting on the shore and the seagulls soaring and diving. Some day when Uncle Ran was better, Julia decided, she must accept Mrs. Brett's invitation and go to Gemscoombe—it sounded such a lovely place.

CHAPTER 33

1

THE day passed remarkably quickly. Maggie returned at tea-time full of praises for the Westchester Home and for the comfortable quiet room and the 'wise-like nurse' that had been allotted to Uncle Randal. She was somewhat worried about the expense of these amenities, but Julia was able to reassure her by explaining that she had arranged all that with Mr. MacTavish.

'Do you mean you're paying yourself, Miss Julia?' asked Maggie in astonishment.

'Yes, I've got enough in the bank—it's all arranged,' replied Julia confidently.

The next morning Julia had her breakfast in bed as usual and then went downstairs to dust 'the room' (the little task had become part of her daily routine). She chatted to Maggie and to the painters, who already were working busily in Uncle Ran's bedroom, and went out to do the shopping.

A great many people in the town asked anxiously about Mr. Harburn; everybody seemed to know he had gone to Edinburgh to have an operation. It was obvious that Mr. Harburn was well known and well liked in the little town, not only because of his own delightful personality but also because the Harburn family had been closely associated with Leddiesford for hundreds of years.

Mrs. Brown in the dairy explained this by saying, 'Well, ye see, Miss Julia, the Harburns are oor ain folk—that's the way of it. There was mony a sair hairt in Leddiesford when the big hoose was sold to the London gentleman, but that's what happens nowadays. It was too big for Mr. Randal to live in, himself; it would have been different altogether if he'd been married.' She wrapped up the butter and put it into Julia's basket.

'Mind you it's a pity,' she added. 'It's an awful pity his marriage never came off.'

Strangely enough the idea that Uncle Randal might have married had never occurred to Julia, but now she began to think about it. He was so attractive, so interesting and so kind, and he must have been very good-looking when he was young. Why had he never married? Julia thought about what Mrs. Brown had said; it almost sounded as if he had been engaged to be married and the engagement had been broken off . . . but perhaps Mrs. Brown had not meant that; perhaps it was just her way of putting it. Julia still found Looking-Glass language puzzling at times.

2

When Julia got home there was a small parcel, heavily sealed and registered, lying upon the hall table. How quickly it had come! She pounced upon it in delight and ran upstairs to her bedroom so that she could open it in private.

The parcel had been so securely fastened that it was quite difficult to open. Inside the brown paper covering was a white box and inside the white box was the little chamois-leather bag which had been made by Mrs. Brett. Julia untied the string and the sapphire rolled out onto her dressing-table and lay there, glowing in the noonday sunshine.

How beautiful it was! It was even more beautiful than she remembered—it was even more like 'a blue red-hot coal'—but perhaps that was because she had seen it before by lamplight and now it was in the sunshine. 'This is a gem that feels the influence of the air and sympathises with the heavens and does not shine equally if the sky be cloudy or bright.' It was shining now with a soft velvety sheen—cornflower blue—quite, quite beautiful!

For some time Julia gazed at it, marvelling that any stone could be so exquisite . . . a tiny thing, not much larger than a good-sized pea, but somehow complete in itself and containing its own glowing light. Would it shine in the dark, she wondered. She felt sure that it would shine in the dark.

The dinner bell roused Julia from her enchantment. She put the sapphire back in the little bag; she found a black ribbon, and fixing it firmly to the string of the bag, tied it round her neck. Fortunately the ribbon was exactly the right length, so the little bag fitted very comfortably underneath her clothes. Indeed there was a little hollow which might have been specially designed for a sapphire in a little chamois bag.

It will be safe there, thought Julia. It's very valuable, of course, so I must take the greatest care of it.

Having made sure it was perfectly safe and completely invisible Julia went downstairs to have her lunch.

CHAPTER 34

IT HAD been arranged that Julia should visit Uncle Randal in the afternoon, so she went up to Edinburgh in the bus and found her way to the Westchester Nursing Home. She was surprised when she was shown into his room and found he had a visitor. A tall thin man with grey hair and grey eyes was sitting beside his bed.

'Come in, come in, my dear!' exclaimed Uncle Randal when he saw her hesitating at the door. 'I'm glad you came just now. This is a very old friend of mine, Henry Baird. I wanted you to meet him.'

Mr. Baird rose and shook hands with Julia; she was aware of the grey eyes looking at her with keen interest.

Julia liked him (in a way he resembled Uncle Randal, so she was not surprised to hear they were friends), but all the same she hoped he would go away soon, for she wanted a private chat with Uncle Ran. There were all sorts of things she wanted to ask him: whether he was being well looked after; whether he had slept well; whether he liked his 'special nurse.' The room seemed comfortable, bright and airy and well furnished.

'If there's anything I can do for you while your uncle is laid up you have only to let me know,' said Mr. Baird.

'Oh, thank you,' replied Julia, politely.

'Yes, just ask him,' said Uncle Randal. 'He'll give you whatever you want.'

Julia was glad to see that Mr. Baird was gathering up some papers which had been lying on the bed and putting them away in a brown leather brief-case.

'You know all about everything, don't you, Henry?' asked Uncle Randal, anxiously.

'Yes, yes, it's perfectly simple and straightforward. I'll get it done immediately.' He said good-bye and went away.

'He's one of the best,' declared Uncle Randal. 'We were friends when we were boys. The Bairds had a fine place not far from Leddiesford, so we saw a lot of each other in the old days.'

'How are you getting on?' asked Julia anxiously. 'Are you quite comfortable here?'

'Very comfortable indeed.'

'Have you got a nice nurse?'

Uncle Ran chuckled. 'You mustn't call her a nurse; she's a sister. Sister Don is her name. She looks after me like a baby. She's a bit strict—I'm not allowed to do this and I'm not allowed to do that—but we're getting to know each other. Now, sit down, my dear, and tell me all the news. I feel as though I'd been away from home for weeks.'

Julia smiled. He had left home only yesterday, so there was not much to tell him except that everybody had been making kind inquiries about him.

'That's good of them.'

'Mrs. Brown asked for you. She talked about you a lot.'

'She would,' nodded Uncle Randal. 'She's a gas-bag. What did she say about me?'

'Well, for one thing, she said it was a pity you had never married.'

'Did she? As a matter of fact Mary Brown knows well enough why I never married.' He hesitated, and then continued, 'I've been wondering whether or not I should tell you, Julia. At first I decided not . . . but now that you're staying on in Leddiesford and chatting to people I think it might be as well for you to hear the true story in case you hear a garbled version of it from somebody else. The reason I never married is because there was only one woman I wanted. It was your mother, my dear.'

'Mother!' exclaimed Julia in astonishment.

'Yes, Anne Chesterfield. I met her when I was staying with some friends at Bristol and we fell in love with each other. Anne was a good deal younger than I, but she had had a sad life and in some ways she was older than her years, so it didn't seem to matter. She was an orphan— she had no relatives at all—so my parents suggested that the wedding should take place in Leddiesford. My mother was particularly anxious to have the reception at Harburn House, because she enjoyed weddings and she had no daughter, so it was all arranged.'

'It was all arranged!' echoed Julia. 'Uncle Ran, you don't mean—'

'Yes, my dear, it was all arranged and everybody was pleased. Anne came to stay at Harburn House and my parents loved her—as I knew they would. I introduced her to all my friends and received their congratulations. Everybody in Leddiesford was delighted at the prospect of a marriage at Harburn House. One old woman told me there had not been a marriage at Harburn House for eighty years. I was very happy; there was no cloud in my sky.'

'Uncle Ran!' exclaimed Julia in alarm. 'What—'

'My dear, you had better let me finish,' he told her. 'Now that I've started, you had better hear the whole story. Well, it so happened that Andrew was not at home at the time. He was studying English law at London University and had the promise of being taken into a well-known firm. But he came up to Leddiesford for his holiday, and the arrival of Andrew made my happiness complete. Andrew and I were devoted to each other. He is eight years younger than I am; I can remember the day he was born; I can remember him as a small child running after me and wanting to help me with whatever I happened to be doing; I can remember him as a schoolboy, captain of the rugger fifteen. Then, when he grew up, he was a fine fellow and I was proud of him. He was full of fun and gaiety. There was never a dull moment when Andrew was there. My father was proud of him too, he was a son to be proud of. My mother adored him.

'Well, Andrew came up to Harburn House for his holiday—as I told you—and he and Anne took to each other at once. Of course I was delighted when I saw them getting on so well . . . the two people I loved best in all the world! Naturally I wanted them to be friends. You can understand that, can't you?'

Julia gazed at him in dismay. 'What happened?'

He sighed. 'Nothing much happened. I never suspected anything; they never said a word to anybody. They just went away.'

'Went away!'

'They just got into Andrew's car and drove away. They went to London. Andrew wrote to me and said that he and Anne had discovered they loved each other, so to save any trouble they had been married by special licence. Those were his very words, Julia: "To save any trouble."

'I should have left it at that,' he continued sadly. 'I ought to have accepted the fact and made the best of it. I ought to have realised that it was natural for those two young creatures to fall in love with each other. To tell the truth I believe I could have accepted it if Andrew had come to me bravely and told me what had happened . . . at any rate I would not have minded so much. It was the way Andrew did it that made me so angry; it was mean and cowardly—that's what I felt. I was almost demented with rage and grief, all the more so because I loved them. It's a terrible thing to be angry with somebody you love; I hope you'll never know what that's like, Julia.'

He paused and looked at her and she shook her head. She could not speak.

'So I went to London,' he continued. 'I saw Andrew and we had a blazing row. We both said things that should never have been said—dreadful things. Well, I've lived to regret my foolish words; I regret them deeply and sincerely; I would give a lot if I could go back and wash out my part in that terrible quarrel. I've done my best to make amends. I've written to Andrew several times and begged him to let bygones be bygones, but he has taken no notice of my letters.'

'Oh, why did they do it!' Julia exclaimed.

'Why did they do it? They were in love, Julia. Have you never been in love? Have you never felt that the world was well lost for love? No, I can see you've never felt that.'

Julia could not reply. She had believed herself to be in love with Morland, but it certainly had not been the overmastering passion for the sake of which one was willing to give up everything in the world.

'They were in love,' repeated Uncle Randal. 'They gave up everything for love. I hope they were happy. I couldn't say that at the time, but I can say it now. They were happy together, weren't they, Julia?'

'Yes, of course,' she replied, but without much conviction: for to tell the truth she had never considered the matter before, and now that she was forced to consider it she felt increasingly doubtful about it. The happiest times had been when she and her mother escaped from Manor Gardens and went abroad together. However, it was no use saying that to Uncle Ran.

Julia changed the subject. 'What did you do?' she asked.

'It must have been difficult for you to come home.'

'It was much too difficult. I went abroad and wandered about the world. You see, I wanted to escape from everybody. I couldn't face my friends; I couldn't bear their sympathy. That was wrong, too,' he declared, shaking his head. 'I should have been here with my parents. They had to bear it. I left them to bear it alone. My mother was quite ill with distress; my father was furious. He had always been proud of his name and lineage, he had enjoyed the respect and affection of the people in Leddiesford; he felt that Andrew had disgraced him. In one of his letters to me he said, "My son has made me ashamed to walk down the street and meet my neighbours. I have written and told him so."'

'How dreadful!' Julia exclaimed.

'Yes, poor Andrew! I can see now what a bitter pill that must have been. He had always been his father's pride and joy.'

'Oh, Uncle Ran, I don't know what to say!'

'There's nothing to say,' he replied. 'You mustn't worry about it, my dear. It's an old, old story; it all happened long before you were born and it has nothing to do with you . . . but you can see why Andrew is so angry with me, can't you? You can see why he's so angry with you. I expect he feels you've deserted him and gone over to the enemy.'

'I haven't deserted him, Uncle Ran. He doesn't want me.'

'Doesn't want you?'

'Father never wanted me,' said Julia in a low voice. 'He wanted a son, so I was a disappointment from the very beginning.

He wasn't unkind to me—you mustn't think that—but he just wasn't interested in me. He scarcely ever spoke to me.'

'I can't believe it!'

'It's true—honestly. I tried hard to—to be friends with him, but it was no good. He just wasn't interested.'

'It doesn't sound like Andrew.'

'I know,' she agreed thoughtfully. 'I mean you've told me a lot about "Andrew" but it doesn't sound like Father at all. He must have changed. People do change, don't they?'

'Don't grieve about it, Julia. Don't think about it too much. Maybe I shouldn't have told you, but all the older folk in Leddiesford remember what happened so you were bound to hear the story sooner or later and it seemed better that you should know the truth.'

'I'm glad you told me. It explains a lot of things that have been puzzling me . . . things that I couldn't understand.'

'What things?'

'There was a picture of Harburn House in the attic,' said Julia in a voice that was little more than a whisper. 'Uncle Ran, he tore it up.'

'Poor Andrew,' said Uncle Randal sadly. 'Well, well, don't let's talk about it any more.'

CHAPTER 35

1

UNCLE Randal was in the home for several days undergoing various tests and examinations, and Julia went to Edinburgh to see him every afternoon. He was peaceful and cheerful and very comfortable, Sister Don looked after him well. To Julia she seemed alarming, tall and angular with very bright brown eyes, but Uncle Randal liked her.

On the fourth day Neil came to supper at The Square House and Maggie gave them salmon and green peas. This was very different from Maggie's usual frugal catering, but on making inquiries Julia was informed that a fine salmon had been caught in the river by Mrs. Inglis's cousin and three nice steaks had been delivered at The Square House that morning 'with Mrs. Inglis's cousin's compliments and he hopes Mr. Harburn is keeping better.' The peas had been sent by Mrs. Dow, who lived opposite and kept lodgers.

Julia was touched at this kindness on the part of her neighbours and said so to Neil.

'Yes, they're a decent lot,' agreed Neil, as he tucked into the delicious food with enjoyment. 'And of course they all love Uncle Ran. What have you been doing with yourself, Julia?'

'Reading and writing letters, working in the garden and talking to Maggie.'

'Uncle Ran is afraid you may be worrying about what he told you. I mean about the feud and all that. Of course I've known about it for ages but it wasn't my business to tell you.' Neil smiled and added, 'I've often wanted to talk to you about it because it's so interesting.'

'Interesting? What do you mean?'

'Here are two brothers,' explained Neil. 'Andrew steals Randal's bride, and makes off with her like young Lochinvar, and twenty years later Randal steals Andrew's daughter.'

'It's horrid to say that!' cried Julia. 'Nobody has stolen me—nobody could! I belong to myself. I'm here because Uncle Ran needs me.'

'I know, I know,' agreed Neil in soothing tones. 'I didn't mean it in a horrid way. Of course you belong to yourself; you're quite a different kind of person from your mother.'

'Uncle Ran said I was like her.'

'You may be like her to look at,' said Neil . . . and left it at that.

There was silence for a few moments. Julia had been very fond of her mother and would have liked to defend her, but what could she say? Hitherto Julia had blamed her father for what had happened (he had behaved even more badly than young Lochinvar, for it was his own brother's bride he had stolen); everyone seemed to blame him, and him alone; yet Julia realised that this was unfair.

'I can't understand it,' she said at last with a heavy sigh. 'It was a dreadful thing to do. They must have been mad—both of them.'

'He was frightfully attractive—everybody says so,' Neil reminded her. 'And of course he was used to having his own way. Old Mrs. Hepburn told me that Andrew was thoroughly spoilt. She said, "Andrew was everybody's darling."'

'Then—afterwards,' said Julia thoughtfully. 'Afterwards people in Leddiesford were angry with him.'

'Furious with him. Everybody knew about it—all his friends—everybody! He could never go back to Leddiesford; he was an outcast.'

'But he must have known that would happen!'

'I wonder,' said Neil. 'Perhaps he thought he could do what he liked and get away with it because he was "everybody's darling."'

2

They had finished supper by this time, so they went into the study, and in spite of the fact that it was a lovely fine evening Maggie had lighted the fire. (For in this respect—but in no other—Maggie resembled May Martineau and was of the opinion that a nice fire was conducive to a comfortable chat.)

'There are other things that puzzle me,' said Julia as they sat down together. 'For instance, it seems so queer that Father is the one who is unwilling to make up the quarrel. It was Uncle Ran who was the injured party.'

'It isn't queer at all,' replied Neil without hesitation. 'Surely you realise that it's much harder to forgive somebody you've injured than somebody who has injured you. Besides, the two brothers were quite different. Randal was a fine character, so he was able to get over it; Andrew was spoilt by too much admiration.'

'That's another thing that puzzles me,' Julia declared. 'I mean Uncle Ran told me a lot about "Andrew"—all about how gay and cheerful he was—and you say he was "everybody's darling." He isn't like that now. He's miserable.'

'Miserable?'

'Yes, he's silent and moody. He wraps himself up in a big brown blanket. . . . Sometimes he doesn't hear what you say to him.'

'A big brown blanket,' said Neil thoughtfully. 'I know what you mean. That's really an illness.'

'An illness?'

'A sickness of the brain. It's not surprising under the circumstances . . . in fact it's just what I would expect to happen to a man like that.'

'What could have changed him?'

'The quarrel, of course. You know, Julia, they did things much more sensibly in the old days. When two men quarrelled they went for each other with swords.'

'You mean duels! But that was terribly wicked!' cried Julia.

'Not at all. It was much better than going for each other with words—much healthier.'

'But Neil, they killed each other!'

'Not always . . . in fact not often,' said Neil cheerfully. 'They just wounded each other and the blood flowed. There's nothing like blood-letting to calm over-heated tempers. After that, honour was satisfied and they went their ways in peace. That's what would have happened if your father and Uncle Ran had lived two hundred years ago . . . and it would have been better for both of them. As it was they belaboured each other with words and wounded each other inwardly. Wounds like that are very unhealthy indeed. They fester.'

Julia was silent. Of course Neil was talking nonsense, but all the same she saw what he meant.

'Your father ought to consult a psychiatrist,' said Neil.

'He wouldn't dream of doing such a thing!'

'That's what he ought to do. A psychiatrist would get to the bottom of the trouble. I expect it's a feeling of guilt and resentment—in fact I'm sure it is. You may not know it, Julia, but it's a well-known fact that a feeling of guilt can react upon the body or the mind and make a person physically ill.'

'I see,' said Julia thoughtfully. 'Yes, it might be that.'

'I'm sure it's that,' declared Neil. 'I remember reading about the case of a woman who had been paralysed for years by a subconscious feeling of guilt. When the cause of her trouble was discovered and removed she recovered and—'

'Oh, of course!' cried Julia. 'Like the man at Capernaum whose friends let him down through the roof!'

'Let him down through the roof? What happened?' asked Neil eagerly.

Julia was surprised that he had forgotten the story; she was about to remind him of it when the door opened and Maggie came in.

CHAPTER 36

MAGGIE's entrance put a stop to the conversation. Julia was quite pleased to see her, for to tell the truth she had had enough. It was exhausting to talk to Neil for long and he had given her plenty to think about. Neil felt differently; he was very much annoyed at the interruption.

'What on earth do you want, Maggie?' he exclaimed. 'Can't you see we're talking?'

'The only time you're not talking is when you're sleeping,' retorted Maggie, smiling good-humouredly. 'I wouldna have bothered you, but there's a letter come for Miss Julia and I thought it might be important. The lad from the Black Bull brought it. I said he was to wait till I saw if there was an answer but he was away off down the road like a scalded cat. It's yon football,' she added scornfully, as she went out and shut the door.

Julia had taken the letter and was holding it in her hand unopened, gazing at it in dismay.

'Why don't you open it?' asked Neil.

She did not reply. She was afraid to open it. The address: 'Miss Julia Harburn, The Square House' was written in Morland's handwriting. Morland! Morland here at Leddiesford! Morland at the Black Bull—of all places!

Neil was getting impatient. 'Why don't you open it?' he repeated. 'What's the good of sitting there and staring at it like that! Who is it from?'

'From—Morland,' said Julia with a little gasp. 'Neil, it means he's here, at the Black Bull! What can he be doing at the Black Bull?'

'If you open it you'll see. It's that fellow you were engaged to, I suppose?'

'Yes . . . but why has he come to Leddiesford?'

'For pity's sake open the letter! If you can't open it yourself give it to me and I'll open it.' He held out his hand and repeated, 'Give it to me.'

This was out of the question, of course, so Julia was obliged to open it herself.

> The Black Bull,
> Leddiesford

My dear Julia,

    You will be surprised to hear that I am at Leddiesford. The reason for my coming all this distance is twofold: namely to give you a message from your father and to have a talk with you about our own affairs. I have very good news for you.

My intention was to call upon you at your uncle's house but, on second thoughts, I decided to write to you as I fear your uncle may be prejudiced against me and I am doubtful of my reception. Perhaps you will be good enough to name an hour at which it will be convenient for you to see me.

Yesterday I called upon your father at his office. He and Retta have returned from their cruise and are now in residence at Manor Gardens. I found him very much distressed at your sudden and ill-considered departure to Scotland—you will remember I warned you that he would be displeased—but he is willing to forgive you and let bygones be bygones if you return at once. I am sure you will agree that this shows a very forgiving spirit on his part.

We had a long talk. Your father asked me to go to Leddiesford and persuade you to come home and, although it was inconvenient for me to leave Town, I considered it my duty to accede to his request.

I have found a youth who is willing to deliver my letter and await a reply. It is unnecessary for you to remunerate him for his trouble as I have already done so.

This inn is exceedingly uncomfortable and dirty—I had no idea that such an uncivilised hostelry could exist in modern times—but fortunately I need not stay here long.

With all good wishes, believe me, my dear Julia.

Yours sincerely,

MORLAND BEVERLEY

Julia read the letter twice, then she raised her eyes and looked at Neil.

'What am I to do!' she exclaimed. 'Oh, Neil, what *am* I to do? He wants to see me!'

'Well, of course he wants to see you! You don't suppose he came all the way from London for the pleasure of staying at the Black Bull? What else does he say? Here, give me the letter!'

Julia hesitated, but not for long; she was aware that Neil would give her no peace until he knew all about it, so he might as well read the letter himself.

Neil took it from her half-reluctant hand and read it. 'Great Scott!' he exclaimed. 'What an extraordinary letter! Does he talk like that?'

'Like what?'

"'I considered it my duty to accede to his request,'" quoted Neil. "'It is unnecessary for you to remunerate him for his trouble.'"

'No, of course he doesn't talk like that,' said Julia indignantly. 'He writes like that because he's used to writing business letters.'

'But this isn't a business letter.'

'Besides, I expect—I mean you can see he's feeling rather embarrassed,' added Julia.

'Yes, that's true,' agreed Neil, who was always willing to consider other people's difficulties. 'I can see it's a bit embarrassing for him, and of course the Black Bull is all he says—and more. He ought to have gone to the Harburn Arms, which is very comfortable indeed. I expect they told him at the station to go to the Black Bull. The ticket collector is Rab's brother-in-law.'

'Rab?'

'Rab Sinclair, the innkeeper, of course. Come on, Julia,' added Neil rising to his feet. 'We'd better get moving.'

'Get moving?'

'To the Black Bull, of course.'

'Go to the Black Bull!' cried Julia in horrified tones. 'But Neil, I don't want to—'

'You'll have to see him.'

'Not now!'

'Yes, now; this minute,' said Neil cheerfully. 'Come on and get it over. If there's something unpleasant to be done it's better to do it at once, whether it's getting a tooth out or facing a difficult interview. You can't possibly refuse to see the fellow when he's come all the way from London.'

'I could see him to-morrow.'

'No, to-night. You won't sleep a wink if you don't get it over to-night.'

This was so true that she made no attempt to deny it. She rose reluctantly and went to put on her outdoor shoes.

2

When Julia came downstairs Neil was waiting for her in the hall.

'I've spoken to Maggie,' he said in muted tones. 'I told her we were going for a walk and might be a bit late. There's no need for her to know anything about it. Here's the latch-key; you can put it in your pocket. Come on, Julia!'

'But you aren't coming, Neil!'

'That's where you're wrong, my girl! We're cousins, aren't we? Besides, I'm not going to let you out of my sight. It wouldn't be safe.'

'Wouldn't be safe?'

'Well, you never know,' explained Neil, putting his arm through hers as they walked along together. 'If the man is such a desperate character he might abduct you and carry you off to London. We can't risk that.'

In spite of her distress Julia could not help smiling at the idea of Morland as a desperate character, at the idea of Morland abducting her! Morland who, even when they were engaged to be married, considered it unseemly to walk with her arm in arm (as Neil, though not engaged to her, nor ever likely to be, was walking with her now).

'But seriously, Julia,' said Neil, giving her arm a little squeeze. 'Seriously, you're not going back with him, are you? I mean it's so frightfully important for you to be here because of Uncle Ran. You realise that, don't you? If he has this operation it will be touch and go. Mr. MacTavish says quite frankly that there's only a fifty-fifty chance of his pulling through.'

'A fifty-fifty chance! Oh, Neil, perhaps we shouldn't—'

'If he doesn't have the operation he'll die,' declared Neil in a hard, strained voice. 'You know that yourself. Maggie knows it too.'

They walked on in silence.

'I don't want to go,' said Julia at last. 'I was frightfully unhappy at home—I told you that, didn't I?—but I was just wondering whether I ought to go and try to persuade Father to make up that dreadful quarrel. I don't know whether I could persuade him, but perhaps I ought to try.'

'You mustn't go,' declared Neil with conviction. 'If Uncle Ran was all right I'd say yes, go and do what you can—but he's very ill and he needs you.'

'Really and truly needs me?'

'Yes. Your being here might just tip the scales in his favour. He's terribly fond of you . . . but you don't need me to tell you that.'

'I'm terribly fond of him.'

'Well, that's settled, then,' said Neil with a sigh of relief.

Now that it was settled they walked on more quickly and conversed about other matters. Neil did most of the talking, as he always did, and his talk was cheerful and enlivening. It was impossible to feel gloomy when Neil was in an entertaining mood, and Julia's spirits rose accordingly.

They walked down the hill and through the outskirts of the little town, and presently arrived at the bridge and the inn which was situated on the bank of the river.

'Here we are,' said Neil. 'Allow me to introduce you to the Black Bull, the historic hostelry where Jamie the Saxth is said to have broken his journey on his way to London to get his crown. Much more likely to have broken his crown on one of the oaken beams in the ceiling.'

'I don't know what you're talking about,' declared Julia in bewilderment. 'Who is Jimmy the Sacks?'

(Julia had become acquainted with Bill the Fish and Tom the Milk and others of their kidney, who rushed about madly on bicycles all over Leddiesford delivering their wares and occasionally were to be met with in Maggie's kitchen enjoying a 'fly-cup' and discussing the latest gossip, but Jimmy the Sacks was a new one on her.)

'Lassie, lassie!' exclaimed Neil in dolorous accents. 'Did they niver lairn ye hist'ry at skulh?'

At any other time Julia would have laughed, as she always did at Neil's Doric, but they were now actually standing outside the door of the historic hostelry and the approaching ordeal was so heavy on her mind that she could think of nothing else.

'You aren't coming in, are you?' she asked in sudden alarm; for although it would be bad enough to face Morland alone, it would be twenty times worse if Neil intended to be present at the interview.

'No, no, of course not,' said Neil. 'I might lose my wool and hit him on the head; but I won't be far off, so just scream if you want help. I'll nip into the bar and wait for you. Don't be too long,' he added. 'Beer doesn't suit my constitution and I can't afford whisky.'

Julia was aware that all this nonsense was designed to encourage her, but it encouraged her none the less. She was almost smiling when she pushed open the shabby, ill-fitting door of the inn.

CHAPTER 37

1

THE front door of the Black Bull opened straight into the lounge, a large room with black oak beams across the ceiling. It had once been the taproom where stage-coach passengers refreshed themselves before proceeding on their journey, and in those bygone days it was probably a cheerful place with a sanded floor, noisy with the sound of voices and laughter and the clink of tankards on the wooden tables; now it was a dismal apartment, dingy and badly ventilated, furnished with small rickety tables and uncomfortable chairs. Outside in the street it was still daylight, but the ceiling was low and the windows were small and dirty. The room was dark except for one small lamp on the table in the farthest corner, where a man was sitting reading a newspaper.

At first Julia was not sure whether or not the solitary man was Morland, but when she approached she saw that it was.

'Hallo, Morland!' she said; and was annoyed to find that her voice was trembling.

'Julia!' he exclaimed in astonishment, dropping the paper and rising to meet her. 'Julia! I didn't expect to see you to-night!'

'I thought I'd just—come,' she explained. 'I thought it was better to—to—' (She had been about to say 'get it over,' but that seemed unnecessarily rude.)

'Yes, of course,' he agreed. 'Much better to come. I don't suppose your uncle would want to see me. That's why I wrote. This is a frightful place, but everyone seems to sit in the bar, so we can talk here comfortably in private.'

In private perhaps, thought Julia, but not comfortably. Morland seemed just as uncomfortable as herself.

'Would you like tea or—or something?' he asked as they sat down. 'I don't suppose they've got sherry. There's plenty of whisky, of course— it's the only decent thing in this ghastly hole—but I don't suppose you would care for that?'

'Nothing, thank you. I mustn't stay more than a few minutes. I just came to tell you that I can't go home at present because my uncle is very ill indeed and may have to have a serious operation. I couldn't possibly go away and leave him.'

'Your father wants you to come home immediately.'

'But he doesn't understand. I must stay with Uncle Randal until he's better.'

'You can't do that,' declared Morland. 'It's your duty to obey your father and come home at once.'

'It's my duty to stay here until Uncle Randal is better. It is, really. You see he sort of depends on me; he hasn't got anyone else belonging to him. Perhaps you could explain that to Father. I've written and told him about it, but perhaps he doesn't understand. If you could explain—'

Morland was leaning forward in his chair. 'Listen, Julia,' he said eagerly. 'This is what I want to tell you; I said I had good news for you, didn't I? Well, I've been given the partnership. Isn't that splendid? We can be married quite soon.'

'Married!'

'Yes. I told your father yesterday—it was one of the matters we discussed. When I told him about the partnership he was delighted. He talked about very generous marriage settlements, and agreed that we should be married as soon as possible. He said—'

'Morland!' cried Julia. 'I don't know what you mean! Our engagement was broken off.'

'We had a little misunderstanding, but that was nothing. People often have misunderstandings, don't they? We both got rather heated and said things we didn't mean . . . but that's all over now. It's stupid to quarrel, isn't it? Look, Julia, here's your ring. Let's make it up and be friends.'

'Oh no!' she cried. 'No, I couldn't! I mean of course I'm willing to be friends—nobody hates quarrelling more than I do—but I couldn't marry you. I couldn't possibly!'

'You couldn't marry me?' asked Morland incredulously.

'I couldn't! I couldn't bear it!'

'Julia, what do you mean? We were engaged for months.'

'Our engagement was broken off.'

'It was just a misunderstanding.'

'It was more than that.'

'It was a misunderstanding,' repeated Morland. 'I was annoyed because you wouldn't listen to my advice. I should have been more patient—I see that now. You had just got the letter from your uncle and you were upset to hear he was so ill; you were sorry for him—that was natural. You didn't understand that it would offend your father if you came to Leddiesford without his permission; you didn't realise what you were doing. I should have explained it to you carefully; I should have been more patient . . . but it's all over now, isn't it? You'll come home and your father will forgive you and we can be married quite soon. We love each other—that's all that matters. I've got the partnership so we needn't wait any longer. Everything is all right now.'

Julia listened in dismay. Poor Morland, she had not expected this . . . never for a moment!

Oh, poor Morland! It was so strange to see him in these dismal surroundings; it was so strange to see him here that she could scarcely believe he was real. There he sat in his immaculate brown-worsted lounge-suit, his trousers creased and pulled up a little showing the crimson silk socks which exactly matched the crimson silk tie. He looked as if he ought to be walking down Regent Street instead of sitting in the Black Bull Inn in Looking-Glass Country, where everything was the other way round.

The puzzling thing was that he had been part of Julia's life for so long and she knew him so well! Yet now she felt as if she were seeing him for the first time. She knew every cadence of his voice; every gesture was familiar to her; she could smell the faint scent of the soap he always used for shaving. Why, even that suit he was wearing! She had been with him when he chose the material and had waited for him while he went away with the tailor—a short red-faced man with a tape-measure round his neck—to be measured.

All this passed through Julia's mind as she listened to him saying over and over again that it was all a mistake, it was just a misunderstanding and he should have been more patient; saying that they loved each other and there was no need to wait any longer, they could be married quite soon; saying that they would look for a nice flat; his mother had promised to help them to find one. . . .

Oh, poor Morland! Julia had never felt so sorry for anyone before.

'No, Morland, I'm frightfully sorry,' said Julia. She said it several times. She said it whenever he paused for breath. 'I'm frightfully sorry, Morland. I had no idea that you felt like this. No, Morland, I can't marry you—really I can't.'

'But we love each other!'

'No, really. It isn't any use.'

'You've changed, Julia.'

'No, I don't think so.'

'What do you mean? We were engaged for months! We were everything to each other!'

'I don't think I ever loved you. I thought I did, of course, but—'

'Of course you loved me!'

'No, Morland,' said Julia desperately.

'You did love me! I know you did! You've changed.'

'No, I haven't changed. I like you very much but—but I don't love you. It was all a mistake. I knew that, when you said there was no prospect of happiness for us—'

'But I didn't mean that!' he exclaimed. 'I didn't mean we shouldn't be married. I was never so surprised in my life as I was when you held out the ring and told me to take it. I didn't mean that at all. I only meant—'

'But I did,' she declared. 'I saw then that you were right; there was no prospect of happiness for us in marriage. There isn't *really*, Morland. I'm not the sort of wife you want.'

'Surely I'm the best judge of that!'

'No, honestly. You want someone who will always do exactly as you say. I couldn't do that. I couldn't really. I'm not that kind of person.'

He was silent for a few moments and then he said angrily, 'There's only one explanation, of course. You've met someone else.'

Julia hesitated. She had been wondering how to break off this frightful conversation. Could she tell a lie and invent 'someone else'? There seemed no other way to convince Morland that she could not and would not marry him. That would convince him. He would see then that it was hopeless and the interview would come to an end . . . and it would save Morland's face. She wanted to save his face; she was so sorry for him. There was something quite dreadful in a humiliated Morland. If he could go home and say she had 'met someone else' it would be much less humiliating than if he were obliged to slink home, defeated, because she found the thought of him as a husband intolerable. All this flashed through Julia's mind in a moment . . . if only she could say she had 'met someone else,' or not say anything at all and let him think it! But Julia could not bring herself to deceive him.

'No, Morland, you're mistaken, absolutely mistaken—' she began.

But it was too late. She had hesitated and he drew the obvious conclusion.

'So that's what it is!' he exclaimed. 'It's a pity you didn't tell me at the beginning; it would have saved a lot of trouble! Now I understand the whole thing!'

'You don't understand anything at all!' cried Julia.

'I understand the whole thing,' he repeated furiously. 'I can only hope that the fellow—whoever he may be—can afford to support you in comfort, because you won't get a penny from your father. He told me himself with his own lips that unless you came home immediately and behaved yourself he would have nothing more to do with you.'

They had both risen from their chairs in the heat of the argument; Morland had said his say; Julia was too angry and upset to speak. It was at this moment—a somewhat unfortunate moment—that the door opened and Neil came in.

'Hallo, Julia!' he said. 'Oh, I'm sorry. I thought you must have finished the palaver. I've been waiting for ages . . . but it doesn't matter. I can go back to the bar if you haven't finished.'

'I think—we've—finished,' said Julia, putting out her hand and seizing hold of the back of a chair.

'Quite finished, thank you,' declared Morland, with a scornful laugh. He turned and went out.

'Julia!' exclaimed Neil. 'What's happened?'

'I think—I'm—going to faint—'

'No, you're not,' said Neil briskly, taking her firmly by the arm. 'You can't faint here; it would be silly. You want fresh air, that's all. I don't suppose they've had those windows open since the place was built.'

'Let me—sit down—for a minute—'

'Nonsense, you want air,' he repeated, opening the front door and dragging her into the street. 'Brace up, Julia! Take a few deep breaths . . . that's the stuff! You're better already, aren't you?'

Neil's arm was round her waist and it was so strong (like steel, thought Julia vaguely) that she felt like a puppet. He was walking her along the street slowly but inexorably. For the first few steps her legs were wobbly, and she could scarcely put one foot in front of the other, but the air was so crisp and fresh that in a few moments she began to recover.

'Good girl,' said Neil. 'Breathe in . . . breathe out. You'll be all right now. If there's one thing more certain than another it's the fact that human beings can't exist without fresh air. I don't know why they should want to, I'm sure, but quite a lot of them seem to like shutting themselves up in hermetically-sealed rooms and breathing fug. Daft, I call it. If I'm ever the Prime Minister I shall make a law forbidding people to shut their windows.'

2

Julia felt a great deal better by this time. The air was lovely, she felt it cool on her flushed face; she breathed it deeply into her lungs.

The light was fading and it was getting dark; it was what Maggie called the gloaming—a lovely word. The roofs of the houses were sharply outlined against a sky of turquoise, shading into palest primrose towards the west.

'What a heavenly night, Neil!' said Julia with a little sigh.

'Yes, heavenly,' he agreed. Now that she was better he had taken his arm from round her waist and drawn her arm through his. Thus linked they were able to walk faster.

'You always seem to be rescuing me,' Julia said. 'You must think I'm awfully silly. It's just that I can't bear scenes and people getting angry. It upsets me and makes me feel ill.'

'Yes, I realised that. There's quite a simple explanation for your abnormality. The condition is the result of the excitability of the adrenalin gland . . . but we won't go into that now. To-night of course there was not sufficient oxygen in that room; anybody might have felt queer.

If I had sat there long I'd have felt queer myself. Sorry I butted in,' he added. 'I'd been waiting for hours—at least it seemed like hours to me.'

It had seemed like hours to Julia also, so she could not blame him for becoming impatient.

'I'd been waiting for hours,' repeated Neil. 'I couldn't think what had happened. I thought you must have gone—so I went to look. I saw at once I had butted in at the wrong moment.'

'If you'd come a few moments later you'd have found me lying on the floor!'

'Nasty, dirty floor!'

They walked on for a short time in silence.

'Was he beastly?' asked Neil at last. 'Ought I to have given him a sock on the jaw?'

'Of course not!'

'Well, I didn't know what to do,' complained Neil. 'I didn't know what you wanted me to do. I'd have knocked him down if I'd thought he'd been beastly to you.'

'I wouldn't have minded so much if he'd been beastly.'

'Was he pathetic? Did he go down on his knees in that smart brown suit?'

'Don't be ridiculous!'

'You spurned him,' said Neil. 'It's a good word, that! I can just see you doing it—spurning him,' repeated Neil with relish.

'I did nothing of the sort! I tried to be kind but I couldn't possibly say I'd marry him.'

'Marry him! Good heavens, was that what he wanted?'

'Yes.'

'So that was why the sparks were flying?'

'Yes.'

'I see,' said Neil thoughtfully. 'Yes, I see . . . but I wonder why he gave me such a dirty look as he went out. I had nothing to do with it, had I?'

Julia was silent.

'If looks could kill I'd be lying dead on that filthy dirty floor. How do you account for that?'

'I wish you would be quiet.'

'Perhaps he thought I was to blame for the spurning. That would account for it, of course. Nobody enjoys being spurned.'

'You're annoying me frightfully; you really are the most annoying person I've ever met. Why can't you leave things alone?'

'I never leave things alone until I get to the bottom of them,' replied Neil. 'I never could, even when I was a child. Maggie would tell you that.'

'Well, if you must know,' said Julia impatiently, 'he had just said the only explanation of my refusal to marry him was that I must have "met someone else," and he hoped that the fellow—whoever he was—had enough money to support me in comfort, because unless I came home immediately and behaved myself my father would have nothing more to do with me . . . and I had just begun to tell him that he was absolutely mistaken when the door opened and you came in and said you had been waiting for ages. That's all,' added Julia. 'So now you know, and we can change the subject.'

'Great Scott! I should have trusted my instinct and knocked him down. I could have done it easily. We're too civilised nowadays—that's what's the matter with us—too conventional, too—er—'

'Namby-pamby,' suggested Julia sweetly.

Neil chuckled. 'I like you, Julia. You amuse me a lot. Do you know this: if I had two thousand a year I'd marry you to-morrow.'

'I wouldn't marry you if you had ten thousand a year.'

'Why not?'

'Because you annoy me—frightfully.'

'I do it on purpose,' explained Neil. 'It's such fun annoying you and seeing your eyes flash like sapphires. I bet you tuppence nobody has ever told you that your eyes were like sapphires before.'

'You've lost your bet.'

'Really? How frightfully interesting! Who was it, I wonder. It wasn't that stuffed peacock, was it?'

'Mind your own business.'

'I thought not,' said Neil. 'I could see at a glance that the fellow has no imagination, no perception. Probably he has never noticed the colour of your eyes—thinks they're brown or something! It beats me why you ever thought of marrying him.'

Oddly enough the same idea had just occurred to Julia.

'I suppose it would be no use asking who it was that said your eyes were like sapphires?' inquired Neil.

'None whatever . . . and anyhow we're going to change the subject.'

'Yes, of course,' agreed Neil without hesitation. 'What shall we talk about? You choose.' He stopped for a moment or two in an angle of wall, produced two coppers and handed them to her.

'What's this for?' she asked in surprise.

'I always pay my bets promptly,' he replied. 'They're debts of honour, you see. I wouldn't sleep a wink to-night if I had a debt of honour on my conscience.'

'How silly you are!' exclaimed Julia, giggling.

'What are we going to talk about?' he asked.

'Nothing,' she replied. 'I can go home the rest of the way by myself. I'm perfectly all right now, and it isn't far. You've been very kind and—and helpful. I'm really very grateful, Ned.'

'That's all right. It's been a pleasure; besides we're cousins, aren't we? I think I shall kiss you, Julia.'

'Oh, no!'

'Yes, really. Cousins do. It's the right thing.'

Julia made no more objection (he really had been very kind and helpful; in fact she could not think what she would have done without him), so Neil stooped and kissed her lightly on her upturned cheek. The cousinly salute was not at all unpleasant.

'Well, thank you again—and good-bye,' she said, smiling at him.

'No, not good-bye; not even *au revoir*. I'm afraid you'll have to put up with my company a bit longer.'

'But I'm quite all right now!'

'I must see you safely in at the door of The Square House before we say good-bye.'

'But why?' she asked. 'It isn't far.'

'Because we're being followed.'

'Being followed!' echoed Julia incredulously. 'Do you mean there's someone following us?'

'Yes, I'd have told you before but I didn't want to alarm you.' He took her arm and they walked on.

'Why should anyone follow us? There's no sense in it. You must be mistaken.'

'I'm not mistaken,' declared Neil with conviction. 'You see, he's not doing it very well. I mean you read in books about people being "shadowed," and of course in books the "shadowers" creep along silently, unheard by their quarry. This chap—whoever he is—doesn't know his job. I can hear his footsteps quite clearly. You'd hear them yourself if you stopped talking for a minute.'

Julia felt inclined to point out that it was not she who had been talking incessantly, but she was rather frightened so she refrained . . . and listened . . . and now that they were silent she could hear footsteps coming along behind.

'Neil, are you sure?' she whispered. 'I mean it could just be someone who happened to be going this way, couldn't it?'

'It couldn't, really. Perhaps you haven't noticed that I've been hurrying you along and then dawdling and then hurrying again. If it had just been somebody going this way he would have passed us or been left behind . . . and when we stopped and I paid my debt of honour the footsteps stopped too. I was hoping he would pass but he didn't.'

'Oh goodness! What had we better do?'

'If I were alone I'd know what to do,' declared Neil savagely. 'I'd turn round and go after him, I'd seize him and shake him till his teeth rattled . . . but I've got to get rid of you first.'

He was hurrying her along again so that she was almost breathless.

'Need we—go—quite so fast?' she gasped.

'No, of course not—sorry—it's just that I want to get rid of you,' explained Neil, slowing down.

'Do you think it's a tramp?'

'No, I don't.'

'Well, who could it be?'

'I don't know.'

'Neil, who could it be?' asked Julia urgently.

'Well, as a matter of fact there was a burglary last night at Dunbar. A house was broken into and some jewellery stolen. There's a lot about it in the *Evening Despatch*.'

'Neil, you don't think—'

'Well, you never know,' said Neil cheerfully. 'It might be the fellow or it might not. The police have been warned to keep a lookout for him. That's why I want to get rid of you before I tackle him—see?'

Julia saw. The sight did nothing to allay her fears, but fortunately by this time they had reached the gate.

'You must come in,' she declared, as they went up the path.

'Neil, you must come in—he may be desperate—you can't tackle him alone. You must come in and we'll ring up the police. That's the sensible thing to do.'

Neil took the latch-key from her trembling hand, opened the door and pushed her inside.

'Neil, you must come in!' cried Julia, clinging to him with all her strength.

'Nonsense!' cried Neil, laughing and shaking her off as if she had been a kitten. 'Away with you, Julia! I can't wait to get after him! Now that I've got rid of you safely it's all right—it's fun!'

The door banged between them and he was off.

Julia fled upstairs to her bedroom window and leaned out. She could see the figure of a man in the distance; he had turned and was walking away quickly; Neil was running after him. Hunter and quarry had changed places! She wondered what would happen when Neil caught him . . . but they both disappeared round the corner leaving the road empty of life.

Oh dear! thought Julia. How awful men are! No wonder there are wars! It was distressing, but all the same you could not help admiring courage. If Neil had come in and rung up the police it would have been sensible—but tame. A tame man would be simply horrible, thought Julia as she undressed and prepared for bed. Neil certainly was not tame, whatever else he might be. She was not worried about what was happening to Neil—not the slightest bit—in fact, when she saw the bruises on her arm where Neil had gripped her, she felt just a tiny bit sorry for the burglar. Perhaps at this very moment he was being shaken till his teeth rattled.

Serve him right! thought Julia, smiling to herself as she snuggled down comfortably in bed.

CHAPTER 38

As a matter of fact Julia was entirely mistaken. The interview which was in progress beneath one of Leddiesford's infrequent lamp-posts did not necessitate physical violence. Neil—by no means certain of the fellow's identity—decided that it might be as well to make sure before doing anything that he might regret. He moderated his speed and timed his approach until the lamp-post was at hand before seizing the man's arm in a vice-like grip. By this time Neil's vague suspicions were confirmed and he knew exactly whom he had got hold of . . . and it certainly was not a housebreaker!

'Let go of me!' exclaimed the victim, struggling to free himself and failing. 'Let go of me at once or I shall call the police.'

'Who are you?' demanded Neil. 'What do you think you're doing, skulking about like this and frightening girls!'

'Frightening girls!'

'Yes, that's what I said. Here, let me have a look at you!' Neil swung his captive round and surveyed his face in the light of the lamp. 'Good heavens!' he exclaimed, feigning intense surprise. 'Good heavens! It's Mr. Morland Beverley!'

'Yes. Let go of my arm at once.'

Neil released him, aware that he could catch him again if necessary.

'I suppose,' said Mr. Morland Beverley with elaborate sarcasm, 'I suppose there isn't a law in this benighted country forbidding a gentleman to go out for an evening stroll?'

(So he really does talk like that, thought Neil. I can do it too.) Aloud he said, 'Most certainly there is a law forbidding a gentleman to follow a lady and frighten her. I should have thought there was a law of that nature in most civilised countries.'

'I had no intention of frightening anyone.'

'Your conduct was extremely unconventional to say the least of it. My cousin and I were—'

'Your cousin?'

'My cousin, Julia Harburn. I was escorting her home when—'

'I had no idea she was your cousin. As a matter of fact I was not aware she had a cousin. It seems strange that she never mentioned the fact.'

'I see nothing strange about it,' declared Neil with absolute truth. 'And anyway that is not the point. You have not explained your behaviour. It was most alarming.'

'Alarming?'

'I was taking my cousin home,' said Neil (resisting the temptation to say that he had been escorting her to her uncle's residence). 'I was taking her home after her interview with you at the Black Bull when suddenly we discovered we were being dogged.'

'Dogged?'

'Yes, dogged,' said Neil emphatically. 'Shadowed—if you prefer the word. Believe me it is an unpleasant experience.'

'You are making a great deal of fuss about nothing.'

'Not at all, Mr. Beverley. Perhaps you don't read the *Evening Despatch*. In to-night's edition there is an account of a case of house-breaking at Dunbar and the police have been warned to keep a lookout for a man who was concerned in the crime.'

The *Evening Despatch* was not a paper with which Morland was familiar, but it so happened that he had found a copy in the lounge of the Black Bull and, having nothing else to read, he had read it from beginning to end.

'Oh yes,' he said, taken aback. 'Yes, I see. Yes, I did happen to—to notice it. But I wasn't following you—or at least not in the sense you mean. I merely wanted to ascertain where Miss Harburn was living.'

'It's quite impossible for you to see my cousin again to-night,' said Neil firmly. 'It's getting on for eleven o'clock; she'll be in bed by this time. I only hope she'll be able to sleep after her terrifying experience.'

'Terrifying experience? Really Mr.—er—'

'Being dogged like that. She was extremely shaken. I was obliged to take the latch-key from her hand to open the door. Your conduct was most reprehensible for any man who calls himself a gentleman.'

'But I've told you!' exclaimed Morland, whose high-flown language had deserted him completely. 'I've told you I didn't mean any harm and I never intended to try to see Julia again to-night. I only wanted to find out where she lived so that I could call and see her at a reasonable hour to-morrow morning.'

'Couldn't you have asked your way to The Square House?'

'I did,' replied Morland. 'I asked the landlord—or whatever he calls himself—but I couldn't understand a word he said.'

'What!' exclaimed Neil in astonishment. 'Rab Sinclair did that to you! I wouldn't have believed it!'

'I don't know what you mean. The man was speaking in his own extraordinary—'

'The man was offering you a deliberate insult.'

'An insult?'

'Yes, you must have riled him. I mean you must have annoyed him beyond the limits of his endurance. That same Rab Sinclair can speak as good English as yourself—or very nearly. He sits with his eyes and ears glued to his fine new television set for hours at a time.'

'Then, why—' began poor Morland in bewilderment.

'Never mind, Mr. Beverley,' said Neil quite kindly; for now that his victim was subdued and was talking like an ordinary human being and was looking so harassed, he had not the heart to persecute him any more. 'Never mind, there's no need to worry about it . . . but I had better see you safely back to the inn.'

'Thank you, but I am quite capable of walking back alone,' said Morland, gathering the shreds of his dignity about him and turning away.

'I doubt it,' replied Neil, falling into step beside him. 'It seems to me that you're not very capable of looking after yourself. For one thing there's that burglar—possibly a pretty desperate customer—and for another, the inn will be closed and Rab asleep in his bed. It's a cold night to spend out of doors, Mr. Beverley.'

'Do you mean he will have locked me out?' exclaimed Morland in dismay.

'I wouldn't wonder. If he's riled with you he's quite capable of bolting all the doors and snibbing all the windows (he's a black-tempered customer, is Rab). But never mind,' added Neil in soothing tones. 'We'll get in somehow. If the worst comes to the worst I can throw a few stones at Pat's window; he's the barman and sleeps in a wee room at the end of the passage. Pat owes me a good turn for sobering him up and keeping him out of jug on Orange Day.'

Morland had given up trying to understand the peculiar ways of Looking-Glass Country. He said, 'It's all quite ridiculous, but if they have locked me out I shall ring the bell and knock on the door and waken everyone in the damned place.'

'I believe that would be best,' admitted Neil. 'Just you take a firm line with Rab and throw your weight about and if you can't understand what he's saying tell him to speak plain English.'

'I shall,' said Morland.

They walked along in silence for a while.

So far so good, thought Neil. He had done as he had intended; he had bewildered the fellow and given him a fright, which he richly deserved, but how was it possible to prevent the fellow from calling at The Square House to-morrow morning? The last thing Julia wanted was another interview with Mr. Morland Beverley. Her previous interview with him had upset her so much that she had almost fainted on that filthy dirty floor, so it was up to Neil to spare her another scene with the fellow if he could manage it.

'About to-morrow,' said Neil. 'I wouldn't advise you to go and see Julia to-morrow.'

'But I want to see her. There's something I want to explain.'

'It will do no good. My cousin Julia is a girl who knows her own mind, Mr. Beverley.'

Mr. Beverley knew this already—none better—so it was in doubtful tones that he began, 'Yes—er—that's true, of course. I was just wondering whether Julia has—er—met someone else. I can see no other explanation of her extraordinary behaviour. It was so unlike Julia to rush off to visit an unknown uncle in defiance of my wishes . . . and her father's wishes, of course.'

'I thought the same when she told me about it.'

'Did you?' asked Morland with interest. 'Did you, really?'

'I thought it was out of character.'

'Of course it was—completely out of character!'

'I couldn't understand it at all until she told me her reason.'

'What was her reason?' asked Morland eagerly.

'My dear sir!' exclaimed Neil indignantly. 'I hope you are not asking me to betray my cousin's confidence. If my cousin has not told you her reason it is not my business to inform you.'

Poor Morland! He had been led up the garden path and left in the air—so to speak. He certainly was no match for Neil in guile.

'Oh—er—no, I suppose not,' he muttered, 'It was just that I have been wondering whether—whether she had met someone—'

'Good night, Mr. Beverley,' said Neil in a dignified manner.

'I have brought you to your door. You will observe that there is still a light in the lounge, so you will have no difficulty in gaining admittance.'

Neil bowed and walked away. He was obliged to walk quickly, because there were little bubbles of laughter rising up inside him, but being of a merciful disposition he lurked in a neighbouring archway until he saw the door of the Black Bull open and his victim safely inside. Then he strode on his way home to Dunraggit, whistling softly but cheerfully, for in truth he was pleased with his evening's work. Unless he was very much mistaken Mr. Morland Beverley would trouble Julia no more but would return to his own proper *milieu* convinced that she had 'met someone else.' (Not Neil, of course, but some other.)

It was delightful to be able to do a good turn for Julia, besides being his duty as a cousin. The cousin idea was a good one. Neil had no family; Julia had been cast off by hers. They had nobody belonging to them except Uncle Ran. Neil could look out for himself; he was supremely confident of his own abilities, but girls had to be looked after. Therefore it was absolutely essential that Julia should have somebody to look out for her—somebody to whom she could turn if need be—in other words a cousin.

And I'm sure we are cousins, thought Neil as he strode along through the darkness. I'll get out that tree and have a look at it some day when I've time.

CHAPTER 39

1

THE day after the interview with Morland was wet and miserable; Julia spent the morning darning linen, quite unaware that but for Neil she might have had a visitor. She thought about Morland and all that he had said, but she did not worry unduly; probably he was on his way home by this time.

In the afternoon Julia went to Edinburgh by bus as usual and called at the nursing home to see Uncle Ran.

Sister Don was waiting for her on the landing outside the patient's door. 'I'm very glad you've come,' she said. 'He has been wearying for you and wondering whether it would be too wet. Will you come into the pantry for a minute, Miss Harburn? I want to speak to you.'

Julia followed her into the little pantry.

'Mr. MacTavish asked me to tell you that he has decided to operate,' said Sister Don. 'He meant to see you and tell you himself but he was called away to an urgent ease. He said you had given him permission to do as he thinks best, so the operation is to be performed to-morrow.'

'To-morrow!'

'If a thing has got to be done it's better to be done quickly. Mr. MacTavish thinks it would be unwise to delay. You said he was to do as he thinks best, didn't you?'

'Yes, of course, but—'

'It's better to get it over, Miss Harburn.'

'Oh dear, I suppose it is,' said Julia miserably.

Sister Don nodded. 'Mr. MacTavish asked me to tell you that he would like you to be here to-morrow at two o'clock or soon after. Will that be all right?'

'Yes, of course. Does my uncle know he's having the operation to-morrow?'

'Mr. MacTavish told him this morning and he's being very good about it. Don't stay with him too long this afternoon and don't upset him, will you?'

'No, of course not,' said Julia indignantly.

Sister Don smiled rather grimly. 'You have no idea how foolish some people are,' she declared.

The little pantry was private. Julia spent some minutes there. She had hoped against hope that perhaps an operation would not be necessary and that Mr. MacTavish would be able to suggest some treatment instead, so the news that it was to be done—and done to-morrow—had come as a shock. However, it was no good being foolish, and it was no good lingering here and thinking about it, so Julia put on a bright smile and went into Uncle Randal's room.

His face lighted up when he saw her. 'Julia!' he exclaimed.

'I was afraid it would be too wet for you to come.'

'Did you think I was made of brown paper?'

'I thought you were made of sugar and spice.'

'I'm much more durable,' said Julia. She kissed him and added, 'Maggie sent her best respects as usual.'

'Give Maggie my love; she's a dear kind creature and she's been a good friend to me.'

As usual he wanted to hear 'all the news,' so she told him what she had been doing (but not about Morland nor the curious adventure last night). She told him about the salmon, which interested him greatly; he wanted to know how large it was and where Sam Fraser had caught it, but unfortunately Julia did not know. Then she told him about an old book, all about Leddiesford, which she had found on the top shelf in the study and they talked about that for a while.

'Have you heard from your father, Julia?' asked Uncle Randal suddenly.

This was a little difficult to answer. 'I haven't had a letter yet, but perhaps he'll write soon,' she replied.

'I've been lying here thinking about it. I've been wondering if I did the right thing in telling you that old story. Maybe I should have left it alone.'

'I'm glad you told me.'

'Listen, Julia. I want you to make it up with your father:'

'I've written several limes.'

'I know, but I'm sure if you went and saw him you could win him round,' said Uncle Randal earnestly. 'Promise me you'll go and try.'

'Yes, I'll try,' she said, nodding. 'But I can't go until you're better. I couldn't go away and leave you until you're better, could I?'

'Have they told you about to-morrow?'

'Yes, darling. I shall be thinking about you—but you know that, don't you?'

'You're my own dear wee lassie!'

'Mr. MacTavish is very clever; everyone says so.'

'Yes, yes.'

'And you like him.'

'He's a fine man.'

'It's a good thing to get it over, isn't it?'

He sighed. 'Yes, I suppose it's just as well . . . but I'd have liked to stay with you a little longer, my dear. We've not had very long together.'

'I'll be there waiting for you when you come home,' Julia told him, smiling as cheerfully as she could. 'We'll have a lovely time when you come home. You'll be so much better and stronger that we shall be able to go for little walks together. That will be nice, won't it?'

Uncle Randal did not reply.

'I must go now,' she added. 'Sister Don said I mustn't stay too long.'

'Just a little longer,' he said. 'Tell me about the garden.' Julia told him about the garden, but she had a feeling he was not really listening, he was just lying and looking at her, so presently she got up and kissed him. He took her hand and clung to it for a few moments, and then he let her go.

She paused at the door and looked back. '*Au revoir*, darling,' she said, smiling and blowing him a kiss.

2

When Julia got outside the door her smile faded. Uncle Ran had been wonderfully cheerful, but she did not like the way he had said, 'I'd have liked to stay with you a little longer.' The words haunted her. She went on thinking about the words, and the sad way he had said them, as she walked down the street to get her bus. She thought, too, of the earnest manner in which he had begged her to go and see her father 'and make it up with him.' It was easy to see what he had been thinking when he said that.

Julia was so lost in her unhappy thoughts that she would have allowed the bus to go without her if a completely unknown woman had not taken her by the arm and said, 'Here's the Leddiesford bus, Miss Harburn!'

Julia awoke from her trance, thanked the unknown woman and scrambled in.

'You'll have been in seeing Mr. Harburn,' said the woman, sitting down beside her. 'Is he keeping any better?'

Julia gave what news she could about the patient.

'Oh dear!' exclaimed the woman. 'It's to be to-morrow, is it? I could see you were feeling a bit upset. But Mr. MacTavish is just wonderful. Everybody says so. I must tell the boys,' she added. 'They were saying this morning they wondered how he was keeping. Maybe a few nice fresh eggs would come in useful?'

'I'm afraid he isn't allowed eggs.'

'Oh well, it'll just have to be sweet-peas then. I'll send up one of the boys with a bunch. Maybe it would cheer him a bit and you could tell him that Mrs. Lang and the boys were thinking about him and wishing him well.'

'I'm sure it would cheer him,' declared Julia. She herself was beginning to feel considerably less woebegone under the influence of Mrs. Lang's sympathy. 'It's very kind of you,' she added.

'Not at all, Miss Harburn; you see I've got three boys,' replied Mrs. Lang as if the fact that she was the proud mother of three boys explained the matter fully.

'How lovely for you to have three boys. What are their names?' asked Julia.

This subject proved very fruitful; Julia heard all about the boys (the eldest was called Randal) and what they were doing and how much they enjoyed going to the boys' club in the evenings . . . and how much better it was to have a nice place like that to go to instead of hanging about in the street and getting into mischief.

After that they talked about gardens; Jamie Lang had reported that he had seen Miss Harburn working in the garden at The Square House.

'Yes, I'm digging up the weeds,' said Julia. 'I've got some packets of seeds but I haven't planted them yet.'

'You'll be wasting your time, Miss Harburn. There's nothing'll grow in yon garden unless you get dung.'

'Unless I get dung?'

'Manure,' explained Mrs. Lang. 'You'll need to get a cart of manure and dig it in thoroughly. There's no goodness in the soil; it's been neglected for years. But I tell you what, Miss Harburn; you get the dung—manure, I mean—and the boy's'll come and dig it in. That's the plan.'

'How very kind!'

'Not at all,' replied Mrs. Lang cheerfully. 'When would you like them to come?'

Julia hesitated. 'I don't quite know,' she said vaguely. 'I shall have to see. . . .'

'Yes, of course,' nodded Mrs. Lang. 'You'll need to wait till Mr. Harburn is better. Just let me know. The boys can come along any evening and they'll be glad to do it.'

It certainly was very kind, but Julia could not accept the offer without finding out how much it would cost to buy a cartload of manure. She had begun to feel worried about money. Sometimes, when she thought about it seriously, she felt very worried indeed. Seven hundred pounds had seemed a vast sum to Julia but it had begun to dwindle away.

Julia had discovered that the housekeeping at The Square House had been conducted in what seemed to her a most extraordinary manner. 'I just ask him for money when I'm wanting it,' Maggie had explained. 'He gives me the cheque and I take it down to the bank and Mr. Edgar gives me the money. I keep it in a soap-box in the dining-room cupboard and take it out when I'm needing it to pay my wages and the shops. That's the way we do it, Miss Julia. It's easiest for him. He's not wanting to be bothered with bills and such-like.'

Julia was somewhat horrified at this revelation; she was much more horrified when she was told that there was now no money left in the soap-box, Maggie's wages were in arrears, and the shops had not been paid for weeks.

'I just didn't like to bother him when he was not so well, and that's the truth,' explained Maggie apologetically.

Julia had put matters right and was now paying the housekeeping bills regularly; they were not very large, for Maggie was economical to a fault, but all the same it was a constant drain upon her resources. Furthermore Julia had inquired at the nursing home how much Uncle Randal's room and treatment were costing per week and had been absolutely staggered at the reply. How long would she be able to carry on—that was the question—and would she have enough money to pay Mr. MacTavish's fee? To make matters worse, she had received a short note from Mr. Silver informing her that the allowance from her father had been discontinued. This was no surprise, of course, it was what she had expected, but somehow it seemed the last straw.

CHAPTER 40

1

THE waiting-room at the Westchester Nursing Home was a comfortably furnished apartment with easy-chairs and a big round table with a pot-plant in the middle. Julia had arrived there at two o'clock and had been sitting there for hours waiting for news of Uncle Randal. The operation had taken place in the morning; Mr. MacTavish had told Julia that it was successful but Mr. Harburn was very weak. Mr. MacTavish had looked different to-day; he looked tired and anxious, his manner was grave.

'Will he be all right?' Julia had asked.

'I hope so,' he had replied . . . and that was all.

The matron was a little more communicative. She looked in and asked if Julia was comfortable.

'It's a very comfortable room,' replied Julia politely.

'Would you like a book to read?'

Julia shook her head. 'I'd like to see him,' she said. 'Why can't I see him, Matron?'

'It would be no use at present. Mr. Harburn is still under the anaesthetic. Mr. MacTavish wants you to be here when he recovers consciousness.'

'Oh, I see!' exclaimed Julia. She had been wondering why they wanted her to be here, if she was not to be allowed to see Uncle Ran.

'You won't go away, will you? Mr. MacTavish is very anxious for you to be here.'

'Of course I shall be here.'

'You may have to wait for hours.'

'It doesn't matter,' declared Julia. 'I'll do whatever you say.'

'Just wait,' said Miss Johnstone. 'I know it's one of the hardest things to do. I'll send you in some supper.'

It certainly was one of the hardest things to do. Julia walked about the room, she stood and looked out of the window. The prospect was not enlivening, for the room was at the back of the house and looked out onto a small garden with bushes and trees all wet and dripping with the rain which was falling, not hard but persistently, from leaden skies. She took up a magazine which was lying on the table, but she found she was reading the words without taking in their sense, so she put it down again.

A young girl came in with a tray of supper. There were lamb cutlets and green peas and a dish of trifle, it was nicely cooked and served and looked very appetising, but it tasted like sawdust and stuck in Julia's throat so that it was almost impossible to swallow it. When she had swallowed as much as she could she rose and walked about again.

Then suddenly she remembered the sapphire; she was wearing it all the time in the little bag, tied round her neck. She sat down and took it out and looked at it, holding it in the palm of her hand. It was beautiful, of course—it was always beautiful—but to-day it did not shine and glow as brightly as usual. Well, of course not! thought Julia. 'This is a gem that feels the influence of the air and sympathises with the heavens and does not shine equally if the sky be cloudy or bright.' Poor sapphire! How could it shine when the sky was leaden and the rain was running down the window?

Julia held it in her hand and thought of Stephen . . . and wondered if by any chance Stephen happened to be thinking of her. She thought about Gemscoombe and tried to remember all that Stephen had told her about his home: the old rambling house with the huge cellars where the 'Gentlemen' had kept their smuggled wares; the orchard at the back with the old gnarled apple trees; the cliff with the sea below. She thought of the waves lapping on the rocks and the seagulls soaring and diving.

The hours dragged on. The daylight faded and the room became dim . . . and still Julia waited. She began to think they must have forgotten about her. She began to wonder what she should do. Supposing they had forgotten that she was here, waiting! Perhaps she would be left here all night.

Suddenly the door opened and there was Neil . . . and Neil looked so strange, so haggard and drawn and old, that she scarcely recognised him.

'Come quickly,' Neil said.

She was so frightened that she was turned to stone.

'Come,' said Neil, seizing her hand. 'Mr. MacTavish sent me to fetch you. Come quickly.'

2

The room was very quiet and shadowy; there was a light on the table beside Uncle Randal's bed. The window was wide open. Mr. MacTavish was there—and Sister Don.

Mr. MacTavish came forward and put his hand on Julia's shoulder. 'I want you to speak to him,' he said. 'Speak to him; tell him who you are. Try to rouse him.'

She went and knelt beside the bed.

'Speak to him,' repeated Mr. MacTavish. 'Speak loudly.'

'Uncle Ran, darling!' cried Julia.

He lay there without moving; his eyes closed; his face as white as paper. Even his lips were colourless.

'Uncle Ran! It's me—Julia! Uncle Ran, you know me, don't you?'

His eyelids flickered for a moment; his eyes opened but they were vague and wandering.

'Speak to him,' said Mr. MacTavish urgently. 'Take his hand.'

She took his hand, it was cold and limp, and she went on speaking. 'Uncle Ran! You know me, don't you! It's Julia. I've been waiting for you to wake up. You're awake now, aren't you? Look at me, darling! You know who I am. I'm Julia.'

His eyes found her face and slowly a look of recognition dawned in them. His lips moved and formed a word, 'Julia . . .'

'Yes, darling,' she said clearly. 'It's Julia.' She gave his hand a firm squeeze. 'Dear, darling Uncle Ran, I'm here beside you. I'm your very own Julia. You're pleased to see me, aren't you?'

His lips moved. 'It's a joy . . .' he whispered.

Julia tried to go on talking but she could say no more. The lump in her throat was choking her.

For a few moments he looked at her in the old kind way and then his eyelids flickered and closed. . . .

She knelt there gazing at him in consternation, too terrified to speak, too terrified to move.

Neil had been standing behind her, he lifted her up and half-carried her out of the room.

She heard Mr. MacTavish say, 'Poor lassie, she's upset—and no wonder! Bring her in here, Logan. This room is empty. You had better stay with her a while till she feels better.'

'I'm all right,' she said. 'Neil, I'm all right. I'm not going to faint or anything silly.'

'Of course you're all right,' declared Neil, putting her down on the bed. 'Just lie still for a few minutes.'

'Neil, I did my best. I tried to—to speak to him.'

'You did exactly what we wanted you to do.'

'But—but it was no use,' she said in a choking voice.

'It was splendid,' Neil told her. 'He went to sleep—'

'He went to sleep! Are you sure?'

'Of course I'm sure; I was watching. He recognised you and then he drifted off to sleep, holding your hand.'

'Neil, you must go and see!' exclaimed Julia. 'See if he's really and truly asleep. Come back and tell me.'

Nell went away and Julia lay there waiting for him to come back; her heart was thumping so hard that she could scarcely breathe.

Presently he came back and shut the door. 'He's asleep and Sister Don says the pulse is slightly stronger. If he's better in the morning they'll be able to give him a transfusion.'

'Does that mean . . .'

'It means he has a chance,' said Neil seriously. 'There's a chance of his pulling through. Mr. MacTavish says you're to stay here for the night . . . just in case they want you again. See?'

'Stay here?'

'Yes, you don't mind, do you?'

'I don't mind anything,' said Julia. She lay still with the tears flowing out of her eyes and down her cheeks unchecked.

3

Some time later Sister Don came in and turned on the light. 'We'll get you to bed,' she said briskly. 'Matron lent me a nightdress for you, and here's a new toothbrush. It's lucky this room happens to be empty; you'll be quite comfortable here.' She helped Julia to undress and to put on the very large blue cotton nightdress, and tucked her up in bed.

'You ought to have a strong sedative,' she declared. 'That's what you need, but Mr. MacTavish said not unless it was absolutely necessary, in case you're wanted in the night.'

'Of course not! If he wakes you must come for me at once.'

'Yes, I'll come for you. Don't you worry about that.' Suddenly Julia sat up in bed and exclaimed, 'Oh goodness! How frightful! I'd forgotten poor Maggie!'

'It's all right about "poor Maggie,"' said Sister Don, smiling. 'Mr. Logan asked me to tell you that he had phoned to "poor Maggie." I had no idea who she was, but he just said that was the message and you would understand.'

'Oh, thank you! It was awful of me to forget.'

'Mr. Logan didn't forget. He's a great lad is Mr. Logan.'

'Yes, he is.'

'We're all pleased about his good fortune; nearly everybody is pleased. Of course there are a few who were hoping for the post themselves and you couldn't expect them to be pleased, could you?'

Sister Don had been tidying the room as she spoke and now she came and looked at Julia. 'Don't worry too much,' she said kindly.

'Do you think he's going to get better?'

She nodded. 'I think so,' she said. 'In my experience—and I've had a good deal of experience—it's spirit that counts. I've seen patients give up the struggle and lie down and die . . . but he's not that kind. There's plenty of spunk in Mr. Harburn. So don't worry too much but just turn over and go to sleep.'

'You'll waken me if you want me.'

'Yes, that's what you're here for, isn't it?' said Sister Don, smiling.

Julia turned over but she did not go to sleep. She lay awake thinking of all that had happened. Something very mysterious had happened; Uncle Ran had been a long way off and he had come back to her when she called to him . . . so perhaps now he would stay with her. 'I'd have liked to stay with you a little longer'—that was what he had said—so that was why he had come back.

Julia had prayed earnestly that Uncle Ran might stay with her; and now, as she lay quietly in bed, a peaceful feeling crept into her heart—and she knew—yes, she knew quite definitely that her prayer was answered.

4

Several hours passed. Everything was quiet except for occasional soft footsteps in the passage and the sound of a church clock striking. It struck twelve and one and two. Soon after that the door opened and Sister Don looked in.

'Are you awake, Miss Harburn?' she whispered.

'Yes. Shall I come?'

'He wakened and I gave him a drink but he's a little restless. It might put him off to sleep if you came in and let him see you. Speak to him quietly for a minute or two. You could say a poem to him or perhaps a psalm. It's the sound of a familiar voice that matters, not the words.'

He was lying on his back as before. Julia knelt down and took his hand . . . this time there was no need to tell him who it was.

'Julia!' he whispered in surprise.

'Yes, darling, here I am. It was too late to go home to Leddiesford last night so they gave me a room next door. I'm very comfortable there. You're better, darling; I can see you're better. It makes me so happy. You mustn't talk . . . not a word. Sister wants you to go to sleep again, see?'

There was a slight pressure on her hand.

Sister had told her to say a poem or a psalm—it was the voice not the words that mattered—but what should she say? Not the twenty-third psalm, though that was her favourite. She would never be able to say that. 'Yea, though I walk through the Valley of the Shadow of Death' . . . no, no! Impossible! She began to say the first thing that came into her head (though why it should have come into her head Julia did not know). She had not said it since she was a child, had not thought of it, did not even know that she remembered it until she began:

> 'Then the little Hiawatha
> Learned of all the birds their language,
> Learned their names and all their secrets,
> How they built their nests in summer,
> Where they hid themselves in winter,
> Talked to them when e'er he saw them,
> Called them Hiawatha's chickens . . .'

She saw a tiny smile curling round the corners of his mouth, so she went on—forgetting a few words here and there but remembering most of it: all about the beavers and the squirrels and the rabbits, and about Hiawatha walking through the forest 'proudly with his bow and arrows and the birds sang round him, o'er him, "Do not shoot us, Hiawatha!" Sang the robin, sang the blue-bird, "Do not shoot us, Hiawatha!"'

Presently she saw that he had fallen asleep, so she stood up.

Sister Don's arm went round her and led her back to bed.

'You'll get a sedative now, anyway,' she said, blowing her nose violently.

'Perhaps I'd better not. I mean—'

'You'll do as you're told,' said Sister Don crossly.

Julia did as she was told. Who could gainsay Sister Don when she spoke like that?

CHAPTER 41

THE following morning Julia was obliged to go home without seeing Uncle Randal. Sister Don told her he was stronger and was having a blood transfusion.

'Come and see him to-morrow,' she said.

Unfortunately, however, Julia was unable to go to Edinburgh as had been arranged. That night when she was sitting in the study she began to feel rather queer.

'You're just worn out; that's what's the matter with you,' declared Maggie. 'You'll go to your bed and maybe you'll be better in the morning.'

Julia went to bed and awoke with a raging cold. Besides feeling ill and miserable she was very angry indeed . . . how maddening to get a cold just now—just now when it was so important that she should be fit and well so that she could go and see Uncle Ran! Julia scarcely ever had colds, which made it a great deal more maddening. She explained all this to Maggie.

'It's just ridiculous,' said Julia. 'Where on earth can I have got it?'

'It doesna matter where you got it; you've got it,' replied Maggie sensibly. 'You'll just need to keep your bed till you're better. It would be a deal more ridiculous to go and see him and maybe give him a cold.'

This was true, of course, so Julia was obliged to give in and to content herself with sending messages and hearing news by phone from Neil and Sister Don. One day Uncle Randal was better and the next day not so well; the following day he was a good deal better . . . so it went on. Julia was worried, she longed to go and see him with her own eyes.

It was a whole week before Julia felt it was perfectly safe for her to visit the patient and she had heard so many varying accounts of his condition that she did not know what to expect . . . but when she walked into his room and saw him sitting up and reading his beloved *Blackwood's* her delight knew no bounds. 'Darling, you're simply marvellous!' she exclaimed.

He chuckled. 'Yes, I'm fine. The old horse has been given a new lease of life. I thought he was just about ready for the knacker's yard but it seems I was mistaken. Are those violets, Julia? What a kind wee lassie! I'll have them near me on the table so that I can smell them.'

Julia found a little vase and arranged the violets as he wanted.

'Are you better, my dear?' he asked anxiously.

She nodded. 'It was only a cold, that's all. I was furious about it! Fancy getting a stupid cold just now, when I wanted to come and see you!'

'These things happen,' said Uncle Ran, smiling. 'Did Maggie look after you well?'

'Maggie and I are getting on fine. We're very chief.'

'You're not to make me laugh!' he exclaimed in alarm. 'It's sheer agony to laugh.'

'Oh, I'm sorry. I'll speak plain English. We're great friends, Maggie and I. She tells me all about her relations.'

'Maggie's relations are no great shakes.'

'I gathered that. Sometimes in the evenings she comes and sits in the study and we have a chat.'

'That's good of you, my dear.'

'It isn't good of me; we both enjoy it. She tells me stories and—'

'Tells you stories!' exclaimed Uncle Rap, in horrified tones.

'What sort of stories?'

Julia laughed. 'Stories about things that happened long ago in Leddiesford. It's very interesting, Uncle Ran.'

He shook his head as much as to say there was no accounting for tastes.

'Oh, I met Mrs. Lang one day,' said Julia. 'We went down to Leddiesford together in the bus. She said she was going to send you some sweet-peas to cheer you up and to remind you that she and the boys are thinking of you.'

Uncle Randal nodded. 'They're a nice family. The eldest lad was a bit wild and troublesome for a while but he's settled down now. Did she say how wee Jamie was getting on at school?'

Julia tried to remember what Mrs. Lang had said about Jamie's progress, but it was difficult, for she had been worried and upset. She remembered about the boys' club, so she told him that.

'Yes, yes, the lads enjoy it,' said Uncle Randal, nodding. He smiled and added, 'How's the little Hiawatha, Julia?'

'It was a silly thing to say to you, wasn't it?'

'It was a nice sleepy thing to say. I'm very fond of the little Hiawatha so it was pleasant to be reminded of him.'

'I didn't know you were listening—not properly listening,' Julia explained. She rose as she spoke, for she thought he had talked enough.

'I was listening in my dreams,' he told her. 'Julia, you're not to go yet!'

'I thought you were looking a little tired.'

'Sit down,' he said. 'It's important . . . and it won't take long. I don't want you to go back to that job in London—selling hats. Those girls were disagreeable to you.'

'Yes, but it's quite a good job and it would be difficult for me to get anything else. That's the trouble.'

'There's no need for you to get a job at all,' he said earnestly.

'I'd like you to feel that The Square House was your home.'

'Oh, how kind of you, Uncle Ran!'

'It's sheer selfishness,' he told her. 'Of course I'm not suggesting that you should stay with me all the time—you can come and go as you please—but just make it your headquarters until you get married and have a home of your own.'

'Who said I was going to be married?' cried Julia in alarm.

'Nobody. Nobody at all,' he replied, with a little chuckle. 'But there's always a chance that some misguided man might take a fancy to you.'

Julia laughed.

'Well, anyway,' he said. 'You'll not go back to that hat-shop, will you, Julia? I just can't bear the thought of it.'

'I promise not to leave you until you're quite well,' said Julia reassuringly.

'In that case I'll take my time about getting quite well.'

For a few moments there was silence.

'I'm a bit sleepy. I think I'll just—take a wee nap,' said Uncle Randal dreamily.

She looked at him and saw to her surprise that his eyes were closed; he had begun to breathe rhythmically. Beyond doubt Uncle Ran was fast asleep! She tiptoed out of the room and closed the door very carefully.

Sister Don was in the pantry arranging flowers, so Julia stopped to speak to her.

'He's asleep,' said Julia anxiously. 'He was talking . . . and then suddenly he was asleep. Is that all right?'

'Oh yes, they often doze off in the middle of a conversation. He can't have too much sleep: it's the best thing for him. He's looking wonderful, isn't he?'

'Wonderful.'

'It's his spirit,' declared Sister Don. 'He's made up his mind to get better and that's a good deal more than half the battle. He often talks about going home and being with you and going for little walks with you, Miss Harburn. You must have mentioned it to him some time.'

'Yes, I did.'

'It's a good thing to have something like that to look forward to,' said Sister Don, nodding.

2

Uncle Randal's request that Julia should make her home with him was very kind indeed. She knew that he really meant it and that it would give him pleasure; he was looking forward to coming home and being with her. Julia herself was looking forward to it; she was devoted to him, and of course it would be delightful to feel that The Square House was her home . . . but how could she pay her way unless she had a job? Yes, that was the trouble. Her only source of income was the hundred pounds a year which had been left to her by her mother, and that would not go far.

Madame Claire was willing to keep her job open indefinitely—which was extremely kind—but Julia could not leave Uncle Randal until he was perfectly well: it would be impossible for Maggie to look after him in addition to her other work. For all her briskness and efficiency Maggie was by no means young and it would be most unfair to saddle her with so much responsibility . . . besides (thought Julia), it was very important for Uncle Ran to have the right kind of food to build up his strength, and Maggie's ideas of catering for an invalid were unimaginative to say the least of it.

Julia sighed. How difficult it was! She wondered if there were any sort of job she could get in Leddiesford. However, she could not feel unhappy for long; Uncle Ran was getting better, that was the main thing.

Quite definitely Uncle Ran was getting better, there were no more ups and downs, he went ahead slowly and steadily. Mr. MacTavish was delighted with him and went to see him every day and talked to him. Sometimes Mr. MacTavish made him laugh, which was extremely cruel of Mr. MacTavish because he knew—none better—that it was painful for his patient to laugh.

One day when Julia returned from Edinburgh she found a letter waiting for her; it was from Stephen. Letters from Stephen were always a joy, they were long and interesting and full of Stephen, so when she opened the letter and saw that it was quite short she was disappointed. However, when she read it she understood. Stephen apologised for 'just a few lines' and explained that the roof was finished—it had taken much longer than he had expected—and he was just off to London to see the family lawyer. He intended to be in Town for a week. Was there any chance of Julia coming south? It would be lovely to see her. Would she write to him at his club and tell him her plans? He was very glad indeed to hear that 'Uncle Randal's' operation had been so successful and hoped he was making good progress. As usual he was 'YOURS EVER, Stephen.'

The letter was short but it seemed to Julia that the YOURS EVER was even larger than usual and, on comparing it with the other letters, she discovered that it was almost twice as large.

Julia smiled and thought about Stephen . . . and wondered.

She still had not told him that she had broken off her engagement. The reason was that she did not know what Stephen would do when he heard . . . or perhaps she did have a sort of vague idea of how he would react to the news! At any rate something might happen, something that would take her mind off Uncle Ran. This would not do. While Uncle Ran was so desperately ill Julia felt that she must give him her whole attention; she must think of him—and him alone. She felt that if she took her mind off him and thought of someone else he might slip back into the shadows. But now Uncle Ran was better; he was out of danger; he was making good progress, so it would be quite safe to spare a thought for Stephen.

I wonder, thought Julia. I shall have to write to him at his club and tell him I can't come to London. Shall I tell him about Morland . . . or not? Perhaps I had better wait a little longer; perhaps I should wait until Uncle Ran comes home and gets comfortably settled. Yes, that's the best plan; I shall wait until Uncle Ran comes home.

CHAPTER 42

THE next day was Wednesday. It had been arranged that Maggie was to go to Edinburgh and see 'him.' She was very excited about it and went off by the afternoon bus laden with a sponge cake, a parcel of clean pyjamas and a large bunch of sweet-peas which had been delivered at The Square House by Jamie Lang.

No sooner had Maggie gone than the door-bell rang, and when Julia went to answer it she found Mr. Baird standing on the step. She had seen him before, though only for a few minutes, in Uncle Randal's room. Now that she saw him again she remembered him quite clearly; he was the sort of man one did not forget.

'Oh, Mr. Baird!' exclaimed Julia. 'How kind of you to call! Do come in.'

'I happened to be down in this direction so I thought I'd take the chance of finding you at home. There are several things I want to discuss with you, Miss Harburn.'

'It's lucky you came to-day,' she told him. 'Usually I go and see Uncle Randal in the afternoon, but to-day Maggie has gone instead.'

'Mrs. Maggie Walker?'

'Yes, do you know her?'

'I've heard of her,' replied Mr. Baird.

By this time they were in the study. They sat down, and for a few minutes they talked of Uncle Randal. Mr. Baird said he had rung up the nursing home and had been delighted to hear that his old friend was making satisfactory progress.

'Do you think he would like me to go and see him?' asked Mr. Baird.

'I'm sure he would, but it would be better not to stay more than a few minutes. He still gets easily tired.'

'I'll do that,' replied Mr. Baird, nodding. 'You see, Randal and I are very old friends. When we were boys we used to go camping together. The only trouble was that Randal's ideas were a bit too rough for me.'

'Too rough?'

'He enjoyed roughing it,' said Mr. Baird, smiling reminiscently. 'He could lie down on the hard ground and go to sleep without the slightest difficulty. I must admit I preferred to be a little more comfortable.'

'He's still like that!' exclaimed Julia. 'He doesn't mind discomfort. You have no idea how uncomfortable his room was—quite dreadful! I'm having it done up for him while he's away.' She laughed and added, 'It will be interesting to see whether he notices the difference.'

'The whole house needs doing up, Miss Harburn. It's in an appalling condition; I saw that as I came up the path. Randal shouldn't allow his property to deteriorate like this; I must speak to him seriously about it.'

'Oh, don't do that!' cried Julia in alarm. 'We mustn't worry him about anything just now. Besides, it would cost a lot of money to have the whole house painted and put in proper order and he can't afford it. Honestly, Mr. Baird, you mustn't worry him about things like that!'

'I won't mention it till he's better, but it will have to be done fairly soon. What do you mean when you say he can't afford it?'

'I mean he's so terribly badly off.'

'What makes you think so?' asked Mr. Baird in surprise.

'I wouldn't say Randal was wealthy, but he has quite a good income.'

'Quite a good income!'

'Yes.'

Julia gazed at him incredulously. 'I can't believe it!' she cried. 'Mr. Baird, there must be some mistake!'

'I'm not in the habit of making mistakes, Miss Harburn. I've looked after Randal's business for years and I think I may say that I know a good deal more about his affairs than he does himself. What on earth made you think that your uncle was a pauper?' asked Mr. Baird, laughing.

Julia was still incredulous. 'He had to sell Harburn House, hadn't he? And look at this house! And—and there are other things—'

'I've explained that,' interrupted Mr. Baird. 'This house is in a very bad condition, but that's not because Randal can't afford to keep it in proper repair; it's because he can't be bothered; it's because he doesn't notice his surroundings. Give Randal an easy-chair and a log fire and a book to read—preferably an old book about history—and he's perfectly happy.'

Julia knew this to be true. 'Yes, but Harburn House! He didn't want to part with it but he was obliged to sell it. He said so.'

'Of course he was obliged to sell Harburn House,' replied Mr. Baird impatiently. 'A great many people have had to sell their family estates and move into smaller houses. Naturally it's a wrench to part with a place which has been in one's family for generations—I know that only too well, for I had to do the same thing myself—but it's no pleasure to live in an enormous house without an adequate staff; besides, the taxes on large estates are crippling. Randal has a reasonably good income but he's not a millionaire by any means. Only a millionaire could afford to live in a place like Harburn House nowadays and keep it up in the old style.'

'Yes,' said Julia. 'Yes, I see.'

'As a matter of fact I begged him to sell the place. It was nothing more nor less than a white elephant to a man with no family.'

'Yes, I see,' repeated Julia thoughtfully. 'But why did Neil say he hadn't enough money to pay for the nursing home and his operation?'

'Neil Logan said that!' exclaimed Mr. Baird. He snorted contemptuously and added, 'I have no idea why Neil Logan should say such a thing. That young man talks too much, and most of it is rubbish. I have no use for him at all. He annoys me.'

Julia was silent. She herself was very fond of Neil but at times she found him annoying . . . and it was easy to see that Mr. Baird might find him very annoying indeed.

'I see you still don't believe me,' said Mr. Baird crossly.

'But may I ask who is supposed to be paying the fee for Randal's operation and the bills for the nursing home?'

'Oh, I arranged all that with Mr. MacTavish.'

'You arranged it? You mean you're paying for it?'

'Yes. You see, it was so important for him to have a nice quiet room, and I thought . . . Oh dear, I've been very silly, haven't I?'

Mr. Baird looked at her and smiled. 'It was a delightful kind of silliness, Miss Harburn. However, I can assure you that Randal is quite able to pay for it all himself. In the last few years he has spent little more than half his income upon his personal expenses; he gives away the surplus to charitable institutions and he has other interests as well. For instance he bought that house in Leddiesford and started the boys' club . . . but you know about that, I expect.'

'No,' said Julia. 'I had no idea . . .'

'Oh well, that's what he did. He's very interested in boys. He used to go down to the club in the evening and chat to the boys; he taught them to play badminton and helped them to produce plays. They did carpentry and photography—all that sort of thing, you know,' said Mr. Baird vaguely. 'Of course latterly, when he was ill, he wasn't able to go, but I managed to find a man to run the place for him and I hear things are going on quite satisfactorily.'

Julia nodded. So that was what Mrs. Lang had meant!' Well now,' said Mr. Baird, pulling himself together. 'Let's get to business, Miss Harburn. I had better give you a cheque and you can open an account at the local bank.'

'Are you sure Uncle Randal would want that?'

'Quite sure. As a matter of fact that was one of the reasons I came to see you; I was wondering why you hadn't asked me for money nor sent me any bills.'

'I've been paying the bills myself.'

'That's absurd,' said Mr. Baird, and so saying he produced his cheque-book and proceeded to make out a cheque.

Julia watched him. She was still feeling slightly dazed, but she was also very much relieved, for she began to realise that there was no need to worry any more; this would solve all her difficulties.

Perhaps it had been silly of her to have got it fixed firmly in her mind that Uncle Randal was very badly off . . . but, no, when she thought about it she decided that it had not been silly. She had received the impression on reading Uncle Randal's letter, saying he had been obliged to sell the old house which had belonged to the Harburn family for generations, and the impression had been strengthened when she saw the conditions in which he lived. The Square House was in a deplorable state and Maggie's housekeeping was economical in the extreme. Poor Maggie had been counting every penny, trying to make the money in the soap-box last as long as she could!

'That will keep you going for a bit,' said Mr. Baird as he handed Julia the cheque.

'Five hundred pounds!' she exclaimed, looking at it in astonishment.

Mr. Baird smiled. 'It's a good thing to have a substantial sum in the bank and you'll find it will melt away quite quickly, what with one thing and another. You had better get the gate repaired and try to find a man to trim the hedge; and I noticed a slate had fallen off the roof, that should be seen to at once.'

'Oh yes, I know,' agreed Julia. 'I'd have had it done before, but you see I was so worried about money.'

'Randal should have made proper arrangements with you,' said Mr. Baird, frowning. 'It was ridiculous to leave you here without proper arrangements . . . but I don't suppose he ever thought of it. He's the most unbusiness-like man on earth.'

Julia knew this already. She nodded and said, 'Yes, you would be horrified if you knew the way the housekeeping was done.'

'No doubt I would be,' agreed Mr. Baird. 'But things will be different now. You'll put everything in proper order.'

'Are you sure it's all right?'

'I'm certain of it. Randal wouldn't like you to be short of money. He said you were to have as much as you wanted, or words to that effect. You heard him say so.'

'When did he say so?'

'It was that day when we met in his room at the nursing home before he had his operation.'

Julia tried to think. Of course she remembered meeting Mr. Baird in Uncle Randal's room, but she could not remember what had been said.

'Well, never mind,' said Mr. Baird. 'I dare say you were a bit upset that day so it's no wonder you can't remember . . . but that brings us to another matter. You see, Miss Harburn, I was there with Randal for quite a long time before you came in. He had sent a message saying he wanted to see me both as a solicitor and as a friend. As I told you before, Randal is one of my oldest friends, so I know all about his private affairs as well as his business. He wanted to talk to me about all sorts of things.' Mr. Baird hesitated for a moment and then added in a low voice, 'Poor old Randal didn't expect to recover from his operation.'

Julia nodded. 'I know. He didn't say it to me—he was wonderfully brave—but I knew what he was thinking.'

'He talked a great deal that afternoon. He talked about the old days and about your mother. I suppose you know what happened?'

'Yes, Uncle Randal told me.'

'He talked about you,' continued Mr. Baird. 'He told me that he had written to you and asked you to come and see him . . . and you had come at once. I could see that your doing so had touched him deeply; I could see he was very fond of you. He said rather sadly that if things had not gone wrong you might have been his daughter. That was how he felt. He added that he could not have been more fond of you if you had been his daughter, so I wasn't surprised when he went on to say that he wanted to make you his heir.'

Julia was so astonished that she was speechless. She was absolutely stunned with amazement. Her expression was so blank that Mr. Baird thought she had not understood. He said, 'Randal made a will leaving you his money, Miss Harburn. There are bequests to Neil Logan and Mrs. Maggie Walker and one or two others, but you are the residuary legatee.'

'Me!'

'Yes, you,' said Mr. Baird, smiling. 'Why are you so surprised? I thought it perfectly natural, especially when he told me his reasons. You may think it indiscreet of me to tell you about this, but Randal asked me to tell you. He said quite frankly that if he died he wanted you to know why he had made you his heir and if by any chance he recovered he still wanted me to explain the whole matter to you and make sure that you understood. He wanted you to know that he looks upon you as his daughter, but he didn't want to tell you himself. It was all arranged that afternoon when I saw him at the nursing home, he was giving me instructions to draw up a new will in your favour, and we had just finished when you came in. You can imagine how interested I was to see you!'

Mr. Baird paused and looked at Julia. 'You understand, don't you?' he said. 'If there's anything you don't understand just ask me.'

'Oh, darling Uncle Ran!' she exclaimed. 'What am I to say to him? How can I thank him?'

'He doesn't want thanks . . . and if you take my advice you'll say very little. You can just say I've told you and you're very pleased. It's difficult to thank people for leaving you money in their wills,' added Mr. Baird, smiling. 'Randal is not giving you his money. He's leaving it to you in his will because he wants you to have it when he's dead. Now that he is getting better it may be years before—'

'Oh, I hope so! I hope it will be years and years and years!'

Mr. Baird laughed. 'Tell him that, Miss Harburn.'

Soon after they had finished their business talk Mr. Baird went away. Julia offered him tea, but he replied that he wanted to get home.

'All that I've told you this afternoon is confidential,' said Mr. Baird very seriously. 'You realise that, I hope. Randal wouldn't like anybody else to know about his private affairs.'

Julia nodded. 'I shan't tell anyone,' she said.

When she had seen her visitor off at the gate Julia stood there for some time looking round and thinking. Quite suddenly the world seemed to have turned topsy-turvy. It was a very odd sort of feeling. She had been worrying about money, wondering how she was going to make ends meet, and now she found she had plenty of money—enough and to spare. She could do anything she wanted. First of all she would buy a new carpet for Uncle Randal's bedroom. The room was ready, except for the carpet, and looked delightfully fresh and bright. She had been pricing carpets in some of the Edinburgh shops, but they were so expensive that she had decided to buy a second-hand carpet at a sale. There was no need for that now. Uncle Ran should have a lovely new carpet . . . not that he would notice it, of course, thought Julia, smiling. Then there was the gate. She must get a new gate—the old one was literally falling to pieces—and she must have the tool-shed repaired; she must get a man to look at the roof (several slates had fallen off and there was a patch of damp in Maggie's bedroom); she would have the hedge trimmed—Mr. Inglis would do that—and she would order a cartload of manure and ask Mrs. Lang if her boys would come and dig it in. What else should she do?

I must ask Neil, thought Julia . . . and then she remembered that she must not ask Neil. She must not tell Neil a word about it, nor Maggie either. She had promised not to tell anyone. Neil and Maggie would just have to go on thinking that she was paying for everything herself. Julia did not feel very happy about this, but it could not be helped.

CHAPTER 43

'MAGGIE,' said Julia. 'Who is Jimmy the Sacks?'

'Jamie the Saxth, Miss Julia?'

'Yes, Neil said something about him one day and I wondered who he was. I've never seen him.'

'You've never seen him!' exclaimed Maggie in astonishment. 'What are you thinking of, Miss Julia? How could you see him? He's been dead for hundreds of years. Did you never lairn about him in history?'

'No, never.'

'Well, there now!' exclaimed Maggie. 'That's strange. We had about him at school.'

'Who was he, Maggie?'

'He was a king, of course. To tell the truth I was always interested in Jamie the Saxth. I felt sorry for him.'

'Sorry for him!'

Maggie nodded. 'He was awful human, for all he was a king.'

Maggie had come into the study to clear away Julia's supper and had stayed to chat.

'You had better sit down and tell me about him,' said Julia, smiling. 'I can see there's a story.'

'Och, there's a story all right—and a good one too,' declared Maggie, and, nothing loath, she sat down and began without delay.

'Well, maybe you'll have heard of Queen Elizabeth?' asked Maggie—a trifle doubtfully, for her confidence in Miss Julia's education had been severely shaken by her lamentable ignorance of Jamie the Saxth.

'Yes, of course,' nodded Julia. 'She was the daughter of Henry the Eighth—Good Queen Bess.'

'That's her . . . but she was not all that good, to my way of thinking; cutting off Queen Mary's head! And all because she was jealous of the poor pretty creature.'

Julia had heard a somewhat different version of this affair and was about to say so.

'Well, never mind that,' said Maggie hastily. 'The story starts when Queen Elizabeth lay dying . . . and maybe regretting her sins. She lay on a heap of cushions, dressed up in all her finery, and wouldna go to her bed; but at long last, when she was near her end, her ladies took her by main force and carried her to her grand bed with the velvet curtains and the velvet counterpane. There she lay with the doctors standing round shaking their heads and the ladies on their knees praying. The great high counsellors were there too, and they all had grave faces, for the truth was, not one of them knew what was to happen when she died.

'There were several who were wanting the crown of England and some of the counsellors thought it should be this one and some of them thought it should be that one; but the Queen had never said which it was to be and it was for her to choose . . . and now it was too late—or so it seemed—for she was too far gone to speak a word. At last one of the counsellors had an idea, so he went forward and said to the poor lady that he would say the names of all the different people and when he came to the right one—the one she wanted to rule England in her place—she was to raise her hand a wee bit and they would know her wish. So he said the names clearly, one by one, and when he came to "His Majesty King James of Scotland" she raised her hand. So that was that,' declared Maggie triumphantly. 'And it's my belief she did it to make amends . . . because she was sorry she had cut off his mother's head.'

'But that was James the First!'

'Well, maybe you know him as James the First but he was Jamie the Saxth in Scotland.'

Julia was under the impression that the story was finished and was beginning to thank Maggie and to say it was very interesting indeed. . . .

'But there's more to come, Miss Julia,' Maggie told her, 'It's the best part, to my way of thinking. There was a man there in the palace, Sir Robert Carey his name was; he was great friends with Jamie the Saxth and he had promised to bring news about what happened as quick as ever he could. So he waited till the Queen was dead, and without waiting a minute longer he was up and away to Scotland on his horse. He rode like a madman till the poor beast could bear him no longer and then changed to another horse, and then another and another and scarce paused for bite or sup, galloping and galloping night and day. I'm not very sure how far it was, but it was two and a half days he took to do it—that was all. Two and a half days galloping and galloping with the horses almost dying beneath him, changing to a fresh one and on the road again. The road was not a proper road in those days, you'll understand, it was little better than a cart track; there were rivers he had to cross and there were deep ruts and bogs and rocks. He took a bad fall at one place and bumped his head, but up he got and on he went with the blood pouring down his face.

'Meantime Jamie the Saxth was waiting for news. He had heard that Queen Elizabeth was desperately bad and not expected to live, and he knew well enough that she had never said who was to come after her . . . so there he was, walking the floors of the great grand rooms of Holyrood Palace, back and forth, biting his fingers, nearly demented. Would it be him? That was the question. Maybe the Queen had named somebody else or maybe she had died without saying who was to have the crown! Oh, what could have happened to Sir Robert Carey who had promised to bring the news? Back and forth went Jamie the Saxth like a restless spirit, and not a creature in the Palace dared speak to him for he was half crazy with the worry of it all.

'It was dead of night when Sir Robert Carey reached Holyrood Palace and hammered on the gates to get in—and you may be sure he was not kept waiting long. They took him straight up the stair to the King's bedroom just as he was, unkempt, unshaven, muddy from head to foot with the bogs he'd come through, and his face all smeared with blood . . . and that's the way Jamie the Saxth heard the news that he was to be King of England and Scotland and Ireland.'

Julia had been listening enthralled to the saga. She had never heard it before! History books seldom concern themselves with the romantic details of events but merely with hard facts and dates which are liable to go in at one ear and out of the other. Maggie's story would be recorded in a school history book as the fact that Queen Elizabeth of England had named King James of Scotland as her successor and the kingdoms had been united. Julia had forgotten this—important though it was—but now, thanks to Maggie's vivid recital, she would remember it all her life.

'You're an awfully good story-teller,' she declared.

'Och well, it's just because I can see it all happening,' replied Maggie. 'I can see the old Queen dying in her grand bed and I can see Sir Robert Carey galloping—I can hear the sound of the horses' hoofs—and I can see poor Jamie pacing back and forth in yon big dining-hall at Holyrood

Palace, back and forth like a demented ghost. It's easy enough to tell about it if you see it happening. . . .

'Maircy, it's ten o'clock already! Away you to bed, Miss Julia! I'll go and warm your milk.'

(A glass of hot milk and a couple of Marie biscuits was a refreshment forced upon Julia every night and, to be truthful, appreciated and enjoyed by the recipient.)

Perhaps it is not to be wondered at that when Julia had drunk her milk and eaten her biscuits she lay down and went to sleep and dreamed about Sir Robert Carey's ride . . . the gallop of horses' hoofs went through her dreams . . . but the odd thing was that when the rider turned his head and she saw his face in the moonlight it was Stephen's face. Stephen's face, set in lines of stern resolve and determination, as he pressed forward to Scotland 'o'er moor and fen, o'er crag and torrent,' and scarce paused for bite or sup.

The dream was so vivid that Julia woke from it with a little cry—a cry of delight! Why should Stephen be on his way to Scotland . . . unless he was coming to see her?

Chapter 44

1

Julia awoke to find Maggie standing by her bed with the breakfast tray.

'You were dreaming!' Maggie exclaimed.

'Yes, I was dreaming about Sir Robert Carey,' said Julia sleepily. 'I saw him galloping along in the moonlight. It was rather a nice dream.'

'It must have been nice. You were smiling to yourself.'

'Are there any letters this morning?'

'There was just one. It was for me—and I could have done without it,' replied Maggie as she put Julia's breakfast before her.

'It's from ma nephew in Canada; he's got himself into a fine pickle and no mistake.'

Julia knew all about Maggie's relations; there was 'ma sister in Skye' and 'ma niece in New Zealand' and several cousins in different parts of the world. They were for ever getting into some sort of trouble and appealing to Maggie for financial assistance, but 'ma nephew in Canada' was the worst of the lot . . . and Maggie's heart was so tender that she was unable to say no.

As a matter of fact Julia felt very much annoyed with Maggie's relations, so she listened with mixed feelings to Maggie's recital of her nephew's woes.

'You see, Miss Julia, I'll need to send him the money straight off. He's borrowed it out of the club funds and if he doesna pay it back before the end of the month there'll be an awful to-do about it.'

'Maggie, how frightful!' exclaimed Julia in horrified tones.

'It is that. He was wanting the money so he just borrowed it. I'll need to get a money order at the post office and send it away to-night.'

Julia did not approve of this at all; she was of the opinion that 'ma nephew in Canada' should be left to stew in his own juice; it would do the young man a lot of good if his sins were brought to light and he received just retribution. She said so to Maggie as tactfully as she could.

'But, Miss Julia, he's ma nephew!' exclaimed Maggie in surprise.

It was useless to say more.

'Mind you, it's difficult,' continued Maggie thoughtfully.

'It'll just need to be the money I set aside for a new winter coat. I'll get ma old one sorted and it'll do for another year.'

It was Maggie's problem, of course, but now it had become Julia's problem. She thought about it as she ate her breakfast and all the time she was dressing; she was still thinking about it as she stood and looked out of her window at the drizzling rain. How strange it was that Maggie Walker, upright and honest as the day, should be afflicted with such disreputable relations! How much stranger it was that Maggie should condone their misdemeanours!

Yes, it was very strange indeed . . . but this was not Julia's problem. Julia's problem was how she, herself, ought to deal with the situation. She had seen Maggie's winter coat (it was in a deplorable condition) and was aware that Maggie had been 'putting by' for a new one. Now, alas, the carefully hoarded money was to be dispatched forthwith to Maggie's scapegrace nephew . . . and Maggie would shiver in the winter winds. Julia's first impulse had been to give Maggie the money to send to her nephew, but on second thoughts she decided that it would not be right. It was against Julia's principles to provide money to save the young blackguard from the consequences of his sins.

How difficult it is! thought Julia . . . and then she thought, but of course I could give Maggie a new winter coat! Good. That's what I shall do.

Her problem solved, Julia was just turning away from the window when she saw a car draw up at the gate. It was a long low car with a cape-hood—a speedy-looking car—and so bespattered with mud that she could not determine its colour. It drew up at the gate and a man got out, a large tall man in a burberry coat. He stood for a moment stretching himself as if he were cramped.

Julia waited not a moment longer, she rushed downstairs and out of the front door like a whirlwind and flung herself into his arms as he was walking up the path from the gate—flung herself into his arms and felt his arms close round her.

'Stephen!' she cried. 'Stephen!'

'Julia, Julia, Julia!' murmured Stephen's voice in her ear.

They stood there on the path, oblivious to their surroundings, oblivious of the fact that their meeting had been observed by quite a number of interested spectators.

Maggie, peeping from the window in the dining-room, where she was laying the cover for Julia's solitary lunch, was transfixed with astonishment for at least half a minute; then, pulling herself together, she laid two places on the table and rushed into the kitchen to see how the half-pound of round steak which she had intended to stew in brown gravy could be made to feed three people . . . and one of them a man. Curry, she thought. That's the thing. It's as well I've got enough rice.

Tom the Milk stopped whistling while he stood and stared. Meta Young, who had 'been a message' for her mother fell off her bicycle sideways and only just managed to save herself from falling onto the road. She also stood and stared; it was exactly like the movies! Quite half a dozen other people happened to be in the vicinity and reacted in much the same manner . . . and the old gentleman who lived opposite in Mrs. Dow's rooms and was done for by that lady seized his pen and wrote a long letter to *The Scotsman* deploring the Lack of Decorum Shown by Young People Nowadays.

However, the old gentleman was in the minority of one; everybody else was pleased and wildly excited and the news went round Leddiesford like a prairie fire, improving every minute, so when it reached the ears of Mrs. Inglis (who most unfortunately had chosen that *very* morning to turn out her back bedroom) she was informed by Bill the Fish on good authority that Miss Julia's young man, who was a sailor in the Navy and had been reported lost at sea, had been saved miraculously by an Aberdeen trawler and landed at Dunbar that very morning. He had borrowed a racing-car and made straight for Leddiesford and had just that moment arrived . . . and if Mrs. Inglis didn't believe him she could ask Tom the Milk who had seen them hugging and kissing on the path outside The Square House with his own eyes. 'And they're to be married next week,' added Bill the Fish providing his own little quota for good measure before hastening away to carry his story to other cars.

'Well, I never saw a ring on her finger and that's the truth,' declared Mrs. Gowan, who had called in to borrow a flue-brush from Mrs. Inglis. But as Mrs. Inglis pointed out, when she was retailing the story to Mrs. Wilson,' You'll always get wet blankets to pick holes in everything they hear.'

2

Meanwhile the principal actors in the drama had awakened to the fact that it was raining, and arm in arm strolled into the study and sat down together on the old leather sofa.

'Darling Stephen, my eyes nearly dropped out when I saw you. How did you get here?'

'From London, driving all night.'

'Driving all night?'

'I only stopped once—I'm not sure where—for a cup of coffee and a roll. Then off again as hard as I could pelt. The car went like a race-horse.'

Julia sat up and gazed at him, wide-eyed. 'Oh, Stephen. I saw you!'

'You saw me?'

'I dreamt about you. I did really! You were riding, like Sir Robert Carey.'

'Riding a motor-bike?' asked Stephen in bewilderment.

'No, it was a horse. He rode all the way from London to Edinburgh. I saw him in my dream galloping along like mad and when he turned his head I saw it was you.'

'It's impossible. No horse could do it,' declared Stephen.

'He kept on changing horses all the time and scarcely paused for bite or sup.'

'Some ride! Did he do it for a bet?'

'No, he did it . . . but never mind that now,' said Julia, abandoning the intrepid Sir Robert. 'Tell me why you did it—all of a sudden like this.'

Stephen was only too ready to obey her command. 'Well, you knew I was in London, didn't you? I was frightfully busy, but last night I called in to see Miss Martineau to ask her if she knew your plans. It was nearly eleven o'clock by the time I got there, but she seemed awfully pleased to see me. She took me up to her parlour and we sat there and talked.'

'Oh, you mean she told you—'

'She told me quite a lot, but the main thing was that you had returned the Rajah's ring—I never liked that ring—so naturally when I heard that glorious piece of news I came as quickly as I could. I had to go back to the club and pack and I had to go to the garage and get the car, so it was after two o'clock before I got started. I thought of flying, of course, but I might have had to wait at the airport for a plane, so I decided that what with one thing and another it would be just as quick by road. I'd have come before—I'd have come at once if you'd told me. Why on earth didn't you tell me?'

'I wanted—a little time,' replied Julia, trying to explain.

'You see, I'd been engaged to Morland for months and months, so it was difficult to feel disengaged all of a sudden . . . and Uncle Ran was desperately ill; I was so worried about him. Then Morland came to Leddiesford and there was an awful scene. It was all such a muddle. Besides, I didn't really know I wanted you so much and loved you so much until I saw you at the gate. Then suddenly I knew.' She looked up at him with dewy eyes. 'You understand, don't you, Stephen?'

Stephen did not understand in the least, for his own feelings had been entirely different; he had loved her and wanted her more than anything on earth from the very first moment when he had seen her sitting on that seat in Kensington Gardens, looking rather forlorn but as beautiful as an angel. . . . However, it did not matter; the only thing that mattered was that she loved him now and wanted him now, and she had left him in no doubt of that. So he just said, 'Darling, Julia!' and kissed her again, which was quite a good way of answering her question.

'What else did May tell you?' asked Julia. 'You see, Stephen, I've sort of got into the habit of telling May everything because she's so cosy.'

'Yes, she is cosy . . . and this is cosy,' said Stephen, drawing her closer. 'I'm a bit tired for some reason or other and I'm not quite sure if I'm awake or dreaming. I suppose we really are engaged all right?'

'Engaged!' cried Julia, sitting up and looking at him indignantly. 'Of course we're engaged! You don't suppose I'd have let you kiss me like that—'

'No, of course not,' said Stephen hastily. 'It just seemed too good to be true. I've been driving for hours and hours,' he added pathetically. 'You get a bit dazed when you drive for hours and hours.'

'Oh, darling, it was marvellous of you to come so quickly.'

'Seven hours,' said Stephen. 'Not bad going for nearly three sixty miles—and stinking bad weather most of the way.'

'Wonderful!' said Julia, admiringly. 'Tell me about it, Stephen.'

3

Stephen had just begun to describe some of the adventures he had met with during the night when there was a very discreet knock upon the door. Julia and Stephen immediately sprang apart and took up their positions at opposite ends of the sofa.

'Come in!' cried Julia.

The door opened slowly and Maggie's head appeared. This behaviour was so unlike Maggie's usual method of entry that Julia was surprised.

'Come in,' she repeated, rising and smiling at Maggie. 'This is Mr. Brett; he has come all the way from London to see me. Stephen, this is Mrs. Walker.'

'How do you do, Mrs. Walker,' said Stephen, shaking hands cordially. 'Julia told me so much about you in her letters that I feel I know you quite well.'

Perfect Stephen! thought Julia, looking on with shining eyes. Absolutely perfect! If he had said, 'Miss Harburn told me . . .' it would have been wrong; if he had not shaken hands with her it would have been frightful. How did he know how to behave in Looking-Glass Country?

'Tell her, Stephen,' said Julia.

Stephen laughed delightedly. He said, 'Mrs. Walker, prepare yourself for a shock. Julia and I are engaged to be married.'

'Well, I never!' exclaimed Maggie, trying her best to look surprised.

'You're the first person to know,' declared Julia. 'You're the very first. Nobody else has any idea of it.'

It was true that Maggie had been one of the first to know, but it was very far from the truth that nobody else had any idea of it.

'Well, it's nice that you've told me,' said Maggie with most unusual tact. 'I'm sure I wish you every good wish; health and joy and a long life together. Nobody could say more than that.'

They both agreed that nobody could possibly say more than that, and shook her hand warmly. Julia would have liked to kiss her nice rosy cheek but, being uncertain as to whether this would be considered the right thing, she refrained.

Now that Maggie had said her little speech, which had been prepared most carefully beforehand, she went on to matters of immediate importance.

'Will Mr. Brett be staying, Miss Julia?' she inquired.

'I could easily put up at the hotel—' began Stephen.

'There's no need for that,' declared Maggie. 'Where's the sense of spending good money at the Harburn Arms? They're just robbers at yon place. It's for you to say, Miss Julia.'

'You mean he could stay here?'

Maggie nodded. 'He could sleep in his room and air his new bed for him—that's what I was thinking. It might be a bit cold and damp, you see. I've had hot-water bottles in it, of course, and I'll go on putting them, but there's nothing like a body for warming up a bed and we're not wanting him to take cold.'

Julia was giggling, so she could not reply; but Stephen, though confused by all the pronouns, had understood enough to realise that he was being invited by Mrs. Walker to stay at The Square House; he would willingly have slept in the coal cellar for the pleasure of sleeping under the same roof as Julia, so he accepted with alacrity.

'I never catch cold,' he declared. 'So if it won't be a bother—'

'It's not you, it's him, Mr. Brett,' said Maggie. 'And it'll be no trouble at all, for the kitchen is thronged with folk and one of them can give me a hand with sorting the room and laying the sheets.'

'I didn't know you were having a party, Maggie!' Julia exclaimed.

'Nor me, neither,' declared Maggie, grimly. 'But there's some folks that likes to poke their noses into everything.'

'Perhaps we had better go to the Harburn Arms for lunch,' said Julia, who had suddenly remembered the small piece of meat which she herself had procured yesterday from Butcher—Wilson.

'There's enough to eat, Miss Julia—that's to say if Mr. Brett can take curry and apple-pie—and you'll be more private.'

Mr. Brett declared emphatically that curry and apple-pie and privacy were what he would like better than anything in the whole wide world.

This was an extravagant way of talking (quite daft in Maggie's opinion); but of course it was only natural that Mr. Brett should be a bit above himself, so Maggie forgave him and smiled and went away, closing the door very carefully behind her.

4

'What a pet!' exclaimed Stephen.

'Yes, isn't she?'

'But you said in your letter that it was difficult to understand what she said.'

'So it is—sometimes. If you could hear them now, all talking together in the kitchen, you wouldn't understand a word. I wonder why she's having a party,' added Julia thoughtfully.

'Perhaps it's her birthday or something.'

Stephen was not interested in Mrs. Walker's party—birthday or otherwise—so he drew Julia down beside him on the sofa.

'Now we must be sensible,' he said. 'I've got such a lot to tell you . . . but first of all let's decide when we're going to be married. This is Scotland, of course, so we could be married to-morrow at Gretna Green.'

'To-morrow at Gretna Green!' echoed Julia in alarm. 'No, we couldn't possibly. For one thing I can't leave Uncle Ran until he's quite fit and strong and comfortably settled at home, and for another thing I don't believe you can be married at Gretna Green all of a sudden like that. But anyhow that doesn't matter. It's Uncle Ran that matters. I can't leave Uncle Ran—'

'Oh, Stephen!' she exclaimed, sitting up and looking at him in dismay. 'Oh, Stephen! I don't think I shall be able to marry you after all!'

'What do you mean?' gasped Stephen.

'Because I can't go out to Africa with you, that's why. I simply couldn't go so far away—'

'But I've decided not to go back to Africa—I was going to tell you that. You see, Father is getting old and Mother isn't as strong as she might be, so I shall have to try to get a job near home.'

'Good,' said Julia. 'That's lovely because I don't want to be too far away from Uncle Ran.'

'We'll be together!' exclaimed Stephen, suddenly struck all of a heap at this amazing fact.

'Well, of course we'll be together, darling Stephen. We're going to be married, aren't we?'

'We're going to be married,' said Stephen fatuously. 'We're going to be married. We're going to be together all our lives.'

There was a slight pause in the conversation.

'Do be sensible, Stephen,' said Julia at last.

'Yes, we must be sensible,' he agreed. 'Let's see now. There's the sapphire, of course. I must have it set in a ring.'

'Yes, of course,' agreed Julia, and so saying she pulled the black ribbon and produced the sapphire from its hiding place.

'There it is, safe and sound,' she added, smiling at him fondly.

'Do you mean it's been there—all the time?'

'All the time,' nodded Julia. 'It's so valuable, you see, and it seemed safer to wear it all the time; besides, I love it. I love it because it "feels the influence of the air and sympathises with the heavens and does not shine equally if the sky be cloudy or bright." It's perfectly true, Stephen. The dear darling sapphire likes sunshine and blue skies.'

'You've been wearing it all the time,' said Stephen in a dazed voice.

Julia looked at him in surprise. 'I've told you—'

'I know,' said Stephen. 'It's just so—so amazing. I can't help wondering if it really has magical properties.'

'Magical properties?'

'Yes, but we must be sensible. Listen, Julia, I want to get it properly set in platinum for you (the setting is very important indeed, so it can't be done in a hurry). Meanwhile you must have a ring immediately, so that any stray male who comes your way will realise that you're booked good and proper.'

Julia giggled.

Stephen had always adored her silly little giggle and the dimples which it displayed, and now he discovered that it was a hundred times more adorable than he remembered. In fact it gave him quite a severe pain in the region of his heart—so he was obliged to kiss her again several times.

'I thought we were going to be sensible,' she said.

'Yes—well—I'll show you,' said Stephen, and with that he produced a ring from his pocket and slipped it onto her finger.

It was a little gold ring, rather solid and old-fashioned, with a small red stone set in a cluster of diamonds.

'Oh, Stephen, what a darling ring!'

'Mother gave it to me for you.'

'Gave it to you—for me! But how did she know! I mean she couldn't have known that we were—'

'She didn't know,' explained Stephen. 'But I think she hoped. You see, one evening when I had been talking about you and—and telling her about you she took out her jewel-case and found the ring and gave it to me. She said that perhaps some day I might need it in a hurry so I had better keep it safely in my pocket.'

'It was sweet of her,' Julia declared. 'I must write and thank her and tell her how much I value it.'

'Oh, it isn't valuable. It's just a garnet and tiny diamonds. Mother has much better rings, but she said they would be too big for you. This ring belonged to my grandmother, so it's very old-fashioned.'

'It fits beautifully,' said Julia, holding out her hand.

'So it does! How on earth did Mother know the size?'

'I love it,' declared Julia, evading the question. She loved it because she loved Stephen and because Stephen's mother had given it to him for her (which was tremendously important because it meant that Stephen's mother thought she was good enough for Stephen). She loved it because Stephen's grandmother had worn it and, last but not least, because it was so delightful and so unusual and fitted so snugly on her finger. 'Look how nice it is!' said Julia, displaying it with pride. 'You know, Stephen, I think if you don't mind I'd like to have this as an engagement ring—'

'Not the sapphire?' The tone was slightly disappointed.

'Of course I want the sapphire! But it would be too grand and beautiful to wear all the time. I want an engagement ring that I can wear night and day, always, all the time. You see that, don't you?'

Thus explained, Stephen saw it at once.

'There's another thing I want to talk to you about,' he continued. 'It's important, so listen carefully, Julia. When we're married I don't want you to say "obey." I'm told that nowadays you can have a different kind of service.'

'But I don't mind—' she began.

'I do,' he declared emphatically. 'We're going to be equal partners to discuss things and decide everything together. That's my idea of marriage.'

'Are you sure it wasn't May's idea?' asked Julia, sitting up and looking at him anxiously.

'No, it's my idea,' he replied.

This was perfectly true, of course. It was Stephen's own idea . . . and, although it had been inspired by May Martineau's disclosures, there was no necessity to mention the fact. May Martineau's information had been very interesting indeed—and very helpful—but it had been given in strict confidence, so even if Stephen had wanted to tell Julia what she had said he could not have done so without breaking his promise. Stephen could almost see Miss Martineau sitting in her parlour in the pink plush chair with her plump little feet on the pink plush footstool; he could almost hear her voice as she told him the history of the broken engagement and about Julia's declaration of independence. 'But you must promise faithfully that you'll never, never tell her I told you,' Miss Martineau had said, wagging her plump little finger at him . . . and of course Stephen had promised.

Miss Martineau had been so kind to him and so encouraging and so delighted at the news that he intended to dash straight off to Scotland that Stephen had kissed her when he came away—and she had been pleased—but he decided not to tell Julia about that either.

It was only afterwards, when he was rushing along the Great North Road, that the Idea had come to Stephen and he had made up his mind that if Julia agreed to marry him he would not allow her to stand before the altar and utter the word 'obey.'

'It's my own idea. It's my idea of marriage,' repeated Stephen.

'It doesn't seem very important to me,' said Julia thoughtfully.

'It's vitally important to me,' declared Stephen. 'I don't want a slave; I want a partner. Can do?'

'Can do,' replied Julia, nodding.

They shook hands on the pact with due solemnity.

THE END

AN AUTOBIOGRAPHICAL SKETCH
by D.E. Stevenson

EDINBURGH was my birthplace and I lived there until I was married in 1916. My father was the grandson of Robert Stevenson who designed the Bell Rock Lighthouse and also a great many other lighthouses and harbours and other notable engineering works. My father was a first cousin of Robert Louis Stevenson and they often played together when they were boys.

So it was that from my earliest days I heard a good deal about "Louis", and, like Oliver Twist, I was always asking for more, teasing my father and my aunts for stories about him. He must have been a strange child, a dreamy unpredictable creature with a curious fascination about him which his cousins felt but did not understand. How could ordinary healthy, noisy children understand that solitary, sensitive soul! And as they grew up they understood him even less for Louis was not of their world. He was born too late or too early. The narrow conventional ideas of mid-Victorian Edinburgh were anathema to him. Louis would have been happy in a romantic age, striding the world in cloak and doublet with a sword at his side, he would have sold his life dearly for a Lost Cause—he was ever on the side of the under-dog. He might have been happy in the world of today when every man is entitled to his own opinions and the Four Freedoms is the goal of Democracy.

My father was old-fashioned in his ideas so my sister and I were not sent to school but were brought up at home and educated by a governess. I was always very fond of reading and read everything I could get hold of including Scott, Dickens, Jane Austen and all sorts of boys' books by Jules Verne and Ballantyne and Henty.

When I was eight years old I began to write stories and poems myself. It was most exciting to discover that I could. At first my family was amused and interested in my efforts but very soon they became bored beyond measure and told me it must stop. They said it was ruining my handwriting and wasting my time. I argued with them. What was handwriting for, if not to write? "For writing letters when you're older," they said. But I could not stop. My head was full of stories and they got lost if I did not write them down, so I found a place in the box-room between two large black trunks with a skylight overhead and I made a little nest where I would not be disturbed. There I sat for hours—and wrote and wrote.

Our house was in a broad street in Edinburgh—45 Melville Street—and at the top of the street was St. Mary's Cathedral. The bells used to echo and re-echo down the man-made canyon. My sister and I used to sit on the window-seat in the nursery (which was at the top of the house) and look down at the people passing by. I told her stories about them. Some of the memories of my childhood can be found in my novel, *Listening Valley*, in which Louise and Antonia had much the same lonely childhood.

Every summer we went to North Berwick for several months and here we were more free to do as we wanted, to go out by ourselves and play on the shore and meet other children. When we were at North Berwick we sometimes drove over to a big farm, close to the sea. We enjoyed these visits tremendously for there were so many things to do and see. We rode the pony and saw the farmyard animals and walked along the lovely sands. There were rocks there too, and many ships were wrecked upon the jagged reefs until a lighthouse was erected upon the Bass Rock—designed by my father. Years afterwards I wrote a novel about this farm, about the fine old house and the beautiful garden, and I called it *The Story of Rosabelle Shaw*.

As we grew older we made more friends. We had bathing picnics and tennis parties and fancy dress dances, and of course we played golf. I was in the team of the North Berwick Ladies' Golf Club and I played in the Scottish Ladies' Championship at Muirfield and survived until the semi-finals. I was asked to play in the Scottish Team but by that time I was married and expecting my first baby so I was obliged to refuse the honour.

Every Spring my father and mother took us abroad, to France or Switzerland or Italy. We had a French maid so we spoke French easily and fluently—if not very correctly—and it was very pleasant to be able to converse with the people we met. I liked Italy best, and especially Lake Como which seemed to me so beautiful as to be almost unreal. Paris came second in my affections. There was such a gay feeling in Paris; I see it always in sunshine with the white buildings and broad streets and the crowds of brightly clad people strolling in the Boulevards or sitting in the cafés eating and drinking and chattering cheerfully. Quite often we hired a carriage and drove through the Bois de Boulogne. My sister and I were never allowed to go out alone, of course, nor would our parents take us to a play—as I have said before they were old-fashioned and strict in their ideas and considered a "French Play" an unsuitable form of enter-tainment for their daughters—but in spite of these annoying prejudices we managed to have quite an amusing time and we always enjoyed our visits to foreign countries.

In 1913 I "came out" and had a gay winter in Edinburgh. There were brilliant "Balls" in those far off days, the old Assembly Rooms glittered with lights and the long gilt mirrors reflected girls in beautiful frocks and men in uniform or kilts. The older women sat round the ballroom attired in velvet or satin and diamonds watching the dancers—and especially watching their own offspring—with eyes like hawks, and talking scandal to one another. We danced waltzes and Scottish country dances and Reels—the Reels were usually made up beforehand by the Scottish Regiment which was quartered at Edinburgh Castle. It was a coveted honour to be asked to dance in these Reels and one had to be on one's toes all the time. Woe betide the unfortunate girl who put a foot wrong or failed to set to her partner at exactly the right moment!

The First Great War put an end to all these gaieties—certainly nobody felt inclined to dance when every day the long lists of casualties were published and the gay young men who had been one's partners were reported dead or missing or returned wounded from the ghastly battlefields.

In 1916 I married Major James Reid Peploe. His family was an Edinburgh family, as mine was. Curiously enough I knew his mother and father and his brothers but had never met him until he returned to Edinburgh from the war, wounded in the head. When he recovered we were married and then began the busiest time of my life. We moved about from place to place (as soldiers and their wives and families must do) and, what with the struggle to get houses and the arrival—at reasonable intervals—of two sons and a daughter I had very little time for writing. I managed to write some short stories and some children's poems but it was not until we were settled for some years in Glasgow that I began my literary career in earnest.

Mrs. Tim was my first successful novel. In it I wrote an account of the life of an Officer's wife and many of the incidents in the story are true—or only very slightly touched up. Unfortunately people in Glasgow were not very pleased with their portraits and became somewhat chilly in consequence. After that I wrote *Miss Buncle's Book* which has been one of my most popular books. It sold in thousands and is still selling. It is about a woman who wrote a book about the small town in which she lived and about the reactions of the community.

All the time my children were growing up I continued to write: *Miss Buncle Married, Miss Dean's Dilemma, Smouldering Fire, The Story of Rosabelle Shaw, The Baker's Daughter, Green Money, Rochester's*

Wife, A World in Spell followed in due succession—and then came the Second Great War.

Hitherto I had written to please myself, to amuse myself and others, but now I realised that I could do good work. *The English Air* was my first novel to be written with a purpose. In this novel I tried to give an artistically true picture of how English people thought and felt about the war so that other countries might understand us better, and, judging by the hundreds of letters I received from people all over the world, I succeeded in my object—succeeded beyond my wildest hopes. My wartime books are *Mrs. Tim Carries On, Spring Magic, Celia's House, Listening Valley, The Two Mrs. Abbotts, Crooked Adam* and *The Four Graces*. In these books I have pictured every-day life in Britain during the war and have tried to show how ordinary people stood up to the frightfulness and what they thought and did during those awful years of anxiety. One of my American readers wrote to me and said, "You make us understand what it must be like to have a tiger in the backyard." I appreciated that letter.

Wartime brought terrible anxieties to me, for my elder son was in Malta during the worst of the Siege of that island and then came home and landed in France on D-Day and went through the whole campaign with the Guards Armoured Division. He was wounded in ten places and was decorated with the Military Cross for outstanding bravery. My daughter was an officer in the Women's Royal Naval Service and was commended for her valuable work.

In addition to my writing I organised the collection of Sphagnum Moss for the Red Cross and together with others went out on the moors in all weathers, wading deep in bog, to collect the moss for surgical dressings. This particular form of war-work is described in detail in *Listening Valley*.

After the long weary years of war came victory for the Allies, but my job of writing stories went on. I wrote *Mrs. Tim Gets a Job, Kate Hardy, Young Mrs. Savage* and *Vittoria Cottage*. All these books were quite as successful as their predessessors and *Young Mrs. Savage* was chosen by the American Family Reading Club as their Book of the Month. My new novel *Music in the Hills* is in the same genre and all those who have read it think it is one of my best. A businessman, who lives in London, wrote to me saying '*Music in the Hills* is as good as a holiday and, although I have read several other books since reading it, the peaceful atmosphere lingers in my mind. I hope your next book will tell us more about James and Rhoda and the other characters for they are so real to me and have become my friends." The scene of this book is laid in the hills and valleys of the Scottish Borders and the people are the rugged individualistic race who inhabit this beautiful country. For a long time it has been in my mind to write a story with this setting and to try to describe the atmosphere, to paint an artistically true picture of life in this district. Now it is finished and I hope my large and faithful public will enjoy reading it as much as I have enjoyed writing it.

Sometimes I have been accused of making my characters "too nice". I have been told that my stories are "too pleasant", but the fact is I write of people as I find them and am fond of my fellow human beings. Perhaps I have been fortunate but in all my wanderings I have met very few thoroughly unpleasant people, so I find it difficult to write about them.

We live in Moffat now. Moffat is a small but very interesting old town which lies in a valley between round rolling hills. Some of the buildings are very old indeed but outside the town there are pleasant residential houses with gardens and fine trees of oak and beech and elm. From my window as I write I can see the lovely sweep of moorland where the small, lively, black-faced sheep live and move and have their being. Every day the hills look different: sometimes grey and cold, sometimes green and smiling; in winter they are often white with snow or hidden in soft grey mist, in September they are purple with heather, like a royal robe. Although Moffat is isolated there is plenty of society and many interesting people to talk to and entertain and it is only fifty miles from Edinburgh so, if I feel dull, I can go and stay there at my comfortable club and see a good play or a film and do some shopping.

There are several questions which recur again and again in letters from friends and acquaintances. Perhaps I should try to answer them. The first is, why do you write? I write because I enjoy writing more than anything. It is fascinating to think out a story and to feel it taking shape in my mind. Of course I like making money by my books—who would not?—but the money is a secondary consideration, a by-product as it were. The story is the thing. Writing a book is the most exciting adventure under the sun.

The second question is, how do you write? I write all my books in longhand, lying on a sofa near the window in my drawing room. I begin by thinking it all out and then I take a pencil and jot it all down in a notebook. When that stage is over I begin at the beginning and go on like mad until I get to the end. After that I have a little rest and then polish it up and rewrite bits of it. When I can do no more to it I pack it up, smother the parcel with sealing wax, and despatch it to be typed. I am now free as air and somewhat dazed, so I ring up all my friends (who have been neglected for months) and say, "Come and have a party."

Another question is, do you draw your characters from real life? The answer is definitely NO. The characters in a novel are the most interesting part of it and the most mysterious. They must come from Somewhere, I suppose, but they certainly do not come from "real life". They begin by taking shape in a nebulous form and then, as I think about them and live with them, they become more solid and individualistic with definite ideas of their own. Sometimes I get rather annoyed with them; they are so unmanageable, they flatly refuse to do as I want and take their own way in an arbitrary fashion.

All the people in my books are real to me. They are more real than the people I meet every day for I know them better and understand them more deeply. It is difficult to say which is my favourite character, for I am fond of them all, but the most extraordinary character I ever had to deal with was Sophonisba Marks (in my novel *The Two Mrs. Abbotts*.) I intended her to be a subsidiary character, an unimportant person in the story, but Miss Marks had other ideas. In spite of the fact that she was plain and elderly and somewhat deaf and suffered severely from rheumatism, Miss Marks walked straight into the middle of the stage and stayed there. She just wouldn't take a back seat. She is so real to me that I simply cannot believe she does not exist. Somewhere or other she must exist—perhaps I shall meet her one day! Perhaps I shall see her in the street, coming towards me clad in her black cloth coat and the round toque with the white flowers in it and carrying her umbrella in her hand. I shall stop her and say loudly (because of course she is deaf) "Miss Marks, I presume!"

It will be seen from the foregoing sketch that my life has not been a very eventful one. I have had no hair-raising adventures nor travelled in little-known parts of the world, but wherever I have been I have made interesting friends and I still retain them. Friends are like windows in a house, and what a terribly dull house it would be that had no windows! They open vistas, they show one new and lovely views of the countryside. Friends give one new ideas, new values, new interests.

Thank God for friends!

Someday I mean to write a book of reminiscences; to delve into the cupboard of memory and sort out all the junk. There is so much to write about, so many little pictures grave and gay, so many ideas to think about and disentangle and arrange. Looking back is a fascinating pastime; looking back and wondering what one's life would have been if one had done this instead of that, if one had turned to the left at the crossroads instead of to the right, if one had stayed at home instead of going out or had gone out five minutes later. Jane Welsh Carlyle says in one of her letters, "One can never be too much alive to the consideration that one's every slightest action does not end when it has acted itself but propagates itself on and on, in one shape or another, through all time and away into eternity."

FICTION BY D.E. STEVENSON

Miss Buncle Married (1936)

The Empty World (1936, aka *A World in Spell*)

The Story of Rosabelle Shaw (1937)

The Baker's Daughter (1938, aka *Miss Bun the Baker's Daughter*)

Rochester's Wife (1940)

Crooked Adam (1942)

Celia's House (1943)

The Two Mrs Abbotts (1943)

Listening Valley (1944)

The Four Graces (1946)

Amberwell (1955)

Summerhills (1956)

Still Glides the Stream (1959)

The Musgraves (1960)

Bel Lamington (1961)

Fletcher's End (1962)

Katherine Wentworth (1964)

Katherine's Marriage (1965, aka *The Marriage of Katherine*)

The House on the Cliff (1966)

Sarah Morris Remembers (1967)

Sarah's Cottage (1968)

Gerald and Elizabeth (1969)

House of the Deer (1970)

Portrait of Saskia (collection of early writings, published 2011)

Found in the Attic (collection of early writings, published 2013)

* see Explanatory Notes

EXPLANATORY NOTES

MRS. TIM

Mrs. Tim of the Regiment, the first appearance of Mrs. Tim in the literary world, was published by Jonathan Cape in 1932. That edition, however, contained only the first half of the book currently available from Bloomsbury under the same title. The second half was originally published, as *Golden Days*, by Herbert Jenkins in 1934. Together, those two books contain Mrs. Tim's diaries for the first six months of the same year.

Subsequently, D.E. Stevenson regained the rights to the two books, and her new publisher, Collins, reissued them in the U.K. as a single volume under the title *Mrs. Tim* (1941), reprinted several times as late as 1992. In the U.S., however, the combined book appeared as *Mrs. Tim of the Regiment*, and has generally retained that title, though a 1973 reprint used the title *Mrs. Tim Christie*. Adding to the confusion, large print and audiobook editions of *Golden Days* have also appeared in recent years.

Fortunately no such title confusions exist with the subsequent Mrs. Tim titles—*Mrs. Tim Carries On* (1941), *Mrs. Tim Gets a Job* (1947), and *Mrs. Tim Flies Home* (1952)—and Dean Street Press is delighted to make these long-out-of-print volumes of the series available again, along with two more of Stevenson's most loved novels, *Smouldering Fire* (1935) and *Spring Magic* (1942).

SMOULDERING FIRE

Smouldering Fire was first published in the U.K. in 1935 and in the U.S. in 1938. Until now, those were the only complete editions of the book. All later reprints, both hardcover and paperback, have been heavily abridged, with entire chapters as well as occasional passages throughout the novel cut from the text. For our new edition, Dean Street Press has followed the text of the first U.K. edition, and we are proud to be producing the first complete, unabridged edition of *Smouldering Fire* in eighty years.

FURROWED MIDDLEBROW

*titles available in paperback only

Printed in Great Britain
by Amazon

37557644R00145